FORSAKEN

Fall of Menevilen Series

Book One

MaKenzie McCroskey Jones

DEDICATION

To my mother, for your fervently unyielding confidence and encouragement in my writing. For your overall love and support. For truly believing in me and pushing me to achieve my dreams.

To two of my best friends, Allie and Katie, for your steady belief in my capabilities and your sincere interest in my work. For having more faith in me and my talents than I could ever possess.

And finally, to two of the most profound teachers I've ever had the honor to know, Mrs. Crane and Coach Mac, for your genuine intrigue in my capabilities, your unwavering support, and for truly caring about the craft you teach.

CONTENTS

Acknowledgments

I would like to thank the very talented Marylin Lopez for all of the hard work she put into creating the artwork and covers for my series. I have no idea what I would do without her help.

My gratitude is extended to Katie Spieckermann for all of the time she spent editing this book. Her blunt critiques and support have helped shaped this book into what it is now.

The Traitor

Comforting smiles and a dreamy gaze
While his thoughts are running
He mindlessly betrays

Caught in a tangled web of hopeless desperation
He regretfully understands the gravity of his situation

Deceitful eyes
Are the elusive disguise

That shackles his heart in chains

He plasters on a grin
And the deception begins

And yet
His heart has never felt so much pain

Prologue

The girl's irises flashed maroon with fright.

Twigs snapped in the distance, startling her into a heart-pounding sprint. The sound of footsteps was rapidly approaching, an eerie voice spewing through the cold air. She could see the Wall ahead, the pale marble radiating through the darkness and illuminating her path. She was so close to freedom, so close to safety, she could feel the sweetness of the notion dancing across her dry tongue.

But the girl's hopeful thoughts of escape were shattered as she suddenly lost control over her tumbling body. She fell to the ground hard, ragged breaths escaping her cracked lips. She attempted to scramble to her feet, but it was too late—a shadowy figure had already emerged from the depths of the forest. A twisted dagger suddenly cut through the darkness, aiming directly for the girl's chest. She screamed, helplessly petrified with fear. She closed her eyes, wincing, waiting for a jolt of immeasurable pain—but there was nothing. Silence hung heavy in the air, drawing open the girl's uncertain eyes. The body of a man blocked her vision, a puddle of crimson blood staining the fabric of his cloak.

"You can't always protect her," a harsh voice slithered through the calm, the sound of it filling the girl's chest with unbridled fear. "She *will* fall by my hand. The longer you prolong it, the more brutal her end will be."

"Then she will leave Menevilen until she is strong enough to destroy you," the man spoke loudly, his body heaving as he tore the dagger from his torso. "Leave now. Your mortality is susceptible, and you know I cannot perish until my time has run out."

An indignant scoff sounded, but the vile attacker retreated

into the shadows of the forest without protest. "Until we meet again, *princess*."

The man's hand softly fell on the girl's forehead, his blue eyes studying her frightened expression. "For now, you must forget," he whispered. "Clear your mind. Relax. Let the past slowly slip away. You must forget."

The girl stared at the man in confusion, dizzying waves spreading through her limbs. Her mind was growing foggy, her vision blurred. She could hear the pulsating beat of her heart, yet she didn't feel as though she were alive. Her body felt foreign. She could feel the framework of her life rapidly disintegrating into vague recollections. Her identity was suddenly swallowed by a smothering flame of uncertainty, ripping apart the seams of reality. She felt numb and misplaced, and although she could not recall a single fact about herself, she felt as though something terrible had occurred— something terrible that had left an irreversible mark on her life.

Chapter One

The Death of a King

The charred log roasting in the hearth crackled and split, tossing sparks through the chilled winter air. Wind howled in the distance, sending cold tufts of air spewing through gaping cracks in the barn walls. The frozen hay beneath Kiara's feet crunched as her boots stomped against the ground, unsettling the eerie stillness of the room. She crossed the length of the barn, stopping beside a wooden table bearing three weapons: a wooden bow coupled with countless arrows sheathed inside a leather quiver, a two-handed sword with a thick blade, and a slick silver knife brandishing an intricately decorated hilt. Her fingers naturally itched to grasp the knife, but she had entered the barn with the burning desire to revise her sloppy form with the heavy sword, and besides she couldn't afford to waste time as it was rapidly ticking away.

Kiara's small hands wove around the sword's hilt, heaving the weapon off the table. The colossal sword was nearly half of Kiara's diminutive frame, but she was miraculously able to sustain its weight. She leveled the blade forward, extending her hands carefully, as she eyed a dummy constructed of worn canvas and hay standing with its back to the fireplace. She lurched forward suddenly, swinging her hands downward, as the blade tore through the dummy's shoulder, ripping apart the canvas. Mounds of hay escaped through the tarnished seam, pelting Kiara's body as she sourly eyed the injured mannequin.

"Useless!" she chided, kicking the dummy's legs. It fell over with a thud, provoking a cry of frustration from her lips.

Kiara's seventeenth birthday was mere hours away, and she

could feel the onslaught of apprehension billowing through her chest. At seventeen, she would become an adult—a legal, decision-making citizen of Menevilen. She would apply for a position in Enevale's army—the only kingdom within walking distance—and hopefully abandon her dismal life in the small, pointless village she had been trapped in since childhood. Her chances of becoming a soldier were fairly high, considering her Evalseman Specialty *was* immense strength, but she disastrously knew her Nonae eyes would provide her with the label the village had given her: *freak*.

She was all too aware of the bitter rivalry between the Nonae and Evalseman races. Kiara had learned about the bloody history multiple times throughout her years in the academy; had even witnessed a violent brawl between a rogue Nonae and an Evalseman from the village. The approved statement taught throughout the Evalseman-inhabited regions of Menevilen was simple: Nonae were the enemy. And Kiara suspected the Nonae's stance carried the same hatred. If not, the Nonae empress wouldn't have launched a war with Enevale's king—a war that had persisted for nearly eight years.

With the eminence of the Nonae and Evalseman feud taking a tight grip on Menevilen's society and its citizens' mentalities, Kiara could not fathom how her parents had managed to fall in love. She had naturally assumed she was half-Nonae, half-Evalseman, as her Nonae-like irises shifted colors to display her inconsistent moods, but no one could offer her any insight into her past. She was just as oblivious to her unnatural existence as the rest of the village, which only fueled the flames of prejudice the villagers wafted in her direction. Luckily, her mentor, Brin, held a respected position in the village's society, and had bravely taken her under his wing. She couldn't remember a time before living with Brin and his daughter, Anya. Everything before her ninth birthday was a mysterious abyss shrouded in ambiguity.

A lighthearted chuckle filled the room, startling Kiara so

badly that she dropped the sword. She spun around, discovering her adoptive sister, Anya, standing in the doorway.

"What did you think would happen if you slashed through a dummy constructed of flimsy canvas?" she asked, laughing. "Did you think it wouldn't tear?"

Kiara sighed, her shoulders slumping downward. "Honestly, I don't know what I was thinking," she admitted. "My anxiety is seriously draining my common sense."

Anya snickered, her blue eyes lightening with humor. "You mean the tiny amount of common sense you possessed in the first place?"

Kiara scowled, but she couldn't argue. Anya was correct— Kiara really *did* lack a below average amount of common sense, which accounted for her absent-minded behavior and straightforward mannerisms. "I have to correct my form by tomorrow," she said quietly. "I'm useless with a sword."

Anya crossed the room, stopping beside her sister. Her fingers comfortingly stroked Kiara's shoulder, her face pulled into a concerned expression. "You're brilliant with a sword," she praised. "You're going to do just fine. Besides, it's a long walk to Enevale. You can practice on the way."

"Thanks, sis," Kiara mumbled, smiling softly.

"Of course. Now, come back the house. Dinner's ready, and you need rest." Anya prepared every meal in the household, considering neither Kiara nor Brin held any culinary skills.

Anya turned toward the exit while Kiara grudgingly followed suit. Anya unsealed the barn door and was instantly assaulted by the harsh winter wind outside. Snow danced through the air, dotting the dark sky. Anya shivered, hugging her cloak nearer to her body, as she began walking toward the house. Kiara tightly closed the barn door behind her, wishing she had remembered to recover her misplaced cloak from the depths of the house. She blew hot breath against her icy fingers, rubbing her hands together and roughly running her palms across her chilled arms. She followed after Anya through the darkness, her eyes locked on the illuminated window of the house glowing in the distance.

As they reached the back door, Kiara's frigid body yearned for the comfort of the heated home. Anya pulled open the door, dashing inside as she yelled for Brin. Kiara's hand gripped the doorknob, but a gust of harsh wind halted further movement—the wind had seemingly shrieked Kiara's name. Her eyes widened, flashing yellow with panic, as she stared desperately into the shadowed yard. There was nothing in sight. She furrowed her brow in confusion, peeling her gaze away as she entered the house.

*****

Avian surveyed the tense atmosphere of the room, watching his colleagues' familiar faces glance upward as he hovered in the doorway. The three young dukes were present, reclined tensely in velvet-padded chairs. The dukes met regularly, as they were all very close friends, but they seldom convened under the king's direct command.

Avian crossed the room, taking his place beside Aiden, his eyes glued to the king's closed bedroom door. Avian folded his legs across his lap, tapping his foot against the marble floor impatiently. "What do you think has happened?" he inquired loudly. "He hasn't summoned us together since Blade's father passed."

Blade stared up at his friend through a curtain of silvery hair. "And that was nearly four years ago."

"Perhaps the princess has been discovered," Ace offered.

Avian automatically shook his head. "No, I would know about *that*—undoubtedly."

The boys' chattering was instantly silenced as the door to the king's bedroom creaked open. King Kyan exited his room, a small silver necklace clutched in his fist, his face pulled into an uncharacteristic frown.

"Kyan!" Avian exclaimed, quickly jumping to his feet. "What's happened?"

Kyan's light blue eyes slid over his advisor. Unbridled sadness clung to the depths of irises, his coppery eyelashes downcast. "Boys..." he spoke hoarsely, his lips trembling, "I am dying."

*****

A malicious laugh filled the silence of the campsite, signaling Vyntrx's delight. Demmonai soldiers stopped in their tracks, taking a momentary break in patrolling as they sent confused expressions in the direction of their empress's tent. Vyntrx rarely showed any emotion beside deranged madness, and the sound of her jovial laughter chilled the bones of all who heard it.

"Vyn?" Murdock spoke tentatively, hovering in the doorway of Vyntrx's tent. "What's going on?"

Vyntrx turned to face her comrade, her unnatural black eyes sparking with excitement. Her blood-red lips curled into a wide grin, a high-pitched chuckle escaping her throat. "Kyan is dead!" she cried shrilly. "Kyan is *dead!*"

Murdock shook his head, his mouth falling open in disbelief. "H-how?" he stammered. "He was still so young."

"The details are meaningless," she hissed, hurrying to Murdock's side. She pulled him into the tent, dancing around the room with her hands held high above her head. "His daughter's been discovered, too! Right under our noses! Kyan may have told everyone she was in another world, but he was *l-y-ing*," she drew out the last word, practically singing. "No wonder my locating spells never went through! I never even searched Menevilen!"

"This is unbelievable," Murdock murmured. "Your goals have *actually* become achievable."

If Vyntrx had been in a worse mood, she would have swatted at her companion for his pessimistic remark. But she was so elated, she could think of nothing but the productive future. "I have to get started right away. Murdock, fetch me one of my servants—one I can dispose of."

Murdock raised a skeptical eyebrow. "Why?"

"Don't question me. Also, find my bird. I wonder where he's flittered off to. We can't continue without him."

Murdock nodded comprehensively, bowing slightly. He turned toward the exit, dashing into the darkness of night. Little did Vyntrx know, her bird was sitting outside the tent, listening—and his heart was sinking through his chest.

*****

Kiara awoke to the sound of bells. They rang solemnly, ominously, droning through the quiet calm of morning. Her eyes opened slowly, her small bedroom pouring into view. Faint light trickled in from the window, casting shadows across Anya's empty bed.

Kiara yawned, rubbing sleep out of her dull brown eyes. Her auburn hair fell past her shoulders in messy heaps, sending chills across her bare flesh. She lazily climbed out of bed, pulled on a warm pair of leather boots, and headed down the stairs to the kitchen.

Anya was draped over the stove, industriously frying several pieces of half-cooked meat. Her hair was pulled away from her face, tucked beneath the straps of her apron. She barely glanced at her sister as she entered the room, but motioned to a cup of nillamee sitting on the table.

Kiara's face lit up with surprise. She gratefully snatched the warm cup in her hands, breathing in the delicious aroma of a delicacy her family could rarely afford to indulge in. "Thank you so much," she spluttered, allowing the hot liquid to slosh against her chilled lips.

"Happy birthday," Anya replied, smiling. She flicked her wrist, flipping the meat into the air. She caught the food on the skillet, allowing the pink sides of the meat to be exposed to the heated iron.

Kiara slowly sat down at the table, grateful for the heat of the stove to warm her bare arms. "Where's Brin?"

"He went outside to speak to the blacksmith. I believe they're discussing the reason behind the ringing of the bells."

"Oh," Kiara's voice was barely audible. She stared into the swirling, honey-brown liquid of her favorite beverage, unable to summon enough motivation to actually consume it. She tapped the mug with her finger half-heartedly, sighing. "Something's wrong with me, Anya. It's my birthday—my most important birthday—and yet, I feel..." she trailed off, searching for the correct word to describe her emotions.

"Sad," Anya finished, eyeing her sister's shimmering sapphire irises. "Your eyes are dark blue."

"They are?" she muttered, her hand instinctively flying to her cheek. She couldn't *feel* the color of her eyes, yet she could never fight off the impulse to try. "How strange..."

Anya shrugged, lowering the cooked meat onto a chipped plate. "You've become an adult. You're leaving the innocence of your childhood behind. It *is* sad, in a way."

"I suppose," Kiara sighed, taking a small sip of her nillamee. She was so pleasantly overwhelmed by the prevalent vanilla tang, she nearly drained the entire cup with her next drink.

Anya set the plate of meat in the center of the table, sending streams of steam swirling through the room. Kiara eyed the food hungrily, secretly wishing her sister had prepared a large loaf of bread instead.

"Happy birthday, Kiara!" Brin's booming voice abruptly filled the silence. He entered the kitchen, his dark eyes radiating compassion, his hand reaching out to pat his daughter's head.

She smiled up at him, her eyes automatically flashing purple with happiness. "Thank you," she replied softly. "Why were the bells ringing?"

Brin frowned, the lines on his forehead pulled tightly together as he slowly sat down in the chair opposite Kiara's. "The king of Enevale passed away this morning," he said delicately. "He was a friend of mine…"

"That's awful," Kiara gushed, her stomach knotting at the thought of death. "Did that vicious Nonae woman kill him?"

Brin shook his head, resting his chin on his upturned palm. "No, I'm afraid the cause of death hasn't been identified. He didn't appear to be wounded, however."

"Poison?" Anya offered, joining her family at the table. She laid down a plate bearing a chunk of bread in front of each person, her hands moving mechanically as her eyes stared fixedly at her father.

"I doubt it," he replied, picking up a piece of meat from the center of the table and laying it across his plate. "Kyan was very talented at apprehending poison in foods—which is why Vyntrx never bothered attempting to poison him."

Kiara gratefully picked up her bread, biting off a piece. "Who will rule Enevale now?" she asked through mouthfuls of food. "The princess is still missing, right?"

Every creature within a week's walk from Enevale knew the tragic story of King Kyan and his family. The king had taken a Nonae wife who had been unwelcomed by the Evalseman people, especially considering her sister had been the self-proclaimed ruler of the Dark Forest—or the inhabited territory of the Nonae. Kyan's wife had died during childbirth, and his daughter nearly suffered the same fate. Miraculously, the princess lived—but she had been hunted by her malicious aunt until Kyan had been forced to unwittingly send her to another world in an attempt to save her delicate life.

"I suppose Avian will take the throne, temporarily," Brin explained. "Aside from being the king's advisor, he *was* raised by Kyan."

"Oh, Avian," Anya swooned, staring dreamily into the distance. "He'll be a brilliant king."

Kiara snickered, picking up a piece of meat and biting into it. "Have you ever even *seen* Avian in person?"

Avian Knight, the king's advisor, was just as famous as the king he so dutifully served, although *his* past was mysteriously curtained. He was constantly featured in tapestries and paintings, loyally at the king's side. His stunning looks and reportedly charming personality had provided him with countless suitors and fans. He was seemingly the charismatic "prince" the masses cheered for, and with no heir in sight, his temporary position as king would be widely accepted.

"Well, no," Anya mumbled, stuffing her mouth with food.

"Things will definitely change," Brin said decidedly. His face was locked in a mixed expression, dripping with emotions Kiara couldn't read. "Nothing will be the same."

Anya was busy hiding her blushing face, and didn't catch Brin's unusual visage, but Kiara's eyes were locked on her adoptive father. Her hazel irises were brimming with confusion, but just as she was about to question Brin's foreboding speech, Anya politely asked Kiara if she would fetch a bucket of water from the well outside.

Normally, Kiara would have argued with her sister for several minutes over the excursion, but she wished to momentarily relieve herself from the tense atmosphere.

"I found your cloak!" Anya called as Kiara hurried through the living room. "It was under the couch!"

As Anya's voice succumbed to silence, Kiara's eyes fell upon her disheveled cloak lying on a chair in the living room. She grasped the garment, relieved she wouldn't have to dart into the cold weather with bare arms, carefully winding the fabric around her body. She snatched up a small bucket from the front room, hugging the item against her chest.

She opened the front door, her eyes squinting in an attempt to adjust to the sunlight. The village square was visible from Kiara's house, and the communal well was merely a stone's throw away from her front door. Not an overwhelming amount of people had decided to brave the vicious weather, but a handful of villagers were crowded around a makeshift memorial for the deceased king.

She crossed the cobbled stones of the square, nodding politely at the mourners as they glanced in her direction. She was tempted to pay her respects, but she knew the villagers would only spew hateful remarks regarding her Nonae eyes—especially if her irises happened to reflect any other emotion beside the sharp sapphire of sadness.

Her hands trembled, frozen from the cold, as she began to tie the rope around the handle of the bucket. Her fingers were shaking so badly, she nearly dropped the bucket into the well. After she had secured the bucket, she began lowering it into the water below. The stone of the well had been constructed of a material that was immune to cold, which provided the villagers with lukewarm water every day of the year. Evalseman born with inventing Specialties had created the magical stone, among many other creations, and had provided Menevilen with advanced technology.

"Kiara?" a strange voice spoke suddenly, immediately drawing her attention away from the well. She was caught off guard, startled so badly, she released her grip on the rope, sending the bucket splashing into the water.

A middle-aged man was staring directly at her, his hand resting on the edge of the well. He possessed a wild look, his eyes a familiar hazel; he was eerily pale, his flesh nearly translucent, as though he had lived in a cave all his life. He was clothed in black, tattered garments, the darkness of his robes a striking contrast to his pallid skin. "You're Kiara, right?" he persisted, his hand reaching to grab her wrist.

She impulsively flinched away, narrowing her gaze. "Who are you?"

"Show me your name," he demanded, eyeing her booted feet. "Take off your shoe."

Her eyes widened, flashing yellow with astonishment. "How

do you know the location of my name?"

Evalseman were born with their name birth marked in varying locations on their bodies. Parents were not able to name their children; they were born with their names already engraved in their skin. It was the mark of an Evalseman, and while some names were proudly displayed, others were readily concealed each day by clothing. Kiara's name was sprawled across her left ankle, typically hidden beneath her favorite pair of brown boots. Only Brin and Anya had ever seen it exposed.

The man grinned, his eyes flickering a humored, deep purple. Kiara stumbled backward, realizing that the man was a Nonae. His previously hazel eyes had displayed his curiosity, but the change in the color of his irises suggested that Kiara had accidentally given away information and he was thoroughly delighted.

He reached into the depths of his cloak, withdrawing a pointed dagger. His smile magnified, distorting his already deranged expression. "My master has ordered your death," he explained, raising the weapon high above his head. "Time to die, princess!"

The dagger swept downward, but Kiara expertly darted out of harm's way. She grasped the man's arm with one hand, twisting his wrist forward as she held his forearm back with her other palm. He winced in pain, dropping the dagger into the snow.

Kiara lashed her leg forward, landing a powerful kick in the middle of his torso. His body flung backward, giving her time to snatch the dagger from its buried location in the cold snow. She hurried over to where he lie, flicking the point of the blade underneath his chin, barely scraping his neck. "Your master should've sent a better assassin," she spoke thickly, appearing braver than she actually felt. She could hear the concerned whispers of villagers nearby, the low hum of their voices buzzing above the sound of her pulsating heartbeat. "Who are you?"

Despite the delicate situation he had been thrust into, the man's grin had not been vanquished. He stared up at Kiara, giggling, as a torrent of wind suddenly blasted her backwards. The dagger flew out of her reach as she was flung into the snow, but she didn't have time to recover the weapon before the Nonae sprang forward.

She recalled a lesson on Nonae she had been taught at the academy—the students had been informed about the abilities and characteristics of the species. She had already been aware of their inconsistent eyes that constantly shifted to reflect their emotions, but she was amazed to discover that Nonae could manipulate the energy around them to create a form of magic. There were common spells taught widely amongst the masses, but she had been warned of darker magic—spells that could destroy lives and temporarily raise the dead.

As the man reared his hand backward, summoning a spell, Kiara began to wonder what type of magic he possessed. She had never seen someone conjure magic before, and she wasn't sure how to fight against a bodiless entity.

Fire grew in the man's palm, the flames flickering ravenously, his hands miraculously unscathed. "Can't fight against this, can you?" he jeered.

"She may not be able to, but I can," a masculine voice abruptly declared, instantly demanding the attention of Kiara and her attacker.

Her head swiveled to the right, her eyes latching on a strikingly gorgeous young man. He was standing several yards away, his light brown hair falling into his eyes. Even from a distance, Kiara could tell his irises were mismatched—his right eye was an emerald green while his left was a vibrant blue. He held a confident expression on his strangely familiar face, the shadow of a smirk hugging the corners of his lips.

"*Avian?*" the Nonae man spoke incredulously. "What are you doing here?"

Kiara's eyes widened as her rescuer's name was revealed.

14

The *Avian?* she thought disbelievingly, suddenly very aware that she was still wearing her nightgown.

"The princess's safety is my top priority," Avian spoke calmly, his voice tinged with an accent iconic of Enevale. He hurriedly walked toward the Nonae, his eyes glaring darkly. "And you're compromising it."

Princess? Kiara wondered silently. *Who is this princess they keep going on about?*

"But, Avian, I—" the man's voice was silenced as Avian's hand suddenly grasped his throat. He had moved so quickly, so gracefully, Kiara had barely witnessed his body sliding across the snow.

The crowd of villagers loitering in the streets had increased noticeably, and a purr of hushed whispers infiltrated the silence. Kiara fought off the urge to glance over her shoulder to see if Brin and Anya, curious about the noise, had exited the house, but she was afraid if she peeled her eyes away for even a second, she would miss Avian's next move.

Avian tossed the man against the ground as though he were weightless. The Nonae gasped for air as if the action had drained his lungs of oxygen. His hands clawed his throat, his forehead breaking into a nervous sweat. As Kiara realized the man was actually unable to draw a breath, she suspected Avian of possessing Nonae magic—but she distinctly recalled hearing a rumor about the famous "prince": Avian was believed to brandish many mysterious and unique Evalseman Specialties. Having more than one Specialty was a rarity, but possessing an uncountable amount was unheard of. If Avian's good looks and royal connections hadn't provided him with a celebrity status, his unrivaled abilities would have.

Avian's smirk widened, his eyes flitting in Kiara's direction. She felt her cheeks instantly burn under his intense stare, felt her eyes shift downward as though they lacked the capability of returning his gaze. *He's just another Evalseman,* she reminded herself pointedly. *Don't let your guard down.*

The sound of a loud, desperate gasp tore Avian's attention away from Kiara. While she had been chiding herself for losing her head over the prince's presence, *he* had clearly allowed his mind to be distracted. The Nonae had managed to free himself of Avian's control and had regained the ability to breathe. He stood up shakily, holding his hand forward as he summoned a spell. A wall of pointed blades suddenly appeared from thin air above the man's hand. He flung his hand forward, sending the projectiles whirling directly at Avian.

Avian laughed, cavalierly raising his hand. A wall of ice appeared in front of his body, shielding him from the onslaught. The blades pelted the icy partition one by one, but the shield was so thick, not even one blade penetrated the surface of the other side. He snapped his fingers and the shield, bearing the weapons, instantly vanished. "Clever," he spoke sardonically, "but not enough verve."

The Nonae desperately attempted to summon another spell, but before he could fully raise his arm, Avian sent a fleet of sharp, cylindrical icicles speeding toward the man's body. The man shrieked, unable to think of a way to escape before the hurling icicles burrowed into his body. The Nonae's torso and left arm had been brutally tarnished with broken flesh and blood by the attack, weakening his limbs as he crumpled to the ground.

Avian casually sauntered over to the man's body, glancing up at Kiara from under downcast eyelashes as he past her. She watched him eagerly, identifying the notion of murder flickering in his eyes. Her stomach knotted at the thought—she had never witnessed a death, and the concept of dying was a disquieting topic she had trained her mind to avoid.

"Do you realize what you've done?" he roughly demanded an answer, folding his arms as he stared down at the injured Nonae writhing in pain. "Do you understand the gravity of the situation you have put yourself in?"

The Nonae, unable to respond, clutched his bleeding chest.

His eyes were bright maroon with terror, his body trembling.

"You attempted to murder the sole heir to the throne of Enevale," Avian explained, his cheeks dotted red with anger. He lifted his arm, pointing his finger in Kiara's direction. "You attempted to murder Princess Kiara Fable!"

Kiara's eyes widened mechanically at his words. She could feel her irises shift color, but she wasn't sure what emotion she was exuding. Her brain felt foggy, her body completely numb. There was a distant ringing pulsating through her ears, the sound growing so loud it was nearly deafening. Unrivaled ambiguity turned her heart to lead, filled her head with pandemonium, and shattered her balance. She could distantly feel her body falling, hitting the snow below. She could vaguely see Avian in the distance, unaware of the plague she was suffering as he sauntered toward the Nonae. His hands were held high above his head, ready to deliver his enemy's fate.

But Kiara's eyes slid shut before she could witness the man's death, and her consciousness was abruptly devoured by darkness.

Chapter Two

A Forsaken Destiny

Avian's heart was fluttering wildly in his chest. His reunion with the lost princess hadn't occurred even remotely how he had hoped it would, but being in her mere presence frayed his nerves and tugged at an emotion he had long since bottled down.

She had changed since he had seen her last. Her wavy hair had grown slightly, cascading across her back instead of hugging the ends of her shoulders as it had during childhood. Her face had become slimmer with cheekbones more prominent and lips fuller. Although her height had barely increased since she was nine, her body had become that of a woman's—narrow shoulders, small waist, proportionate hips, shapely legs—the only amenity she was lacking was a developed bust.

Avian sighed, wondering if Kiara's personality had shifted as drastically as her physical appearance. She had always been brave, always overestimating her abilities and putting herself in dangerous situations. He hadn't been surprised to find her attempting to ward off the Nonae on her own. But he couldn't fight the feeling that something about her was different. She had lived her life so differently than he had led his. While he was enjoying a life of luxury in the castle, she had been trapped in an isolated village, completely unaware of her destiny. He had thought of her every day, fondly recalling the time they had spent together, yet she only knew of him from paintings and stories.

Avian's fingers wove tightly around the small crown pendant the king had entrusted in him to deliver to the princess. He had often caught Kyan staring into the silvery depths of the necklace, and as Avian's downcast eyes bore dreamily into the metal, he could vividly picture his expression matching the solemn king's. The necklace rightfully belonged to Kiara, and the memory of her childhood lingered within the chain's cold touch.

"I was expecting you to come sooner," Brin's voice abruptly dissolved Avian's musing, drawing his eyes upward. Brin was standing in the doorway of the sitting room, lines of worry creasing his forehead as he surveyed the king's advisor.

After Avian had punished the Nonae for his offense, he had been confronted by Brin, who revealed that he knew Kiara's true identity. He had suggested they conduct their business indoors, and had carried Kiara's listless body to her room while Avian waited patiently on the couch.

"I was not aware of Kiara's location," he explained coldly, tucking the pendant into the pocket of his trousers. "We were all convinced that she was lost in a foreign world. I believe you and the king were the only two who were aware of her presence in Menevilen. But I—*I* should've known."

Brin crossed the room, tentatively sitting down beside Avian on the sofa. "Kyan was wary to inform me, although she was living under my guidance. It was the most important secret I have ever been ordered to keep."

"I was his advisor," Avian spoke coolly. "He raised me as though I were his son. He knew how deeply I cared for the princess, and yet he kept her out of my reach for so many years..."

"Don't be upset with Kyan," Brin advised. "He was protecting her. If you visited her frequently, someone would have caught on—and she would have been suspicious, undoubtedly. She's under your guidance now. I've raised her very well. She's an excellent warrior."

Avian sighed, running a hand through his orderly light brown hair. "I've no doubt she is. Once she awakens, we'll leave for Enevale."

"Enevale?" Kiara's confused voice spiked through the room, instantly grasping the attention of Avian and Brin. "With *you*?"

Avian tilted his head in her direction, the sight of her sending his heart on a rampage. Her eyes were bright orange with bewilderment, her eyebrows sharply narrowed. She folded her arms across her chest, making her appear incredibly small. He had to swallow down the urge to wrap her body in his arms. He cleared his throat, chiding himself for allowing his emotions to stir so rampantly. "You should sit down, Ara. We have a lot to discuss."

"Ara?" she muttered in confusion, hurriedly sitting down in a chair facing the couch. "Are you going to tell me what the hell is going on?"

"You know the stories of King Kyan and the lost princess, yes?" he asked rhetorically, knowing fully well she had undoubtedly heard the legend several times. She nodded, urging him to continue. "The princess in the story is you."

Kiara's mouth automatically unhinged. "I didn't hear you incorrectly earlier?" she spoke frantically, her irises shifting yellow with shock. "You're telling me that I *am* King Kyan's heir?"

Avian nodded stiffly. "The one and only. You are Kiara Sparrow Fable, princess of Enevale, daughter of King Kyan and Queen Raiyx, and one of the only half-Nonae, half-Evalseman in existence."

Kiara's head fell limply into her palms, her mind rushing with questions, her brain reeling to process the newly acquired information. She could feel the room spinning beneath her feet, but she wouldn't allow herself to fall prey to another fainting spell. "Wh-why can't I recall any of this?"

Avian was suddenly at her side, his arm wound around her waist. "Don't try to remember, it will only make you sick. Just absorb the information as if it were completely new."

"It *is* completely new!" she shouted, pushing his hand away.

"None of this makes sense!"

"It will all eventually make perfect sense, I swear," he whispered assuredly, patting her hand. "Your father erased your memories, Kiara, that's why you can't remember anything before living here. Isn't it strange that you couldn't recall your childhood? Did that ever concern you?"

"No, it did not," she spoke thickly, tucking her hand under her legs and out of Avian's reach. "I thought it was perfectly normal for children to forget most of their memories. It's difficult to recall things from your earliest years. I read that somewhere."

"Yes, that is common. But to completely forget *everything*—isn't that even the slightest bit odd?"

Kiara's eyes slanted downward, her brow furrowed. She appeared to be racking her brain for a proper response, but was coming up blank. "I guess," she huffed. "Well, what about you? Why are you so entwined with my hidden life?" She stared up at him with wide, curious hazel eyes. His face was merely inches away from hers—evoking a stronger feeling within his chest than the one that had overwhelmed his mind when she had observed her from a distance—and up close, he could see the faint cluster of freckles dotting the edges of her cheeks and the bridge of her nose, the light beauty mark underneath her left eye. He was so busy studying her face, he nearly forgot to reply.

"You—you already know that I was your father's advisor," he stammered uncharacteristically. "My family tragically died when I was a little boy, and because my father had been a duke and the king's best friend, Kyan decided to take me in. That's when I met you. You didn't look anything like your father—not really. You had your mother's sincere face, her inconsistent eyes. You were a perfect balance of Nonae and Evalseman, a balance of kindness and discipline. Something about you fascinated me, lured me to your side. You befriended me, cared for me. We were the best of friends, so close it made the other dukes jealous. But, one day, it all changed.

"We had been playing in the Dark Forest. We weren't allowed to venture into it—but you had always been adventurous—and we had discovered a hidden crack in the Wall large enough for us to crawl through. We accidently journeyed deeper into the forest than usual, and as dusk seeped across the sky, we were still helplessly lost. As night settled in, your aunt appeared within the shadows of the forest. She chased after us—knife in hand—and amid the chaos, we were separated. When I was finally recovered by your father, you were asleep in his arms. He told me that he had erased your memories, and that he was planning to send you away from Menevilen until you were ready to claim the throne.

"So long I've waited—desperately, longingly—for that joyful day. The day you would return to your rightful place in the castle, your rightful place at my side. I did not predict the day would also be so tinted in sullenness. I am mournful of your father's death. I am terrified of becoming the temporary king. But I have never felt as helplessly alone as I do when I stare into your eyes—eyes that should arouse nostalgia, eyes that should reflect compassion—and see nothing."

Kiara's expression softened remarkably at Avian's words, her lips parting as she attempted to construct a response. His hair tumbled into his eyes, casting shadows across his pale, unblemished skin. His eyes refused to meet Kiara's, although he could feel her penetrating stare scathing like flames against his flesh.

"I—I meant a lot to you, didn't I?" she questioned softly. The tense atmosphere had quelled her fury, and although she hated to admit it, she felt sincere sympathy for Avian's situation.

He nodded slowly. "More than you could ever realize."

"I'm sorry," she whispered, awkwardly laying her hand upon Avian's. "This is all just so hard to grasp. This morning, I woke up expecting to become an adult, to venture to Enevale and enlist in the military. I never imagined that Avian Knight would show up and surprise me with news of a hidden past. Did you really think I would just accept my heritage? That I would just waltz away with you and readily take the crown?"

"I assumed you would be skeptical," he replied huskily. "I understood that your memories had been eradicated. I was hoping the bond we had shared had not been broken, and that somewhere, deep down, you would feel it, and believe me."

She shrugged, wrapping her arms around her chest and pulling her knees tight against her torso. "I *do* believe you. It's just—it's so difficult to actually act upon it. My entire life was a lie. Who I am—no, who I *was*—it was all fake. There's a part of me that has been locked away. A part of me I didn't know existed. I feel angry, and scared, and confused." She abruptly stood up from her chair, her eyes harshly locked on Brin. "I trusted you, yet you kept something *so* important hidden from me. You let me live a lie!"

"I was protecting you," Brin spoke patiently. "It was imperative that the secret of your identity remain concealed. I received strict orders from your father. If you had been alerted, it would have made it very easy for Vyntrx to track you. Because you were entirely oblivious, because you never once suspected that you were the lost princess, you took on the persona of a completely different person, which made it virtually impossible for anyone to locate you."

"Why does Vyntrx want to kill me at all?" she demanded an answer, an incredulous tone resonating through her voice as she rested her hands against her hips.

"She blames you for the death of her sister," Avian explained, his voice tight. "She had harbored an intense hatred for the Evalseman since childhood, had always wished to launch a war against the entire race—but your mother's death was the push she needed to take action. She wished to wipe out the Fable family, take control of Enevale, and extend her conquest across all of Menevilen."

"Why is it safe for me to know about the truth now?" she questioned. "Doesn't she still want to kill me?"

"You're stronger now," Brin explained. "I wasn't training you so you could join the military and fight Vyntrx's army. I was training you to fight Vyntrx herself."

Kiara's eyes widened, her irises shimmering maroon with fright. Her heart dropped from her chest, her stomach lurching violently. "Me?" she spoke hoarsely. "You actually expect *me* to fight the most vicious Nonae in the Dark Forest? I—I'll die!"

Avian's hand gently clutched Kiara's shoulder, drawing her eyes to his face. "You will have time to prepare yourself. It is my most important duty to protect you—I will not let you be killed."

"How can you expect me to trust you so willingly?" her voice escaped her lips in a harsh whisper as she jerked her shoulder away from Avian's hand. "How can you come into my life and change everything? How can you demand so much of me? Who the hell do you think are?"

Avian's mismatched eyes hardened. His hands clenched so tightly into fists, his knuckles turned white. "I'm Avian," he spat. "There was a time, Kiara, when that actually meant something to you."

Kiara's rage dwindled abruptly, as though her fury had taken a blow from his sharp words. Her eyes searched Avian's, exploring the wealth of frustration and hurt that welled beneath his irises.

"Avian is your advisor now, Kiara," Brin spoke tentatively. "It is his duty to deliver you to Enevale, to educate you about the kingdom, to make you a worthy queen. Above all of that, however, he is your protector. Your safety lies in his hands."

She stole a glance at Avian. His face was downcast; he refused to return her gaze. "My life in your hands," she muttered. "You've got to be kidding."

His eyes flashed upward at her words, his handsome face contorted by a mask of pain. "Could you imagine if that girl you consider your sister were to just forget you? Imagine how you'd feel if she lost all memories of the times you've spent together. Imagine if she looked at you, and instead of friendship and compassion filling her eyes, a hateful glare took its place. Imagine if she vanished for several years, and when the day finally came that you were reunited, she was callous and subjective. What would you do? How would you act? How desperate would *you* be?"

Kiara couldn't bring herself to reply. Avian's words drilled through her mind, effectively cutting away her fury. In the heat of her perplexed rage, she hadn't realized how sharply her words had stung him. She shook her head, attempting to chase away the look of sympathy that was slowly spilling across her face. "I'm going to my room," she declared hotly.

"Do you want—" Brin started.

"I want to be left alone," she decreed, silencing his voice. "If I really am the lost princess you've been going on about, then you'd better heed my warning. I want to be left alone."

Silence weighed heavily on the tense atmosphere as Kiara darted out of the room. She sprinted up the small staircase in the corner of the kitchen, dashed past where Anya sat dejectedly at the table, and entered the small loft she shared with her sister. It was then that Avian's muffled voice sounded from beneath the floorboards, and it was then that Kiara's eyes welled with unrestrained tears.

*****

Anya hovered in the doorway of the loft, watching Kiara's small body heave with sobs. She had pulled her legs tightly against her chest, the way she always did whenever she was upset, and had hidden her face from sight.

Kiara possessed many routine habits and many consistent traits that Anya had managed to note. Kiara didn't cry frequently, but when she did allow herself to succumb to tears, it required a significant amount of effort to suppress her sobs. Anya had been present to soothe her sister on many occasions, when she had possessed the understanding of the situation and means of fixing it. But as she watched her sister cry over a matter that was helplessly out of her hands, she felt utterly useless.

"Kiara?" she spoke gently, taking a timid step into the room. "Are you alright?"

She glanced at her sister with sapphire eyes rimmed in tears. "No," she said plainly. "I am not."

Anya sighed, hurrying over to her sister's bed. She sat down on the mattress, comfortingly running her fingers through Kiara's disheveled tresses. "I overheard your conversation with Brin and Avian. I—I was prepared to see you leave today, but not under this strange ordinance. I always knew you were special..."

"I am *not* special," Kiara argued thickly. "I'm a *freak*. I am the result of a Nonae and Evalseman's love affair. I have the blood of two species coursing through my veins—two species that shouldn't coexist. Wrestling with that fact my entire life was a burden enough—you know the penalties I received, the prejudice I suffered. But now I'm expected to rule an entire kingdom? This is a sick joke. Avian should know fully well a kingdom teeming with Evalseman would not accept a half-breed. They showed Kyan's wife only cruelty."

"She was your mother," Anya whispered. "She endured it. Why can't you?"

"She had my father!" Kiara shrieked hysterically, flinging her body off of the bed. "She was not entitled to rule Enevale on her own! Her life was not being hunted by a bloodthirsty empress! She was not required to single-handedly end a vicious war! Do you even remotely understand the intensity of this world I have been thrust into? I probably won't make it out alive!"

Anya's eyes fell downward, unable to endure the sight of

Kiara's distraught expression. She had rarely seen her sister so distressed, and the occurrence was deeply unsettling. She could *feel* desperation secreting from Kiara's words, and as much as she wanted to offer her assistance, she wasn't sure she could. "I'm so sorry," she spoke softly, her eyes suddenly flooded with tears. "Th-this is your destiny," she choked out the words, burying her eyes in her palms. "It's what you have to do. I'm afraid you don't have another choice."

Kiara mechanically shook her head, unable to fathom that a life of normalcy was so miserably forsaken. "It can't be my only choice," she spoke, her voice merely a whisper.

"It is," Anya persisted, cautiously moving her hand away from her tear-streaked face. "If you don't reclaim the throne and end the war, Vyntrx will rule over all of Menevilen. You and I both know that Kyan was the sole barrier between the Evalseman and Vyntrx's vile crimes. Avian may be able to fend her off for a little while, but ultimately, Enevale needs a monarch. Enevale needs you."

"I—I can't," Kiara stammered, her tremulous legs buckling. She fell to her knees on the wooden floor, her eyes staring directly at the ground. "I'm not strong enough."

Anya exhaled sharply, her eyes narrowing in her sister's direction. "Remember when we were children, and you always wanted to pretend you were a magnificent queen? You would boss me around for hours. You would tell me elaborate stories of wars we had fought and won, of lands we had bravely conquered, of handsome princes we had shyly courted. Once you grew into a young lady, you abandoned idle thoughts of make-believe stories. In its place, you constructed a dream—a dream to become a legendary warrior of Enevale. It was a very real dream to you, to my father, and even to me. You traded in figurines and gowns for knives and fighting lessons. I watched my father mold my vulnerable little sister into a strong-willed, determined warrior. You possessed such fiery passion, the same passion I saw flicker in your young eyes as you imagined yourself as a powerful queen. You have always wanted to escape this mundane village. You have always hungered for adventure, have always thirsted for danger. But now that you have been handed the world you always craved, you have lost your appetite. You're scared—and it isn't like you. For the sake of the Evalseman race, for the sake of the kingdom of Enevale, and by Veinya's name, for the sake of our family, *please* recover your bravery. Because if you don't, not only will you perish, but you will selfishly take all of Menevilen with you."

Anya's words struck Kiara like a painful blow, detangling the knots of apprehension from her stomach. She reclined her weight upon her knees, meeting her sister's pleading gaze. Residual tears stained Kiara's cheeks, but Anya's speech had instilled her body with a newfound sensation of unparalleled strength. "You're right," she exclaimed breathlessly. "You're entirely right!"

Anya smirked, patting her sister's shoulder lovingly. "Of course I am. I am your older sister, after all. *Someone's* got to talk some sense into you when you become irrational. Don't fret, though, I'm sure Avian can fill my shoes perfectly."

Kiara smiled, allowing her sister to help her climb to her feet. At the mention of Avian's name, a bitter pang of guilt swept through Kiara's chest. She instantly regretted the callous demeanor she had possessed during her conversation with him. He had merely been trying to help, while she had returned his kindness with harsh tones and hurtful words. "Thank you for helping me come to my senses," she gushed gratefully. "I need to apologize to Avian. He needs to know that I'm ready to accompany him to Enevale."

Kiara hastily turned toward the door, but Anya caught her wrist. "First, you need to change out of your nightgown. Put on some proper clothes before you gallivant across Menevilen."

Kiara chuckled, turning away from her sister and critically eyeing her wardrobe.

*****

The sunlight cascading across the village was dull, rays of golden sun hidden beneath tufts of cloud. The light that filtered through the sky was grey, casting morose hues across the snowy ground below. Avian's booted foot kicked the ground, loosening a clump of ice. Cold flecks of water sprayed up at his frowning face, but he was undaunted by the action. The cloak hugging his shoulders typically provided enough warmth, but his argument with Kiara had turned his veins to ice. He felt eerily cold, as though her words had stolen away his ability to feel the warmth of contentment.

A harsh gust of wind tore through the village square, tangling Avian's orderly hair. The frozen air cut through his cloak, biting at his flesh and sending chills across his arms. He was tempted to duck indoors, to escape the frigid weather, but he refused to return to Kiara's house—he couldn't handle being so close to her and yet feeling so far away.

"Avian?" Kiara's voice was barely audible above the howling wind. At first, he figured his mind was playing a cruel trick on him, but as her hand fell upon his shoulder, his head immediately swiveled around.

She was glancing down at him with curious hazel eyes, her eyebrows narrowed. She had pulled her hair into a high ponytail, the ends of her wavy tresses brushing against the nape of her neck. "What are you doing out here? It's freezing."

"Just preparing myself for the journey," he responded, forcing a pleasant tone to infiltrate his voice. "I teleported to your village, but that would be a difficult feat to manage with you pinned to my side. We'll have to take a horse to the kingdom."

She wrinkled her nose at the thought, sitting down beside him in the snow. "I'll ask Brin if you could borrow some of his clothes. You'll freeze to death."

"I'll be fine," he assured her. "Are you alright?"

Kiara nodded, hugging her legs to her chest. Avian noticed she had changed out of her plain nightgown and had tucked a pair of tight olive pants into tall leather boots. "I'm alright," she said thoughtfully. "Anya brought me back to my senses. I understand now that it's my duty to return to Enevale and reclaim the throne. I'm sorry I acted callously."

Avian's face brightened instantly. "Ah, so they *did* provide you with an extensive vocabulary in this small village! Wonderful!"

Kiara scowled, lightly elbowing Avian in the ribs. "Shut up! I'm apologizing!" she yelled, fending off a smirk. "But if you must know, I actually studied language and literature on my own. The academy didn't provide me with enough information."

"Your apology is accepted, of course," he replied, laughing as he bumped his shoulder against Kiara's. "That's impressive, though. Why did you only study those subjects?"

She shrugged. "They were the only two that interested me. Did you expect me to be illiterate just because I grew up in a small village? My roots *are* apparently planted in Enevale, though."

Avian chuckled, watching Kiara's lips pull into a smile. The cold wind had turned her cheeks rosy; her eyes were shimmering purple with happiness. "You're coming to terms with it all," he noted. "That's a relief."

"I am," she admitted. Her eyes found Avian's face and he readily returned her gaze. "It's still a bit strange to me, though. You know practically everything about me, and yet I can't remember anything about you."

"We'll just have to become friends all over again," he decided. Although he appeared to be perfectly unabashed by the idea, Kiara could clearly see clouds of pain swirling beneath his seemingly joyful stare. "It'll be easy, really. I'm quite charming."

"So I've heard," Kiara laughed. "Tell me something about

yourself that no one knows. I've heard plenty of rumors about you. I want to know something that isn't whispered by the masses."

Avian sent her a crooked grin, shaking his head. "Something no one knows?" he chuckled. "I have plenty of secrets. You'll come to learn all of them over time, the closer we become..." he trailed off, attempting to recall a fact about himself that he could share. His face abruptly darkened, as though a shadow of anguish had settled within his mind. "Today, however, I will grant you a little insight into my past. It's common knowledge that my parents were brutally murdered when I was a child, but there are two additional points to the story that I have kept hidden from prying minds. First, I had a younger half-brother who was also killed on that dreadful day. Second, my family was massacred by Vyntrx herself."

Kiara's mouth hung open in surprise. She stared at Avian with sympathy, her hand mechanically reaching out to stroke his shoulder. His muscular arms were tight with tension, relaxing slightly under her gentle touch. "I'm so sorry," she spoke quietly. "Vyntrx is a monster. One day, Avian, I swear, I'll kill her and end this bitter war."

"Anya really got through to you, didn't she?" he asked, smiling as his hand lightly patted Kiara's head. "Perhaps I should ask her for some tips on how to handle you."

She shrugged, edging her cloak nearer to her body. "I'm sure you'll figure me out rather easily."

"I certainly hope so," he said confidently. He started to wrap his arm around Kiara's shoulders, but the puzzled expression playing on her face startled him back to his senses. He cursed under his breath, chiding himself as he folded his arms across his chest. "I'm sorry," he grumbled rather grudgingly. "I have to keep reminding myself that we're strangers."

Kiara shook her head in protest. "No, don't tell yourself

that. We aren't strangers; we're acquaintances on a mission to become friends. Besides, to you, I'm the little girl from your memories. What you need to understand is that I am a completely different person than I was then. I've changed. You'll come to terms with the new me, and I'll come to know you as more than just Avian Knight, the charming advisor."

Avian's lips slid into a wide smile, his mismatched eyes shimmering with approval. "Sounds like a plan," he decided. "That reminds me, I have a present for you."

"A present?" Kiara echoed, watching Avian as he scoured his pocket for the mysterious object.

"Here it is!" he exclaimed. There was a wink of silver as Avian withdrew something from his cloak. He held his hand forward, waiting for Kiara to receive the object.

She timidly extended her hand forward just as Avian released his hold on the object. A small, silver pendant cascaded from his palm, landing against Kiara's outstretched hand. Before her eyes flickered to her gift, she caught a glimpse of a delicate birthmark branding Avian's palm—it was his name, his Evalseman marking. Avian had immediately struck her as the type of Evalseman that wouldn't exert any effort to hide his Evalseman signature, but with the location being so naturally exposed, his name was destined to be a spectacle any time he extended his hands. Kiara was suddenly grateful for the readily concealable location of her name. She had never been fond of the attention an Evalseman mark encouraged.

Her eyes fell upon her own palm as she drunk in the sight of a beautiful necklace crafted out of a shimmering, silver metal. It bore a crown pendant the size of a strawberry, held into position by a thick chain. Kiara's fingers danced across the intricate design on the crown emblem, her lips parted in wonder. "This is mine?" she asked breathlessly.

"It is," Avian assured her. "It was made in your honor the day you were born. Your father asked that I deliver it to you. It's a gift—it *is* your birthday, after all."

"It's magnificent," she praised, hurriedly unfastening the latch. "I'm going to wear it every day."

Avian chuckled, watching her fumble as she attempted to fasten the necklace behind her neck. "Let me help you," he whispered, his fingers brushing her own as he reached around her back. He expertly secured the latch, attempting to ignore the sensation that swept through his chest as his cheek rubbed against Kiara's.

"It's fastened," he declared, quickly pulling his body away from hers.

She watched him apprehensively, her fingers winding around the chain of the necklace. "How does it look?"

"It looks perfect," he decided, eyeing Kiara as a bout of strong wind made her shiver. "Let's retreat indoors," he suggested, carefully grasping Kiara's small hands in his own. Her exposed fingers were red and nearly frozen, but she hadn't seemed to notice. He held her hands up to his cracked lips, emitting a cloud of hot breath against her skin. "You're freezing."

Kiara's weather-beaten face flushed crimson. "M-my hands are always cold," she stammered, unable to find enough strength to pull away from Avian's grasp. "You're right, though, we should go back to the house. We should eat a proper meal before we head out."

"Yes, we should," he agreed, instantly dropping his hold on Kiara's hands.

She smiled shyly, climbing to her feet. She waited patiently for Avian to follow suit, but after several minutes had passed, he still sat placidly on the ground, his eyes fixed on something she couldn't see.

Kiara cleared her throat. "You coming?"

"Oh," Avian said quietly, blinking hard. His eyes found Kiara's face and he smiled, but she could tell the expression was forced. "Yes, I'm coming."

Chapter Three

Departure

Kiara stared lovingly at the diminutive loft she had considered her bedroom for eight years. Her bed already appeared forlorn, as though it were entirely aware that she would never sleep within its comfort again. She had memorized the pattern of the cracks in the thin walls, had grown accustomed to the rickety floorboards. Although she had always told herself that she loathed the crowded bedroom, she found herself admitting that she would actually miss it. She sighed, her fingers instinctively tracing the crown pendant lying against her chest.

Avian had advised that she pack lightly—although she had already gathered most of her belongings, and had to weed through the large sack she planned on carrying—and had politely asked Anya to prepare a bag full of food for the journey. Anya had obliged, of course, and Kiara could hear her in the kitchen, hurriedly combing through cabinets.

"You doing alright up here?" Avian's voice suddenly broke through Kiara's reverie.

She turned around, discovering Avian in the doorway of the loft. His signature grin was pinned to his face, his body reclined casually against the doorframe.

"Yes, I'm fine," she replied. "Just making sure I've packed anything I can't live without."

"Ah, but you haven't. You forgot to pack me," he joked, thoroughly pleased at his own humor.

Kiara laughed, shaking her head. She recovered her leather bag from its position on the ground, shouldering the strap. "I just packed some spare clothes and a blanket. I need to grab my weapons from the barn before we leave."

Avian nodded in accordance, allowing Kiara to brush past him toward the staircase. He followed her down the stairs, eyeing Anya as she compiled a stack of bread into a large sack. Brin was sitting at the kitchen table, sharpening the blade of a five-inch dagger. His expression lightened as his eyes fell upon Kiara, a smile forming on his lips.

"I figure you'll be making use of this," he said, turning the dagger handle in Kiara's direction. "I had the blacksmith forge it for you. I thought it'd be a nice birthday gift."

Kiara was wearing an elated expression as she grasped the dagger, exclaiming her gratification. The weapon brandished a sharp, silver blade protruding from an intricately designed hilt that fit perfectly within her small hand. She gleefully examined the dagger before expertly tucking it away inside a sheath tied to her belt. "We're going to fetch the rest of my weapons," she informed Brin.

He nodded his approval. "Anya will have your food ready when you return."

Avian followed at Kiara's heels as she darted out of the kitchen, disappearing behind the back door. The stretch between the house and the barn was minuscule, which Avian was grateful for as a gust of wind tore through his cloak. The barn's exterior was rather shabby—the paint covering the wooden boards had been chipped and worn. A small door stood in the center of the building, inviting Kiara nearer as her hand fell upon the handle.

"I always practice in here," she explained, pulling open the door. "What weapons are you familiar with?"

Avian took a step into the barn, crunching a pile of hay under his boots. The room was spacious, considering there was nothing crowding it besides a small table and a stone fireplace. "I'm familiar with them all, really," he explained. "However, I favor swords."

"You didn't bring a sword, though, did you?" she

questioned, recovering a wooden bow from the table and stringing it across her back. She gathered her arrows, securing them inside a leather quiver that she hurriedly strapped into place in-between her shoulders.

Avian shook his head. "I don't always fight with weapons. I have far too many Specialties to require assistance."

"You're lucky," she mumbled, eyeing the heavy sword lying on the table. She contemplated leaving it there—she felt the weapon merely got in her way—but before she could decide, she was suddenly struck with an idea. "You can use this sword," she suggested. "So you'll be fully prepared if we run into danger."

Avian smiled, his fingers sliding across the padded hilt of the sword. "It's a beautiful weapon," he admired. "Are you sure you wouldn't mind me borrowing it?"

"Of course I wouldn't," she responded conclusively. "You can keep it. I only use a sword if I have to."

Avian carefully retrieved the weapon, examining the blade. "It's sharp enough, I believe," he noted. "You know, I have the same amount of strength as you—well, actually, the strength from your Evalseman Specialty. It's one of my many traits. This sword feels like a feather in my hands."

"Another Evalseman with my Specialty, huh?" she playfully jeered, picking up a sheath from the table and tossing it in Avian's direction. "You may just be my match."

He caught the sheath, his eyebrows rising at Kiara's comment. "Your match?" he wondered, attempting to quell the illogical voice inside his head that suggested she had used the term romantically.

"Yeah, in a fight," she responded, unaware of Avian's confusion.

"Oh, of course," he said quickly, tying the sheath to his belt and sliding the sword into the holster. "Or perhaps I'm your superior," he chuckled.

She scoffed, resting her hands on her hips. "I suppose we'll just have to test your theory."

"Another day, Ara," he promised. "We've got a long journey ahead of us."

Her eyes abruptly gleamed orange with confusion. "Why do you keep calling me that?"

"It's your nickname," he explained briefly, admiring the sword's elegant hilt as it rested against his hip. "Do you not like it? I can stop calling you that if it bothers you."

She shook her head, picking up a small, sheathed knife from the table and tying it into place beside her dagger. "No, it doesn't bother me. No one's ever given me a nickname, so I was just a little taken aback."

Avian smiled kindly, resting his weight against the empty table. "That's not entirely true. All of the dukes—and even your father—called you 'Ara'."

She waved her hand dismissively. "Should we buy one or two horses for the journey?"

"Just one," he decided. "We can only take the horse halfway. Horses refuse to venture into the Dark Forest, and even if they would, the terrain would be extremely difficult for them to navigate."

Kiara's eyes instantly widened, flashing maroon with fright. "Wait, we're going through the Dark Forest? Isn't that Nonae territory?"

Avian nodded solemnly. "Enevale is entirely flanked by the forest and the Kahliar Sea—well, there's also the Eustoripha Plains, but beyond that, there's merely more forest. We'll have to travel quickly through part of the forest. Luckily, we'll be hundreds of miles away from Vitaciel, the Nonae capitol and Vyntrx's self-proclaimed fortress."

Kiara's mouth had grown unbelievably dry at the thought. She attempted to swallow down the spiking fear of Vyntrx and the forest, but the action felt as though she had poured a handful of sand down her throat. "That sounds mildly dangerous," she spoke quietly, her voice raw. "What will we do with the horse once we reach the forest?"

"There are small villages similar to this one scattered across Menevilen. We'll sell the horse in a town near the forest and then we'll be forced to continue on foot."

Kiara nodded comprehensively, taking a step toward the door. "Approximately how long do you think the trip will last?"

Avian obediently followed after Kiara as she exited the barn. "Less than a week, since we'll be traveling on horseback for part of the journey."

"Not too bad," she decided, shivering as she hurried across the yard toward the house. "I'm anxious to see Enevale."

She opened the back door, allowing Avian to duck through the threshold before she shut out the howling winds. Avian smiled, following Kiara into the kitchen. "It's a very beautiful city," he explained. "I think you're going to enjoy living there."

Brin chuckled, overhearing Avian's words. "Yes, I'm sure Kiara will be delighted to live in Enevale. She's always complained about being in such a small village."

Kiara shrugged, resting her back against the wall. "It's boring here."

"Your food is ready," Anya chimed in, standing up from the table and pointing to a large knapsack resting on the counter. "I packed a few loaves of bread, dried meat, and some vegetables. I know Kiara won't touch the vegetables, but I figured Avian might want them. I also poured some water into a weather-protective pouch. I hope it's enough."

Avian smiled gratefully, picking up the bag. "It's definitely enough. Thank you, Anya."

Anya blushed, averting her gaze to the floor. Kiara eyed her sister, laughing quietly. "I'm going to miss you, Anya," she said softly.

Anya's expression saddened as she lifted her face upward. "I'll miss you, too," she whispered, holding her arms forward as Kiara fell into them. "You're going to be a brilliant queen."

Kiara clung to her sister's shoulders, attempting to fight off the cloud of tears lining her eyes. "Thank you," she breathed. "I hope I can make you and Brin very proud."

"You already have," she said assuredly, patting Kiara's back. She gently pulled away, smiling at her sister. "We'll see you soon. Come visit when you get the chance."

"I will," Kiara promised. She wiped at her eyes with the back of her hand, wishing she could collect her emotions as capably as her sister could. She turned her attention to Brin, feeling her eyes swell once again.

"The moment you joined my family, I knew this day would eventually come," Brin spoke nostalgically, beckoning Kiara closer. She wrapped her arms around her father, reveling in the familiarity of his touch. She felt entirely at ease against her father's chest, as though his strong body could shield her from the potential dangers of her newfound world. "I have cared for you as though you were my own daughter. I have trained you, protected you, provided for you—but most importantly, I have loved you. You have left an irreplaceable mark on my life, and I sincerely hope that I have issued a similar impact upon yours. For years, I have understood your fate and have attempted to prepare you for it. I have watched you grow into a young lady your father—your *real* father—would be incredibly proud of. You are strong enough to face Vyntrx and win. If you would push away your thoughts of doubt and replace it with confidence, you would be unstoppable. I know you will become a legendary queen. Always know, wherever you are, Anya and I are thinking about you, praying to Veinya that she will guide you and protect you from harm. I was blessed to have such an amazing young woman in my life, and I am saddened to see you leave. However, I know many great things await you in Enevale. The fate of Menevilen rests on your small shoulders, daughter, but I know you will not falter."

Unrestrained tears spilled from Kiara's sapphire eyes, urging a soft whimper from her lips. Brin's arms extended toward her, catching her small body as she fell against his chest. He stroked his daughter's hair shakily, trying to hold back his own emotions.

"I love you, papa," she whispered hoarsely. "Regardless of what happens to me or Menevilen itself, I *will* see you again."

Kiara felt Brin's lips pull into a smile against the top of her head as his chin brushed her forehead. "I love you, too, daughter."

He held her comfortingly for a long pause before he finally obtained the nerve to release his grip. She stared up at him with bright blue eyes, evidence of saddened emotion dripping down her pallid cheeks. His fingers were warm as they carefully brushed her tears away.

"We should depart before the sun rises too high," Avian advised, his calm voice seemingly misplaced amid the somber ambiance. "We don't want to waste daylight."

Kiara nodded slowly in compliance, averting her gaze from its locked position with her father's eyes. She gathered the knapsack Anya had packed from the table, sharing one last glance with her adoptive sister before she darted out of the room with Avian at her heels and tears in her eyes.

*****

The bitter wind cut across Avian's flushed cheeks, his long eyelashes dusted by white flecks of snow. The temperature had dropped sharply since he and Kiara had left the village, and although the dull sky had remained the same shade of grey, he knew nighttime was approaching.

At the edge of Kiara's village, they had procured a strong horse in exchange for a handful of Avian's money. The horse was sheer black with sleek fur and bulging muscles—utterly intimidating in appearance—but it possessed a calm and obedient temperament, and had proven to be reliable.

Kiara lacked experience with horses and had modestly asked Avian to help her mount the giant animal. He had chuckled, realizing that because of her petite stature, she would have required his help regardless. Once they were settled on the steed, with Avian proudly clutching the reins and Kiara cautiously gripping his shoulders, the horse began marching in the direction of Enevale.

Kiara's hands slipped down to Avian's torso as the horse galloped across rough terrain. Her arms instinctively wound around his stomach, her head resting in-between his shoulder blades. "Don't flatter yourself," she mumbled, feeling his body tighten under her abrupt touch. "I just don't want to fall off."

"Cling as tight as you like," Avian chuckled, stealing a glance at Kiara over his shoulder. She had buried her face in the fabric of his cloak, shielding her skin from the frigid wind.

"Are we going to ride through the night?" she wondered, her voice muffled.

Avian shook his head in response, his eyes carefully scanning the snow-covered horizon. "No, we'll stop to rest once we come across another village. There's no need to sleep in the snow."

"Do you have money for a room?"

Avian chortled loudly. "Of course I do! Being the King's advisor certainly has its perks. Although, I was well-off just being the son of a duke."

"You're lucky," Kiara muttered acrimoniously. "My family has faced much difficulty earning money. There aren't many jobs in my village, and even if you manage to obtain one, the pay is minimal."

Avian's lips fell into a grimace as he was embraced by guilt. "I'm sorry, I didn't realize."

Kiara shook her head, sending chills down Avian's spine as her hair brushed across his back. "You can't help that you're wealthy. I don't blame you for being proud of it."

"I—I'm not proud. Kiara, I don't want you think that I'm bragging—"

"It's alright," she said quickly, silencing him. Although her tone was convincing, Avian felt her grip around his torso lessen. "So, my father raised you, right?"

Avian momentarily stopped chiding himself to respond to Kiara's question. "Yes, he did. After my parents were killed, I had nowhere else to go. Your father was a strong, kind-hearted man. You remind me of him very much."

"It's still weird for me to picture King Kyan as my father," she whispered. "It's odd to think the Great King himself is responsible for my existence."

Her bemused words brought Avian's characteristic smile back to his face. "Kyan would have never considered himself a 'great' king. He was merely serving his birthright, protecting his people. He genuinely cared about the Evalseman, and all of his courageous efforts in fending off Vyntrx were in an attempt to preserve his beloved kingdom. When he interacted with you, he was no different than any other endearing father."

Kiara smiled, attempting to envision the bright-eyed king from the tapestries as though he were as real as Avian, his body warm against her fingertips. "Did you ever meet my mother?"

"As a young child, I'm sure I was around her constantly, since our parents were the best of friends. But the queen died the day you were born, and I was only a little over two years old at the time. I can't remember anything from that time of my life."

"That's understandable," Kiara said slowly. There were tapestries of the queen spread throughout the kingdom, as well, but they weren't as common. She had only seen one image of the queen throughout her entire life, and she hadn't studied the painting long enough to commit her visage to memory.

"She looked like you," Avian explained. "Or, really, *you* look like *her*. There are paintings of her in nearly every hallway of the castle. She's strikingly beautiful."

Kiara snickered, bumping her forehead against Avian's back. "Then I must not actually look like her," she murmured.

"Oh, you certainly do look like her," he insisted. "And you are similarly beautiful."

Kiara's cheeks automatically flushed at Avian's words. She had never extensively spoken to boys her age—most of the people in the village shied away from her at all costs—and she had never heard anyone outside of her family comment on her appearance.

"Th-thanks," she spluttered, feeling Avian's body quiver against hers as he chuckled.

"There's a village in the distance," he spoke abruptly, pointing to a black dot creeping over the grey horizon. "We'll stop there for the night. We've covered enough ground for today, and I'm sure you're exhausted after this morning's pandemonium."

Kiara nodded, longing for the warmth of a heated room and the comfort of a quilted blanket. "I keep thinking that tomorrow I'll wake up and today would have simply been a dream."

Avian laughed quietly, shaking his head. "Well, then, when you wake up tomorrow morning, you will be pleasantly surprised. And, of course, I'll be there beside you, anchoring you to reality."

Kiara smiled, slowly tightening her grip around Avian's torso. To her, Avian was a symbol of her new world, an important beacon guiding her toward her destiny. To her, he was a vital part of her royal life, the only one who could satisfy her crave for knowledge about her mysterious past. To her, he was irreplaceable. And even though Kiara barely knew him on a personal level, something about his demeanor was irresistibly inviting. Something about the charismatic smile on his face—the light kindness in his eyes, the gentleness of his touch—implored Kiara to be close to him, to trust him. And although she had never trusted anyone outside her family before, she could feel the precautionary walls around her heart beginning to deteriorate.

Chapter Four

The Dark Forest

The days slowly crept past like shadows cast against a wall, leisurely slipping further downward as the sun fell in the sky. Although Kiara and Avian had embraced a daily routine—consume a small breakfast, ride toward Enevale, stop at a village near dusk, eat dinner, sleep—time seemed immeasurably unhurried.

Kiara grew restless, her limbs tingling with the desire to move. She had never sat for four days straight on a horse, aimlessly eyeing dull, snowy landscape pass by. She sought solace in communicating with Avian, and after hours each day of extensive conversation, she felt as though she knew no one better. She learned nearly every detail of his childhood, had received vivid recollections of his past. His father's name had been Ariux Knight, a duke of Enevale and King Kyan's dearest friend since infancy. Avian's father had pursued a Nonae woman while he had still been married to Avian's mother, which resulted in the wife's suicide shortly after Avian's half-brother had been born illegitimately. Avian was consequently raised in the Dark Forest until Vyntrx brutally massacred his family, prompting him to live with King Kyan in Enevale.

Kiara learned that Avian had traveled through the Dark Forest countless times, virtually mastering its labyrinth paths while encountering Vyntrx and her minions on several occasions. He had engaged in battle with the majority of them and even been affronted by Nonae magic spun from the hands of Vyntrx herself. She learned that he had been trained in hand-to-hand combat since he was five years old, leading him to be placed in charge of Enevale's military the day he accepted the role of Kyan's advisor. He had excelled so greatly in academics that he had finished even the most complex academy lessons by age fourteen, enababling him to eloquently speak the ancient Evalseman tongue, a language that only the highest class Evalseman practiced. She learned his favorite foods, his least favorite activities, the qualities in others he couldn't tolerate—she regretted to admit that she possessed a handful of these characteristics herself. She became familiar with nearly every aspect of Avian's life, so she rewarded him with a front-seat view into hers. He already knew the basics, having been acquainted with her during childhood, but she had clearly changed since then, otherwise Avian wouldn't act so flustered whenever he couldn't read her.

"Honestly, you don't like *fruit*?" he exclaimed disbelievingly, twisting his neck around to gape at her.

She laughed lightly, shaking her head. "Not a single kind."

"I have never heard of such anarchy," he joked. "You used to enjoy apples."

She shrugged, smirking. "It seems even my taste buds have changed since our last meeting."

He smiled, turning his attention back to the solemn road ahead. "The Dark Forest is in view," he whispered. Kiara's eyes followed his pointed finger, latching on a row of shadowed trees in the distance. "There's a village on the horizon, to the right," he explained, moving his hand toward a small clump of buildings hugging the outskirts of the forest. "We can sell the horse there and replenish our food supply."

Kiara nodded slowly, attempting to bottle down the wave of hysteria rising in her chest. "We'll enter the forest immediately?"

"Yes," Avian said tensely, as though he weren't comfortable with the idea himself. "I don't want to prolong our arrival any longer than absolutely necessary. You've been away from Enevale long enough."

"Sure," she agreed weakly. She had been granted four long

days to mentally prepare herself to enter the Dark Forest, yet the thought still sent shivers crawling down her spine. Throughout her entire life, she had been repeatedly told of the dangers of the forest and listened to bloody stories about wandering Evalseman who had met unfavorable fates at the hands of monsters. The Dark Forest was a deadly place, one she unwittingly knew she would have to cross eventually, regardless of the anxious knot the thought formed in her stomach.

They reached the village too quickly, sold the horse too easily, acquired food too cheaply. It all passed by in a blur of movement and a hub of meaningless noise. In what felt like seconds, Kiara stood at the base of the forest, her feet stubbornly planted to the last snowy stretch of ground before the wintery landscape faded into a white and brown mixture of forlorn snow and unearthed dirt. It seemed even the ice was too timid to fully blanket the forest floor.

"Ladies first," Avian spoke flippantly, attempting to mask his own nerves with a casual tone.

Kiara tried to work her mouth into a smile, but all she could muster was an anxious grimace. "Okay," her voice quivered as it escaped her lips in a rush of unsteady air. *It's just a forest,* she told herself reassuringly, *and you can fight. And you have Avian at your side. He's been through these trails before. He's even faced Vyntrx and lived. You have nothing to worry about.* She sighed, forcing a sense of calmness to cease her pessimistic thoughts. Dealing with anxiety was a hindrance Kiara had been exposed to countless times, yet overcoming its paralytic side effects was an unconquerable feat.

Trembling, she lifted a heavy leg and took a small step forward. She took another step, and another, her pace quickening as she neared the trees. She kept walking until her boots no longer sloshed through the snow, until her body was entirely encircled by the forest's trees, despite the sharp torrents of apprehension shot through her chest with every step.

Avian followed closely behind her. She could hear every step he took and each uneven breath that passed his lips. He was humming the tune of an ancient Evalseman lullaby, one meant to placate young children. Anya had often sung the song to Kiara on stormy nights throughout childhood, but the sound of the sweet melody had always possessed a deeper sense of nostalgia, one she could never explain.

"It's warmer here," Kiara noted hoarsely, eyeing the miniscule patches of snow caught in-between thick tree roots.

"It usually is," Avian explained, suddenly at Kiara's side. His arm gently caressed her shoulder, steering her down a narrow path. "It takes a blizzard in Enevale to accumulate one inch of snow in the forest."

She managed a small smile, her nerves somewhat diluted by the familiarity of the lullaby. "I always pictured the forest as a very dark, cold place."

Avian chuckled. "You're half right. The thick tree leaves block most of the sunlight, even on the sunniest days. There's an old Nonae legend that Veinya changed the temperature of the forest to her liking, otherwise the canopy of leaves would condemn the forest to frigid conditions without the warmth of sunlight. Her mansion resides somewhere in these woods."

Kiara stopped in her tracks, swiveling around and facing Avian head-on. "You're telling me the *death goddess* herself lives in the Dark Forest?"

Avian nodded slowly, confusion evident in his eyes. "Yes. Of course, no one can enter her grounds without her permission—or, naturally, they would have to die first."

"I always assumed Veinya was merely a legend."

Avian laughed, shaking his head. "Of course not. I've seen her mansion with my own eyes—I've never been inside, though, but I'm not in a hurry to. Have you read stories about her?"

Kiara's eyebrows were raised quizzically; she was entirely

unconvinced. "All of them. The sacred texts were part of the required curriculum at the village academy."

"Then you know that her mind is half-benevolent and half-malevolent; she is neither fully good nor fully bad. There are tales of her favoring war heroes and tyrannous villains throughout Menevilen's history. She reportedly picks exceptional people and bestows her favor upon them, which gives them advantages over other mortals. Her good side favored your father throughout his life, but her bad side..." Avian trailed off, his eyes abruptly cast downward, "favors Vyntrx."

"She's not the only one who favors Vyntrx," a high-pitched voice suddenly exclaimed.

Kiara and Avian automatically spun around, their hearts pounding in sync as their eyes fell upon a group of weapon-clad Nonae. Avian's face morphed into a look of sheer fury, his eyes locking on the woman that had spoken. "Harlyt," he growled through clenched teeth.

The Nonae called Harlyt pulled her red lips into a broad smile. She was tall and blonde, a revealing outfit—despite the cold weather—hugging every curve of her well-defined body. "Tsk, tsk, Ave," she spoke condescendingly, "looks like you walked right into our clutches."

"Not yet." The words had barely escaped Avian's lips by the time he had unsheathed his sword, the blade immediately lashing across a surprised Nonae's chest. The injured Nonae shrieked, falling to the ground as blood frothed upward from the gash.

Harlyt readily sent a spell flying in Avian's direction, but he recognized her movement from his peripheral vision, expertly pushing a nearby Nonae directly into the spell as he ducked downward. The spell collided with the flabbergasted Nonae, erupting against his chest in an explosion of mutilated flesh and crimson blood. Avian's face was sprayed red.

A startled scream rocked the eerie silence, and it took Kiara several seconds to realize the sound had been emitted from her own throat. She clamped her lips together, staring at the dismembered Nonae. *That could have been Avian,* she thought, her stomach churning with acidic fear. *That spell destroyed the Nonae instantly.*

Harlyt harrumphed, eyeing Avian critically. Only two Nonae remained at her side, their faces ashen. "Get the princess," she snarled.

Immediately, the pair of Nonae dashed at Kiara while Harlyt sent another spell flying at Avian. He skillfully dodged the attack, but doing so had positioned him further from Kiara. He glanced over at her, calling her name in a desperate attempt to wake her from the unmoving stupor she had worked herself into. While his attention had been diverted, Harlyt had slunk closer to him and managed to wrap her hands around his neck before she recaptured his awareness.

While Avian wrestled with Harlyt, Kiara stared unblinkingly at the approaching Nonae. *One spell, and I could be dead,* she thought grimly. Her hands were itching to grasp her knife, to take action, to fight—but fear had paralyzed her limbs.

"This'll be easy!" one of them exclaimed, grinning. They reached Kiara's side and extended their weapons toward her, eyes glinting purple with glee. One of them snickered, harshly poking his knife into Kiara's arm. The stab of burning pain coursed through her veins, issuing a small whimper from her lips. But the pain did more than injure her—it seemed to awaken her comatose conscience and revitalize her disabled awareness.

In one fluid motion, her leg flew upward, knocking the knife out of the man's hand as her foot collided with his chin. He fell backward, unconscious, hitting the ground with a roaring thud. Before his companion could gauge what had occurred, Kiara slid her knife out of its holster, adeptly swiping it across his chest. Without pausing to take a breath, she thrust her knife forward, directly into the Nonae's exposed neck, and then ducked down to stab the side of his torso. Three wounds—three *deep* wounds—and it was enough to steal the Nonae's life. He crumpled to the ground at Kiara's feet, staining her boots red.

A strange, unfamiliar emotion surged through her body. Her stomach twisted into constricting knots; blood rushed to her head in dizzying waves; her heart throbbed so vivaciously, she could hear nothing but the deafening thump of her heartbeat. One sharp thought kept digging into her mind, provoking her conscience. *I killed someone.*

Kiara's vision had blurred into a mess of red, brown, and white. Distantly, she heard her name being screamed. She felt a faint pressure on her shoulders, felt her body rock back and forth, back and forth.

"Kiara, move!" Avian shouted repeatedly, shaking her. Her eyes were glossed over, bright maroon with terror—two wide, unblinking circles dotting a tormented expression. Avian stole a quick glance over his shoulder, watched the injured Harlyt scramble backwards. He blinked and she was gone. Teleported.

Impatiently, Avian drew his hand across Kiara's cheek. He hadn't slapped her with enough force to injure her, but just enough to startle her out of her reverie. Awareness flooded her eyes as blood rushed to her face, reddening her cheeks. She stared up at Avian in confusion, her eyelid flittering as she examined her surroundings. Her gaze fell upon the dead Nonae and she bit her lip.

"*What* was that?" he asked gruffly.

Her eyebrows pulled together. "What do you mean?"

"First you freeze and can't defend yourself, and look—!" His hands clamped around her forearm, just below the tear in her sleeve where the Nonae had thrust his knife. "And after you won the battle, you blacked out! What if you had been facing an entire fleet of Nonae? You couldn't afford to be overwhelmed by emotion. You'd die!"

Kiara flinched at Avian's harsh tone, jerking her arm away from his grip. "Those Nonae were ten times more powerful than the one I fought in my village," she explained through clenched teeth. "I was caught off guard. I have never killed anyone before."

"Well, you'd better get used to it," he snapped, pointing toward the unconscious Nonae on the ground. "We're at war. You wanted to be a solider, didn't you? And you can't even kill? If this Nonae wakes up, he will stalk us, and attack us again. He means to *kill us*, so he should meet the same fate. Kill him."

Kiara's eyes were burning red with anger. She stared at the Nonae on the floor, his body stained with the blood of his fallen comrade. She stared at the knife quivering in her hand, at its crimson blade. "He's just following orders," she whispered.

"Unlike you," he muttered. He lifted his sword into the high air before bringing it down with a crack, instantly severing the Nonae's head. "You need to get stronger," he said disdainfully. "Let's move."

They walked without speaking, the soft thud of their footsteps against the ground unnaturally loud. Kiara had been fuming since their spat, her scarlet eyes staring blankly ahead. Every couple of minutes, Avian would send a sidelong glance in her direction. She could see his head swiveling toward her, but she refused to meet his gaze. Avian's words had been harsh, the rage behind his expression unforgettable. She wanted so badly to apologize for testing his patience, but she was too stubborn to do so. She wanted to stay mad at him, wanted him to feel the same desolation she had been assaulted with.

"Let me heal your arm," Avian spoke suddenly, tentatively.

Kiara glanced at him from the corner of her eye. He had stopped walking. She slowed her pace, turning to face him. "I'm fine," she said tersely. "Let's keep moving."

Avian's hand moved rapidly, clutching Kiara's wrist. He tugged her toward him gingerly, his fingers lightly tracing her wound. She watched in awe as her arm began to tingle, her flesh stitching back together as though he were using an invisible needle and thread. "I'm sorry I raised my voice at you," he said softly, wiping away residual blood from her skin. "I should have taken your emotions into consideration and tried to view the situation from your perspective. You just scared me, that's all."

"It's okay," she mumbled, grateful he had acquiesced to the post-argument guilt before she could. "Why were you scared?"

Avian shrugged, dropping her hand. "I just didn't want you to get hurt."

"It won't happen again," she said reassuringly. "My wits are fully gathered. No more blacking out."

He nodded his approval, a small smile forming against his lips. "Good."

"How did they know we were in the Dark Forest?" Kiara asked, trailing Avian as he continued walking down the path.

"Vyntrx must be using some sort of tracking spell," he deduced. "We won't be entirely safe until we reach Enevale."

"Why doesn't she just attack Enevale now? The king is dead."

Avian's face possessed an all-knowing grin. "Your mother placed a spell on the kingdom. Malevolent forces cannot breach the Wall that guards Enevale from the Dark Forest unless a crowned heir rests on the throne. Because your father is dead, and because you have not yet been inducted, the Wall is impenetrable. The moment after you are crowned, Vyntrx can easily enter the kingdom."

Kiara slanted her eyes, processing Avian's words. The trail abruptly narrowed, curtailed by unruly tree branches. She swiftly evaded the overflowing foliage, ducking to the side while her shoulder bumped against Avian's arm. "Why didn't my mother just make the spell everlasting?"

"She wasn't strong enough. For such a complex spell, drawbacks were necessary."

She suddenly slowed her pace, her mind reeling. "Wouldn't the kingdom be safer if I stayed away, then?"

"Of course not," Avian said quickly, shaking his head. "Don't think like that. If there were no ruler, Enevale wouldn't need to worry about evil breaking through the Wall because chaos would sprout *inside* the kingdom and poison everyone. Besides, on the throne, you can rescue the Evalseman race from this bloodthirsty war."

She shrugged, stepping away from Avian as the road widened. "That makes sense," she admitted.

"Also," he continued, "I swore to your father that I would bring you to Enevale and crown you queen. If I fail to do so, my soul becomes Veinya's. I swore on my life."

Kiara's hand clutched the crown necklace resting in-between her collarbones. As her fingers traced the icy metal, she felt connected to Enevale, to the father she couldn't remember knowing. "You would put your life at risk for such an unimportant cause?"

"*Unimportant*?" he repeated, speaking as though the word were sour against his tongue. "I serve a noble cause. Enevale needs a queen, and it is my duty, honor, and privilege to secure that position for you. Besides, Kiara, have you forgotten about our childhood friendship? Since we were adolescents, I knew I would readily lay down my life for you. All matters concerning you are of the utmost importance—don't ever believe differently."

Avian's declaration had flushed Kiara's cheeks for a reason she couldn't comprehend. Her eyes shifted orange with embarrassment, but she hurriedly glanced at her feet so Avian wouldn't notice the color change. "Th-thanks," she stammered. "Your loyalty seems unwavering."

His hand fell on her arm, gently squeezing her shoulder. "It is," he assured her, his tone sincere. "It's getting dark. We should stop and rest."

After several minutes of searching, they came upon a cluster of rocks just barely visible through the trees. There was a small opening amid the boulders, just large enough for a grown man to squeeze through. "Coronix and Cobreum tend to flock to dark places," Avian explained, hovering around the entrance. "I'll take a look inside. Wait here."

He flattened his back against the cold stone, slipping into the cave as he was swallowed up by darkness. Kiara watched the shadows anxiously, half-expecting a cry of terror to overwhelm the silence. She had seen renditions of the Coronix inside multiple books in the academy—they were small, quick monsters with razor-sharp claws and fangs, capable of ripping a person apart in a matter of seconds. They traveled in packs, unlike Cobreum, whose colossal size prevented mass migration. Cobreum were undoubtedly less common than the vicious Coronix, and because of their rarity, paintings and sketches of the giant monsters were nonexistent, but stories and accounts spoke of slithering bodies and thousands of clawed hands. Demmonai, another bloodthirsty monster that haunted the forest, were typically not found in caves or enclosed places, as they typically resided in small villages or miniature cities. Demmonai were a mystery to the Evalseman—considering they typically avoided contact with other creatures and feasted on Coronix flesh—but Evalseman and Nonae alike were both weary of the thought of encountering a deadly, towering Demmonai.

Avian's face appeared in the entrance, illuminated by a handful of fire blazing magically above his palm. "It's safe," he decided. "It's a small area, and there're no creatures in sight."

"How're you doing that?" Kiara wondered, pointing to his hand.

"One of my countless Evalseman Specialties," he bragged, chuckling. "Gather some wood before you come inside and I'll start a fire." He disappeared into the shadows once more, taking the artificial light with him.

Kiara stumbled across the rock formation, the uneven floor potentially dangerous for her clumsy feet. She stopped at the nearest tree, tugging at the lowest branches until they broke free. She carried the heap of wood over to the cave entrance, tossing them inside before she slipped in-between the rocks.

Avian quickly retrieved the pile of branches in one hand, flames still blazing above his other. He set the mound down in the center of the room, allowing the fire to spread from his fingertips and alight the makeshift pit. Dim orange light spilled through the small room, casting shadows across the jagged walls. Faint sunlight filtered in from the cave opening, accompanied by bouts of chilly wind. Kiara shivered, wrapping her cloak around her arms and sitting down beside the fire.

"Your Specialties are incredible," she whispered. "Is there anything you *can't* do?"

Avian smiled coyly, joining her beside the rising flames. "Yes, actually," he admitted. "I can't control objects with my mind. And, of course, no reading minds, either."

There had never been a single Evalseman in history that had possessed the ability to read or control minds. It was a common belief that such a Specialty could never be attained. There had been a famous Evalseman, known for his unusual purple eyes, whose Specialty had been the ability to manipulate objects and people with just his mind—but he had died hundreds of years ago and his rare Specialty hadn't been obtained since.

"My Specialty must seem so pathetic," she murmured. "You're stronger than me, why don't you just kill Vyntrx?"

Kiara's question caught Avian off-guard. His mouth twitched, caught in-between a grimace and a grin. "It's *your* destiny," he said plainly. "Vyntrx is incredibly powerful. But she hates you—you're her weakness, the one thing that can blur her thoughts with rage. When she fights you, she will be fighting with her defenses down, and she will make herself more vulnerable. You just need to learn how to control your own emotions so you can defeat her with a clear mind. Besides," he added, "I'll be fighting her alongside you. Between the two of us, we can surely win."

"I suppose so," she said thoughtfully, her curious hazel eyes staring at the fire intently.

"And I'm sure the dukes will volunteer to fight Vyntrx at our side," he continued reassuringly.

She cocked her head in his direction, her eyebrows knitting together. "There are other dukes?"

Avian chuckled softly, withdrawing two pieces of bread from the pouch of food he had strapped around his waist. He handed one to Kiara before taking a bite out of the fluffy dough. "Of course. There are four dukedoms: Knight, Crossingrose, Russett, and Stone. You and I grew up playing with the duke's sons, and now that their fathers have all passed, they have officially taken over the titles. They're talented warriors, all high-ranking in the military, and served the King as his own personal guard. Naturally, their duty is now to serve you."

"I can't ask people I don't know to put their lives at risk for me," Kiara murmured, pressing the bread against her lips. "That would be selfish."

Avian shook his head. "It certainly would not be selfish. You're the future queen of Menevilen. It's their duty to protect you, even if that means there's a chance their lives will be terminated. It's the price they would willingly pay for the longevity of the kingdom."

"I just can't view life the way you do," Kiara admitted, taking a timid bite out of her roll.

He shrugged, finishing his bread with a large gulp. "You will eventually," he promised. "As you are exposed to death, war, and misfortune, you will harden. You will realize that your life does not have value unless you would readily sacrifice it for something that has a higher purpose."

"I suppose," she whispered. Her eyes scanned the sweltering flames, her mind processing Avian's words. She couldn't fathom death, couldn't picture a situation in which she would willingly perish to serve a cause. *Does that make me selfish?*

she thought solemnly. But she couldn't uncover an answer.

*****

"Look at my lovely bird," an ominous voice sang. "An opportunity has finally arisen for him to snatch up his prey."

Out of the darkness sprung a face, her cheeks sallow and nearly lifeless. Blood rolled from beneath her lethargic eyes as though she were shedding spoiled tears. Cuts and contusions littered her pale, exposed skin. Clumps of tangled auburn hair hung across her forehead, dried blood streaked through the tresses. She abruptly shuddered, tossed back her head, revealed her face. The dying girl was Kiara.

"Pity, pity, little worm," the haunting voice spoke mockingly. It was unlike any voice Kiara had ever heard before—it possessed a much more disturbing, dangerous tone. "My bird tore you out of your little hole in the ground."

Kiara's glazed eyes slowly scanned the room, discovering a dank chamber solely constructed of stone. Blood dotted the grey floor like inadvertent ink splotches on a piece of parchment. Her hands were manacled above her head, her body dangling against the rock wall. A cloaked figure emerged from a shadowed archway, its hand clutched around a hidden object. Its wide shoulders curved upward tensely, its step hesitant. Embroidered in silver stitching on the back of the figure's black cloak was the image of a bird trapped in a cage.

Kiara's eyes fell upon the mysterious figure as it approached. Her inattentive eyes sparked with emotion as she discovered the person's face, her irises shifting scarlet, sapphire, rose...

"My little bird," the voice suddenly sang again, "will utterly destroy you."

Kiara's eyelids fluttered open, immediately assaulted by

sunlight. She squinted, reducing the sharp brightness as she rolled her weight onto her backside. The fire beside her had dwindled to mere embers, but the flames were no longer required to provide light. Streams of sunbeams filtered in through the opening in the cave, dousing the small enclosure with illumination. She ran her hands through her hair, undoing and redoing her ponytail hurriedly.

"Finally awake, are you?" Avian's voice teased suddenly. He appeared in the entrance, a smile plastered to his face.

She stood up quickly, dashing over to meet him. "Have you been gone long?"

He shook his head, patting Kiara's shoulder. "I've just gone outside to have a look around. It's not nearly as bright outside as it is in here. The entrance must be positioned just so a handful of sky breeches it without the obscurity of tree leaves." He studied the small opening carefully, his mismatched eyes shimmering. "I have good news. We're about a day's walk away from the Eustoripha Plains—if we walk throughout the night."

"Then we'd better get going," she decided, smiling.

They gathered their supplies, scattered the charred wood from the dead fire, and abandoned the depths of the cave. The light dimmed as they returned to the forest, the sunlight swallowed by shadows as though the trees had taken a deep breath and had forgotten to exhale. Wind swept through the leaves, filling the silence with crumpling noise. A cold chill sent shivers down Kiara's spine as she hurried to Avian's side, attempting to keep up with his long-legged pace.

"Be alert," he advised. "Vyntrx has probably sent her minions to comb the forest."

"I'll try, but I'm not very observant," she mumbled. Her eyes raked the forest scenery, her mind replaying her most recent dream. Something about the shrouded figure had seemed familiar, but she couldn't discern the reason. That malicious voice kept infiltrating her mind, spiking fear in her heart.

She and Avian walked at a quick but steady pace,

occasionally stopping to munch on food or rest their muscles. The sun slipped further in the sky, greatly extending the curtain of shadows with each passing hour. They spoke casually, the light tones of their voices the only sound flitting through the forest.

Night overtook the sky, causing the temperature of the forest to plummet. Kiara shivered, tugging the edges of her cloak together in an attempt to trap her body heat against the fabric. Avian's arm timidly wrapped around her shoulders, his hand rubbing along her shoulder as though he were trying to start a fire. "Do you need to stop?" he whispered.

She shook her head, her jaw locked tight in an effort to avoid chattering teeth. She nestled her shoulder against Avian's torso, feeling a vague sense of warmth emit from his body.

"You're right, it's better to keep moving," he decided. "We should only have a couple of hours left and then you'll be toasty warm inside the castle."

Distantly, the sound of music buzzed through the quiet forest. Avian heard the misplaced noise, immediately stopping in his tracks. His hand fell away from Kiara's body, a quizzical look lining his face. "Stay here," he demanded, slowly creeping forward. "Don't move. I'll be right back."

She stared at him with arched eyebrows, her eyes dark amber, displaying her confusion. "Alright," she complied.

Avian stealthily tiptoed toward the sound of music, weaving in and out of trees, his footsteps utterly silent against the snowy ground. He was grateful for the training he had received in furtiveness, grateful for his vast knowledge of the Dark Forest's paths.

A campsite sprouted out of the shadows, the black tents nearly shrouded by curtains of leaves. Despite its attempted concealment, the glow of a fire gave away the site's location, drawing Avian nearer. Groups of laughing people crowded the campsite, dancing jovially. Loud, carefree voices belted an old Nonae hunting song that had become iconic of the Dark

Forest's rebel force.

"Cylis Septimus," Avian snarled under his breath. As though he had heard his name being called, the rebel leader emerged from a canopied tent, a toothy grin dominating his flushed face. He linked arms with a dark-skinned boy who yanked him toward the fire. Cylis spoke to a group of his followers, but Avian couldn't decipher his words over the roar of the music.

Carefully, Avian snuck away from the campsite. A knot of anxiety had tightened within his stomach, a sense of desperation sparked through his veins. He gravely understood that if Cylis discovered his presence in the forest, he and his rebels would attack—and it would be lethal. Because Cylis harbored an intense hatred for both Vyntrx and King Kyan, and had taken a middle-ground stance in the war, he would not hesitate to assassin monumental players from either side.

Kiara was waiting exactly where he had left her, her arms folded across her chest impatiently. Her eyes glowed light purple with relief when they fell upon his approaching figure. "Is everything alright?" she questioned.

He shook his head. "No, I'm afraid not. Do you know of Cylis Septimus?"

She shrugged, her hands tightly gripping the edge of her cloak. "I've heard the name, but I don't know much about him."

"He's a Nonae rebel. He despised Kyan and wants Vyntrx dead. He doesn't sympathize with either side of the war, and views followers of each with intense disdain. If he discovered us, I'm sure he would readily prepare our execution." Avian's face was lined with worry, a sense of exhaustion evident in his voice. "His campsite is up ahead, so we'll have to carefully sneak around it. We could go off trail and swerve around it, but that would add hours to our trip, and I can't guarantee that we won't become lost."

Kiara nodded, her eyes shifting maroon with fright. Avian understood she would be embarrassed if he mentioned the emotion welling in her irises, so he remained silent, his eyes flittering away from her face. He motioned for her to follow him, bringing his forefinger to his lips.

They crept softly toward the glow of Cylis's campsite, Kiara's lips trembling as she attempted to breathe quietly. Avian walked soundlessly, as though he were hovering, expertly winding his way around the trees. She eyed him enviously, flinching every time her feet crunched loudly against the forest floor.

Music and laughter danced through the air, the sound so jovial, Kiara found it difficult to believe that the producers of such joy could readily extinguish her life. Her fingers scraped along the bark of trees as she carefully weaved her way through the forest, her heart drumming in her chest, filling her ears with a thudding beat. She had heard many stories about Cylis and his group of rebels—rarely had they ended on a positive note. Cylis was painted to be ruthless and determined, a man who would cut down any soul who dared violate his goals.

They neared the edge of Cylis's campsite, revealing rows of multi-colored tents. A fire swelled in the center of the gathering, flanked by dancing bodies and smiling faces. A blonde-haired male stood with his back to the edge of the woods—and although Kiara had never seen paintings of him, she knew with utter certainty that the man she was staring at was none other than the infamous Cylis Septimus.

He was speaking quietly with two of his peers—one, a girl with honey-blonde hair and a pretty face, kept glancing in Avian and Kiara's direction, as though she could somehow sense their presence.

"Is something the matter?" Cylis spoke in a quiet tone as the music halted momentarily while the singers switched tunes. The sound of his light voice tugged at Kiara's chest, filling her body with an emotion she couldn't describe.

The girl shook her head, mumbling something. Her eyes flickered between her comrades, toward the forest, at the floor.

She excused herself, hurrying to a nearby tent.

"She's getting a weapon," Avian whispered morosely. "She'll be back. Let's move—quickly."

He dashed through the thicket soundlessly, his body disappearing in the darkness. Kiara attempted to follow after him at the same hurried speed, momentarily allowing the desire to flee eclipse the importance of stealth. She loudly crumpled through the leaves as Cylis's back automatically straightened with attentiveness. The blonde girl exited her tent, club in hand, but Cylis put up a hand to halt her.

"Kiara," Avian's voice hissed through the shadows. "Carefully step backwards. Hide yourself behind the trees."

She mechanically followed orders, gingerly slipping behind a nearby tree, attempting to create the smallest amount of noise possible. Cylis turned and approached the edge of the woods while his friends stared after him curiously. Shards of light pooling from the campsite fell upon his face, illuminating his puzzled expression. His Nonae eyes were wide and hazel with curiosity.

The sight of his visage struck a heavy chord of familiarity inside Kiara's heart. She could clearly see every angle of his face through the curtain of leaves she had hidden herself behind—and although she could not explain the feeling, she knew with certainty she had seen him somewhere before.

As Cylis approached Kiara's position, Avian's hands gripped the handle of his sword readily. He eyed the rebel with scrutiny, waiting for even the slightest hint that Cylis had discovered the intruder. Kiara slunk away nervously, her back flat against the body of a tree. If the situation spun out of control, Avian would not think twice about exposing himself in order to protect her—he just hoped their presence would go undiscovered so he could avoid rash conflict.

As Avian watched the scene unfurl, he began to wonder if his eyes were failing to communicate the truth. The closer Cylis inched toward Kiara, the more translucent her skin became until finally, she had completely blended in with the forest behind her. When Cylis roughly parted the foliage she was cowering behind, his eyes fell upon empty space. He sighed a mixture of relief and annoyance, releasing his tense hold on the branches.

As Cylis hurried back to his campsite, calling to his friends that they had merely been paranoid, Kiara re-appeared in the exact location she had vanished, breathing shakily. A puzzled expression dominated her face, her eyes the deep yellow of confusion.

*****

"He looked *right* at me!" Kiara exclaimed the second they could no longer see the illumination of Cylis's campsite in the distance. "But he didn't do anything—he just walked away!"

Avian stared ahead solemnly at the shadowy path, his mismatched eyes swimming with unreadable emotion. Times when Kiara couldn't discern what Avian was thinking, when he was absorbed in his thoughts, she wished he had been born with revealing Nonae eyes regardless of his pure-Evalseman heritage. "You weren't there, momentarily," he explained in a dazed tone. "I know you're part-Nonae, but I wasn't aware you had learned magic."

Kiara's eyebrows slanted downward as she attempted to process Avian's claim. She had been so tightly wrapped in fear as Cylis's eyes peered straight at her, it was entirely plausible that something could have occurred to her body without her notice—but to turn *invisible*? She had never been taught a single spell of Nonae magic, had never even been introduced to the basics of summoning energy through her will. To be told that she had conjured Nonae magic without even the slightest memory of doing so seemed an utterly ludicrous accusation. "What are you talking about?" she stammered. "I've never produced a single spell!"

"*Consciously,*" he corrected. She halted in her tracks, her eyes glaring at him through the darkness. His smile was tight as he returned her heated gaze. "Look, I'm just telling you what I saw. You *are* half-Nonae, after all, you could be prone to bouts of subconscious magic release—most young Nonae between the ages of two and eight create such a ruckus—"

"I'm not like ordinary Nonae!" Kiara interrupted loudly. "Most Nonae grow up around magic, so it's no doubt they would pick it up—just like how they learn our language. But I— I grew up in an Evalseman village that shunned the practice of magic."

"Then it makes perfect sense why you were able to turn yourself invisible," Avian declared, picking up a hurried pace as he trampled through the forest. "You've finally witnessed magic with your own eyes. Until now, you couldn't fathom what magic was like because you had never seen it. But now that you've gotten a taste of it, your inner nature has taken over."

"I don't know," she said slowly, trailing Avian at a leisurely pace. The gathering of trees had grown scarce as they neared what Kiara hoped was the edge of the forest. A cold chill had swept through the air and the thin layer of snow that blanketed the floor was accumulating progressively. "Is that *normal*?"

Avian shrugged, stealing a glance at Kiara over his shoulder. He beckoned for her to quicken her speed, pausing momentarily as he waited for her to reach his location. "You're not a full-blooded Nonae, so it's very difficult to determine what is and isn't normal for you. I simply know that naturally, you will be drawn to magic."

Kiara's mind processed Avian's words, but she refrained from speaking as she followed him through the outskirts of the forest. The darkness of night was dense, the wind howling through the air incredibly guttural and cold. Abruptly, the trees of the Dark Forest faded into the shadows, and in the distance, Kiara could vaguely see the outline of a glistening city.

Chapter Five

Enevale

The guards swung open the set of heavy stone doors that shielded Enevale from the treacherous conditions of the Dark Forest. Although Kiara's eyes were riddled with exhaustion, and although her body yearned to scamper across the village and bury herself within the warmth of the castle, she could not swallow the desire to stop and gape at the city she had dreamt of visiting.

Wide cobble-stoned streets wove through the town, leading the way to variously designed buildings, homes, and shops. The majority of the buildings were constructed from large stones or painted wood and possessed arched doorways and windows. Lamps littered the streets, illuminating the nearly deserted city in a soft yellow glow. Loud, inebriated villagers crowded the open door of taverns, spilling the contents of their mugs onto the roads. Aside from the late-night drinkers and pub owners, all of Enevale's citizens were locked away in their homes.

"Don't just stand there," Avian's voice suddenly whispered in her ear. His breath was hot against the back of her neck. "The castle's that way."

Kiara's gaze followed his extended pointer finger, her eyes falling upon Fable Castle in the distance. The palace was constructed from a mysterious material, shimmering brilliantly through the haze of snowflakes and the thick shadows of night. The castle was positioned on top of a sloping hill, a stone pathway weaving its way along the incline, which led to a smaller wall that separated the castle grounds from the kingdom.

Avian's arm wove around Kiara's shoulders, steering her

down the road. As she sped past the dimly lit houses, she found herself attempting to imagine the interior of the castle. She had heard several villagers elaborate about Enevale, heard them complain about the crowded streets and strict laws, but she had never been graced with any sort of description of the castle.

After trekking for nearly half an hour through the ornate pathways of the village, Avian and Kiara halted in front of the guards who stood beside the gate of the palace walls. The soldiers recognized Avian immediately and promptly bent their torsos downward in respectful bows. They quickly opened the iron gates, revealing a carefully kept garden dotted with unusual plants, granite statues, and tinkling fountains. Kiara sucked in her breath at the sight of the beautiful garden. Despite the cold, the plants flourished with life, and she suspected they were artificial.

"Come along," Avian chuckled, taking Kiara's weather-beaten hand into his own.

They walked through the gates, entering the castle grounds. A nostalgic sensation surged through Kiara's body as she climbed the steep hill toward the wide, polished wooden doors of the castle. Up close, the palace was twice as breathtaking. Arched windows were spread across the shimmering material of the castle walls, framed by dark wooden panels. Spires rose upward from soaring towers, so tall they were nearly unidentifiable against the dark sky.

The guards posted at the castle doors identified Avian as he was approaching and readily opened the doors before he and Kiara had reached the entrance. Avian nodded his head politely, his grip around Kiara's hand tightening as the guards scrutinized her curiously.

They entered the castle, passing through a dull stone hallway that, Kiara noted as she glanced at the ceiling, could be sectioned off from the rest of the castle by iron gates that hung, unused, from thin slots in the archways. Beyond the drab entrance emerged an extravagant foyer possessing granite walls heavily adorned with oil paintings and woven tapestries. A wooden and glass chandelier hung in the center of the arched ceiling, emitting a soft glow throughout the room. Several archways tapered in dark wood led out of the entry hall, revealing endless passages.

"It's beautiful," Kiara whispered, mesmerized.

Avian's grip around her wrist tightened as he laughed lightly. He pulled her through one of the archways, leading her down a dimly lit corridor as she imbibed the sight of the castle. She was embedded in amazed silence as they steadily made their way through the labyrinth halls, her eyes brimming turquoise with excitement.

"The castle surely seems impossible to maneuver, but trust me, after a few days of exploring, the halls will be as familiar to you as your own face," Avian spoke tenderly, expertly weaving his way around a curve in the hallway. "Our suite is on the third floor. Your parents had the room constructed before you were born. It's spacious enough—there're two bedrooms, a bathroom, a kitchen, and a living room. I'll be sharing the suite with you, of course. My chambers were always in your father's suite, but his room became inaccessible after his death."

Avian's words managed to penetrate Kiara's scrutinizing mind. Her eyes flickered to his face, shifting light yellow with shock. "You and I are *sharing* a room?"

His laughter echoed off the high ceiling. "You seem so startled, Ara. We're sharing a *suite*, not a room. The suite possesses two bedrooms; I'll simply be a few steps away. If Vyntrx were to ransack the castle, it would be imperative for me to be near you. Your safety is my top priority."

At the mention of Vyntrx's name, a lump of apprehension formed in Kiara's throat, blocking the air from escaping her lungs. Anytime Avian mentioned her malicious aunt, Kiara felt as though Vyntrx were standing behind her, positioning a blade between her shoulder blades. She reluctantly admitted to herself that Avian's presence significantly dulled the terror her aunt incited. "That makes sense," she mumbled.

"Also," he continued, "we need to keep your identity a secret. I plan to inform the dukes, as they will be charged with your safety, but the rest of the kingdom will be kept in the dark until you are fully prepared to be crowned queen. We will commence physical training sessions, lessons in etiquette, and informational sessions about Enevale's history until you possess the proper demeanor of a queen. Once you have accomplished that, we will hold a coronation ball and unveil your identity to the entire kingdom."

"Sounds like a lot of work," she muttered, trailing Avian as he climbed a wide, wooden staircase. "What's the cover story, then?"

"Well," he smirked, "I'm still *ironing* out the details. On a completely unrelated note, how would you rate your cleaning skills?"

She stared at him quizzically, attempting to decipher his level of seriousness. "Are you honestly going to condemn me to a life of scrubbing the castle floors?"

He laughed loudly, thoroughly humored by Kiara's aghast expression. "That would be a sight, wouldn't it? The sole heir to the throne of Enevale industriously sweeping the floors of her own castle!" He paused to snicker, eyeing Kiara's heated glare. "I'm kidding, Ara."

She unlatched her mouth to fire a curt reply, but Avian abruptly stopped in front of a large doorway, causing her to bump against his back.

"Your suite, my queen," he said slowly, withdrawing a small silver key from the depths of his cloak. He handed the object to Kiara; the metal was icy against her upturned palm. "Your mother cast a spell on that key. It is impossible to lose. If you misplace it, it will return to your pocket automatically. It was a precautionary action, in case you inherited your father's absentminded tendencies—which, after accumulating a mound of evidence, I've concluded you have."

She smiled shyly, her eyes raking the magical key. Her initials were embossed into the metal, a declarative stamp that linked her vague past with the present. "She was clever," she whispered. "If only I had inherited that trait instead."

Avian's hand gently rubbed her shoulder, a comforting smile pinned to his face. "Don't view yourself so harshly. I'm sure you possess many of your mother's best qualities." He nudged her toward the door, his fingers wrapping around her wrist as he steered her hand to the doorknob.

She shoved the key into the lock, twisting it back and forth. She had always hated keys, had never been capable of successfully unlatching a lock without excessive rattling. She felt her cheeks flush as Avian watched her struggle, a tinge of humor coursing through his eyes. "Let me," he offered, chuckling. He skillfully twisted the key in the latch and was rewarded by a resonating *clink* that signaled the door's opening. "After you," he said, bowing slightly and depositing the suite key in Kiara's cloak pocket.

She timidly pushed open the double-doors. As though her movement had trigged some sort of mechanism, the lights abruptly flickered to life, drenching the suite in illumination. She slid into the suite, finding herself in the center of a circular room flanked by four wooden pillars whose surfaces had been carved into ornate designs. A glossy table was positioned in the middle of the room; six cushioned chairs had been pushed up against the edges. A swooping, wooden chandelier dangled from above, casting hues of light and shadow upon the hall.

Two archways trailed off from the main room; one led to an apparent kitchen riddled with unfamiliar metal appliances; the other led to a spacious room that possessed a set of plush sofas and a wide fireplace constructed of colossal stones.

Kiara passed through the second archway, discovering a pair of doors on either side of the vast fireplace. Avian pointed to the one on the right. "That'll be my room. It's nothing special.

It hasn't ever been occupied before. Your room is to the left."

She hurriedly pushed open her bedroom door and was instantly startled by its extravagance. The room was a sharp comparison to the petite loft she had shared with Anya throughout her childhood. A massive, canopied bed took the place of the narrow, mangled cot she had occupied night after restless night at the village. The bedposts appeared to be handcrafted and were draped by a canopy that met the floor in a puddle of ivory fabric. Countless pillows crowded the headrest, and even from a distance, Kiara could easily discern their pliable structure.

She and Anya had barely managed to cram their small beds and a dingy dresser into the confinements of their loft, so the endless amount of empty space inside her new bedroom utterly baffled Kiara. A long couch rested in the corner of the room, nestled beside a small door that Kiara speculated led to her closet. Another door stood catty-corner from the closet, nearly unnoticeable between a wooden armoire and vanity table.

"This is spectacular!" she spluttered, swiveling around to find Avian hovering in her bedroom doorway. "It's unreal."

He chuckled softly at Kiara's enthused reaction. "You'll find an array of clothing in your closet. A spell was placed on your clothes so that their measurements would shift as your body did. You can easily find a nightgown, I'm sure."

Her eyes shifted in the direction of her closet, a bemused expression crossing her features. "Nonae magic never ceases to amaze me."

"It's very late," Avian observed, eyeing the bleak early morning sky through Kiara's bedroom window. "If you don't require any further assistance, I'll leave you to rest."

"Actually," Kiara's voice escaped her lips before she had a chance to fully process her words, "would you mind lying on the couch until I fall asleep? I've always had difficulty falling asleep, because my mind refuses to shut down, but I'm so used to having Anya sleep near me, I'm afraid of what may happen once I'm fully alone with my thoughts."

A humorless smile traced Avian's lips. "I've always believed we are merely slaves to our own minds. If you believe my presence will quell any potential anxiety, it would be my duty to stay by your side."

"Thank you," she mumbled awkwardly. "Just stay until I fall asleep."

*****

Kiara had scoured the depths of her never-ending closet for nearly a half-hour before she had finally located a row of nightgowns. She had changed hurriedly, grateful to peel off her tattered, snow-caked clothes. Her hair was mangled and damp, but as she was far too exhausted to bathe, she merely tied her tresses into a loose bun.

She climbed into her fortress of a bed, her eyes lingering on Avian as he reclined comfortably along the couch. The mattress nearly swallowed Kiara's small body—a vast improvement from her weathered, lumpy bed at the village.

Avian had dimmed the lights, and the only illumination caressing the room was a sliver of silver from the full moon spilling in through the window.

"It's still so surreal—" Kiara mumbled into the fabric of her blanket, "—everything that's happened."

Avian's form was vaguely distinguishable through the shadows, but as Kiara's eyes adjusted to the darkness, she could just barely decipher the features of his smirking face. "You'll grow accustomed," he promised quietly. "It's surreal for me, as well. For a long time, I began to doubt that we would ever be reunited."

"Am I even remotely how you expected me to be?"

He chuckled lightly. "You've certainly changed since childhood. During your absence, I imagined several scenarios of our reunion; created multiple personalities you may have adopted. I had absolutely no idea what to expect. You did not disappoint."

Her lips pulled into a satisfied grin as her eyelids slowly slid shut. "I'm glad," she managed to whisper before a yawn worked her mouth into silence.

"It's late, Ara," Avian's voice was gentle, as though he were lulling her into slumber. "You need your rest."

She nodded in compliance, her mind growing foggy with exhaustion. Despite the unfamiliar environment of the castle and the foreign feel of the warm bed sheets, Avian's comforting presence managed to work Kiara's mind into a state of placid dormancy.

*****

Kiara waited anxiously beside a guillotine, her eyes sharp maroon with unbridled terror. Her small body was draped in a thin white dress plastered with mud, her hands fettered so tightly by chains that a line of dried blood ringed her wrists. Her hair hung in tangled heaps, sticking to the tear stains streaking her cheeks.

The executioner gruffly ordered that she move closer, his gloved hands beckoning toward the machine that would heartlessly deliver her demise.

"Be brave," she reminded herself breathlessly as she shuffled her tremulous legs in the direction of the guillotine. Shakily, she fell to her knees before the wooden block. Her eyes latched on the semi-circular slope devised for cradling her neck. She nearly threw up her heart.

As the executioner roughly pulled her hair behind her neck, she allowed her eyes to scan the audience, to drink in the sight of life one final time. Her eyes raked the frontline of onlookers, discovering a handful of solemn prisoners, their hands manacled in chains; their eyes, full of heart-wrenching familiarity, were pinned on Kiara.

The executioner announced that someone was waiting to bid her farewell, his abrupt voice breaking her reverie. She tilted her head, her eyes falling upon Avian. He was hovering above her, his mismatched eyes blazing with desolation. He fell to his knees, pulling her frail body into an intimate embrace. She wondered if he had begun sobbing—his body was shaking with every breath. He remained embossed in silence; he simply held her body as close to his as he could physically manage. She could feel his heart fluttering rampantly in his chest and the warmth of his body against her chilled limbs. She couldn't muster enough energy to wrap her arms around his back or gather enough strength to do anything. She wanted so desperately to beg for his help, but her vocal cords tightened rebelliously in her throat.

He whispered a short sentence in her ear, his tone soft and yearning, but she couldn't decipher his words. Startled, she jerked her head upward, preparing to ask Avian to repeat his phrase, but the executioner roughly grabbed her neck and slammed her against the hard wood of the guillotine. Her throat constricted violently as she spluttered for air.

As Kiara prepared for death, the onlookers celebrated, their hands ramming together in spasms of applause as their mouths shouted a chorus of cheers. Her skin crawled as her ears were filled with the sickening sound of the guillotine's blade sliding toward her exposed neck. She waited disastrously for one last conclusive sensation of pain as she fought off the unbearable urge to scream, to flee, to cry, and then—

Kiara's blood-curdling scream sliced through the silence, sharply shoving Avian's mind into consciousness. Kiara's bedroom poured into view in a wave of color. His eyes immediately found her body writhing spasmodically, trapped in a state of hellish slumber.

He instantly flew to her side, his hands gripping her

shoulders as he shook her repeatedly. He yelled her name, begged her to wake up. After an eternity of Avian's pleading, Kiara's eyes finally flashed open.

Her lungs greedily swallowed buckets of air as her mouth hung open in a startled gasp. Beads of sweat coated her panicked expression, her bright eyes revealing her terror. Her hands clutched Avian's fervently, her entire frame quivering. "I—I died!" she spluttered.

"*What*?" Avian's eyebrows narrowed. His hands gently caressed her cheeks, his forehead bumping against hers as he forced her to meet his gaze. "Calm down, Ara. Breathe. You're not dead."

"It felt so real," she whispered hoarsely. "I—I could *feel* it—"

"Shh," he cooed soothingly, wiping away a stray tear as it trickled down her face. "It wasn't real. *This* is real. You're in the castle—*completely safe*—with me."

She released a shaky huff of air. She nodded slowly, the frightened shade of her irises shifting as Avian managed to soothe her disturbed psyche. "Was I screaming?" she asked, her voice barely audible.

He nodded. "I heard you—from my room. I heard you screaming and it woke me." He didn't understand why he had lied so mindlessly. He hadn't been in his room, he had fallen asleep in hers. Had he simply not possessed enough energy to trek through the suite to his room, or was he secretly terrified to leave her side in fear that he would wake up and find her missing? He didn't have the answer. He could have told her that he had acquiesced to exhaustion, but for some unexplained reason, he wanted her to believe—no, he really wanted *himself* to believe—that he had obtained enough willpower to depart her side, regardless of the irresistible lure of slumber.

"Thank you for waking me," she murmured.

"Do you want to talk about it?"

She shook her head as Avian's hands fell away from her face.

She slowly disentangled herself from the bed sheets, pulling her body into a sitting position. Strands of her hair had escaped the barriers of a half-hearted bun, tumbling past her shoulders in messy waves. "I just want to forget about it."

Avian nodded compliantly, crossing the room and pushing a silver button on the wall that summoned light to the ornate chandelier dangling in the center of the ceiling. "The dukes will attend breakfast in the dining hall in about an hour. I figured we could join them, if that's alright with you?"

Kiara shrugged, her hand lingering over the doorknob of her bathroom. "I have no objections. I'll get ready and meet you in the living room."

He smiled in approval, departing her bedroom as she slipped through the washroom door. She bathed slowly, scrubbing off the film of dirt that had blanketed her body during the journey to Enevale. In her closet, she uncovered tight, stretchy pants, a pair of lace-up boots, and a corset top. She plaited her wet hair away from her face, critically eyeing the dark smudges of unrest that stood out against the pale planes of her cheeks. Her hand automatically fell to the crown pendant resting loyally against her collarbone, the feel of the cold metal oddly comforting.

Avian stood facing the fireplace, a thoughtful expression playing on his features. He had taken the time to tidy his appearance and change outfits, but the sword Kiara had given him was still proudly stamped to his waist. His eyes darted in Kiara's direction as she departed her bedroom, his lips working into a welcoming grin. "You look lovely."

She couldn't fight the smile spilling across her face at Avian's abrupt compliment. "The clothes in my closet are made from more luscious materials than the outfits Anya stitched together for me."

His smirk broadened at Kiara's inexperience with flattery. He waved her closer, taking several steps in the direction of the dining room. "The castle inhabits the royal family, the dukes—

who each have a wing of the castle for their own families—the castle personnel, and the military. There is a cooking staff on duty for each meal of the day, and because most of the suites occupied by workers don't possess kitchens, the dining hall is continuously busy. Even though the dukes have their own personal kitchens, they've adopted the dining hall as their daily haunt."

As they departed the suite, Kiara reached into her pocket to retrieve the enchanted key that had loyally appeared at her side whenever she had changed clothes and accidentally left it in her discarded pants. Locking the door behind her, she hurried after Avian as he expertly maneuvered his way through the castle halls.

"Do you think the dukes will recognize me?" she wondered. Sunlight streamed in through countless windows lining the halls, filling the castle with a homey feel—a sharp contrast from the dark, intricate corridors she had explored upon her arrival. Several people scurried past, unfailingly bowing their heads in Avian's direction any time their eyes fell upon the temporary king. None of them seemed to notice Kiara's presence. "Did they notice when you left to retrieve me?"

"Of course they were informed," he explained, waving at a pair of castle guards as they stood to attention. "Moments before his death, your father called all of the dukes into his chambers. He told us where he had sent you, and reminded me of the promise I had made him—the promise to bring you back to Enevale and crown you queen. However, the matter of them actually *recognizing* you is a completely unpredictable event."

The end of the corridor was suddenly swallowed by a wide, arched opening. Beyond the archway, rows of tables and a horde of loitering people were visible. A buzz of noise emanated from the dining hall—Avian hadn't exaggerated the busyness of the room.

Avian led her through the bustling cafeteria, weaving around the crowded tables. Kiara noticed a separate room at one end of the dining hall that was clustered with jars of liquid and trays of steaming food. "That's where you order your meals," Avian explained, catching her eyeing the room. "We'll get some breakfast in a bit. I want to reunite you with the dukes first." His hand abruptly clamped around Kiara's, his gaze locked on a group of three young men talking animatedly in the center of the room.

"I'm not saying I have a thing for Harlyt, you ass!" Kiara overheard a boy with silvery hair declare, loudly slamming his fist against the table. "All I said is that she is an extremely sexy woman who shouldn't be wasting her time working for Vyntrx."

A blonde man, who was sitting beside the speaker, raised a quizzical eyebrow. "Blade, you obviously let your guard down around her. We were supposed to be spying on Vyntrx, to gather information about her current plans. It's no surprise our mission failed, considering you stood around gawking at Harlyt long enough for her to stab you in the stomach."

"It was merely a flesh wound," Blade muttered. "It healed quickly. Besides, she was really talented at handling that sword."

The third boy chuckled. "Does that have a double meaning?"

"Hello, my minions!" Avian interjected, startling his friends into silence. Blade's hands jerked into the air dramatically, while the other two boys merely stared at Avian with shocked expressions.

The blonde's gaping face pulled into a grin, his eyes flickering to Kiara momentarily before he met Avian's gaze. "You're back already? We were expecting you to be absent for at least two more days. The princess didn't require much convincing, I assume?"

Kiara smiled shyly. "I was pretty bent on disbelieving Avian. He certainly didn't have an easy time."

The other two dukes scrutinized her as she hovered

awkwardly behind Avian. She was suddenly very conscious of his hand pressing gently against hers. Blade's gaze shifted across her figure, noticing their interlocked fingers. His eyebrows narrowed. "This is the brat?" he asked. "She grew up."

"I honestly don't remember what she looked like as a child," a boy with glistening tawny eyes admitted, "but I didn't see her as much as you and Avian did, Blade."

Blade rolled his eyes. "My parents were always encouraging me to play with the princess." He turned his attention to Kiara, a serious expression pinned to his face. "I'm lucky your father requested Avian to marry you, otherwise I may have been forced into an arranged marriage."

Kiara's head immediately snapped in Avian's direction, her hand falling out of his reach. "We were *engaged*?"

He hurriedly unhinged his mouth to reply, but Blade cut him off. "Never mind that, how *did* you wind up so short? Your parents were both rather tall."

"What's wrong with my height?"

"It's lacking,"

"Oh, shut up, Blade," Avian said irritably, swinging back the empty chair that sat beside the silvery haired duke. He gestured to Kiara, implying she should sit down.

She sent him a half-hearted smile as she reclined in the cushioned chair, her thoughts still glued to the notion of an arranged marriage. She couldn't understand why Avian had refrained from revealing such a vital piece of information. *If he plans to follow through with the engagement, shouldn't he have my consent?* she wondered silently.

Avian occupied the chair beside her, and as his leg brushed against hers slowly, she felt her cheeks flush. "Well, it seems Blade has made his identity quite apparent, courtesy of his characteristically rude demeanor. He is the head of the Crossingrose dukedom, which has historically been in charge of surveying the kingdom's crime rates and dealing with security issues the military can't handle. Blade's Evalseman Specialty is manipulation of all forms of water, but we've speculated he also has an inhuman ability of furtiveness. That is, of course, if he doesn't allow himself to be distracted by pretty girls."

"He really just likes to stare at them," the blonde muttered. "He's all talk, no action."

"And this," Avian continued, pointing to the blonde man as Blade huffed a slew of insults under his breath, "is Aiden Stone. He's the oldest of us dukes and he's been in charge of his dukedom since a very young age. He is solely responsible for the kingdom's finances and the castle treasury. He has a younger sister, Akanine, who is the *real* brains of the family. With her intellect and Aiden's management skills, they are able to successfully maintain an abundant economy. His Evalseman Specialty is the ability to create and control fire."

Aiden smiled proudly, his scarlet eyes shimmering flames. "You flatter me, old friend."

"And finally," Avian nodded in the direction of the yellow-eyed boy, "this is Ace, the head of the Russett dukedom. His family hails from a long line of Kyraix, which are an extremely rare species that is too complex to simply describe. His dukedom is charged with the responsibility of public relations and establishing communication with the citizens of Enevale. Each day, he wades through piles of papers bearing complaints, suggestions, or requests, and he addresses them all."

Kiara's eyebrows were perched high on her forehead, her lips parted, displaying her amazement. "You're all so impressive," she breathed. "I had absolutely no comprehension of responsibility until my past was revealed and my destiny thrust upon me. The four of you grew up understanding your purpose in this kingdom, and you're all apparently quite efficient in your respective fields. I'm afraid all my inexperience will only deter your hard work."

"We're your royal court, your majesty," Aiden said gently. "It's our duty to serve you. If you feel you aren't fit for the throne, then it becomes our responsibility to prepare you."

Avian nodded his approval. "Yes, I planned to post-pone the coronation until I feel she is undeniably ready. She can learn from all of us. I suggest we each meet with her for a few hours every day. You're going to need to work with her on stealth, Blade, she's the clumsiest person I've ever met. We can discuss our plans in depth later, however."

"Has anyone else been watching her eyes change color?" Blade randomly interposed. He rested his chin in his hands, his icy eyes sliding over Kiara's features. "I've never noticed how frequently Nonae eyes shift. They must be a pretty emotional species."

"I think everyone is emotional, regardless of his or her race," she replied coolly.

Blade shook his head. "Evalseman are more composed. Nonae have always struck me as bipolar."

Kiara's eyes narrowed, flashing black with annoyance. "What would you know? You've only dealt with hostile Nonae, haven't you? They're not all malicious."

He shrugged casually, Kiara's rising temper clearly not affecting his mood. "An overwhelming amount of Nonae side with Vyntrx. It seems those who don't are defective."

A wave of crimson rage clouded Kiara's eyes. "Are you saying my *mother* was defective?"

"She certainly wasn't a typical Nonae—but even though she was kind, she was still hated by the kingdom."

"This is unbelievable!" she shouted, standing up from her chair angrily. "I would have figured that a sophisticated city like Enevale would carry less prejudice than the hell of a village I grew up in! It seems all of you pure-blooded Evalseman share the same haughty mindset!"

Avian was suddenly at her side, his hand pressing against her shoulder tightly. "Kiara, calm down. You're causing a scene." His eyes nervously scanned the crowds, watching several people send curious glances in their direction. "It's in Blade's nature to be an idiot. Don't let it upset you."

"How can you ask that of me, Avian?" she implored. "How can you when you're fully aware of the discrimination I faced? Blade's opinions are surely echoed throughout the entire kingdom! I will *never* be accepted by the Evalseman race—let alone Enevale!"

Avian shook his head, twisting Kiara around so she stood facing him, her scarlet eyes burrowing into his. "You are Enevale's beloved king's daughter! You are the rightful heir to the throne. The kingdom will accept you with open arms!"

Blade scoffed. "Or they'll charge her wielding pitch-forks."

Kiara jerked her body out of Avian's grasp, her furious eyes glued to Blade's uncaring face. She spun on her heel, hurrying through the cafeteria before Avian could fully process her actions. She slipped out of view as she rounded the corner of the archway, sending one last menacing glance in the direction of the dukes.

"Brilliantly done, Blade," Avian muttered tersely. "You've pissed off the queen."

He shrugged. "Not my fault she's overly sensitive."

Avian sighed exasperatedly. "I'll recover her. You know, Blade, I figured you would've been excited about the heir's return to Enevale. She's experienced life in an utterly different manner than we have. Direct your callousness to someone who won't take it to heart." He departed the table, leaving Aiden and Ace to further scold Blade while he muttered in annoyance.

*****

Kiara charged blindly ahead, unsure where her legs were carrying her. She couldn't divulge her location in the castle or recall the path that led back to her suite, yet she couldn't force her body to stop moving. Her limbs appeared to be invisibly controlled by the puppet strings of her rampant emotions.

After she had taken an innumerable amount of turns, passed a thousand doors, conquered never-ending stairwells, the flame of anger burning wildly in Kiara's heart finally died down, scattering ashes of insecurity and loneliness throughout her chest. Her legs felt heavy as they slowed to a halt in the middle of a dim, abandoned hallway. A frustrated sigh spilled from her lips. *Which way did I come from?* she wondered, eyeing each identical end of the corridor.

She slunk against the wall, sliding to the floor on her knees. Her heart was hammering anxiously in her chest; her thoughts sped by so quickly, they were hazed blurs. A single, core notion flooded the front stage of her mind: she was unwanted by the kingdom she was allegedly forsaken to protect.

"Lost?" Avian's voice abruptly reverberated through the silence. Kiara wearily glanced upward at him; his hand rested against the wall above her head, a half-smile timidly clutching his lips. "I assumed I'd find you sobbing."

"I'm not *that* weak," she mumbled. "At least he was speaking honestly."

"It still bothered you," he observed. "You were practically forced into this life, and then Blade stupidly runs his mouth and makes you feel as though you're not welcome at all. Am I correct?"

Kiara unhinged her mouth to protest, but as a wave of desolation swept through her chest, her voice forcefully escaped her lips in the single syllable she had attempted to hide: "Yes."

Avian's lips extended the barriers of a smirk, breaking out into a full-fledged smile. "Wow, I'm brilliant."

"Oh, don't sound so arrogant," she advised hotly. "I'm not that hard to figure out."

He sighed, stooping beside Kiara as his hand lovingly fell upon her head. "Calm down, Ara. I was simply attempting to cheer you up."

"Sorry," she huffed, pouting as she avoided Avian's persistent gaze.

He chuckled, ruffling the crown of her hair. "You're so stubborn. Kiara, I understand that you're scared. You just need to realize that I will be at your side every step of the way."

"What if the kingdom really does hate me, Avian?" she whispered sincerely, worry evident in her light blue irises. "What if Blade's opinion is only magnified among the masses?"

Avian's lips parted, a reply hesitantly forming in the base of his throat. "They may be a bit prejudiced toward you, at first," he explained, "but they will undoubtedly warm up to you. I'm sure of it."

"How do you know?" her small voice pleaded.

He smiled softly, his mismatched eyes pools of compassion and sincerity. "Because it isn't fathomable that someone would meet you and not immediately love you."

Kiara's cheeks were alight with fire as she half-heartedly fought off the urge to replace her scowling face with a goofy grin. "Th-that's not true," she spluttered. "My aunt despises me—and all of the Evalseman in my village certainly didn't send a speck of affection in my direction. And Blade is obviously *not* my biggest fan."

"Your aunt is a deranged murderer. Your village didn't know you on a personal level, they merely judged you because you were different—the kingdom won't be able to do that, as you will make many public appearances and speeches. And Blade..." he trailed off, rolling his eyes, "was simply being himself."

She shook her head, her humored eyes shifting to a light purple hue. "You think far too highly of me."

"Nonsense. My thoughts of you are entirely the correct height," he chuckled at his joke as he gently nudged Kiara's shoulder. "There's no point in hovering in the hallway. Let's go back to the suite. There's something I would like to show you."

Chapter Six

Ambiguity

Kiara sat placidly on her bed, her fingers absentmindedly stroking the metal of her crown necklace. She had already grown accustomed to the feel of the pendant against her chest and been familiarized with the heavy tug of the chain. She speculated that within a handful of days, the weight of the necklace would feel just as natural as her skin.

"Recently, I've been staring at this letter your father gave me a week before he died," Avian's voice abruptly declared as he strode into her room. He had told her to wait while he dug through the desk in his bedroom to uncover what she discovered was a crumpled piece of parchment.

"What does it say?" she wondered, climbing to her feet.

"Here," He handed her the letter, closely scrutinizing her face as she drank in the sight of the page.

Kiara's eyes raked the parchment. The intricate, penned scrawl wasn't even remotely similar to her sloppy handwriting. She stared at the arched letters enviously, nearly forgetting to actually *read* the contents. Whenever her mind had finally processed her father's words, she was thoroughly confused by the message. Avian's name dominated the top of the page, followed by three sentences that were concluded with a magnificent signature.

"*Avian,*" she read aloud, trying desperately to picture her father slumped over a desk, writing away at a piece of parchment. "*My time here has nearly been concluded; my debt must be paid in full. I am leaving with my daughter the utmost protection from my deadliest enemy. Her voice must reverse the name she had been given, unlock the metal key, and melt away the royal silver. Sincerely, Kyan Fable.*"

"A few parts I understand," Avian informed her before she could voice her response. "He had gained the specifics of his eminent death—he had known for years—but he wouldn't tell me *how* he knew. I don't know what debt he had to pay, but I'm certain he paid it with his life. The second sentence indicates that he made certain you would be protected, which most likely implies that he planned to leave your safety in my hands, but I haven't the slightest idea about the significance of the third sentence."

"Why would he give you—his *adviser*—a cryptic message?"

Avian's thoughtful expression fell into one of melancholy. He shrugged, his light brown tresses tumbling across his eyes. "He didn't necessarily...*trust* me."

Kiara's eyebrows narrowed. "Why?"

His signature smile suddenly returned, reappearing as quickly as it had faded. He pushed his hair out of his eyes, the strands neatly falling into place. "That's a very long story."

"Go on," she urged.

Avian laughed, but Kiara couldn't discern a trace of humor in the sound he produced. "I'm afraid you're not ready to hear my tale. It's complicated and confusing, and it wouldn't benefit you to know it yet. Some day, Ara, I promise you, you will know every sharp detail of my life. But for now, let the past remain in the shadows where it belongs."

"Now I'm even more curious," she grumbled, "But I won't press you further. Do you have any clue at all about what my father may have meant?"

"Well, 'her voice must reverse the name which she had been given' could suggest speaking your name in the ancient Evalseman language. However, I cannot divulge the meaning behind the 'metal key' or 'royal silver'."

She shrugged. "I've never been good at riddles."

"Neither was your father, which leads me to wonder if it's even a riddle at all. I'm nearly positive his words aren't as complicated as we believe—we're just over-analyzing." He appeared genuinely flustered as he spoke, his lips twisted into a scowl. "I'm quite clever, so it deeply perturbs me that I can't unearth the logical explanation behind his message."

"You're also extremely humble," Kiara noted sarcastically, smirking.

Avian's lips pulled into a heartened smile. "I'm glad you noticed."

"Look, let's not worry about my father's letter too much," she decided. "We'll figure it out eventually. He wouldn't have written it if he hadn't been absolutely positive we could decipher it, right?"

He nodded in accordance. "You're right."

"Can I..." she started, staring down at the crumpled piece of paper with admiration. "Can I keep it, though? It makes me feel a little closer to him."

Avian smiled, chuckling lightly. "Of course you can. I'm sure he wouldn't have objected to that."

"I wish I had known him," she whispered longingly. "What was his Specialty?"

"He had many," he explained. "Not as many as I have, of course, but he had a handful of Specialties even I didn't know about. The only person who knew all of them was your mother."

Kiara sighed, her eyes shifting dark sapphire with sadness. "My father is such a mystery to me..."

"He loved you," Avian spoke gently. "He loved you more than anything."

She shrugged her shoulders, sighing. "I've heard about the king all of my life. It isn't fair that I never knew my father on a personal level. I've only ever seen exaggerated paintings and tapestries constructed in his honor, but I want to see what he *really* looked like—without the dramatic poses and elaborate crowns."

Avian chuckled, crossing the room in three long strides. He

stopped next to the vanity, opening a drawer and digging through the contents. From the depths of the dresser, he withdrew what appeared to be a sheet of glass framed by gold. He walked over to the edge of the bed, where Kiara was sitting, extending the glass clutched in his hand toward her open palm. "Your father," he said softly. "The way he appeared almost every day."

Kiara's hands shook with anticipation as she timidly gripped the gilded frame. She tilted the glass forward, her eyes starving to capture a glimpse into the personal life of the father she never knew. What she held was an intricately crafted painting—she could see the magnificent brush strokes flicking across her father's copper hair, capturing every reddish hue; his eyes were the palest blue, nearly translucent, staring up at her with friendliness. A splash of freckles dominated his cheeks and the bridge of his small nose, accenting his rosy skin. His mouth was pulled into a tight smile that held no arrogance. Although a silver and sapphire crown was nestled in his fiery tresses, he did not look like a king. To Kiara, he bore more resemblance to a youthful prince who hadn't yet gripped the responsibilities and regulations of royal life.

She had inherited a very small faction of his freckles, although hers were not so bright or unruly. Besides the red hues to her otherwise brown hair, she did not possess any of his other physical traits. Her face was oval in comparison to his square features, her nose was rounder than his, her ivory skin void of the pink tones that were present in his. She had a sinking suspicion that she resembled more of her mother, and was incredibly tempted to ask Avian if he had a portrait of her, as well, but before she could voice her question, he cut her off.

"I don't have a picture of your mother," he informed her regretfully. "Your father had one in his bedroom, but after his death, I couldn't locate it. Who knows what he did with it."

She nodded comprehensively, her body feeling weary and heavy. Her eyes stung, but she couldn't tear her gaze away from the portrait of her father. Her mind was reeling dizzily, attempting to recall the memories of her father that had been snuffed out.

"Are you okay?" he questioned, a concerned tone infiltrating his voice.

Her legs suddenly went numb, her body wavering precariously. She felt a faint pressure against her shoulders, causing her eyes to snap away from the image of her father. She found Avian bent toward her, his hands firmly wrapped around her small arms as he held her steady.

"I—I'm okay," she stammered. "It was just a bit overwhelming to look at that painting. It was very nostalgic."

"You can keep the picture," Avian decided, rubbing his palm across the bare skin of her shoulders. "It's yours, anyway."

She smiled. "Thank you," she spoke softly, shying away from Avian as she walked toward the vanity. She put the picture on top of the counter, the image of her grinning father winking up at her. She laid his letter down beside it, her eyes dark purple with happiness as she gazed at the sight.

"You need food," Avian declared abruptly, drawing her attention away from the newly decorated counter. "Would you like to accompany me back to the dining hall? If you don't feel like facing Blade, I will collect food for you and bring it here."

She shook her head. "No, I'll go, I would like to apologize for my outburst."

Avian smirked, sighing. "Blade won't apologize, though."

"Forget about Blade. I'm worried I offended Ace and Aiden. Will you show me the way to the dining hall? I need to remember the path."

He chuckled, interlacing his arm around hers as he turned her in the direction of the doorway. "Of course."

*****

"Where'd you run off to, princess?" Blade asked sardonically as Kiara and Avian appeared in front of the duke's table. Ace and Aiden were still present, staring up at the pair with curious expressions, but a new face scrutinized Kiara through wide, red eyes. The newcomer was a pretty girl who possessed wavy blonde hair and a striking resemblance to Aiden.

"*Someone* had to scour for your dignity," Kiara jeered nonchalantly, a bittersweet smile crossing her lips. "Regretfully, I couldn't recover it. I'm terribly sorry."

The table erupted into laughter as Blade glowered in annoyance. "She's witty," Ace noted approvingly to Aiden as they chortled.

Avian, a humored smile stubbornly hugging his lips, withdrew Kiara's chair from the table—which was again beside Blade—before he reclined in the seat beside her.

The blonde young woman sitting across from Avian rested her chin against her upturned hands, her crimson eyes falling in Kiara's direction. "My name's Akanine. I'm Aiden's little sister. Blade's been going on about you for nearly an entire hour. It's safe to say you don't match up with how he described you."

Kiara grinned, her eyes shifting to a dark purple hue. Akanine's expression narrowed as she witnessed the change in Kiara's irises. "Nice to meet you. I'm Kiara Fa—"

"*Knight*," Avian corrected hurriedly. "She's Kiara Knight."

Akanine redirected her confused countenance to Avian. "She's your sister? I thought you were an only child, Avian."

"Oh, I have been an only child for quite some time," he said reassuringly. "Kiara is—well, she's—she's my wife."

Kiara's eyes widened in bewilderment. He cautiously glanced in her direction momentarily, pleading for her to play along with his facade.

"She's your wife?" Akanine repeated, unconvinced. "I thought you've been hung up on the same girl for years. That's why no one in the castle has ever tried to pursue a romantic relationship with you, even though, trust me, you're incredibly popular."

"That's right," Avian said confidently, wrapping his arm around Kiara's shoulders. Her tense muscles relaxed slightly at his gentle touch. "This is the girl. We met years ago when her family traveled to Enevale to collect materials for her village. We began a weekly correspondence and would meet whenever we could find time. After years of involvement, I finally proposed and we were married by her family in her native village. She decided to move to Enevale with me."

Akanine appeared doubtful, but she shrugged her concern away, turning her attention to Kiara. "You're a lucky girl. He's leaving a trail of broken hearts behind."

"I hadn't the slightest idea my *husband* had so many girls chasing after him," Kiara spoke delicately, peeking at Avian through the corner of her eyes.

Blade, who had been exerting an absurd amount of energy in an attempt to conceal his humor, suddenly burst into a roar of laughter.

"What's his problem?" Akanine demanded an answer, eyeing him critically.

Kiara's sharp black eyes fell upon Blade disdainfully. "He has far too many to count."

He caught her glare, returning her heated gaze with an innocent smirk. "I won't give you away," he whispered, his voice so low, he practically mouthed the phrase.

"Blade, would you stop howling like a Demmonai any time soon?" Aiden cut in, rubbing his temples in exasperation.

"I'm going to get a drink," Blade declared suddenly, his smile vanishing. He abruptly stood up from the table, disappearing into the crowds of castle staff as he hurried off in the direction of the shop.

"I'm terribly hungry, Avian," Kiara announced, her gaze trailing Blade's vanishing figure. "Would you accompany me?

I'm unfamiliar with Enevale's food."

Avian automatically abandoned his chair. "Of course," he said, sliding Kiara's chair out from under the table. She stood up beside him, smiling pleasantly at Akanine as she promised they would return momentarily.

They sought solitude inside the nearly abandoned food shop. A large wooden slab occupied a single wall, a list of meals painted onto the surface. A counter flanked the menu, crowded with trays and jars of herbs. Three servers stood behind the counter; two of the women leaned against the wall, speaking casually to one another and eyeing their co-worker as he hurriedly prepared Blade's drink. Blade lounged lazily against the counter, his elbows resting against the wood. His icy eyes fell upon Kiara and Avian as they approached.

"What the hell was that?" Kiara demanded angrily, her hands tossing into the air dramatically as her eyes blazed crimson.

Blade suddenly appeared behind Avian, peeking his head over his friend's shoulder. "I'd like to know, as well," he decided, seeming mildly interested.

Avian shrugged away Blade's reclining chin, his mismatched eyes locked on Kiara's. "It was a brilliant idea. You'll be with me every hour of every day, and if everyone believes we are married, no one will question your presence in the castle."

"I still would've liked to have been informed about this plan *before* you told Akanine," she grumbled. "Why couldn't you have just told her the truth, anyway? She's Aiden's sister—she's part of the Stone dukedom!"

Avian sighed. "I only want those whom I have charged with your safety to know your identity."

"He doesn't trust Akanine," Blade cut in. "He has trust issues. I don't blame him, though, Akanine's basically the queen of gossip."

Avian spun his head around, glaring at his friend. "Will you stay out of it, Blade?" he demanded hotly.

"Won't we actually have to be married now?" Kiara questioned, her face paling. Although she *did* consider Avian her closest friend, and although she couldn't deny she *did* harbor unexplained feelings for him, she did not feel as though she were mentally prepared to be married to a boy she hadn't even known for a month.

The corners of Avian's mouth shot upward; it was obvious he was half-heartedly fighting off a smirk and failing. "What?" he said very seriously, despite his unrestrained grin.

"When Enevale's citizens become aware of my hidden identity, they will assume you're the new king because you're married to me."

Blade snickered. "They'd prefer Avian ruling, anyway."

"Blade, could you *please* hop off the 'Saint Avian' horse for a moment and let me finish my conversation?" Kiara snapped.

"We will simply inform them that our marriage was a cover-story, one we crafted in an attempt to shroud your identity until you were ready to regain control of the throne," Avian explained matter-of-factly.

Kiara's irises flashed black with annoyance as she crossed her arms against her chest. "I'm sure my subjects will absolutely *love* the fact that we lied to them before I was even crowned queen," she spoke sarcastically.

"It isn't really a blatant lie, just a cover-up. I'm certain they will understand. Besides, it wouldn't be a very exaggerated lie..." Avian's voice trailed off, his gaze abruptly darting toward the floor.

"Confession time?" Blade offered, his eyes brightening.

Avian scowled, attempting to silence his friend through gritted teeth.

"How is it *not* a far-fetched lie? I don't recall you proposing to me."

Avian shook his head impatiently. "Your father arranged a marriage between us, Kiara, remember? Blade mentioned it earlier today. You're so forgetful, I swear..."

"No one told me that engagement was on-going," she replied slowly, her eyes shifting hazel with curiosity as her annoyance was replaced with interest.

Blade scoffed. "Like Avian would call it off."

"Blade!" Kiara and Avian shouted simultaneously, identical aghast expressions lining their faces.

He shrugged innocently, the shadow of a mischievous grin clinging to his lips.

"Your father never halted the engagement and I don't have the authority to do so, because I—I gave my consent," Avian spoke awkwardly, his hands twitching. Kiara watched him curiously, realizing she had never seen him acquiesce to nerves. "The only one who can rebuff the engagement is you, and only when you are queen."

She stared up at him with shocked, light yellow eyes. "You gave your consent?" she questioned. "Why would you do that?"

"Can we please talk about this later?" he implored desperately. "My friends are waiting for us to return."

"Oh, my drink is ready," Blade said suddenly, sensing a lull in the conversation. He headed toward the counter as the server sent him an annoyed look. His drink had clearly been sitting there, forlornly, throughout their entire conversation.

Kiara's eyebrows narrowed as she shifted her attention to Avian. "Promise we *will* talk about it soon?" she urged.

"I promise," he assured her with a small smile. "What would you like to eat?" He reached Blade's side in two sweeping steps, his eyes grazing the menu.

Kiara shrugged, hurriedly assuming her position beside Avian. "At the village, we only ate basic foods—meat, bread, eggs, and other noncomplex meals. I don't recognize anything on this menu. Could you just order me something I used to enjoy during childhood? Oh, and I wouldn't mind some nillamee."

Avian expressed his compliance with a grin, placing his

order as Blade strode over to Kiara. He stopped at her side, clutching a blue cup in his hands as steam rose from the contents.

"I'm curious about something," Kiara said quietly. "Why did Kyan choose Avian to be the temporary king if Aiden's the oldest duke?"

Blade shook his head impatiently. "You already know that Avian was the king's advisor, hand-chosen by Kyan himself. He was always Kyan's favorite. Age doesn't matter whenever you're the king's proverbial right-hand man."

Kiara studied the duke's face, contemplating whether or not she should ask the question she had been unable to reap from Avian's cautious lips. "Why did Kyan distrust Avian?" she asked suddenly.

His pale eyes narrowed. "What do you mean?"

"Avian told me that my father didn't trust him. Why would he pick Avian to be his advisor if that were the case?"

Blade raised a skeptical eyebrow, his expression entirely bemused. "I wasn't aware of Kyan's distrust."

"Breakfast has arrived!" Avian abruptly announced, clutching a wooden tray crowded with two large plates of steaming, unidentifiable food.

Kiara smiled, following him and Blade as they departed the shop. They hurriedly located their table, settling into their seats. Avian slid Kiara's plate in front of her before he handed her the warm cup of nillamee she had requested. She gripped the hot mug in her hands, glancing shyly at Avian's friends.

"How are you adjusting to life in Enevale, Kiara?" Akanine questioned.

"It's a bit overwhelming," she admitted, stealing a glance at the food Avian had acquired for her. "But I'll get used to it, I'm sure."

Akanine smiled. "Good. If you need any help with anything, don't hesitate to ask."

"Thank you, Akanine. I really appreciate it."

She nodded in response before turning to her brother and starting a new conversation. Kiara cut into the pile of golden rolls that occupied her plate, spilling thick syrup from the punctured cake. Curiously, she bit into a piece of the pastry and was rewarded by a delicious cinnamon tang. "What is this?"

"Tahsam Cakes," Avian informed her. "It was your favorite meal as a child."

"It may be my favorite meal now," she chuckled.

Aiden abruptly stood up from his chair as though he had been prickled by a needle. His eyes were locked on something in the corner of the dining hall. "Excuse me, I have to meet with Lisette," he declared. His eyes briefly swept downward. "It's nice to meet you, Kiara," he said, following through with the façade Avian had implemented in front of Akanine. He departed the table, hurrying through the thinning crowds of the cafeteria.

"Who's he meeting?" Kiara whispered to Avian, her curiosity piqued.

"Lisette," he said, his response immediate. "She's Aiden's long-time girlfriend."

She nodded thoughtfully. "Are they going to get married?"

Blade's sudden laugh was absent of humor. "Those who willingly serve the royal court through military service are not permitted to marry during wartime—it's seen as a distraction for the soldiers."

"Avian's married," Kiara noted, attempting to divulge a flaw in the pretense Avian had crafted about their relationship.

"He was the king's advisor and now he's the temporary king," Blade explained in a dull, bored tone. "His position on the throne requires his military service, so the rules don't apply to him. Technically, his involvement with the soldiers is part of his job description, not a voluntary decision."

She frowned. "That's not fair."

Blade shrugged. "It's an old rule. The war has been very

quiet lately, though, ever since yo—" he stopped mid-sentence, his eyes flashing to Akanine wearily, "—ever since the princess left."

"If the princess's absence from the throne is the vehicle needed to muffle this war, then I'm sure the entire kingdom is ready to accept it," Akanine immediately declared. "Vyntrx has been quiet for years, but we all know that she's planning something. She was terrified of Kyan, but now he's dead. No one knows what her next move will be."

"She won't stay quiet for long," Avian's tone was solemn and unnaturally serious. "Soon we'll be needing the princess and her soldiers more than ever."

Akanine narrowed her eyes. "How do you know?"

"It's my job to know," he explained, his tone shifting as his characteristic smile swept across his face. "If you're finished eating, Kiara, we should head back to the suite."

"Alright," she replied, glancing down at her devoured entrée.

"I'll see you tomorrow," Avian assured Ace and Blade, standing up from the table and pulling out Kiara's seat.

She waved good-bye to the boys and Akanine, protesting quietly as Avian picked up her empty dishes and placed them on the wooden tray.

They headed through the cafeteria, stopping beside the archway. A wide counter was placed beside the entryway, holding trays identical to the one Avian was grasping. After he had placed their tray next to the others, he and Kiara headed out of the dining hall and into the Master Room.

"Blade was right," Kiara mumbled as Avian led her through the labyrinth of hallways. "The citizens of Enevale don't want me for the throne."

"What made you say that?"

"You heard Akanine. The war hasn't been violent in Enevale since I left. When they know I'm back, they'll expect Vyntrx to return, as well."

"You're going to protect the Kingdom from her. Without you here, Enevale wouldn't stand a chance. Besides, none of them realize the war has been ongoing in the outer regions of Menevilen."

Kiara narrowed her eyes. She could feel the weight of responsibility crushing her mentality, sending shocks of fear through her limbs. "What good will I do? I'm one person."

"Vyntrx doesn't want anyone else. The root of her hatred for the Evalseman race has always been planted, but your mother's death created an intense bloodlust for those she deemed *responsible* for her sister's untimely end–you and your father. Your demise is much more tantalizing to her than the notion of destroying Enevale."

Kiara swallowed hard. The thought of having a disturbed killer constantly chasing after her chilled her to the bone. It made matters drastically worse that it was her aunt—her own flesh and blood—that so desperately wanted her dead. "I can't fight her," Kiara admitted. The fear she had chased away before entering Enevale had abruptly swept back into her heart as though the cork of placations she had used to bottle down her worries had been blasted off by the profusion of her terror.

"I'm afraid you don't have a choice," Avian's voice was husky. He sounded pained, as if he wished he could have given Kiara a different option but knew disastrously that he couldn't.

She glanced up at him, finding his mismatched eyes shining under a pool of light brown hair. "I'm going to die," she whispered, her voice quavering with unbridled fright.

"Always the pessimist," Avian said lightly, attempting to smile and failing miserably. "You won't die. You're going to beat Vyntrx and save Enevale."

"I hope one of your many Specialties is fortune telling," she muttered, turning her head away from Avian and watching the corridors dart past as they walked steadily through the castle.

Avian's eyes still lingered on Kiara's turned face. His hand found hers and he squeezed her palm gently, a silent promise that she would be all right. Although his hand was in-between hers comfortingly, Kiara could have sworn she heard him whisper, "I hope so, as well."

Chapter Seven

Changes

Avian had permitted Kiara to spend the remainder of her first day in Enevale roaming the halls and grounds of the castle. He led her through every hidden corridor, walked leisurely with her through the gardens, and told her countless stories as he revealed the military's training grounds. She was introduced to so many unfamiliar, quizzical faces, she found it impossible to even remember a single name. As dusk settled in the sky, Kiara felt her eyelids droop with exhaustion as she quietly suggested to Avian that they should return to the suite for the evening.

Before she had been able to seek solitude in the confinement of her bedroom, Avian had asked her to sit at the dining table with him and discuss the arrangements for the following months. Wearily, she reclined in her chair and listened as he explained that he and the dukes would undertake the task of "properly" educating her before she could claim the throne. According to Avian, her required curriculum would consist of lessons in Enevale's history, etiquette, dancing, the ancient Evalseman tongue, public speech, stealth, strategy, identification of weapons and creatures, recognition of important figures in Enevale, and of course, physical combat. He decided her schooling would take several months, and throughout the duration of her education, he would put his role of advisor as far aside as he safely could.

After agreeing to Avian's conditions, Kiara had retreated to bed, bitterly cognizant of the fact that the next few months would undoubtedly be mentally—if not also physically—grueling.

Avian had, upon her request, agreed to lie on the couch in her room until she fell asleep. He waited until her breathing grew steady and her restless body finally fell still to creep out of her room and ransack the armoire in the corner of his bedroom.

His hand grasped the small black box he had carefully stored in the depths of his dresser since the day he had given his word to marry Kiara. His fingers lovingly traced the delicate arch of the box before he flicked open the latch. At the bottom of the box, two ornate, silver rings winked up at him through the darkness.

Kyan had been planning the engagement between his daughter and his advisor since the day he had taken the recently orphaned Avian into his family. Being the son of Kyan's closest friend, Avian had secured a place in Kyan's heart since birth, and the potential joining of the Knight and Fable families was a welcomed notion to the king. Kyan had prepared engagement rings for the couple, but in Kiara's absence, Avian had securely locked away the handcrafted jewelry, as wearing the ring proved to be merely a sharp reminder of the constant vacancy of her presence.

His downcast eyes burrowed into the metallic bands, scrutinizing the intricate design that wove across each ring. The rings were nearly identical, the obvious difference being variation in size, but the name of the owner's significant other was engraved in the inside of the band. Avian's fingers traced his ring, following the chain of curves that linked together Kiara's name.

He slid the band onto his left ring finger, reveling in the feeling of security and completeness it stirred within his heart. He smiled softly, closing the box as he attempted to chase away the thoughts of self-loath and guilt that always darkened his short-lived bouts of bliss. *Tomorrow, I'll give her his ring for the sake of the facade,* he thought, cramming the box into the depths of his pocket, *but I will not confess my true feelings for her until the time is right.* And although his bargain with himself appeared necessary, he understood he was asking of himself a difficult feat—for every confusing hour he spent with Kiara further propelled him into the scope of love's merciless whim.

*****

Kiara sat uncomfortably in one of the wide, padded chairs that encircled the table in the suite's dining room. Her fingers fidgeted nervously. Avian sat placidly across from her, his hand wrapped tightly around an object she couldn't discern. "I wanted to give you this before the dukes arrive," he said softly, sliding a small black box across the smooth wooden surface of the table.

Avian had shaken her awake in the early hours of morning and informed her of the duke's expected arrival around midday. He advised she dress casually and invited her to eat breakfast with him in the suite while solemnly declaring he had a present to give her.

They had eaten their small breakfast of toasted bread and nillamee and had pushed the plates aside before Avian had withdrawn her gift from the pocket of his trousers. Kiara stared at the box as he deposited it in front of her. "Is this it?" she wondered, fingering the velvety material of the object.

"Yes," he spoke tersely. "It's for the little facade we've implemented about our relationship. Open it."

Kiara's fingers immediately unlatched the box, her gaze falling upon a small silver ring carefully nestled in swathes of sapphire satin. She withdrew the piece of jewelry, examining the strange design engraved in the band and discovering Avian's name scrawled into the inner circle of the ring. Her eyes flashed upward, light yellow with surprise, as she noticed a nearly identical ring was present on the ring finger of Avian's left hand. "Wedding bands," she said clumsily. "You had actual wedding bands made? Overnight?"

Avian's expression darkened. "I was hoping you wouldn't ask about that," he muttered. "No, I did not have them crafted overnight. These rings were forged many years ago, after I..." he trailed off, his eyes suddenly downcast. "Yesterday, you discovered that I had given your father my permission to be engaged to you. After I gave my consent, he had these rings created. I've kept them in my possession since that day. I figured it would make our *marriage* appear convincing."

Kiara's eyebrows narrowed as she scrutinized Avian's words. She slid the band onto her left hand, marveling at how perfectly it fit her small finger. "I still don't understand why you gave your consent." Her sentence was a declaration, but Avian could tell from the curious hazel hue in her eyes, from the inquiring tone that had captivated her voice, that she had indirectly poised it as a question.

"Another time, Ara," he said quickly, feeling a whirl of apprehension stir inside his stomach at the thought of divulging his reasons behind their engagement. "Just know that our arranged marriage is not in effect unless you declare it to be."

Kiara opened her mouth to respond, but her voice was silenced as a torrent of loud knocks sounded against the main door of the suite. She glanced to the side, sighing, as Avian hurriedly jumped to his feet. "The dukes are early," he commented, his hand falling upon the doorknob.

She nodded, standing up from her chair as the front door swung open and the three dukes loudly forced their way into the suite. Their eyes fell upon Kiara as they shouted a chorus of greetings. "Good morning," she replied quietly.

"Hope we weren't interrupting anything," Blade joked, noting the flustered expression pinned along Kiara's face.

"You weren't," Avian responded automatically, ushering everyone into the living room. He had summoned a glistening fire to the wide hearth in the corner of the room; the soft crackle of the flames infused the atmosphere with a sense of serenity. "I thought we could open with a lesson over Enevale's history. For some subjects, I will only require one of you to assist, but for today, I thought it would be appropriate if we tackled the teaching collectively."

Aiden and Ace nodded comprehensively while Blade shrugged without enthusiasm. He sent Kiara a sidelong glance that suggested he had as little interest in teaching as she had in sitting through the courses.

"However, first I would like to create a weekly schedule, so each of you know whenever your expertise is needed," Avian explained, reclining against the edge of the couch as he gestured for everyone to settle down beside him. "On the first day of each week, Kiara will have morning classes focusing on etiquette with Aiden, followed by a strategy lesson after lunch that I will instruct. On the second day, Blade will inform her about the art of identifying weapons, and that afternoon, Ace will teach her all she needs to know about public speech. On the third day, she'll learn how to identify creatures and herbs with Aiden, and afterward, she will receive lessons on stealth from Blade. On the fourth day, Ace will familiarize her with the faces of important figures in Enevale's society and other nearby kingdoms, and that evening, I will teach her how to dance. On the fifth day, I will not require your assistance, as I will be spending most of the day teaching Kiara the ancient Evalseman language. On the sixth and seventh days, we will exercise with her at the training fields, but we will save the actual lessons on combat and weapon control for whenever she has completed her schooling."

Avian glanced around the room as he concluded his speech. Ace had withdrawn a small pad of paper and a feathered pen from a pouch at his side and was hurriedly scribbling down the schedule. Aiden nodded comprehensively, embedding the schedule into his memory. Blade was staring ahead blankly, his boredom heavily evident on his absent expression. When Avian stopped talking, Blade snapped to attention, cleared his throat, and loudly said, "Sounds like a plan."

"Were you even paying attention?" Kiara asked, attempting to conceal her amusement as she observed Blade's actions.

"Doesn't matter," he replied casually, shrugging. "I'll be where I'm supposed to be."

"Anyway," Avian chimed in, sending his friend a critical glance, "Enevale's history isn't too dense, so if we start now, we can certainly finish by dinner."

The dukes nodded in compliance as Avian jumped into action. He withdrew a heavy book from the depths of his bedroom, handing it to Kiara and informing her that she should follow along as he taught.

Avian and the dukes took turns giving lectures over different events in Enevale's history, and as the material became so overwhelming, Kiara unearthed a pad of paper and began taking notes. Avian had informed her that at the end of her courses, she would be presented with a test that she must pass in order to be deemed ready for the throne, so she exerted her utmost effort in an attempt to remember the information.

Kiara learned about the founding of Enevale hundreds of years ago. According to the texts, some far-off relative of hers had actually built Fable Castle and the oldest buildings in the kingdom and had been the official ruler. She heard stories of the first battle between the Nonae and Evalseman—it had been a short battle, more or less a small squabble over land, but it was repeatedly attributed as being the cause behind the species' irrational hatred for one another.

At the end of the day, Kiara's mind felt fuzzy, as though it had been thoroughly overloaded with information and was refusing to further cooperate. The dukes departed the suite as dusk settled in, promising they would adhere to Avian's carefully designed schedule for as long as he deemed necessary.

Avian prepared a small dinner of seasoned meat and frothy soup. They sat in exhausted silence at the table as Kiara marveled at Avian's exquisite culinary skills. The meat had been perfectly heated until it had reached the perfect texture; the soup had been filled with herbs and spices to permeate a unique, bold flavor. A slice of puffy bread had been placed on each of their plates next to cups brimming with heated liquid. The spread was delicious; a much-needed reward after a long day filled with extensive studying.

"How do you like the meal, Ara?" Avian asked, taking a small bite off his fork.

She smiled, ripping off a chunk of bread and depositing it into her mouth. "It's wonderful, really," she complimented. "You have astounding cooking skills."

Avian chuckled. A lacking quality in his personality was certainly humbleness—in order to not appear boastful, he had to exhume the small supply of bashfulness from the depths of his psyche to forcefully mask his naturally arrogant tendencies. "Your father taught me," Kiara watched the constrained expression playing on his face as he spoke. "I'm not nearly as talented as he was."

She laughed lightly. "You don't have to hold yourself back around me, you know."

"What do you mean?"

"I can tell you don't want to appear proud, so you're being unusually modest," she paused, eyeing his startled expression. "I know you want to brag about your culinary abilities, so go ahead."

Avian shook his head, laughing. "You know me better than I imagined."

"We *did* spend four days just talking during our journey here," she reminded him hastily. "And each minute I spend with you, I feel I understand you better. I enjoy trying to sort you out."

The shy grin that slid across Avian's face at Kiara's words was not forced. A vague glow of crimson clouded his clear skin. "I'm glad," he whispered, abruptly standing up from the table.

"It's been a long day, Ara. I'm heading to bed. Don't stay up too late." He recovered his half-empty dishes, placed them on a counter in the kitchen, gently ran his hand across the crown of Kiara's head, and disappeared behind his bedroom door. Kiara stared after him curiously, her eyebrows furrowing as she attempted to comprehend Avian's sudden departure.

Avian's back was pinned to his bedroom door, his heart beating rapidly. His eyes hadn't adjusted to the suppressive shadows of his bedroom, but he didn't turn on the light for fear that he would find *her* waiting to scold him. *This is dangerous,* he thought miserably. *It was different when this was one-sided, but the situation is changing. If I let her too close, all it will lead to is unbearable pain for us both. But I can't push her away. I can't.*

You're weak, a taunting voice echoed through his head.

Maybe, he agreed, *but perhaps my weakness will give me strength.*

*****

The following weeks progressed at a hastened pace. The dukes obeyed Avian's structured schedule, appearing at the suite on the exact times and days their audience had been requested. Kiara quickly became familiarized with the assorted qualities of the dukes—she learned how to appeal to Ace's innate kindness, how to carry on a sophisticated conversation with Aiden, and most importantly, how to handle Blade's volatile personality and harsh jokes.

After just one week of classes, Kiara determined which subjects were enjoyable and which were nearly unbearable. She was naturally drawn to lessons on etiquette, recognizing important figures, and the ancient Evalseman language, but as hard as she tried, she couldn't even master the basics of stealth, dancing, and strategy.

"I can hear you shuffling your feet," Blade continually

scolded as Kiara attempted to sneak up on him. She would shout in frustration and he would snap, "Yelling gives away your location, idiot."

She would watch Blade's sleek movements as he soundlessly crossed the room, but regardless of how much effort she funneled into mimicking his actions, she could not force her body to match his grace. Being naturally clumsy, she repeatedly tripped over nothing, an error that stirred Blade's rage and was the cause of many heated lectures.

Even though she continually failed at dancing and strategy training, she was gratefully able to seek solace in Avian's endearing, patient demeanor. On just her second day of dancing lessons, she had already lost count of the amount of times she had accidentally stomped on his feet. Unlike Blade, Avian never acquiesced to frustration, and would laugh as she fumbled across the ballroom.

At first, Kiara could only manage to timidly wrap her arms around Avian's shoulders as he led her through the moves of the dances, but as the weeks progressed, she found she could practically pin her body to Avian's without feeling the slightest sense of awkwardness.

She could feel her bonds with the dukes strengthening. The more information she absorbed about life in Enevale, the closer she felt to her advisers. Nearly every day, the five royals would trek through the castle into the cafeteria to share a discussion-driven lunch, and Kiara could tell by the light-hearted tones dominating their conversation that she had been accepted into their close-knit unit.

And then there was Avian. Avian—who had initially struck Kiara as an unreachable celebrity, who had been introduced to her as a loyal advisor, who had quickly become her closest friend in a matter of days—had abruptly crafted his own unique location in the deepest chambers of her heart.

She and Avian had continued their façade of being a married couple, and were both extremely cautious about journeying beyond the suite without their rings in place. It appeared as though no one doubted their ploy—aside from the dukes, of course—but after months of spending endless hours at Avian's side, Kiara began to question the falsity of their fabricated relationship.

She had begun to notice a soft gleam in Avian's eyes when he titled his head in her direction. His intense glances would sweep across her frame, sending her gaze plummeting to the ground as a wave of embarrassment overtook her psyche.

Her strange relationship with Avian heated alongside the weather. Humid, stuffy air grazed Enevale, infiltrating the less ventilated areas of the castle. Although it had only barely reached the warm season—and summer was still months away—beads of sweat had already begun to spill down Kiara's back any time she ventured outside the castle. The dukes had occasionally accompanied her on trips into the city—sometimes Ace had taken her on "missions" to test her ability of recognizing important figures and would occasionally take her and the dukes to a local pub to relieve themselves of stress—and it was during these trips that Kiara first noted the change in climate.

Nearly three months, she thought with stark realization as she climbed the steps stretching toward the dining hall, the figures of Avian and the dukes leading the way in front of her. *I've already been in Enevale for nearly three months.*

Time had sped by with haste, having been so crammed with lessons and tiring routines. She had felt so cooped up, even with the excursions into the city, she was desperately looking forward to the day when Avian would declare her ready to abandon her studies and focus on sharpening her combat skills.

Her mind was reeling as she envisioned the penned maps Avian had recently ordered her to study. He had spread out two extensive maps before her—one of Enevale, and one of the Dark Forest, which was nearly five times as large as the kingdom—and a small, conclusive map of Menevilen. Avian had pointed to Kiara's desolate village on the wrinkled parchment as he explained that the landscape of Menevilen was somewhat of a mystery, considering no one knew what lay beyond the Kahliar Sea nor beyond the northern edge of the Dark Forest. She had studied the charts for several hours before Avian had allowed her to take a short jaunt into the city with the dukes.

"Are you alright, Kiara?" Aiden questioned as they simultaneously rounded a corner. "You're being awfully quiet."

Kiara's glazed expression brightened as she was drawn out of her thoughts. "Oh, sorry," she mumbled. "I was just thinking that I've been here a long time."

"*Too* long," Blade muttered.

She sent him a sidelong glare, but she had grown too familiar with his perpetual rudeness to take his comments to heart.

"Well, she's been here long enough, but I still haven't had a chance to meet her," an unfamiliar voice suddenly echoed through the hall.

Kiara and the dukes instantly stopped walking, turning around in perfect sync to face the speaker as she approached. The tallest woman Kiara had ever laid eyes upon was slinking across the hallway, her piercing green eyes cutting through the shadows as her lips pulled into a wide grin. A blonde girl with an athletic build was pinned to her side, her merry expression matching the face of the woman she was trailing.

"Rissa," Avian whispered. There was an unexplained tone behind his voice as he revealed the speaker's name.

Kiara turned toward him curiously, watching his furrowed brow as he studied the approaching women. "Do you know her?"

"Yes," he answered, his response immediate.

"Have you been avoiding us, Rissa?" Aiden wondered heartily as the woman he was addressing and her companion stopped in front of the dukes.

The woman called Rissa laughed, her short black hair tickling the edges of her chin. "Of course not. Sena and I have been on reconnaissance missions in the Dark Forest and only got back a couple of weeks ago. We've heard rumors that there's a new face in town, and that she's supposedly Avian's bride."

Kiara deduced from context that Sena was the smiling blonde at the woman's side. There was a striking difference between the two—while Rissa was tall, svelte, dark, and tomboyish, her companion's well-defined body was of shorter stature and her light hair was long and neatly combed. Both girls were smiling, but for some reason, Sena's grin was the only one that appeared sincere.

"That's correct," Avian admitted, attempting to mask his tense tone. His arm suddenly wrapped around Kiara's shoulders. "Allow me to introduce my wife, Kiara Knight."

Rissa's eyebrows shot upward as she scrutinized Kiara's form. She smiled pleasantly, but her sharp emerald eyes were unforgettably icy. "My name's Rissa. It's great to meet you," she gushed. "You must be impressive if our extremely selective Avian hand-picked you."

"Nice to meet you, too," Kiara replied warily, forcing herself to smile. "I'm sorry to disappoint, but I'm not really anything that special."

"Oh, you don't have to be modest," the blonde chimed in. "My name's Sena. You poor thing, you have no idea who we are. We must seem so imposing! We're friends with the dukes. Rissa is the captain of the military and I'm the lieutenant."

When Kiara smiled at the lieutenant, she didn't have to fake the smile that spread across her lips. There was something about the bright gleam in Sena's hazel eyes that instantly made Kiara feel at ease. "It's nice to meet you, Sena," she replied. "I can't believe I hadn't met the two of you yet, considering your high ranking positions in the military."

"Ah, well, I'm sure Avian's trying to keep you all to himself," Rissa's sentence appeared teasing, but a harsher tone underlined her words.

"She's just been trying to adjust to castle life," Avian hurriedly explained. "It's a significant adjustment from the small village she grew up in. I haven't quite gotten around to introducing her to people beyond the dukedom."

Rissa shrugged, rolling her eyes. "She should be well-adjusted by now."

"A girl needs friends, Avian!" Sena exclaimed critically. "You can't keep her locked away with a bunch of boys." She turned to Kiara, her smile brightening. "If you ever need someone to talk to that isn't one of the dukes, I would be more than happy to oblige. I'm usually either training in the barracks or relaxing in the dining hall."

Kiara was taken aback by Sena's sincere kindness. She had stated a noteworthy point, however—Kiara had honestly become increasingly tired of all-male company, and the prospect of sharing a conversation with another female was tremendously appealing. "Thank you, Sena," she spoke earnestly. "I'm certain I will take advantage of your offer."

Rissa's expression darkened as she watched her lieutenant's smile break into a toothy grin. "We should be going, Sena," she decided suddenly. "We have a training session in a few minutes."

Sena blinked, staring up at the captain with bemusement. "Alright," she mumbled.

"We'll see you around," Rissa spoke loudly, walking backwards down the hallway. "It was nice to meet you, Kiara."

The dukes waved good-bye to the retreating figures as Avian's hand suddenly clamped around Kiara's wrist. His eyes were locked on the distance, watching Rissa disappear behind a corner. The second she vanished from sight, his grip relaxed noticeably. Kiara glanced up at him curiously, but he wouldn't meet her gaze. His visage was set in a far-off expression.

*****

"What's the story with Rissa?" Kiara asked abruptly. She and Avian had returned to the suite after sharing an awkward lunch with the dukes in the dining hall. No one had spoken about the meeting with the captain, but Kiara sensed from the terse atmosphere that the strange encounter was in the forefront of everyone's mind.

Avian's body stiffened beneath Kiara's touch. They had reclined on the couch in the living room, the warm fire crackling in the hearth as they sat in silence. They were seated facing one another, her knees bumping against his, his arm casually drawn across the back of the couch as his fingers skimmed the edge of her shoulders. "What do you mean?"

Her eyes narrowed with impatience. "Don't play coy. You know what I mean."

Avian released a spew of exhausted air. "You know me too well," he mumbled, absentmindedly brushing a strand of Kiara's hair out of her curious, hazel eyes. "Two years ago, Rissa tried to pursue a relationship with me. She had been a soldier for a while and was quickly gaining recognition for her efforts. When she was promoted to captain, she became my second-in-command, ranked above the dukes—it had been Kyan's decision. She looked up to me, admired me. We became friends, but I suppose she wanted more. She asked me to accompany her to dinner one evening in the city, and I—being oblivious of her true intentions—agreed.

"Dinner seemed normal. We kept conversation mainly focused on the military and the war. But right before we finished our meals, she asked me about my personal life. She wondered if I had ever been in love, and I..." he trailed off, suddenly very uncomfortable, "Well, it doesn't matter what I said. Her question should have been my first hint.

"We walked back to the castle together. As soon as we

entered the main hall, I decided we should part ways, but she quickly asked if I would examine a busted weapon of hers to see if it was salvageable. I told her she should go to the blacksmith, but she insisted so fervently, I finally agreed to help. The weapon was apparently in her suite. I followed her to her room, and as soon as we were inside, she pounced like a Coronix tackling its prey. She wrapped her arms around me tightly, forced her lips against mine. I pushed her away, but she kept trying, kept asking me if I had ever been *with* a woman. Of course I haven't. She had stolen my first kiss. I had been saving everything for—" he stopped talking abruptly, his eyes nervously scanning Kiara's attentive expression. "Anyway, I finally managed to distance myself from her, but I was rougher with her than I meant to be. I accidentally injured her. I thought my coarse rejection and departure would have signaled my disinterest, but it didn't. Any time she could, she attempted to seduce me. It was tiring fending her off all of the time. One day, my patience reached its peak.

"I challenged her to a duel. I told her if I won, she would have to leave me alone or else I would suspend her from the military. Kyan wouldn't have allowed me to discharge her simply because she was a pest—she was too valuable a soldier for that. A duel was required, so a duel I arranged. Her terms were straightforward enough—if she won the match, she won the right to do whatever she wanted with me. And I knew what she wanted.

"I hadn't expected her to be so strong. Her Evalseman Specialty is shape shifting. One minute I was fighting a Demmonai, the next I was fighting a Coronix. She was deadly, and I could certainly understand why Kyan regarded her abilities so highly. She nearly won the duel, but my passions were stronger than hers. At the last minute, I managed to injure her so badly, she had no other option than to give up. I felt no remorse, even when she was required to spend nearly a month in the infirmary.

"Once she was discharged, she kept her word. She stopped scheming to win my affections. Instead, she turned on my friends. For a while, she focused on Blade. He, of course, *did* give in to her coaxing, and they were together for a short time, but her eyes were always puncturing me. It's no surprise she made a point to introduce herself to you. I'm sorry, I should have told you that story long ago."

Kiara's eyes were downcast, her expression darkened. Her hands were cold against Avian's forearm. She remained silent for several minutes, replaying his story in her mind as she attempted to form an appropriate response. "Why didn't you just give in?" she wondered, her voice husky. Her irises were red with anger, speckled with green jealousy and hazel curiosity. "What was holding you back?"

"It was..." he trailed off, his fingers lightly tracing the group of faint freckles on Kiara's shoulder. "I'm not sure if I'm ready to tell you."

She furrowed her brow in confusion. "When *will* you be ready?"

"I'm not sure," he whispered. She could have sworn a line of tears crowded his eyes. "Once I tell you, there's no going back. What I tell you will complicate both of our lives forever."

Kiara gently gripped his hand against hers. "You can tell me anything. You're my advisor, my closest friend, my—" she stopped herself, flushing. "You're—you're my guide."

"You're not ready to hear it," he decided. He disentangled himself from her grasp, hurriedly climbing to his feet. He stood at the edge of the couch, staring down at Kiara as her worried eyes turned light blue. He bent down, gently placing his lips against the crown of her head, listening to her sharp intake of breath. "Perhaps you'll know once you've completed your lessons," he suggested, his mouth moving against her sweet-smelling hair. "But for now, don't fret about it."

He withdrew his touch, taking a step away from the couch as his eyes burrowed into Kiara's. "Follow me," he spoke softly, extending his open hand forward, "there's somewhere I want to take you."

She stared up at him inquisitively, her mind whizzing with the elements of Avian's story as she tried to piece together a reason behind his odd behavior. "Alright," she said skeptically, placing her hand within his grasp.

Avian led her through an unfamiliar part of the castle, exiting out a doorway she had never passed through before. She was amazed there were still parts of the palace that she had yet to expose, but the unending halls surely prevented any of its inhabitants from discovering every room.

The chilled night air instantly caressed Kiara's skin as she passed through the threshold. Despite the rising temperature as the season shifted, the nights were still relatively cool, and as she followed Avian across the castle grounds, she wished she had recovered a cloak before departing the warmth of palace halls.

The large garden flanking the edge of the castle slowly poured into view as they began to pass strange, seemingly glowing plants. The entrance to the garden was flecked with a handful of flowers and statues, but the further the pair walked, the more the garden resembled a small forest. Large, thin trees darkened the grounds; ornate fountains dotted the winding trails, the soft sound of running water filling the peaceful silence.

Avian expertly wound his way through the garden, maneuvering the labyrinth-like structure of the trails as though it were second nature. After several minutes of walking, he came to an abrupt halt in front of a life-like statue. Kiara stopped beside him, her eyes grazing the magnificent stone figure—crafted of glistening marble, the sculpture had been carefully molded into the form of a splendorous king. The chiseled face was instantly familiar, and with a pang of realization, Kiara understood that she was observing a life-size representation of her father.

"This was made in honor of King Kyan," Avian declared, smoothing his hand across the unblemished stone. "It's a tribute to his life. It was finished only last week, but we've encountered a problem. You see these flowers?" His hand brushed a thicket of unusual flora brandishing wild, coppery petals. Their vibrancy had begun to deteriorate, splotches of brown decay ringing the green stems. "They keep dying— quickly, too. They were your father's favorite flower, a rare type that only grows in the Dark Forest, which could be exactly why the gardeners can't sustain the flowers' lives."

Kiara's fingers grazed the velvety petals. "That's sad," she whispered. "I'm sure he would've loved for them to flourish."

"I have something I would like for you to try," Avian spoke somewhat timidly. He ruffled the edge of the flower, knocking loose a handful of petals. "I would like for you to attempt to harness your Nonae magic. Try to bend the energy around you to salvage this dying plant."

Kiara's expression was one of incredulity. Never in her life had she been able to employ Nonae magic on command. The first and only time she had summoned her capabilities had been an accident—she wasn't at all convinced she possessed enough skill to bend energy to her will. "Why do you want me to try to use magic all of a sudden?"

"You're nearing the end of your studies," he explained. "Soon, I plan to focus on your physical training. If you could gain enough basic knowledge on the manipulation of magic, we could harness your power into an unstoppable force. We would not only prepare your body for extensive combat, we would strengthen your magic, as well."

"Avian, like I've said before, I'm not a full-blooded Nonae. I can't just pull magic out of the air—"

"You *can*," he argued. "You have the potential—it's innate. Please, just try. For me."

Kiara sighed in exasperation, unable to deny Avian's pleading tone. "Fine." Her hand shot out clumsily, unsettling the group of tarnished flowers. "What do I do?"

"I'm not sure," he admitted sheepishly. "I'm not a Nonae."

She laughed nervously, her hands stroking the delicate curve of the flowers. As her fingers danced across the dull, vein-laden petals, she envisioned them blushed with bright, vivacious hues. She imagined the stems standing perfectly erect, their leaves curling toward the sky. She pictured the plants so healthy that an orb of liveliness forever surrounded their plot.

Avian's startled gasp sent Kiara's mind spiraling into reality. She must have, at some point, clamped her eyes shut with concentration; her eyelids flashed open as she was drawn out of her reverie.

Avian was standing over the flowerbed in amazement. Life had blanketed the foliage as though time had been withdrawn. The flowers were shimmering with exuberance so dazzling, they seemed to glow through the nighttime darkness. "You did it!" he exclaimed. "You used Nonae magic at will!"

Kiara beamed, staring at her creation with bemusement. She felt as though she had unearthed some raw, fledgling ability from the most abandoned corridors of her mind—as though she had decrypted the mysteries of her Nonae power. Avian's smile was overflowing with admiration. His hand clasped hers excitedly, and as his grip tightened around her fingers, she felt as though she could boldly face any challenge the world could toss in her direction—so long as Avian was standing by her side.

*****

Kiara's studies progressed at a hurried pace for another arduous month. While she was unable to master the arts of stealth or strategy, she gained as tight a hold around the subjects as she could manage. At the end of each day, Kiara would retreat into her bedroom to practice harnessing magic. After just a week of practicing, she was able to lift small objects through telekinesis using a minimal amount of concentration. She could feel her power strengthening as though her magic were a muscle subjected to strenuous exercise. Having finally been able to overcome her fear of speaking to large crowds and having excelled in most of her classes, she could feel herself becoming more deserving of her rightful position on the throne.

Outside of her classes, Kiara had begun to meet with Sena several times each week. Sena had proven to be a genuinely kind person and she found a bond was quickly being forged between them. She discovered that despite Sena's bubbly personality, she lacked true friends, which fueled her desire to spend time with Kiara. Sena was admittedly Kiara's sole female friend—someone she could vent to, confide in, and laugh with for hours.

Regardless of their friendship, Kiara had been unable to tell Sena about her true identity. Scared Avian would be irreversibly angry if she gave away the secret, Kiara had glued her mouth shut. She couldn't hide, however, the fact that she was part-Nonae, as her constantly shifting eyes immediately gave away her guise. Kiara was relieved when Sena failed to express even a hint of contempt after discovering her friend's true heritage.

One afternoon, after having been briefly visited by Rissa as Kiara and Sena shared lunch in the dining hall, Kiara had asked her friend if she understood the strange relationship between the captain and Avian. Sena had responded that there was a rumor floating around Enevale that Avian had been in love with an unknown girl for years, which was apparently why he had shied away from female companions and had denied Rissa's persistent affections.

Her curiosity heavily piqued, Kiara had planned to confront Avian about the rumor over dinner. She had assumed she and Avian would be the only two in attendance, but as the three dukes sat down alongside them at their habitual table, Kiara felt her heart drop with disappointment.

"There's something very important we must discuss, Ara," Avian abruptly announced, setting a filled plate down in front of her.

She stared up at him with curious hazel eyes. Her gaze darted between each of the dukes, attempting to decipher their expressions, before she turned her attention back to Avian. "What is it?"

He exchanged solemn glances with his friends before finally unhinging his mouth to respond. The atmosphere had built with tension. "Kiara," he started, his tone utterly grave. "The dukes and I would like to inform you..." he trailed off, watching Kiara's eyes flash light blue with worry, "that you have obtained all of the knowledge necessary for completing your courses."

Kiara issued a heavy sigh of relief, feeling as though a pair of shackles had been reprieved from encircling her wrists. She laughed lightly, slamming her fist against Avian's shoulder. "You scared me!"

"I couldn't help it," he chuckled. "I have the final tests prepared for you to take tomorrow. Congratulations, Ara, you're on the path to being crowned queen!"

Her lips spilled into a bashful grin. "It's been a lengthy process," she noted, taking a small bite out of a piece of bread. "I'm grateful for all of your help."

The dukes smiled in response, busying picking at the food laden on their plates. "Would you like to do anything to celebrate?" Ace wondered.

"Ah, it'd be bad luck to celebrate prior to her passing the tests," Avian advised. "But I suppose we could fulfill a *small* request, if her majesty commands it."

Kiara scrunched up her face in concentration as she worked through her thoughts and memories, attempting to fathom an appropriate request. As she replayed her time in Enevale, she recalled Avian stating that "perhaps" she could be granted the reason behind his definitive rejection to Rissa's advances. She had been presented with an opportune moment to gain insight into Avian's psyche while divulging information about the mysterious girl Sena had claimed he was in love with. "Avian, do you remember when I asked you about your history with Rissa?"

His eyebrows sloped downward. "Yes."

"You never told me why you were so adamant about distancing yourself from her. I've heard rumors that you're supposedly in love with someone—and have been for years— and that's the reason behind your lack of involvement with romance. So, essentially, I'm asking if you *are* in love with someone, and if that was the reason you wouldn't acquiesce to Rissa's charm."

The dukes collectively drew in their breath, their eyes plastered on Avian's face. Blade brandished a mischievous grin, but lines of concern and bewilderment crowded his face.

An unusual expression crossed Avian's visage—one Kiara had never seen darken his features. His face mimicked one of an animal captured in a snare. "Yes," he said slowly, tentatively. "Yes, I'll admit, I am in love. And while that fact surely steered my decisions regarding Rissa, I'm certain I would not have given myself away so cheaply regardless."

Avian's words sent a surprising blow to Kiara's chest. Her stomach tangled into a knotted mess; her body heated with sudden, unexplained rage. She felt guilty—because the citizens of Enevale believed Avian to be married, she was solely responsible for keeping him apart from the one he truly loved. A question automatically formed along her tongue, but a small part of her tried to bottle it down. After struggling with her conscience and plaintively losing, Kiara suddenly exclaimed, "Who is it?"

Avian's mouth worked itself into a reply, stopped before he had commanded his vocal chords to cooperate, and fell to shattering silence. He didn't possess enough strength to meet

Kiara's gaze. After being encompassed by an unbearably tense atmosphere for several unending minutes, Avian abruptly stood from his chair with a clatter. "I can't do this," he muttered. He departed the table, skirting through the dining hall and disappearing into the hallway before Kiara could manage to blink away the tears that clouded her eyes.

Chapter Eight

A Flightless Fall

"You should go after him," Aiden advised, gently resting his hand against Kiara's shoulder. He exchanged glances with Blade and Ace, who were surveying the situation in silence.

She shook her head mechanically, an unrestrained tear spilling down her pale cheek. "No, he doesn't want me to," she mumbled. "And I don't think I can face him like this."

Aiden sighed, rubbing his temples. "You two are the most complicated couple I have ever laid eyes upon," he muttered. "Just go after him. Trust me, it's what he wants, and I'm sure you will pleasantly surprised at what happens. *Go.*"

"Couple?" she repeated as though she had fallen into a mind-altering daze. "We're not a couple. He's in love with someone."

"And we all know who it is," Blade cut in, impatience coursing through his tone. "But it isn't our place to say. So, for the love of Veinya, move your ass!"

Kiara jolted to her feet at the sound of Blade's harsh persuasion. Although her eyes were sharp cerulean with sadness, a determined expression was painted across her features. "Alright, fine, I'll find Avian," she decided, her voice trembling slightly.

The dukes burst into a chorus of cheers as Kiara spun on her heel, retracing Avian's steps through the cafeteria. As she rounded the corner into the dimly lit hallway, she could still hear the dukes' applause ringing through her ears.

*****

Kiara's legs automatically led her toward Avian. Her body seemed detached from her thoughts, as though her physical form and mentality had become two separate, self-sustaining entities. Her legs carried her in the direction of the garden—she was unexplainably positive he had ventured there—while her mind attempted to script the upcoming conversation with Avian.

The sun had been eclipsed by a collection of gray storm clouds; a chilled, bitter wind swept the distinctive smell of rain across the land. Under typical circumstances, Kiara would have felt cold beneath the touch of the persistent wind, but as her mind was so preoccupied, she didn't notice the chills birthing across her unclothed arms.

Several yards away, at the training grounds, a group of soldiers was sparring under the watchful eye of Captain Rissa. At the sight of her, Kiara's heart accelerated with fiery rage. She was tempted to dart across the grounds and unleash her frustration on Rissa, but as the garden entrance poured into view, she was sharply reminded of *why* her emotions were so frazzled.

Kiara maneuvered her way through the labyrinth-like trails of the garden. The dirt-covered ground had been disturbed—light footprints dotted the floor, but Kiara didn't need to study the imprints to understand where Avian had headed.

Kyan's life-like memorial crowded Kiara's line of vision. Youthful, healthy flowers swayed in the breeze beside the statue, their bright colors a sharp contrast to the dark sky above.

"Why did you follow me?" Avian's voice dominated the silence.

Kiara froze, unable to find enough strength to turn around and face him. The wind howled, summoning a light drizzle of the sky's tears. "Who do you love, Avian?"

"Kiara…" his voice trailed off. He stood merely inches away from her, her small body stubbornly turned away from his. Her auburn hair was repeatedly tossed by the wind, her tightly clenched fists weather-beaten and red. He extended his arm, timidly, his fingers lightly falling upon the middle of her back. She tensed under his touch. "Do you really want to know?"

"You think I would be here if I didn't?" her voice was harsh; she had clearly been offended.

Avian sighed loudly as he gathered his wits. The light rainfall had dampened his clothes, and although the wetness had yet to seep through the fabric and soak his skin, his body felt unusually cold. "I didn't mean for it to happen like this," he whispered.

"It doesn't mater what you *intended*," she chided. Her body was trembling with every breath. "This is how it is."

Avian's arms wound around Kiara's waist as a clap of thunder crashed through the sky. Rain abruptly poured from the clouds in thick sheets, instantly drenching Avian and Kiara as they stood in muddled silence.

Kiara's heart thumped wildly as Avian's grip tightened around her torso. His head fell upon her shoulder, his lips grazing the base her cheek. She was unsure what emotions were swarming her mentality—she could feel the color of her irises shifting rapidly. "Avian, what—"

"It's you, Ara," he breathed into her ear, the sound almost inaudible above the deafening roar of heavy rainfall. "You're so dense. How didn't you figure it out? I've all but told you how I feel. I gave my consent to marry you, and you didn't suspect anything? I've told you I would readily sacrifice myself for you—and I made that decision before I had even entered adulthood. You've consumed my thoughts since the day we met, Ara. I fell in love with you during childhood, and I'm in love with you still. I was heart-broken when your father erased your memories and sent you out of Enevale. I remember the way you looked at me that day—your eyes held no remembrance of our past, of our memories. That was the last expression that crossed your face before I lost you and the first expression that crossed your face when I found you. I wanted nothing more than for you to remember, for you to feel for me as I felt for you. I had preserved my feelings. I wanted to give every aspect of my being to you, the girl who unintentionally stole my heart so many years ago. I love you, Kiara. I love *you*."

Kiara, embossed in baffled shock, was unable to untangle her vocal chords and fell to silence as she attempted to sort out her jumbled thoughts. She couldn't deny that she had suspected Avian's affections, but she had never assumed he had been *in love* with her. *What is Avian to me?* she wondered. He was her closest friend, her advisor, and admittedly the person she cared about most. Undeniably, she was drawn to him. Having never been in love—or, for that matter, having never pursued any sort of romantic relationship—Kiara couldn't describe why Avian's presence made her heart flutter, why his touch sent chills down her spine, why she had to fend off the urge to throw herself into his embrace. *Is this love?*

Turning slowly in Avian's arms, Kiara wound her hands around his neck as they stood face-to-face in the pouring rain. He observed her pallid face, her eyes downcast, her lashes speckled with drizzle, her hair plastered to her forehead. Beads of water dripped down her neck, streaking across her chest and disappearing beneath the fabric of her blouse. His hands explored the natural curves of her body, her wet clothes clinging to her frame. She felt so small beneath his wide palm.

Her gaze flashed upward as she glanced at him tentatively. Her irises were deep pink, displaying the love she unwittingly felt for him. He immediately noticed the distinctive hue of her eyes as they were unwaveringly fixed on him. A shy smile caressed her chattering lips. "Avian, I—"

His lips halted her declaration. He pulled her body tightly against his, her hands weaving through his hair as she deepened the kiss. Their lips moved in sync, fueled by fervent passion, as the rain crashed down around them. Kiara had never held someone so close or felt another's lips dance across her own. Her heart was pulsating madly, her veins rushing with heated blood. She was amazed she was able to refrain from pulling away out of embarrassment. Strangely, she felt entirely at ease, as though kissing Avian were the simplest action in the world.

A sensation of euphoria bloomed in Avian's chest, the feeling so overwhelming, he nearly tumbled to the ground. He fell against Kiara, his lips still working against hers, as she supported his dizzied body. He hadn't felt true happiness since prior to that fateful day, the day everything changed. To feel such ecstasy seemed surreal, and as the skin along Avian's chest burned with guilt, he was reminded that this unparalleled, fleeting bliss would be shattered alongside his heart.

Bending the rules, are we? a malicious voice infiltrated his thoughts, instantly snuffing out the flame of elation that had momentarily blazed through his heart. *What a naughty, naughty boy.*

Avian's eyes flashed open with fear as he unintentionally yanked his lips away from Kiara's. That painfully familiar, antagonizing voice kept playing through his mind as the pit of stomach was subjected to the sickly sensation of anxiety.

"Avian?" Kiara's voice was tinged with worry. Her hands were pinned to his shoulders, her eyes glued to his solemn expression. "What's wrong?"

"I—I—" he stammered, his eyes wide and wild. He gently directed Kiara's hands away from his body, moving as though he had fallen into a mind-numbing haze. "I need to be alone." Without bothering to give an explanation, Avian brushed past Kiara's stunned figure, sloshing through the puddle-strewn garden while his heart fluttered in his chest like a startled bird's wings.

*****

The suite door slammed against the wall with a sharp crack. Residual water sprayed from Avian's arms as he hurried into the room, pelting the wooded floors with beads of rain. He noisily closed the door, arching his back against the frame as he slid down the wall and collapsed into a miserable heap on the floor.

What a pathetic sight, that hauntingly jeering voice sounded through his head. *You'd better stop visualizing the future and start taking advantage of the situation while you still can. She won't be able to look at you with those pink eyes for much longer. Just don't get let your emotions cloud your judgment, or you'll find yourself in Veinya's manor faster than you can scream the girl's name.*

Avian's eyes clenched tightly shut as he tried to force that voice—the one he so disastrously hated—out of his mind. *Get out of my head,* he thought harshly. *I thought you agreed to stop infiltrating my thoughts.*

My dear boy, when have I ever kept my word?

Avian's hand tightly clutched the fabric of his shirt, directly above the wild pulsating of his heartbeat. *I can think of one occasion,* he replied sullenly.

Get a grip, Avian. She can't suspect that something is troubling you. If you're going to sulk, stick to doing it alone. We won't jeopardize everything just because of your spineless ability to rebuke such a trivial emotion as love.

Avian felt trapped, cornered. He thought of Kiara, of how he wanted nothing more from the world than to be able to be with her. But as his chest ached, and that vicious voice kept echoing through his psyche, he regretfully realized it was impossible for the world to start being kind to him so late in the game. In the back of his mind, a little voice was repeatedly reminding him that above all, he was just a bird in a cage that had mistakenly believed he had gained the ability to fly.

*****

Kiara stood in baffled silence. Torrents of rain pelted her chilled body, but she couldn't feel anything beyond the constricting barriers of her tumultuous thoughts. She had watched Avian retreat into the distance, had wanted to chase after him defiantly, but her feet had been sewn to the ground.

She couldn't comprehend Avian's unexplained mood swings. *He* had initiated the kiss, yet *he* had been the one to pull away. She had replayed the scene over and over in her mind, scrutinizing every minute detail in an attempt to discover some sort of misdemeanor that could have signaled his detachment, but she could not divulge an explanation.

Frustration bit deeply into the pit of Kiara's stomach. *Maybe he only wanted me so long as I was unattainable,* she thought dejectedly. *Or maybe when he kissed me, he didn't feel anything. Maybe I'm a terrible kisser. But if he loved me—like he claims—would he really let that push him away?*

Even with a whirlwind of uncertainty swarming Kiara's mentality, she was absolutely certain of one thing—she wanted answers. She had played by Avian's terms for too long, and as a sensation of determination surged through her body, she took a wide step forward in the direction of the castle. She planned to confront Avian, to demand a thorough explanation, and she would *not* accept any of his excuses.

*****

A sharp rattling noise filled the oppressive silence, instantly drawing open Avian's wet eyes. A sliver of light cut through the darkness, the brightness painfully blaring into his unadjusted irises.

"Avian?" Kiara's voice echoed through the unresponsive room as her hand fumbled against the wall in search of the illuminator.

His heartbeat accelerating wildly, Avian hurriedly unwound

himself from the curled position he had pulled himself into along the floor, climbing to his feet. He practically dove into the living room, landing on top of the couch as the lights in the dining room flickered to life. He clamped his eyes shut, evening his breathing as he pretended to be asleep.

"Avian?" her voice called a second time, accompanied by a clamor of footsteps. "Hello?" The floorboards creaked as she crossed through the archway and entered the living room. Light seeped through Avian's tightly closed eyelids. She issued a small, startled gasp as she noticed his body sprawled out on the couch. He felt her fingers lightly stoke his shoulders. "You're not actually asleep, are you?"

He reluctantly peeled open his eyes as a drenched, trembling Kiara poured into view. She had sat beside him on the couch, her fingers wrapped in the fabric of his damp shirt, her eyes blazing that exceptional shade of rose. "No," he admitted shyly.

"We need to talk," she said abruptly, hugging her arms around her torso, her gaze unwavering as she watched Avian pull himself into a proper sitting position.

He nodded tensely. "Yes, we certainly do." He paused, his eyes raking Kiara's panic-stricken face. It was strange to him—she was blatantly worried, but because love was the strongest and most overpowering emotion, her eyes refused to shift colors so long as her gaze was cast on him. "I'm sorry for running away from you—for the second time today. I'm sorry my emotions have been capricious. I was just scared—*terrified*, really—of complicating the situation between us. For years, I imagined finally confessing to you—and of course, I imagined you would return my feelings—but I was afraid that once my daydreams escaped my head, everything would change for the worse. I was afraid that nothing would be how I had hoped, how I had planned. I was fearful of hurting you—fearful you would hurt me. Being in love is a delicate situation, and I let my concerns get the better of me. I'm sorry my clumsy actions confused you. I want nothing more than to be with you." He paused, the edge of his pointer finger gently caressing the curve of her cheek. His expression suddenly darkened as his mouth worked into a sad, foreboding smile. "I hope you can find it in your heart to forgive me, Kiara."

Her palm clamped around his hand as a small smile brightened her features. She was relieved he had apologized before she had brazenly demanded answers. His apologetic explanation appeared sincere, and she could not dismiss the desolation flooding his eyes. "Of course I forgive you," she breathed. "I understand. I don't know how I managed to be so oblivious to my own feelings." She paused, her cheeks flushing with embarrassment. "I—I didn't get a chance to tell you earlier, but...I love you, Avian."

Avian's hand fell to her chin as he tilted her face toward his. Their lips met softly, swiftly—a small conclusion to their declarations. "I love you, too, Kiara," he whispered, brushing his fingers through her damp hair. Without being able to restrain himself, he allowed his lips to sweep across hers with much more enthusiasm.

Kiara's eyes fluttered shut as she wound her arms around Avian's neck. As their gentle kisses escalated, she lowered herself against the cushions of the couch, pulling his body against hers. As her heart thumped wildly beneath Avian's chest, he felt, paradoxically, as if she could not be farther out of his reach. Although he was closer to her than he had ever been—as close to her as he always dreamed—he felt worryingly estranged. And as his lips moved effortlessly against hers, one repeating thought kept surfacing in every corridor of his mind: *I hope, for my sake and hers, she will never stop being so forgiving.*

Chapter Nine

Vyntrx

Kiara's heart quivered with anticipation as she followed Avian onto the training fields. She was fully prepared to begin her combat exercise—she had been subjected to lectures in the castle for far too long and had finally passed the required tests in each subject—but after she discovered that Rissa would be leading the lessons on combat, apprehension had nestled deep into her chest.

The idea had been Blade's. The dukes had been hurriedly making preparations for Kiara's training when he had suddenly been struck with a "profound" realization. "Rissa should teach her," he had declared loudly. "She teaches soldiers every day—it's really second nature to her. None of us have ever taught anyone else how to fight. Plus, we may push Kiara too hard because we don't know her strengths and weaknesses, but Rissa is used to handling a variety of people. Say what you want about her, but Rissa's an amazing fighter—she's better than all of us. She even nearly beat Avian. I'm ninety-six percent sure it's a good idea."

"I'm one hundred percent sure you're an ass," Kiara had grumbled. "Why can't Sena do it?"

"You and Sena are good friends, so she'll take it easy on you," Blade had continued fluidly, as though he had already thought everything out. "Whoever teaches you has to be strict enough to make a difference."

Avian had agreed—rather reluctantly—that Blade had made a valid point, despite the circumstances. They had taken a vote over the situation, and after Kiara had been outvoted one to four, an edict was made: Rissa would be in charge of Kiara's physical training. They had decided that they would simply tell Rissa that Kiara wanted to strengthen her combat skills so she would be able to defend herself in the event of an invasion—and Rissa would *not* be made aware of the true situation. Avian had planned to oversee each session, which would occur for two hours, four times a week.

Two days later, Kiara awoke in a disheartened mood, somberly pulled on appropriate attire for sparring, and grudgingly followed Avian as they departed the suite.

"Try not to let your sour mood show," Avian advised as they descended down the knoll that led to the training fields. "She'll feel accomplished if she knows her presence perturbs you."

Kiara nodded comprehensively, admiring the comfortably warm weather. If she were going to be forced into spending *quality* time with Rissa, at least she didn't have to do it in frigid or blistering temperatures. "I just hope she doesn't stare at you the entire time and forget to train me."

Avian chuckled. "I'll try to stay out of her line of vision."

By the time they reached the training grounds, Kiara's legs were quivering with anxiety. It had been far too long since she had picked up a weapon or executed a proper kick. She disastrously understood that her defined abilities had dwindled, and if that fact weren't enough to concern her, the notion that Rissa would be scrutinizing her every movement was.

As Kiara stepped onto the wide, barren training grounds, Rissa's long-limbed figure fell into view. She was resting under the shade of a small shack—used for storing weapons and other necessary materials—while she waved over the pair as they approached.

"Welcome to the training fields, Kiara," she spoke pleasantly, that iconic fake smile plastered to her lips. "I hope you're ready to work."

"Oh, I am," she said reassuringly, forcing her scowl to shift upward into something that resembled a grin. "What're we working on first?"

"Avian informed me that you have somewhat of a background in combat, but that you haven't been honing your skills recently, so I thought we would just run through some drills. We'll refresh your memory on all of the kicks, punches, jabs, or blocks that you may use during hand-to-hand combat."

Kiara nodded in compliance. "Sounds easy enough."

"Well, I'll just leave you ladies to it, then," Avian announced, lightly patting Kiara's back before he strode across the field and rested his back against the exterior wall of the shack.

Rissa quickly commenced the training session, immediately launching into in-depth instructions. She was impressed by Kiara's innate kicking abilities, but critiqued the lack of effort driving her punches. Much to Kiara's surprise, Rissa was a patient and honest instructor—she didn't allow her undeniable dislike for Kiara cloud her judgment or sway her attitude.

After nearly an hour of vigorous training, Rissa allowed Kiara to take a break and catch her breath. Avian hurried over to Kiara's side, praised her for her efforts, and offered to recover a glass of water for her from the castle. She accepted his proposal, watching him swiftly maneuver his way across the castle grounds before she hesitantly turned to face Rissa.

"Do you know the history between me and Avian?" Rissa abruptly questioned, her emerald eyes wide and speculative.

Kiara hesitantly nodded. "He may have summarized it, yes."

"Oh, good." She released a heavy sigh. "It would be awkward to think that you didn't know he and I had slept together. It would feel like we were keeping some massive secret from you."

Kiara's lungs, suddenly deprived of air, began to shrivel into dust as her throat fought stubbornly for oxygen. "Wh-what?" she managed to gasp. "You and Avian never—" she broke off, attempting to steady her breathing. "He said you didn't—"

"He said we *didn't*?" she responded coldly, regarding Kiara with an astounded expression. "Why would he lie to his wife? We most certainly did, and not just once. It was a reoccurring event. Honestly, I don't know why he would hide that from you."

Because you're lying, Kiara immediately thought. But the pessimist that ruled her consciousness kept suggesting that Rissa was actually telling the truth. Unable to form an appropriate response, Kiara succumbed to silence as she attempted to bottle down the cynical thoughts that were assaulting her mind.

"You're a Nonae, aren't you?" Rissa interrogated, her tone callous as she changed the topic of conversation. "Your eyes kept changing colors. They're bright blue right now, but they were pink when you were looking at Avian."

Kiara's brow lowered, unwanted tears forming on the edge of her eyes. "No," she said cautiously, "I'm *half*-Nonae."

"Maybe Avian doesn't really have feelings for you, then," she suggested heartlessly. "Maybe he only married you because he thinks you'll be an advantage to him in the war. Perhaps he's training you to be a double agent, since you'd easily pass for a full-blooded Nonae. I mean, if he *really* loved you, he wouldn't have kept our little liaison a secret."

Unparalleled anger burned through Kiara's veins. She was so furious, her vision began to turn hazy. Her body temperature rose dangerously. A wall of fire suddenly burst from her hands, as though the flames had escaped through her pours. The fire momentarily burnt wildly in the air—startling Rissa so severely, she nearly toppled over—before fizzling out in the tense atmosphere. "I'm the *princess*," Kiara rashly confessed, "not some little tool that Avian plans to use! I am King Kyan's lost daughter, heir to the throne of Enevale, and Avian's rightful fiancé!" she broke off, breathing heavily, her heart thudding so loudly, she could hear it ringing in her ears. She caught a glimpse of Avian as he descended the hill flanking the castle. He was yelling something incomprehensible. "I don't care if you're telling the truth or if you're lying. All I know is that I need a break from all of this. I'm leaving."

Rissa's eyes were wide and unblinking as she watched Kiara spin on her heel and stomp toward the Wall. Avian's voice kept breaking the silence, slowly burrowing its way through Kiara's buzzing ears. She heard her name being called repeatedly, but she refused to turn around. She listened to Avian screaming at Rissa, asking her what she'd done and reprimanding her for her actions. His thudding footsteps sounded loudly as he chased after her.

After hurriedly trekking across the training field, the Wall suddenly blocked further movement as she came to an inevitable halt. She surveyed the cracked stone, finding persistent leaves from the forest trees poking through. Her mind pulsated as though someone had placed a hot iron to her brain. She couldn't find the strength to turn and face Avian, to run in the direction of the castle. She was mortified of what he may say—mortified he may prove Rissa's claims to be true. Time seemed to tick to a standstill as her eyes raked the Wall. If she could find a way through it, would she risk entering the Dark Forest just to escape an undesirable situation? *Of course not,* she automatically decided.

Coward, a chilling voice suddenly echoed through her head. *The Dark Forest is just as much your home as the Evalseman kingdoms. You claim there isn't anything wrong with being a Nonae, yet you've allowed those Evalseman to stain your view on your own kind. Come into the Dark Forest, Kiara, and you shall see.*

Feverishly, as though someone else were promoting her actions, Kiara fingers scraped the rough marble as she tried to force her way through the Wall. *How do I get through?* she asked the mysterious speaker.

There's a hole, the voice echoed. *You've found it once before, you can find it again.*

Kiara's fingers trailed a narrow but deep crevice in the Wall.

The sliver grew wider as she traced the crack until it vanished behind a row of hedges. Parting the foliage as Avian's footsteps neared, Kiara's eyes imbibed the sight of the forest floor visible through a gaping hole in the Wall.

With her mind whirling with curiosity spurred by the voice and emotions rampantly roused from the unfavorable encounter with Rissa, Kiara stole a glance over her shoulder before she spontaneously ducked into the underbrush.

The hole was wide enough for a grown man on his knees to easily fit through. Crawling through the fissure was practically effortless for Kiara, but the fabric of her pants was dirtied and torn in the process. After wading her way through a thicket of bushes, Kiara emerged into the Dark Forest.

She had felt immeasurably brave before she had entered the forest, but as she stood—defenseless—at the edge of enemy territory, her heart began to thump with anxiety. Suddenly overwhelmed with fear, Kiara turned to depart, but before she had taken the first step, her mind was abruptly engulfed with flashes of a broken memory. She heard the same voice that had lured her into the forest, but instead of sounding convincing, the tone was malicious and threatening. Distorted images clouded her eyes—a child-like version of herself was screaming as she sprinted through the forest, her irises shimmering maroon with terror. A dark figure emerged from the shadows of her memory, the harsh silver of a blade winking through the dimness. A pool of crimson blood stained a sapphire cloak, the edge of a knife poking through the tarnished fabric. Choruses of screams assaulted the silence, the roar utterly deafening.

Abruptly, as though the misplaced visions and sounds had been swallowed up by a vacuum of absolution, there was nothing but silence. After being tormented by sound, the lack of noise was jarring.

Kiara's eyes flashed open. She had fallen to her knees on the dirt-covered ground, but in her dazed stupor, she had apparently propelled herself further into the forest. Any way she twisted her head, Kiara could not distinguish a single difference in the landscape. She couldn't discover the path that led back to the kingdom, and the stone of the colossal Wall was no longer visible through the thick foliage. Feeling vulnerable and trapped, a wave of hysteria rose in the acidic chambers of her stomach, creeping up her throat and forming a constricting knot that blocked the oxygen's path to her lungs.

Lost, are we? the chilled voice tolled through Kiara's mind.

"Who are you?" Kiara spoke aloud. Although she felt entirely asinine speaking to an unresponsive forest, she had an increasing suspicion that the mysterious voice was present, watching elusively in the shadows.

You know me, the voice responded lithely. Kiara deduced that the speaker was a woman—she noted the gentle, lighter tones that appeared miserably out of place with the underlying guttural sound of the voice. *We've met before. I've known all about you, dear—before you were even born.*

"No," Kiara argued, her eyes carefully scrutinizing the forest as she searched for even the smallest sign of life. "No, I'm sure I would remember your voice."

Oh, most people do, the woman agreed. *You would, too, I'm certain, if it hadn't been for that significant day in your life when your father decided to suppress your memories.*

"How are you in my head?" Kiara demanded an answer. "Did *you* put those horrific images into my mind?"

A chorus of malignant, chilling laughter echoed through Kiara's thoughts. The sound was so daunting, it cut its way through her skin and turned her veins to ice. *Those weren't simply images,* the voice explained, *they were memories. That's right, dear, I have pieces of your lost memories tucked away into the folds of my mind. And as for how I've managed to play these forgotten scenes in your head—well, that's the beauty of Nonae magic.*

The woman's words played on repeat in Kiara's head. The speaker claimed to possess memories from Kiara's curtained past and was evidently a Nonae. Her voice sounded threatening and malicious. There was only one person—to Kiara's knowledge—that fit that description.

Vyntrx.

"You're my aunt, aren't you?" Kiara's voice quivered as she backed herself against a tree in an attempt to steady her wavering legs before she could manage to tumble to the ground. Her heart rate accelerated dangerously, each startled beat producing an overflowing stream of anxiety. "Sh-show yourself," she demanded, the tone of her voice portraying far more courage than the small supply she had mustered.

An absolute silence fell over the forest. It remained as it had been prior to the attack on Kiara's mentality: dark, frightening, and lacking any sign of life. Kiara called out to the voice for several seconds, but after the noiseless atmosphere refused to respond, she began to convince herself that she had simply crafted the voice out of a conscience burrowed deep within the patchwork of her psyche, sent to the forefront of her mind in order to reprimand her for rash actions.

But as Kiara lifted a weary foot forward, the shadows to her left began to shift and bend until the figure of a woman emerged from the empty space. Her cold, black eyes were piercing and unnatural, her gaze fixed on Kiara. The skin framing her dark irises was so pale, it was nearly translucent. Although barely any sign of age stained her features, her once-beautiful face had been contorted by the cruel stare in the depths of her hollow eyes and the hateful snarl that permanently lined her blood red lips. Her prominent chin and oval-shaped face bore resemblance to Kiara's, but the majority of her features were entirely foreign. She was clothed entirely in black, swathed in a dark dress that fell against the ground in a cloud of fabric. She twirled a strand of her ink-black, pin-straight hair around an outstretched finger, her nails painted a deep scarlet. "Hello, niece," she spat.

"Vyntrx!" The name escaped Kiara's lips forcefully, as

though the unbridled terror pulsating through her chest had scripted her actions. Her hand automatically flew to her side, where she normally kept her knife, as she disastrously recalled that the weapon had been abandoned in the suite.

"Oh, fear is simply radiating from you!" Vyntrx spoke approvingly, clasping her hands together. She slunk forward, laughing with delight each time Kiara flinched. "You don't have to be so scared, dear," she cooed mockingly. "I simply seek a parley."

Kiara's eyes narrowed skeptically. "A truce?" she whispered. "You want to discuss the war?"

Vyntrx emitted a low, humming noise from the base of her throat. "Not particularly. I simply wanted to propose an offer."

"An offer?" Kiara questioned, her eyes transitioning from maroon to hazel as her curiosity was piqued. "What *kind* of offer?"

"A simple one, really," she nearly sang, planting one foot in front the other as she sauntered in a circle around Kiara's trembling body and the small tree she was cowering against. "I honestly don't understand why you're so loyal to those unscrupulous Evalseman. They all treat you the same, riddled with disdain and contempt—simply because of your inconsistent Nonae eyes. They consider it a symbol of the impiety of your parents, of the impurity coursing through your blood. Are you starting to believe their foul words? They would lead you astray from your heritage. Before I articulate my proposal, allow me to ask you a question." She paused for dramatic effect, halting her movement so she stood at Kiara's side. Her black eyes were wide and jovial, but the root of the happiness brightening her features was undeniably corrupt. "Do you consider yourself your mother's daughter or your father's child?"

Kiara's mortified expression shifted into one of shocked confusion. "How should I know? Until several months ago, I didn't consider myself the legitimate offspring of anyone. I don't understand the situation between my parents or my birth enough to speculate about the subject. If what you're *really* asking is if I consider myself more an Evalseman or a Nonae, then again, I can't give you a straightforward answer. I've always been defensive about my Nonae roots, but I have been raised around Evalseman, so I am unquestionably more familiar with their culture. And if you were sneakily trying to discern my opinion about this ridiculous blood feud, then I can assure you, I believe it's pointless."

Vyntrx clicked her tongue. "Augmented your courage, did you? Finally dismiss the quavering tone of your voice?" She chortled loudly as her hand slammed against the tree bark, inches from Kiara's face. "Well, dear, I'd advise you to think carefully about where your loyalties lie. By all means, be crowned queen of the kingdom. I'm not here to convince you to give up your crown—no, we wouldn't want to upset your dead father, would we? What I'm asking runs deeper than that. Once you're on the throne, you should revisit the topic of your Nonae ancestry. Suggest integrating Nonae citizens into the land of Enevale, and watch the upheaval ensue. Watch your subjects call you a traitor. They will patronize you, condemn you— perhaps they will even attempt to assassinate you. You do not understand how coarse, violent, and irreversible this hatred the races share truly is. Some day, Kiara, it will rear its ugly face, and the Evalseman will turn against you. Just understand that when that soiled crown decorates your head, *you* are the one who has declared war upon the Nonae—*you* are the one turning against half of your ancestors."

"I don't understand what you're asking of me," Kiara admitted, returning her aunt's heated gaze with a steady expression. "How could I please both sides of my heritage? There has been an ongoing war between the Evalseman and the Nonae since before you were born, since before your grandparents were even conceived. Are the Nonae, in your eyes, less guilty of prejudice and malice than the Evalseman?

My mother left her home in the Dark Forest to join my father in the kingdom. She *chose* to side with the Evalseman. Would following in her footsteps not be the safest route?"

Vyntrx's unnaturally black eyes bulged, flecks of crimson anger pulsating through her blackened irises. "Don't bring your mother into this," she hissed. "What I'm asking is that you understand the gravity of the situation you're in. If you feel like you can't bear the burden, then give it to me. I'd gladly take the throne from you—then you won't have to worry about anything. You could run away, go back to your little village. You'd never have to concern yourself about Enevale again."

Kiara opened her mouth to accuse her aunt of attempting to steal the throne in an attempt to reign over the Evalseman, but before she could articulate her thoughts, Avian's voice reverberated through the forest, shrieking Kiara's name against the wind.

"That *idiot*," Vyntrx snarled, pacing around the trees as her eyes unblinkingly scoured the distance. "Come to interrupt us, has he?"

"He came to protect me from you," Kiara said thickly, her hand flying to the pendant on her necklace as though the action diluted her apprehension. "You murderous fiend. You weren't trying to negotiate with me at all, you were simply attempting to lower my guard. I know you want to win this war, to destroy my kingdom and me. What made you think I would trust you with the tainted reputation you bear?"

Vyntrx turned on Kiara, her expression wildly irate. "How dare you speak to me with such insolence!" She leaned down to her niece's height, her crimson-flecked eyes level with Kiara's. "Who do you think you are?"

"I am Kiara Fable—as well as Elbaf Araik—" she hotly shouted her name in the ancient Evalseman tongue, "—queen of the kingdom Enevale!" she spoke boldly, abrasively, her irises blazing red-orange with determination. Her necklace suddenly felt heavy and hot to the touch, but she ignored it, continuing, "I am equal to you on all levels, aunt. We both hold positions of power, and we stem from the same bloodline. Don't make the mistake of belittling me again. If I had a knife, I'd run it through your heart!"

Vyntrx's eyes suddenly widened, fixed on Kiara's hand as she clutched her necklace. The pendant felt different in her palm—heavier, somehow, and oblong—yet the burning sensation had subsided. Glancing at her hand, she discovered she was brandishing a silver knife in place of the necklace. The only sign of the missing article was a small crown motif stamped onto the hilt of the weapon.

"That necklace—" Vyntrx started, reaching her hand forward as she attempted to pluck the recently shifted weapon from her niece's hands. Kiara instinctively flinched backward, slamming into the tree trunk, as a panic-stricken Avian suddenly appeared.

Without pausing to examine the situation, Avian immediately launched into action. Snatching Kiara into his arms, he quickly distanced her and himself from Vyntrx, placing several yards in-between them in a matter of seconds. Glaring at each other across the empty barrier, Avian and Vyntrx's enraged expressions were nearly identical.

Kiara squirmed in Avian's constricting arms, careful to keep the edge of her blade pointed away from his body. "Avian, I—" she started, but his voice instantly silenced her words.

"Vyntrx, you cunning fiend," he severely admonished. Although his mismatched eyes did not shift to reflect his emotion, Kiara could clearly see the distress welling beneath his irises. "Did you really think you could kill the princess so easily?"

Vyntrx's scowling face twisted into a villainous grin. "*Kill* her? My dear boy, if I had wanted to murder her, she'd be dead."

"She was trying to steal the throne," Kiara whispered. Punctured with guilt for her rambunctious actions and shaken from the encounter with her deadly aunt, she was unable to meet Avian's gaze. "She was persuasive. I'm nearly certain she lured me into the forest so she could test my strength."

Avian nodded comprehensively, his fixed glare never departing Vyntrx's face. "I suggest you scurry back to Vitaciel, Vyntrx, before you find your life terminated." He loosened his grip on Kiara's tremulous body, extending his palm forward as he beckoned for her to deposit the weapon in his reach. She passed the hilt onto him, but the second it touched his skin, the knife shifted back into her crown necklace. Startled, Avian nearly dropped the piece of jewelry, but Kiara hurriedly recovered the item before it made contact with the ground.

Vyntrx, chortling madly, withdrew a pointed dagger from the folds of her dress. "My weapon isn't so volatile, niece," she said sardonically. Catching Kiara entirely off guard, Vyntrx darted forward, flourishing the tip of her blade.

As Kiara fumbled with her makeshift weapon, Avian impulsively hurled his body on top of hers, absorbing the blow that had been destined for her heart.

Kiara's chest was sprayed red with Avian's blood. The end of Vyntrx's dagger poked out unnaturally from the fabric of his shirt, the silver stained crimson. His face was scrunched up in a display of pain, his mouth wrenched open, blood frothing from his lips. His grip around Kiara's shoulders weakened, as though vitality had instantly been drained from his body. He slid forward, falling into her stunned arms, as Vyntrx heaved the weapon out of his chest.

For a renowned vicious killer, Vyntrx appeared unusually disturbed. Bits of shocked yellow broke through her black irises. Her mouth hung open, aghast, as she watched Avian struggle to breathe.

Kiara's legs buckled. She and Avian toppled to the ground, landing against a stretch of dirt that had been speckled with crimson. Hysteria bubbled in Kiara's chest, sending her heart on a rampage as her entire body was racked with uncontrollable shivers. "A-Avian," she cooed, her voice breaking. She carefully laid him on his back, unable to examine the gaping wound in his torso. Still anxiously clutching the necklace with one hand, Kiara imagined the knife's arrival and was relieved when she felt the hilt slid into place against her palm.

After bending down to kiss Avian's forehead, Kiara wiped unrestrained tears off her cheeks as she stood to face her aunt, resolutely wielding the knife. Avian's eyes, flittering as he attempted to maintain consciousness, watched in horror as Kiara indirectly challenged her aunt.

Kiara lashed her knife forward—her mind was so encompassed by anguish, she couldn't manage to cultivate enough concentration to summon magic. Vyntrx, anticipating her move, swiped her dagger through air, clanging her blade against Kiara's.

"You bitch," Kiara growled through clenched teeth, pushing the edge of her weapon against her aunt's. Kiara's Evalseman strength allowed her to easily overpower her opponent, knocking Vyntrx's dagger from her reach as it cascaded to the ground. A look of unadulterated bewilderment crossed Vyntrx's face as Kiara flicked the blade of her knife under her chin. "You tried to kill Avian!"

Despite the situation she had been thrust into, a humored smirk contoured Vyntrx's lips. "Oh, I didn't *try*. I'll have succeeded soon enough. That blade's been dipped in poison. He'll be dead by morning." Although she sounded menacing, there was a strange emotion underlying her tone that Kiara couldn't place.

At Vyntrx's words, Avian's body tensed. Pushing himself against the base of a tree, he rested his back against the bark, surveying the situation as he coughed up a wad of blood. "Po-poison?" he spluttered.

"Tell me how to save him, or I'll slit your throat," Kiara demanded, her eyes wildly flashing between crimson infuriation and sapphire sorrow.

"There is no cure," Vyntrx said slowly, the shadow of a snicker curling her mouth. "And if you plan to kill me, niece, you'll have to do better than a measly knife."

Kiara thrust her blade forward, aiming for the soft tissue of Vyntrx's throat, but her weapon simply made contact with a cloud of black dust. Crying out in frustration, Kiara scanned the surroundings for her elusive aunt.

While Kiara's attention was diverted, Vyntrx reappeared at Avian's side. She carefully lowered her lips to his ear, whispering, "Don't worry, Veinya will bring you back to life, but the Fable girl will have to plead with the goddess herself, otherwise she'll be suspicious, so plant the idea in her head. I want to have a little fun with the princess."

Avian grimaced—half out of pain from his wound, and half out of contempt for the situation. "Give Kain back his life, otherwise I'll let Veinya destroy my soul."

Vyntrx frowned, but reluctantly agreed. "Be prepared to die, Avian." Warily eyeing Kiara as she began to give up her search, Vyntrx allowed her body to fade into the shadows, leaving her niece alone in the Dark Forest as Avian's life slowly began to deteriorate.

Chapter Ten

Oblivion

Kiara walked slowly through the forest, Avian's limp arm wrapped around her neck. Her vision was blurred from the uncontrollable waterfall of tears escaping her eyes, and without Avian's guidance and navigation, she would have inevitably been lost among the labyrinth trails.

"I—I don't understand," she stammered weakly. "Why didn't Vyntrx just finish me off when she had the chance? Why would she leave?"

"Be—because—" Avian spluttered, his feet dragging through the dirt as Kiara hauled him toward the Wall. He had lost almost all control over his body to the whim of the poison, but his eyesight had yet to be affected. "She knew—she was at a disadvantage. You were—incensed—and wanted—revenge. With that kind of—motive, she—she knew—she would lose."

Kiara swallowed down the lump of apprehension forming in her throat. She could see the Wall in the distance, could see the illumination of Enevale's lights seeping through the foliage. "I won't need to avenge you. You're not going to die."

A foreboding smile slid across Avian's pallid face. "I'm not so sure about that, Ara."

Fresh, hot tears welled in Kiara's eyes at his premonition. She quickened her pace, tightening her grip around his shoulders. "I-I'm so sorry. If I hadn't been so reckless, you—" she broke off, her vocal chords sharply tightening.

He shook his head, his hair brushing against Kiara's shoulder and sending shivers across her back. "No, it isn't—your fault," he managed to speak in-between contractions of pain. "I-I know Rissa—had been—harsh, and—Vyntrx was using—magic to lure you—into the forest."

"It doesn't matter," Kiara's voice escaped her lips in a choked gasp. "It's all my fault."

"N-no," Avian argued, feeling his lungs constrict as he attempted to steady his breathing. "D-don't think that. I would never—blame you. Kiara, I-I love you."

Kiara's unsteady breathing caught in her throat. "Pl-please, don't say that like it's the last time you'll be able to," she pleaded. "We'll get you to the medic and she'll help. She will. Please, just hang on."

He nodded, his eyelids fluttering. His head fell against Kiara's shoulder as her grip around his waist loosened. She suddenly lifted him with the power of her Evalseman strength, tucking one of her arms under his leg and the other around his elbow as she pulled his torso against her back.

She approached the Wall, her eyes swimming with rampant tears. Sickening apprehension slowly spread through her veins as though her body had been injected with a paralytic poison. She could feel Avian's weakened heartbeat against her back, each *thud* issuing a fresh bout of distress in her mentality. And although his failing body was warm against hers, she disastrously felt as though his spirit had already fled his limbs.

*****

Inside Veinya's manor, the departed souls of the dead stirred restlessly. The goddess paced back and forth, the skirts of her shadowy dress billowing out behind her. Through the darkness, her piercing, light blue eyes shone with anticipation. The manor was entirely dark, the only source of light faintly radiating from the glossy mirror of souls. The spirit of a young man sat beside the artifact, his purple eyes reflecting the mirror's tainted light. He had been dead for far too many years and his vague memories of life had long been pervaded by the omnipresence of death.

"She's nearly here," Veinya's voice sounded as an excited, psychotic whisper. She had been following Vyntrx's movements for nearly an hour, after she had suddenly declared that the empress had worked herself into a tricky situation.

"You mean that monster?" the boy snapped. For most of the deceased, speaking irritably to the death goddess automatically landed them a one-way trip to getting their souls destroyed—but that was never the case for him. He had been introduced to Veinya as a young child and been loyally serving her since. If she hadn't relied on his assistance, his soul would have been reincarnated a decade ago. Veinya had taken pity on his unfortunate life and had granted him the chance to serve in her court until his soul inevitably stopped aging once it reached its maximum age.

"You're so quick to judge," Veinya admonished, tossing her hands into the air dramatically. "I'm curious about this improvised circumstance she's fallen into. What will she do? I can feel her precious bird's soul slipping away."

The boy sent the goddess a side-ways glance. "You're on your bad side, aren't you?"

"It's so hard to stay on my good side when there's no one around to favor. I found myself much more benevolent when Kyan visited frequently," she replied, waving her hand dismissively.

"I can call him over. Your bad side pisses me off."

Veinya glared at the boy with her bright, piercing stare. "It's your duty as my servant to deal with my mood swings."

The boy rolled his eyes. "That's not fair. You don't handle mine."

Veinya's oncoming curt reply was silenced as Vyntrx abruptly appeared inside the manor, a look of sheer indignation crossing her features. "That idiot boy!" she screeched. "Jumped in front of an innocent blade! He was rash! Now he's going to die—and he made *demands* about the situation, after he had been the one careless enough to toss himself into it."

"Oh, it's the bloodthirsty bitch," the boy spoke roughly, refusing to allow his gaze to meet the Nonae empress's eyes.

Vyntrx glowered as she imbibed the sight of the young man's soul sitting beside the glowing mirror. His black hair fell into his averted eyes; his mouth twisted into a scowl. "How are you, you little dead nuisance?" she responded coldly.

"Enough!" Veinya firmly decreed. "While I agree that his actions *were* bold and daft—and verging on insubordination, actually—there is a simple fix to this solution. I will restore his soul, like you *knew* I would. Besides, I am quite fond of the notion of meeting Kyan's daughter. You truly believe she will attempt to salvage his life?"

"Yes, I'm certain, but that isn't necessarily what's concerning me," Vyntrx said slowly.

Veinya raised her eyebrows skeptically. "Go on," she urged.

"Well," the empress started hesitantly, "Avian demanded that his brother's life be restored, otherwise he would opt to having his soul obliterated."

Veinya's immortal eyes swelled with infuriation. She impulsively raised her hand, as if to strike her comrade, but after a movement of conflicted stillness, she swiftly lowered her arm. "He is my most trusted servant. I have not prepared myself to see his departure."

"If you don't return the boy's life, Avian will let his soul perish," Vyntrx explained delicately.

"Command him to give up the idea. He has the mark—he cannot disobey you."

Vyntrx released an frustrated sigh, placing a hand upon her narrow hips. "He would purposely defy me, and then his soul would be destroyed. He has us at a standstill—we can't get around this edict of his."

Veinya, enveloped in silence, understood that she had been defeated. Vyntrx was not lying—Avian's curse possessed the same repercussions as the gift she had bestowed on the empress. "When would the boy's soul depart my manor?" she whispered tersely.

"The day Kiara appears to retrieve Avian's soul," Vyntrx explained, attempting to mask the elated grin that had spilled across her lips. "Three days, at most."

"Wait," the spirit suddenly interjected, climbing to his feet as he abandoned his position beside the mirror. "What's going on?"

"Well, you see, Kain," Veinya whispered tenderly, slowly swinging around on her the balls of her feet as she faced her servant. "Your brother is dying."

Kain's lips split open into the first smile he had formed since prior to his premature death. "What the hell took him so long?"

*****

The white sterile walls of the infirmary did not bring comfort to Kiara's panic-stricken thoughts. Narrow, tightly dressed beds flocked the main room, lined in orderly procession. Several debilitated patients occupied the mattresses, watching wearily as nurses bustled around the room distributing cures.

A startled nurse discovered Kiara while she stood supporting Avian's limp body in the doorway of the infirmary. Hurrying to his side, she whisked the pair into the head medic's office without pressing for details about Avian's physical state. A wide oak desk sat in the corner, nestled tightly between white bookcases full of jars stuffed with herbs and medications. The head medic—a heavy-set woman with unruly hair and a pleasant face—gasped when her eyes fell upon Avian. She immediately stood from her desk, rushing to aid them.

"What happened?" she exclaimed, disentangling Avian from Kiara's back and carefully laying him down on a padded bench in the corner of the room.

"St-stabbed by a poisonous dagger," Kiara explained tersely, dabbing her wet eyes with the edge of her sleeve. She sat down beside Avian on the bench, gently lifting his head and resting it against her lap. Her fingers absentmindedly brushed through his tresses as the medic examined his wound.

"There is no trace of the poison on his flesh," she noted, scrunching up her freckled nose. "It must have been injected directly into the blood stream, making it incredibly difficult to trace. This will sound nosy, but I am inclined to inquire in order to determine what type of poison the perpetrator likely used. Who stabbed him? Where were you when this defilement occurred?"

Kiara sighed shakily. "W-we were in the Dark Forest. Vyntrx discovered our location and attacked."

The nurse's eyebrows shot upward, a shocked gasp escaping her lips. "The Dark Forest?" She shook her head, folding her arms across her chest as she walked across her office. Her eyes raked a large tapestry plastered to the wall behind her desk that displayed an extensive list of herbs. "I'm unfamiliar with any sort of concoction from the Dark Forest. The Nonae's plants are foreign, and Evalseman have little knowledge about their existence, let alone their capabilities." She turned around, facing her patient as her expression darkened. "I'm sorry, I'm not sure I can offer much help."

Kiara's arm wound around Avian's shoulders protectively, her heart screeching to an abrupt halt before it dove into her lungs. Her stomach churned. "Surely as a medic you have healing abilities?"

The medic nodded stiffly. "Of course. It's my Specialty. But when I address cases such as this, I need to be familiar with the poison before I can create an antidote for it. Having no sample of the poison, I am unfamiliar with what it has been made from, the damage it causes, or even the amount of time it takes to erode the body. Regretfully, without this information, my healing abilities will have little effect."

Tears surged in Kiara's eyes as frustration stripped away her mental stability. "You have to do something or he'll *die!*" she screamed hoarsely.

"Calm down, miss," the medic advised. "I'll try to heal him with every antidote I've ever crafted, but I cannot promise favorable results." She placed her hand over Avian's wounds, concentration enveloping her features. After several drawn-out, endless minutes, Avian's body began to shake uncontrollably, his shoulders nearly ripped away from Kiara's reach by jolting spasms. She instantly tightened her grasp, yelling at the medic to cease the trials. The nurse yanked her hand from Avian's stomach, immediately stopping his seizure. His breathing had turned ragged, his body entirely doused in sweat.

"D-do you feel any different?" Kiara whispered, lowering her lips to his frigid cheek.

Avian shook his head in denial, his damp hair plastered to his forehead. He raised his hand as if to touch Kiara's face—but he couldn't maintain enough strength. His arm swung downward, nearly crashing against the edge of the bench. Kiara expertly caught his hand, steadying his movement as she interlaced his fingers with hers.

The nurse frowned, staring at her patient with sincere desolation. "The poison is still in his system," she admitted delicately.

"What can we do?" Kiara's voice was raspy and barely audible.

The medic's face turned solemn, her light eyes drained of all hope. "There's nothing else we *can* do. Unless we're saved by a miracle, I'm afraid your husband will die."

Kiara's hand turned cold inside Avian's grasp. With every rapid pound of her pulsating heartbeat, her vision blurred into incompressible shadows. "No..." she whispered hoarsely. She had been wrestling with the cruel reality of Avian's slowly fading existence, but his death had never been irreversibly imminent. The direct and absolute news of his unstoppable fate knocked her sanity into oblivion. "*NO!*"

"I'm so sorry," the medic spoke softly. "Please allow me to at least heal his bleeding wound. I'll arrange a private room for him to rest."

Kiara was utterly despondent as she stared unblinkingly at the wall. The nurse hurriedly dressed Avian's laceration, stealing concerned glances in Kiara's direction. He flinched slightly at the sudden sensation, his eyes unwaveringly placed on Kiara's distraught expression. He managed to splutter her name, drawing her out of her reverie. She met his gaze, his eyes as damp as her own. They did not speak, but the emotion welling behind their shared stare articulated their despairing thoughts.

The nurse asked for Kiara's assistance, but she couldn't find enough strength to respond. She stood up silently, carefully detaching herself from Avian. Wrapping her arms around his shoulders as the nurse fastened her grip around his legs, they simultaneously carried his feeble body into an abandoned, all-white room rarely used for its initial purpose of housing severely ill patients.

Carefully laying Avian down on the narrow bed, Kiara assumed her position at his side, sliding onto the edge of the mattress. The nurse departed the room, assuring Kiara that if she or Avian required attention, she or anyone on staff would be willing to offer their aid. Watching the door swing shut behind the medic as she vanished into the hallway, Kiara curled her body around Avian's, listening to the unsteady rise and fall of his slowed breathing.

"I-I'm so sorry, Avian," she bawled into the fabric of his shirt. "It's a-all my fault. I-I'm so *stupid*. I'm sorry. Pl-please don't l-leave me, I-I need you here. I love you, Avian. I love y-you..." her voice succumbed to uncontainable sobs as her hands tightly clutched his blouse.

His weak hand found her face, shakily wiping at the line of tears spilling across her cheek. "D-don't cry, Ara," he whispered. "I-I love you. Always remember th-that. E-even if I find myself in Veinya's m-manor."

Her body shuddered with hysterical cries. She wrapped her arms around his neck, pulling his failing body as close to hers as she could manage, as though she were attempting to pass even a sliver of her vitality to him.

Avian slowly pressed his face against hers, breathing in her familiar scent. Her body was trembling beneath his touch, her quivering breath spilling across his paling face. Cupping the crown of her head with his frail hand, he gingerly tugged her lips against his. Although vivacity had fled his bones, he managed to summon enough energy to work his mouth around hers. She responded with heated determination, interlacing her fingers through his hair as she propelled the kiss into the deepest realms of intimacy.

He felt so healthy against her ignorant lips—so warm, so *alive*. The thought that in a mere handful of hours—maybe minutes—his body would be irrevocably cold and still, unresponsive to her pleading touch, filled her mind with unparalleled dread.

As the speed of Kiara's persistent lips quickened, the door to Avian's sick room was tossed open with a resolute crash. Automatically disconnecting her body from Avian's, Kiara sprung to her feet as her eyes fell upon the dukes hovering in the doorway. Far too embedded in anguish to feel embarrassment, Kiara simply stared at her friends with wet, glistening eyes.

Without pausing to examine the situation, Ace hurried into the room, pulling Kiara into a comforting embrace. His eyes glanced in Avian's direction, but the sight was so unbearable, he quickly buried his face in Kiara's tangled hair.

Blade stonily stared at the room, unable to step forward. His body appeared still but his hands were anxiously quavering.

"So it isn't just a rumor," Aiden whispered dejectedly, crossing the room. He sat down on the edge of the bed beside his friend, his eyes clouding with tears. "What happened?"

Kiara gently pulled herself out of Ace's arms, sitting down beside Aiden on the bed. "I-I was stupid. We had been training with Rissa, and once Avian left to get water, she—she turned on me. Her words were harsh. I let my emotions take over. I ran to the Wall, and Vyntrx's voice beckoned me closer—even told me how to get into the forest. Once inside, she assaulted my mind. Avian had followed me. Sh-she tried to stab me, b-but he..." she trailed off, sobbing into her upturned palms.

Aiden's hand lightly stroked her shoulders, his saddened eyes glued to his incapacitated friend. "They can't heal you?" he wondered softly.

Avian slowly shook his head. "N-no, the blade was dipped in p-poison. The m-medic's antidotes d-didn't work."

Kiara slowly lifted her head from her hands, loose strands of her hair falling into her eyes and sticking to her wet cheeks. An idea slowly worked its way through her hazy mind, brightening her eyes and scripting her lips as she quickly whispered, "Maybe the nurse needs to combine every cure she knows into one powerful remedy."

"W-we could try it," Avian suggested. It was evident he was doubtful of salvation.

Kiara readily stood from the bed, wiping at her damp eyes. "I'll talk to the nurse," she declared, departing the room. She hurriedly paced down the narrow hallway that led to the main infirmary. Skirting the edge of the room, she turned into the head medic's office.

Rissa stood facing the doorway, speaking in low voices with the nurse. Her arms were folded across her chest, her eyes dark and etched with tears. As Kiara burst into the room, Rissa's sharp gaze immediately raked her figure.

The nurse, realizing Rissa's attention had been diverted, turned toward the door. "Is he—"

Kiara quickly shook her head in negation. "N-no, he's alright," she stammered gruffly. "I have a suggestion. Would it be possible for you to combine all of the cures into one? Maybe it would have enough power to eradicate the foreign poison."

The nurse pursed her lips. "I can try, but it will be very difficult. I'll need unbroken focus."

Kiara nodded comprehensively. "I'll clear the boys from his room." Refusing to pay Rissa even the slightest fragment of attention, she half-walked, half-ran down the corridor toward Avian's sick room.

She explained the situation to the dukes as she ushered them into the hallway. She instructed them to wait with her in the nurse's office, but as they sluggishly crept down the hallway, she retreated into Avian's room once more.

"I love you," she murmured, placing her hand inside his upturned palm. She bent down, brushing her mouth across his lips.

"D-don't say that like it's the l-last time you'll be able to," he implored, cupping her cheek in his trembling hand.

Kiara's despairing sobs escalated as she clasped his hand in-between her palm and her face. "I-I'm so sorry," she stuttered, her breathing erratic.

"Shh," he cooed. A smile spread across his face, seemingly misplaced amid his sallow cheeks and hallow eyes. "D-don't talk like that. I-I love y-you."

The nurse appeared in the doorway, clearing her throat. Startled, Kiara stood from the bed, still clutching Avian's hand. She kissed his knuckles, her eyes grazing his face one last time before she released her grasp on his fingers.

She brushed past the nurse, retreating into the hall and sealing off Avian's room as she swung the door shut. Her hand instinctively flew to her necklace, the action slightly soothing her anxiety. The events of the Dark Forest felt like years ago, and her mind hadn't been able to think past Avian's precarious situation—but as her hand tightly clamped her crown pendant, she finally allowed her thoughts to replay the scenes from her recent memory.

Her necklace had shifted—unexplainably—into a weapon at her command. She hadn't been able to pinpoint the event that had issued the change, but as she reflected upon the situation, she understood that her parents must have crafted the necklace with magical attributes meant to shield her from harm. She recalled the letter her father had given Avian. *I am leaving with my daughter the utmost protection from my deadliest enemy,* Kyan's words had read. *Her voice must reverse the name she had been given, unlock the metal key, and melt away the royal silver.* Given the details from his message, she imagined he had been referring to her necklace. Although she was still skeptical of the necklace's abilities and was unsure what had spurred the sudden change in its qualities, she was grateful for her newly acquired, easily concealable weapon.

Kiara entered the head nurse's office, attempting to shut out the qualms over Avian's condition with the closing of the door behind her. The dukes' well-defined bodies were smashed together upon the padded bench, their expressions morbidly crestfallen.

Rissa, standing in the corner, glowered menacingly at Kiara as she stepped into the room. "Oh, look, it's Avian's murderer," she harshly reproached.

The dukes' heads snapped upward at Rissa's callous comment. Kiara's eyes shifted scarlet with rage. Without pausing to calculate her actions, she practically darted across the room, her gaze locked on Rissa's stunned expression. She clenched her fingers tightly against her palm, swinging her fist directly against Rissa's cheek with a deafening *crack*.

Rissa was immediately knocked to the ground, a line of blood spewing from her nose and splotching the unblemished wooden floor. Kiara had slightly restrained her strength, to avoid severely injuring Rissa, and although her blow had been damaging, she had managed to not shatter her enemy's consciousness. Rissa stared up at her with a look of incredulity, her palm pressed to her gushing nostril. "Wh-what the hell was that?" she spluttered around a mouthful of blood.

The dukes stood up from the bench in one swift movement. Blade shouted Kiara's name, rushing to her side as if he meant to restrain her. His palm clamped around her shoulder, attempting to push her backwards, away from Rissa. Using her Evalseman strength to resist Blade's tugging, she steadied her ground and refused to buckle. Frustrated, Blade gave up, sighing. "What did Rissa say to you at the training fields?"

Kiara refused to peel her attention away from Rissa's bleeding face. "She had enough audacity to claim that Avian didn't actually love me. She said that she and Avian had slept together and that he was hiding that fact from me. She was unforgivably cruel."

"Dammit, Rissa, why would you lie to her?" Blade chided. "If you had been able to contain your raging jealousy, this entire situation could have been avoided. I hope that this unfortunate predicament teaches you humility and maturity, because you sorely require both."

Rissa huffed indignantly. "I always thought our *princess* would be confident enough in herself and her relationship to not be affected by anything I could say. And I certainly imagined her having more self-control."

"What did she just say?" Aiden gasped. "How does she know your identity?"

Kiara sighed, rubbing her temples. "I may have accidentally told her in a fit of rage."

Aiden opened his mouth to verbalize the displeasure seeping across his face, but his words were silenced as the office door slammed open. The medic appeared in the doorway, appearing utterly unnerved. "I'm so sorry, I tried as hard as I could," she spoke gravely. "My cures have had the opposite effect. He's—I'm sorry—I'm afraid he's dead."

Chapter Eleven

A Risky Adventure

There was a deafening rush of darkness. The world fell away piece by broken piece, leaving nothing behind besides hallowed emptiness. There was only silence—silence so thick and absolute, it was crushing. As the atmosphere increasingly became too heavy to bear, a streak of light cut through the shadows. A soft buzzing noise reverberated through the darkness, relieving the silence. Every inch of the omnipresent shadows dissolved into a flood of bright light, surrounding Avian's disoriented soul as he fell into Veinya's manor.

The blinding lights immediately dimmed, swallowed by the ubiquitous shadows shrouding Veinya's lair. The goddess herself stood beside a large, ironclad mirror, the brightness of the glass curtailed by clouds of smoke swirling beneath its smooth glass.

Avian was struck with unparalleled anxiety as he realized he was dead. He rested his hand against his face, expecting his fingers to fall through his lifeless cheek and was astonished when he felt skin beneath his touch. "Wh-what...?" he started, his voice dying in his throat as Veinya took a wide step closer to his stunned body.

"Fear not," she said icily, "you *are* dead."

Avian exhaled sharply, shaking his head in disbelief. He stood up slowly, his body feeling as light and weak as a flimsy, misused feather. He felt as if one small touch would send him sprawling to the cold floor of Veinya's death manor. "This isn't permanent. Vyntrx promised me that you would return my life."

"You're a fool if you believe anything Vyntrx promises,"

Veinya said dully, cavalierly examining her ink-black nails. "However, you are correct. Your soul will return to your pathetic little life—that is, if your faithful puppet will come searching for my manor."

"The girl will come," Vyntrx's voice abruptly resonated through the room, automatically sending chills down Avian's spine. He spun around rapidly, discovering her standing several yards away, a demonic smirk curving her blood-red lips. "Although predictable, she isn't an imbecile. She won't accept Avian's death, especially knowing the goddess of death resides in the depths of the forest. She'll come for his soul." She paused, her eyebrows lowering critically as her gaze fell on Avian. "You're lucky she's willing to save you, and you're even luckier I decided to negotiate your life. You're lucky you're so valuable to my cause. You're such a careless boy, jumping in front of my blade! Had you forgotten that I cannot eradicate the girl's life until you've crowned her queen? Because of that little promise you made to her father, if you fail to place her on the throne, your soul will be instantly destroyed—ergo, until she's queen, if I kill her, I destroy you." She folded her arms across her chest, impatiently rolling her black eyes. "In the forest, I was simply trying to scare her. When I lashed out, I was expecting you to knock away the blow or pull her out of my reach, not stupidly sacrifice yourself. Has this trivial emotion you feel for her truly diluted your judgment?"

Avian sighed in exasperation, forcing his mind to avoid thinking about Kiara since the action only brought on a paralyzing wave of guilt and desolation. "Of course I was aware that you couldn't kill her. I'll admit I allowed my feelings for her to override my logic. It was an innate response—I ignored all elements of the situation aside from the fact that her safety had been compromised. Yes, I was careless, but I cannot undo the past. Yes, I am obligated to follow your orders for the rest of my miserable life, but it would be impossible to diminish the feelings I have reserved for her."

Vyntrx's eyebrows shot upward skeptically. "I've always known you were weak," she rebuffed. "Your love does not appear unrequited—no, the two of you seem to share this blinding passion. Did you, perhaps, actually listen when I advised you to control her mind so she would be submitted to your thrall?"

"No," Avian automatically responded, his gaze swerving downward as Vyntrx's disappointed glare set his face on fire. "No, I couldn't do it. It was never a direct order, so I chose to ignore it."

Vyntrx smiled sardonically. "Well, *now* it's an order. Control her mind; make her your puppet. We don't want anything interfering with her coronation. You know what happens if you disobey me." She drew a slim finger across her neck, mimicking death.

Avian's unmoving heart dove from his chest. Controlling Kiara's mind would suppress any natural emotion she felt for him and replace it with fabrications. The action was completely unpredictable. After being subjected to such conditions, he was uncertain she would ever be able to feel *anything* for him again. Tears clouded his eyes. A despairing sensation swept through his body, urging his vocal chords to plead for reconsideration—but he tragically understood the act would be futile.

"The princess better kill you—" a husky voice abruptly cut through the tense atmosphere, "—both of you."

Regardless of the fact that Avian's eyes hadn't fallen upon the sight of his brother since the day he had died or heard the sound of his voice since childhood, he instantly recognized his identity. The presence of his dead brother overwhelmed his already deteriorating mentality so tremendously, his light body toppled to the ground with a definite *thud*. "Kain?" he whispered disbelievingly.

"Don't act so shocked, idiot," Kain hurriedly snapped, emerging from the darkness as he strode to where his brother had fallen. "You knew I became Veinya's servant after you had me murdered."

"Kain, I didn't—" Avian spoke frantically as he pushed his weak body off the floor. He stood beside his brother, looming at least three inches above Kain's average stature.

He had matured. He was no longer the frail, lanky five-year-old Avian had despised so vehemently. While Kain appeared to lack muscular physique, his aura screamed possession of strength and brazenness. Although his lack of confidence was evident in the shrug of his shoulders, he effectively covered up his insecurity with intense glares and stoic, conclusive mannerisms.

"What're you gawking at?" Kain barked. "I'm not a child anymore. Did you imagine my soul wouldn't have aged?"

Avian averted his gaze, a handful of tresses cascading into eyes. "You look like your mother," his voice was barely audible.

"You mean the woman you hated so terribly, you—"

"Stop it, Kain," Avian pleaded, torrents of pain coursing through his voice. "I don't wish to relive the past. Especially not now."

Kain scowled, slamming his palm into Avian's chest, directly above his unresponsive heart. "You relive it every single day of your pathetic existence. I know all about your curse."

Avian brushed his brother's hand away, an enraged expression stamped across his features. "You don't know *anything*, Kain. You think you do, but you don't even know half of it."

"I know enough," he retorted, glancing at Vyntrx and Veinya as they fixedly watched the brothers' sour reunion. "You're screwing with our father's godchild's head—the princess."

Unrestrained rage surged through Avian's chest. He clutched the fabric of Kain's shirt within his palm, lifting his brother's light body off the ground. "You don't understand anything, especially regarding Kiara! She—she—" he choked off, attempting to bottle down the sobs that were rising in his chest. "I'm bringing you back to life, and that's all you need to know. Just—just keep quiet about the situation, otherwise you'll find yourself back in Veinya's manor faster than you can say the princess's name."

"I don't know her name," he retorted drily.

Avian angrily unhinged his mouth, but Vyntrx's words killed his voice. "Avian's right. If you want to live, Kain," she said darkly, "there's one little role you'll have to play."

Kain cast his piercing, light purple eyes on the Nonae empress, a curtain of his dark hair falling into his cynical expression. "What is it?"

Vyntrx's red lips spread outward, forming a snakelike grin. Her black eyes glinted as she began to describe how Kain would inevitably become a small factor in the downfall of Enevale's princess.

*****

The air was sucked out of Kiara's lungs. She felt as though her heart had been violently ripped from her chest. The room was whirling unsteadily—she was unsure if she had fallen to the ground or was still standing on trembling legs. A sharp ringing resonated through her ears, utterly deafening her. It was if she had abandoned the realm of reality and stumbled into a horrifying nightmare.

She wallowed in the shadows of the impenetrable, mind-consuming darkness that had invaded her mentality until a persistent streak of light vanquished the gloom. Vision slowly revisited her eyes, the lone sight of a wooden floor pouring into view. Her hearing returned in a voluminous wave of sound, her ears instantly assaulted by the pleading refrain of the duke's voices.

The sight of the wooden floor was replaced by unblemished

white walls as Kiara was abruptly lifted into the air. Every inch of her flesh had been numbed with anxiety, but she vaguely felt someone's arms tight around her body. Ignorantly, she believed she really *had* been asleep, and Avian had rescued her from another paralytic nightmare. Peeling open her sticky eyes, she discovered herself in Aiden's tremulous arms. The hellish situation she had been thrust into was not crafted by the whim of slumber—no, she regretfully resided in reality.

Overwhelmed with desolation and filled with the desire to find Avian, Kiara clawed her way out of Aiden's reach, landing on the balls of her unsteady feet. Her legs still precariously wavering, she barely managed to flee the nurse's office and sprint toward Avian's room. The medic's voice screamed for her to halt, but she didn't listen. She couldn't accept the absolute authenticity of Avian's absence until she witnessed the sight herself.

Standing in the doorway of the room, Kiara's stomach churned acidly as her eyes fell upon the jarring sight of Avian. His body was stiff and eerily pale, his eyes half-covered by dull hair spilled against his face without a careful hand to brush it back. Not a puff of air escaped his lips, not a slight rise or fall graced his chest. Vomit bolted from Kiara's lips, the abrupt action sending her sprawling to the ground. As she heaved uncontrollably, footsteps sounded in the hall and she knew her friends were approaching.

Wiping at her mouth with the back of her sleeve, she half-crawled on unstable legs toward Avian's frozen body. She collapsed on his unmoving chest, her hands stubbornly clinging to his shirt. Beneath the fabric of his blouse, his skin was unnaturally cold.

Just seconds ago, he was breathing, she thought bitterly, drowning in a puddle of her tears. *Just seconds ago, he was here.*

"NO!" she screamed, hyperventilation racking her lungs in a forceful wave. "Come back!" she hoarsely begged, burying her face in his shirt as her tightly clutched fingers nearly tore the cloth. The putrid scent of blood and the forest clogged her nose, gagging her. "*Come back*! Don't leave me! *Please*! Don't leave me!"

The dukes, Rissa, and the medic crowded the doorway of Avian's death chamber. The boys observed Kiara's miserable display with tearful anguish. Blade boldly crossed the room, grasping Kiara's shoulder. "K-Kiara, he's..." he started, his voice quavering. "H-he's gone." He attempted to pry her away from Avian's deceased body, but her grip on his chest was steadfast.

"He's not gone!" she shrieked plaintively, thrusting her elbow into Blade's forearm as she attempted to fend off his persistence.

"He *is*!" he screamed, a mix of indignation and desperation coursing through his voice. "He is *gone*, Kiara! Nothing you can say or do will *ever* bring him back! Unless some miracle strikes and Veinya decides to refuse his soul the process of death, we will *never* see him again!"

Kiara's grasp on Avian's shirt relented at Blade's curt words. She slid down the mattress, collapsing on the floor. She couldn't exhume enough energy to respond to Blade's outburst. She understood he was devastated—Avian had been one of his closest friends. As Blade's arms wrapped comfortingly around her shoulders, she replayed the words he had spoken as an impossible idea formed in the base of her mind: *Unless some miracle strikes and Veinya decides to refuse his soul the process of death, we will never see him again!* If a miracle transpiring were the occurrence required for Avian's revival, then a miracle Kiara would construct. Avian had informed her of the location of Veinya's manor in the Dark Forest. As a child, she had been taught that the examination of one's soul occupied three days' time before Veinya decided if one was fit to be reincarnated or condemned to destruction. Weaving these two important facts together stitched Kiara's loose idea into a solid plan. "Veinya's manor is in the forest," she slowly whispered. "And the forest is beyond the Wall."

Blade gently pulled Kiara's body away from his arms, staring directly into her inconsistent eyes. "No one knows where it's located."

"Vyntrx is tied to Veinya. Avian told me Veinya favors her. If we were to find Vyntrx, we could overwhelm her and demand she lead us to Veinya's mansion. Finding Vyntrx would be insanely elementary for me, considering the woman wants me dead."

A baffled silence absorbed the room. Confused expressions and weary glances were sent and received, but Kiara stared determinedly ahead, her mind reeling with scenarios of a successful escapade.

"You aren't actually considering going after Avian's soul, are you?" Ace said slowly, breaking the quiet atmosphere.

"Yes, I am," she decided immediately, determination curving the contours of her face as her eyes faded from blue to red-orange. She slowly stood on wobbly legs. "I'm leaving as soon as possible."

"This is ludicrous!" Rissa suddenly cried. Her emerald eyes were bright with fresh tears, but she was glaring at Kiara with unadulterated rage. "You must be delusional if you think you can change fate's design!"

Kiara's irises were glazed with black annoyance as she turned toward her foe. "You don't love him, Rissa," she coldly retorted, "or else you'd be willing."

Rissa's face contorted with darkened rage. Her mouth automatically opened, but no sound escaped her lips. After several seconds of struggling to form a response, she gave up, succumbing to silence as she averted her infuriated gaze.

"There is a *very* slim chance you could convince Veinya to return Avian's soul," Blade said slowly, climbing to his feet beside Kiara. "We would only have three days to find her mansion and convince her that Avian's soul is worth bringing back to life."

Kiara shook her head dismissively, strands of her tousled hair sticking to her damp cheeks. "I'm still going to try. I'm not just going to sit here and accept this. I don't care if anyone comes with me. I'm going."

A wave of silence infiltrated the room. The medic stared uncomfortably at the floor, obliged to stay nearby so long as guests were crowding a patient's room. Ace and Aiden were intently staring at Kiara, their faces scrunched up in contemplation. Rissa's irate face bore into the floor, wretchedness and aggravation showcased by her expression.

Blade loudly sighed, the noise cutting through the oppressive stillness. His hand fell on Kiara's shoulder, automatically bringing her eyes to his face. "You're not doing it alone. I'm going with you."

Kiara's mouth, tightened from inexorable sobs, lifted into something that resembled a grin. "Thank you, Blade," she breathed. "We'll leave immediately."

Aiden, pressing the tips of his fingers to his temple, released a huff of exasperated air. "I'm going, too. I can't let you get killed."

"I will, as well," Ace chimed in, nodding in Kiara's direction. A line of half-dried tears streaked his cheeks.

She nodded, her lips widening as she weakly attempted to smile. "Thank you. Let's round up our supplies and head out." She turned toward the bed, gently lowered her lips to Avian's frigid forehead as she whispered, "I swear to Veinya, I *will* bring you back." As she pulled away, she tightly clamped her eyes shut, afraid seeing Avian's dead body would simply steer her in the direction of hysteria.

Blade hurried out of the room, trailed carefully by Kiara. They pushed past the dukes, Rissa, and the medic, who were crowding the doorway. Filing out into corridor, Kiara turned her attention to the nurse. "Keep Avian's body in his room and leave the door shut and locked. Do *not* tell anyone of his death.

If anyone asks—even the medics under your guidance—tell them he's in critical condition and requires solely your attention. We *will* bring him back."

The nurse gaped at Kiara dubiously. "Do you really think you will be able to convince Veinya to return a soul from death? The goddess isn't necessarily known for interacting with mortals or being considerate. How do you plan to defeat Vyntrx, the most villainous creature in Menevilen?"

"Defeating Vyntrx will be the easy part," Kiara said haughtily, her hands automatically clenching into fists at the thought of her aunt. "She'll pay for the pain she's inflicted. I don't care how powerful she believes she is. As for Veinya, I'm hoping she'll be impressed with my fortitude. She *does* favor exceptional souls, and she favored my fa—" she stopped abruptly, warily eying the nurse. She clamped her mouth shut, exchanged nervous glances with the dukes and shaking her head dismissively. She started down the hallway with the boys at her heels. "We'll be back in three days."

"Wait!" Rissa's sudden exclamation resonated through the hall. "I'm going with you, too!"

Kiara immediately twisted around. "What are you talking about? Why?"

"Look, I know you and I have our differences, but I want Avian to return just as much as you do."

Kiara narrowed her eyes skeptically, resting her hand against her hip. "What happened to your opinion that my idea was 'ludicrous'?"

"I'm still doubtful that your plan will be successful, but I would regret it forever if I didn't at least *try* to help." Rissa's eyes were wide and sincere, residual tears clinging to her dark lashes. The neckline of her shirt had been rumpled, revealing a patch of pale skin. Scrawled into the flesh beneath her left collarbone was her Evalseman marking—her name.

As Kiara noticed this birth mark, she recalled Avian stating that Rissa was a lethal warrior whose Evalseman Specialty was the ability to shape shift. "Well, I'm not going to deny myself a strong companion," Kiara decided. "You can accompany us so long as you avoid causing me headaches."

Rissa nodded compliantly, but she attempted to bottle down a look of annoyance. "I'm sure I can mange that."

"Good." Kiara spun on her booted heel, hurrying down the corridor. With Rissa and the dukes following obediently at her side, she weaved through the infirmary and exited through the doors leading into the corridors of the castle.

*****

The Wall seemingly glowed as its strange stone reflected the silvery light of the moon, illuminating the shadows of the castle grounds. Kiara stood alone, tracing the crack that had led her to the concealed fissure in the partition. Warm wind swept across her limbs as she surveyed the stone. Her mind was whirling with the events of the Dark Forest and the devastating aftermath. Her eyes were swollen and red, but the determination coursing through her veins had slightly patched the gaping hole in her chest.

The dukes had scurried to their suites to obtain weapons and appropriate adventure attire while Rissa had been charged with the responsibility of compiling a sack full of food and other supplies needed for their quest. Kiara had suggested Aiden meet briefly with his sister to inform her of the dukes' temporary absence and place her in charge of the throne in case an emergency occurred. They had planned to rendezvous at the training grounds after they had completed their tasks, but Kiara had slunk toward the Wall as she waited for her friends to appear. She hadn't needed to search for a weapon as her necklace's newfound ability provided her with the luxury of traveling light. Before she had trekked outdoors, she had quickly stopped by the suite and changed into a stretchy shirt with quarter-length sleeves and a lace-up front, tight pants, and knee-high boots. Tossing her hair into a high ponytail, she had navigated her way through the castle and emerged into the crisp nighttime air.

Kiara heard her name abruptly shouted in the distance. Turning toward the training grounds, her eyes latched on Blade, Aiden, and Ace as they descended down the small hill flanking the castle. Rissa appeared several yards behind them, walking hurriedly as she clutched a pile of fabric. Kiara waved over her companions, hoping they had remembered to compile the required materials for their journey.

As the dukes and Rissa reached Kiara's side, she discovered that the boys were clutching varying weapons—Blade was wielding a crossbow, Aiden clutched a double-edged sword, a metal pole was strapped to Ace's back—and Rissa was carrying an assortment of cloaks. She distributed the garments, explaining that the forest plummets to icy temperatures at night. Two leather pouches were tied to her belt beside an unsheathed, intimidating mace.

Kiara tied her cloak into place, complimenting Rissa on her planning skills. Rissa, caught off-guard by praise from her enemy, wore an expression of bemused content. She opened her mouth to explain that she had partook in a copious amount of conquests into the Dark Forest, but as she noticed Kiara was unarmed, she posed a question instead. "Where is your weapon?"

Kiara's hand instinctively flew to her necklace. "It's here," she explained, hurriedly unlatching the chain and envisioning a sharp knife in its place. Her companions released a collective gasp as the necklace shifted into a weapon. "I discovered this ability while I was in the forest. I suppose it was the only beneficial incident that came out of today's events."

"That necklace was a gift from your parents!" Blade exclaimed incredulously. "Did your mother enchant it?"

Kiara shrugged, recalling the weapon back to its original state as she fastened it around her neck. "I would assume so. I don't think it just decided to develop magical properties."

Blade mock laughed at Kiara's intended sarcasm. "Are we all ready to leave?"

Kiara nodded, glancing around the assembly to be certain no one was prepared to protest. "Let's head out, then," she decided, fumbling through the bushes surrounding the Wall. The intense darkness handicapped her vision, despite the soft glow of the Wall. Aiden, noticing she was having difficulties, readily sparked a flame inside his palm, extending his arm toward her as he doused her with light. Mumbling her gratitude, Kiara eventually located the winding crack in the Wall, leading her straight to the covert hole.

Hurtling the hedges, Kiara crawled through the opening, advising that Aiden be the last to pass through so he could provide the group with an illuminated path.

Slowly, one by one, Kiara's cohorts joined her on the ground of enemy territory.

"Never knew that hole was there," Blade commented as he inched through the fissure. "We typically go through the city gates and enter the forest through the plains. Once you're crowned queen, we should patch that up, otherwise Nonae may trickle into the city once your mother's protective spell fades."

"That would be an ideal plan, considering Vyntrx is already fully aware of the gap. It was her who directed me toward it," Kiara explained as Aiden crossed through the entrance, flooding the area with warm light.

"Where to now, Kiara?" Aiden interjected.

She shrugged, stepping around a cluster of trees that hid the fissure from the inhabitants of the Dark Forest. She pointed to a worn, almost indistinguishable trail leading toward thick, suppressive darkness. "I'm nearly certain that's the path Avian took to return to this location—but my mind was heavily frazzled at the time, so I can't be sure."

"You're in charge," Ace decided. "Should we head that way?"

"I have a suggestion," Aiden offered. "Naturally, I would propose we venture to Vitaciel, the Nonae capital, in order to find Vyntrx—but given the size of our legion, successful entry or furtiveness would be an unmanageable feat. If we were to stumble across a small Nonae or Demmonai village, they would undoubtedly summon Vyntrx to deal with our punishment, and she would be served to us on a silver platter. Rissa can shift into whichever creature we encounter and we could pretend to be her captives—which would save us from being entirely ensnared by our enemies."

Kiara stared at Aiden, wholly impressed. She patted his shoulder approvingly. "That's a brilliant idea! Are you familiar with this location?"

"No, I'm afraid not, but there should be an encampment not too far from here. The forest consists of small villages and campsites created by clans of Nonae and Demmonai. They're never too far apart, so it would be safe to assume we're only about a day's walk—if not less—away from a gathering of some sort."

Nodding in gratification, Kiara gripped the edge of her cloak and pulled it against her chilled body. Rissa had been correct—the forest appeared noticeably colder than the weather on the other side of the Wall. Avian had informed her that the forest was always warmer than the Evalseman territory, but she assumed this difference was reversed during the dank hours of night. "That's good news," she replied. "Let's walk for a little while to gain some distance and then we should stop walking and sleep. It's been an extremely eventful day and it would be unwise to fight without proper rest."

Her attendants complied with her plan, closely trailing behind Aiden as he led the group through the dense forest. The soft ground refrained from creating the slightest twinge of sound as they trudged across it. Not a single living soul was in sight.

After walking in cautious silence for nearly half an hour,

Aiden abruptly whispered for everyone to halt as he pointed his fire-clad hand to his left. Following his finger, Kiara discovered the outline of a cluster of houses partially hidden by trees in the distance.

"A Demmonai village?" she wondered.

"Either that or a Nonae campsite," Rissa answered. "Only one way to find out."

Kiara sighed a mixture of relief and apprehension. She slowly settled down against the surprisingly soft ground of the forest. "Tomorrow," she declared. "We will venture into the village tomorrow." She turned her attention to Aiden as her friends positioned themselves in a circle around her. "Would it be safe to start a fire?"

He shrugged. "There is an uncountable amount of rogue Nonae constantly roaming the forest. I'm sure they wouldn't find a campfire unusual."

"Please start a campfire, then," Kiara advised, picking up a forlorn twig and tossing it several yards in front of her.

Aiden climbed to his feet, hurriedly gathering discarded wood and adding it to the small pile Kiara had started. Once he had nurtured a warm, glowing fire, the companions huddled around the flames, fastening their cloaks around their bodies in an attempt to garner warmth.

Rissa's hand vanished into one of her small pouches, retrieving a loaf of bread and a handful of sliced, dried meat. She tore chunks from the baked dough and rationed two slices of meat for each comrade, passing the small meal around the campfire.

Kiara balanced her meat against her legs as she slowly chewed through her roll. Her eyes watched the flickering flames as it devoured the wood, crackling and sending sparks through the dark air. A conversation had ensued between Blade, Aiden, and Rissa, but as Kiara's mind was reeling, she did not comprehend their words.

"What does it mean when your eyes are blue?" Ace

whispered, the abrupt sound of his voice breaking through her daze.

She blinked hard, peeling her eyes away from the rising flames. She glanced at Ace, who was slouched beside her, his dark cloak wound tightly around his slim body. Rissa, Blade, and Aiden were reclining on the opposite side of the fire, communicating in loud volumes.

"That depends," she spoke slowly, "on if they are light blue or dark blue. Since I am feeling worried right now, I would assume they are a lighter shade—but the ever-present desolation that has taken control of my emotions since Avian's death could be darkening the hue."

"Are you worried about this quest?" he wondered.

Kiara nodded, a curtain of hair spilling into her eyes as she lowered her gaze—she didn't bother to brush it away. "Yes. I'm afraid I won't be able to succeed. I'm afraid I really will lose him forever." She glanced at her friend through a waterfall of tresses, the red glow of the fire highlighting the copper streaks in her partially brown hair. "Are you worried, too?"

He shrugged, dangling a piece of meat over the ravenous flames. "If anyone can save him, it's you, Kiara."

She tucked her loose hair behind her ear, swallowing the last bite of her bread. She mimicked Ace's actions, holding both strands of her meat over the crackling fire. "Why do you think that?"

"You're one of the most stubborn people I've ever met," he explained, chuckling lightly. "You're almost as steadfast as Blade. You love Avian and you want Vyntrx to be punished—these motives drive you. You're strong. I have faith that with your guidance, we will save Avian's soul."

Kiara worked her mouth into a small smile, watching the dim light reflect Ace's golden eyes. She bumped her shoulder against her friend's, recalling her meal from its location over the fire. Stuffing a large bite of meat into her mouth, she mumbled, "I hope you're right."

Ace's hand gently patted her shoulder, a confident smile curving the corners of his lips. "I am."

*****

Kiara's dreams shifted to a nightmare as Vyntrx's slim, pale hands wrapped around her neck with the stubbornness and deadliness of a noose. Vyntrx hadn't yet killed her niece, but with one quick flick of her wrist, she easily could. "Give it up, Kiara," she snarled sadistically, her wild eyes on fire with anger. "You're not going to save his pathetic life no matter how hard you try."

"I—I—" Kiara spluttered to speak, clawing at Vyntrx's tightly wound hands. "I—will!"

Vyntrx laughed horribly, tightening her grip around Kiara's neck as the scene shifted. An ominous dungeon spilled out of the darkness, bringing with it the disastrous image of the Nonae empress. She stood in the center of the room, standing next to a very startled—very much alive—Avian. Kiara made a sharp move toward him, finding chains tightly clamped over her slender wrists. The bonds tore at her arms, chafing her flesh raw.

"Here he is, Kiara!" Vyntrx taunted, grabbing a fistful of his hair and pulling his face toward hers. "Come and get him!"

Kiara yanked at the chains despite the continuous pain shooting through her exposed wrists—the sensation was unbearable. Her Evalseman strength had faded into pathetic limpness.

Avian was watching her helplessly, tears outlining his eyes. "Give it up, Ara," he whispered feverishly. "Give it up."

"No!" she screamed defiantly, tugging at her chains impotently. "I won't!"

Vyntrx's haggard laugh sliced through the dream, piercing the silence of the dungeon and infiltrating Kiara's ears. Her hands clamped over her head but the sound did not relent. The chuckle grew shrill, threatening to madden her if the persistent noise refused to silence. When the insufferable sound grew utterly intolerable, the dream ended with such swift force it flung Kiara's eyelids open, sending her whirling back into reality.

*****

She had returned to the makeshift campsite, the smoldering fire burning low through the pile of wood. Kiara sat up, rubbing her eyes. Her hands came away wet with tears. Sighing, she pulled her fingers through her tangled hair, releasing it from its messy ponytail. Everyone had fallen asleep. She couldn't remember who had been selected to stay awake to keep watch, but it hadn't mattered. They had fallen sleep anyway. *It was probably Blade,* she thought bitterly, adhering to the natural call to blame the boy who so frequently tempered with her good moods. Despite her hastiness to rebuke him, she couldn't bring herself to wake him from his deep slumber.

She didn't dare fall back asleep—her dreams were far too vivid. She decided she'd walk ahead while the others were resting and scout the nearby village. Slowly creeping away from the campsite, Kiara headed toward the outline of houses tucked away behind towering trees in the distance. She watched her feet carefully as she maneuvered her body through the densely wooded forest. After only a few short minutes of walking, she reached the outskirts of the village. The small town consisted mainly of large, wooden houses haphazardly flocked around a clearing. In the center of the plain, a wide, charcoaled pit baring a roaring fire devoured hoards of wood.

Fortunately, there was not a creature in sight as Kiara crept through the village. Despite the fact that she had never seen a Demmonai in the flesh, she spontaneously peered into the windows of the houses, attempting to discover the mysterious creatures that could be sleeping behind the thick glass. For most of the houses she tried to spy on, curtains blotted out the contents of the room beneath heavy swaths of fabric, making it entirely impossible to peer through the window. However, she managed to locate a single house without drapery, but couldn't find a window belonging to a bedroom.

Frustrated, she delved further into the village. The noise of a twig snapping sounded loudly behind her. She turned on her heel instantly, her hand automatically flying to the cold pendant around her neck.

Kiara's heart dropped from her chest like a dead bird sent sprawling to the dirt-streaked, hard packed ground. Avian was standing a mere few feet away from her, blood absent from his uncharacteristically dark clothes, his chest rising and falling with each misplaced breath. He wasn't smiling for once, and his eyes were lacking the gentle gleam even the smallest fractures of light could manage to capture.

"A-Avian...?" she whispered, feeling her eyes swell. "H-how are you—? Y-you're dead."

"I'm not dead," he countered slowly, his eyebrows pulled into a tight line. "You okay?"

She stared at the sight of Avian with unbridled incredulity. "If you're not dead, then why I am in the Dark For—" her voice immediately relinquished as the village slowly faded out of focus, suddenly replaced by what appeared to be her suite inside the castle.

"What?" he questioned, staring in confusion at her perplexed expression.

She shook her head feverishly, attempting to rattle her brain so fiercely that an explanation would fall from it. "H-how is this happening? You—I saw—" she stumbled over her words, the rampant emotions surging through her body diluting her ability to articulate.

"You must've been dreaming. You're awake now." His explanation was vague, his voice noticeably uncaring.

"No, it was real," she insisted. The cloak Rissa had given her was still draped around her shoulders, sheltering her rapidly multiplying goose bumps. "I *know* it was real. This isn't—This can't..."

Avian carefully strode closer to her, his hands held tightly behind his back. "It's all so complicated, princess. Vyntrx was just trying to upset you."

She took a wide step backwards, her eyebrows furrowing as she shook her head in dismay. "No, Vyntrx succeeded in distressing me when she murdered you. You're not making sense."

Avian shrugged cavalierly. "You're the one talking nonsense. Think about it."

"There is *nothing* to think about!" Kiara roared, her hands trembling from his unexpected presence. Regardless of the fact that the person she was speaking with was not the real Avian and was certainty messing with her mind, the sight of his breathing, moving body set her nerves on edge. "I want the truth! Who *are* you?"

He exhaled, rolling his eyes impatiently. "I'm Avian. You know me."

"Like hell I do!" she fired snappily, her eyes blazing scarlet with frustrated rage. "You don't even talk like Avian, you imposter!"

He continued to saunter toward Kiara, attempting to close the distance between them. "We've only been acquainted for a couple of months. Aside from our childhood friendship that *you* can't even remember, you hardly know me."

"No, you're wrong," her voice possessed more confidence than the diminutive supply she had actually managed to summon. "I know you. I know you better than anyone." She paused, momentarily suspecting that the phony Avian was actually Rissa, as shape shifting *was* her Evalseman Specialty—but as she glanced around the fabricated suite, she understood that the intruder must be someone capable of manipulating one's view of reality.

The fake Avian's mouth curved into a sardonic grin. "See, that's where you're dead wrong, princess. I'm not who you think I am at all. You think you know me, but you haven't even met the *real* me. I have dark secrets. You've only scratched the surface of my personality—the man cowering behind my façade is really just a monster."

Fear, anxiety, and resentment crowded her eyes as she glowered at the imposter. Her hands tightened into clenched fists, irritation surging through her limbs. "You're not Avian! Stop defiling his memory with your fallacies!"

Avian's body bent forward, his head looming above Kiara's as he leaned toward her. His mismatched eyes bore into her fiery, crimson irises. "You're so naïve," he taunted. "You'd believe anything I'd say. You trust me—but you'll soon discover how misplaced that faith is."

"*Shut up!*" she screamed hoarsely, unable to withstand the intruder's slanderous accusations against Avian's life. She thrust her fists forward, intending to make contact with the imposter's torso and send him reeling backwards—instead, her hands helplessly fell through his chest as though he were constructed out of smoke. "What *are* you?" she whispered incredulously, stumbling to rebalance her skewered footing.

The fake Avian shrugged casually, an innocent expression crossing his stolen features. "A ghost," he admitted.

"You're not Avian's spirit," she uttered, hurriedly dismissing the small voice in the deepest chambers of her mind that suggested the imposter wasn't actually a fake. "You're nothing like him."

A dull countenance crossed his handsome face. "Whatever, my little act effectively got your attention. Listen up, princess, here's a warning: saving Avian's soul won't be easy, if you can even pull it off. I'm not your filthy aunt, and I'm not an enemy. Think what you will of me, but I'm on your side. Just don't think this adventure of yours will be effortless. I'll see you again—soon. Bye-bye, princess."

Kiara, confounded into silence, stared with her mouth agape as the mysterious imposter's body diminished into shadows while the fabricated visual of her suite was swallowed by reality.

Kiara's legs automatically buckled as she was returned to the abandoned Demmonai village. She pulled her fingers through her tangled hair, breathing steadily in an attempt to slow her rapidly pulsating heartbeat. The sight of Avian—however tainted it had been—had severely unhinged her emotions.

Who was *that?* she wondered yearningly. The imposter had claimed he wasn't a foe, yet how could she possibly advise herself to believe him? *Allies don't typically tamper with your head before stating who they are.* She sighed, rubbing her temples in exhaustion. Her stomach lurched as the pessimist clouding her judgment began to propose that the fake Avian had really been speaking the truth. Hurriedly pushing down negative thoughts, she wearily dragged herself from the ground. *I'll just discuss this odd occurrence with Avian when he's back,* she thought positively, forcing her lethargic legs to move toward the campsite.

As she neared the huddled gathering of her slumbering friends, fatigue settled into the marrow of her psyche. Wholeheartedly languid, she collapsed beside the ash-ridden remains of the fire, her mind plummeting into the clutches of her dreams before she had closed her eyes.

Chapter Twelve

The Other Knight

Kiara's dream welled beneath her eyelids, a densely shadowed labyrinth spilling from the darkness. Shady walls sped past her as she was rapidly led through the corridors. She felt a light pressure against her extended hand. Glancing down at her arm—so pale in comparison the dark atmosphere—she discovered her fingers carefully intertwined with someone else's. Furrowing her brow in confusion, she maneuvered her attention forward as her eyes fell upon a dark-haired young man.

She drew in a sharp, startled breath. The young man, hearing her exclamation, glanced over his shoulder. His pallid face was pulled into a tight scowl, his strange purple eyes glowing from under a thick fringe of choppy black hair.

"Wh-who are you?" she stammered. "Where are we going?"

"To see Avian," he answered quickly, not bothering to divulge his identity. A harsh tone underlined his words—he seemed as though he'd rather not see Avian at all.

Kiara's heart accelerated at the mention of her lost love—her emotions were still painfully raw from her encounter with the imposter. "Wh-what do you mean?"

"He asked to see you," he muttered, turning back around. "So he can tell you himself that this adventure of yours is going to be a pain."

"Who are you?" she repeated, narrowing her eyes.

The mysterious young man shrugged. "It doesn't matter."

"It does," she hastily argued. "Who are you?"

"If you're lucky, you'll find out, princess," he spoke casually, his words heavy with a cold undertone. His demeanor and speech pattern vaguely reminded Kiara of someone she knew. Combing through memories, her mind latched on her recent encounter with the fake Avian as a pang of realization rattled through her psyche. "You!" she shouted, attempting to pry her hand from the boy's grip and devastatingly realizing her Evalseman strength failed to surface in the realm of her dreams. His fingers merely tightened around hers, locking her in. "You're the one who pretended to be Avian!"

"You're *so* smart," he retorted drily.

She rolled her eyes, her captured hand clenching into a protesting fist. "Why would you masquerade as Avian? Why would you lie to me as him?"

"Are you so sure they're lies?" he jeered, harshly tugging Kiara's hand. "And because I'm not a fan of your beloved Avian."

She studied the back of the young man's head. His shoulders were draped in shadowy cloth, the hue of the fabric nearly matching his black hair. "Why not?" she probed.

He paused, allowing a bout of brief silence to settle amid the dense atmosphere. "Sibling rivalry," he muttered huskily, "or something like that."

Kiara's eyes narrowed. She recalled Avian telling her about the younger brother he had once had, the one he had failed to save from Vyntrx's murderous intentions—but his brother had been dead for over a decade. She stared at the backside of the young man, wishing her persistent gaze would force him to turn around and face her, but he didn't succumb to her penetrating glare. "Who *are* you?"

The boy scoffed. "You keep asking that like you're expecting me to answer."

"I *do* expect you to answer!" she huffed.

He released a small sigh as his grip on Kiara's hand relented noticeably. "I'm a friend."

"A friend?" she echoed, staring at the unidentifiable young man as he led her through an arched doorway. "I haven't met many friends who attempted to unhinge my emotions at our initial encounter. You've left a *wonderful* first impression," she spoke slowly, sarcasm dripping from each clipped syllable.

He sniggered mockingly, his movement halting abruptly as they entered a wide, circular room. Kiara's eyes raked the area as the boy liberated her hand from his constricting hold. As she slowly examined her bearings, her gaze fell upon the sight of an incorporeal form standing placidly in the center of the room.

Her heart pulsated wildly, attempting to hurl itself from her chest. Her throat tightened as the supply of oxygen swirling in her lungs was sharply withdrawn. Numbness crept through her body as though her nerves had been prickled by a needle.

She was staring at Avian.

Cautiously, she took a step forward. Avian's imposter had easily tricked her mind and roused her emotions, and while she forced herself to be guarded, the sight of his nearly translucent body and unwavering chest communicated the possibility that she hadn't encountered a fake.

"Kiara," his voice escaped his transparent lips in a raspy whisper. He bolted toward her, arms extended.

She raced to his approaching figure, tears outlining her eyes. A spark of relief had ignited in her chest—she could discern familiar emotion in Avian's dead eyes, could observe the familiarity of his gait, could hear the desperation in his voice. The arms of the spirit she was hurling herself into were none other than Avian's.

But when their frenzied bodies were just mere centimeters away from collision, Avian's smoky form passed through Kiara's solid stature. She stared, open-mouthed, into the darkness, her hands held outward in vain. Avian steadied his footing, turning toward Kiara with a heavy heart. Their eyes immediately met, frail despondency coursing through their matching expressions.

"Why can't you touch me?" she whispered. "Your brother can."

Avian shook his head solemnly. "He's more..." he trailed off, ransacking his brain for an accurate explanation, "...*alive* than I am. While his soul is solid inside the manor, outside of this realm, it becomes constructed of the same vague material as my form. Spirits cannot typically communicate with the living. In order for to accomplish this feat, one's soul must remain unexamined by Veinya, and only then can one persuade a servant of the goddess to act as a median to the outside world. It's because of my brother that we are able to speak."

Kiara's hand inflexibly reached forward, as though she expected to successfully touch his face. Her hand fell through his cheek as though his flesh were constructed of smoke. A single tear spilled down her face, and when Avian instinctively hurried to wipe it away, his finger merely vanished into her skin. "Why did you summon me here?" she wondered quietly, a thick web of hysteria forming in the base of her throat.

"I wanted to warn you and beg for a favor," he revealed. "Your mission will be incredibly dangerous and life-threatening. I cannot promise that you will retreat safely to the castle—with or without my soul. Before I proceed with the second half of my speech, I must be comforted in knowing that you are unequivocally certain that your quest, however disadvantageous it may prove to be, is absolutely necessary."

Kiara nodded without hesitation. "Yes, of course it is. I'm willing to risk everything."

Avian smiled sadly. "Don't be so blasé about throwing your life away for mine. You have far more potential and significance in this world than I could ever possess."

"It doesn't matter," she admitted. "I want you with me."

He exhaled an anxious breath. "I know your stubbornness. If you insist on trying to save me, then no power in this world except Veinya herself will stop you." He paused, his eyes briefly scanning his brother standing dully in the corner of the room. "If you succeed in convincing Veinya to hand over my soul, then I would like to make a request. My brother died an untimely death. He has served as Veinya's servant since the day he perished, which granted his soul the opportunity to thrive and mature. He was never given the opportunity to experience life. If you could convince Veinya to free my soul, it would mean you had impressed her greatly—perhaps she would even bestow her favor upon you—and she would readily grant you Kain's soul, as well. She has plenty of servants, so I'm sure the absence of one would not greatly affect her."

The dark-haired boy turned his dull gaze on Avian, his purple eyes sweltering with contempt. "You honesty *want* me to come back?"

"This is him?" Kiara wondered, astounded, staring at the young man as he exchanged heated glares with Avian. "The one who was killed by Vyntrx?"

Avian nodded somberly. "This is my half-brother, yes. He'll aid you in your quest, but he won't be able to exist outside of the mansion in his true form, as he isn't exactly *real*. He'll most likely appear as me when he materializes."

Kiara listened carefully to Avian's words as she scrutinized his brother's form. His stature was lacking several inches in comparison to Avian's height and his shoulders were not as broad. While Avian's defined body had been chiseled from years of training, his brother's figure was slim and somewhat gangly. The mysterious boy's unkempt black hair tumbled constantly into his nearly translucent violet eyes, while Avian's light brown tresses were always perfectly swept away from his face. While their features were distinctly different, they possessed the same rectangular shaped face and similarly arched eyebrows. Studying the pair of them closely, Kiara decided that while their appearances were differing, it was evident that they were related.

"I'll try to bring him back," she declared.

Avian smiled. He attempted to brush his fingers across Kiara's cheek and frowned when his hand simply fell through her skin. "Thank you, Ara," he spoke softly, his cloudy eyes glistening. "I miss you."

"I miss you, too," she whispered, her voice unusually raspy. "I promise you I *will* succeed."

His characteristic smile graced his lips. "I know. I'll see you soon, alright? Try to stay out of trouble."

"Given the circumstances, that's utterly impossible," she responded drily, glancing up at Avian from under a fringe of dark eyelashes. "But I'll try to stay safe."

"It's time to go," Avian's brother interjected. He eyed Avian and Kiara callously, pointing toward the dark hallway that led out of the wide room.

Kiara, unable to make contact with Avian's figure, allowed her shimmering pink eyes to express the emotion swelling through her chest. He returned her intimate gaze, yearning for the warmth of her touch to quell the pervading chill that had seeped through his figure since his arrival at the death manor.

"Come *on*, princess," his brother spoke impatiently, breaking through the heavy amorous atmosphere that had fully engrossed the couple.

Kiara sent Avian a sad smile as she relented her stare. She turned around slowly, prompting a sigh of exasperation to escape the mysterious boy's lips. He reached for her wrist, tugging her along as he led her out of the room. She twisted her head around in an attempt to steal one last glance at Avian— but he had vanished.

"So he loves you, huh?" the boy asked suddenly, instantly capturing Kiara's attention as she swiveled her head back around.

"Yes, he does," she answered immediately.

He was momentarily silent. "Strange," he muttered.

"When are you going to tell me your name?"

He sneered, quickening his pace. "Why is it so important to you?"

"It's not," she retorted. "I just need something to call you."

"Too bad, princess. You'll have to wait until you've reached Veinya's manor to find that out."

She huffed, rolling her eyes indignantly. "Fine. Where are we going now?"

"To get your soul back to your body."

Her stomach instantly twisted at the boy's response, her heart screeching to a standstill. "Am I dead?" she wondered despairingly, her voice merely a startled yelp.

"No, not dead," he replied dully, cocking a critical eyebrow as he observed Kiara's astounded reaction. "I just summoned your soul to this realm. I've gotta get your soul back to your body so you can wake up and kick Vyntrx's ass."

She laughed lightly, feeling a bout of relief pour through her veins. "I think I can manage that."

The boy fell silent for several minutes as a slew of dark corridors sped past Kiara's vision. His hold on her wrist loosened progressively as his voice shattered the calm. "About what Avian said..." he murmured, trailing off.

"Which part?"

He glanced shyly over his shoulder at her, his purple eyes glistening beneath the dark strands of his hair. "You don't have to ask about freeing me, okay?"

She inspected his austere expression, evaluating the wealth of concern hiding behind his stoic demeanor. She felt a pang of sympathy for Avian's brother—he had spent the majority of his existence thriving alongside the dead. His situation had been streaked with darkness, isolation, and suffering. She was overwhelmed with the desire to help the boy take a step into the bright world of the living and feel the breath of life infiltrating his sunken lungs. "I want to," she said reassuringly. "You deserve to be alive."

He narrowed his eyebrows skeptically. "Why?"

"You died at a young age. You were never really able to be *alive*," she explained rationally. The young man, unable to meet Kiara's eyes, shifted his gaze forward. "Besides, Avian seems to miss you."

The boy sneered derisively. "Yeah, I'm *sure* he misses me," he grumbled sarcastically. "Whatever, princess. No point in trying to stop you. Vyntrx is one hell of a monster, though. She'll give you a rough time."

A vague smile crossed Kiara's lips. "Not much more than you have."

The boy shrugged, refusing to respond as a lull in conversation assaulted the pair. Kiara, attempting to avoid an awkward silence, shifted their casual banter in the direction of a serious matter. "How exactly *did* you die, anyway?" she asked tentatively.

His body tensed instantly, his fingers sharply curling around her wrist. He remained silent for several seconds as he seemingly collected his thoughts. "Your aunt..." he began hesitantly, pausing. "Your aunt killed my family. Avian and I shared a father, but our mothers were different. My mother was a Nonae—she was actually close friends with your mother. You and I are both half-Nonae, half-Evalseman."

"Really?" Kiara's voice was teeming with wondrous fascination. She had never met another half-breed before, had never even imagined there were others amid the kingdoms of Menevilen. Being born with Nonae and Evalseman blood was a rarity, a phenomenon. She suspected that she and Avian's brother could very well be the only two creatures in existence to be born of both Nonae and Evalseman heritage. She felt instantly drawn to the mysterious boy, as he alone was the only one who could also receive the same biting judgment and isolation issued by both hate-filled races. "We're the same, then."

"Sure," he agreed nonchalantly, clearly not as baffled by their shared roots as Kiara had been. He abruptly stopped walking, releasing his hold on her arm. She slowed to a standstill behind him as her hand limply fell to her side. A large, circular doorway loomed behind him, an eerie abyss swirling darkly beyond the doorframe. "Just pass through here."

She nervously approached the ominous portal, half-expecting the strange void to wrap itself around her body and vaporize her soul. "I'll see you soon."

"Go," he instructed edgily.

Stealing one last glance at Avian's mysterious brother, Kiara hurled her body into the whirling chasm, abrasively thrusting her consciousness out of her dreams and into reality.

hapter Thirteen

Creatures of Shadow

Kiara awoke suddenly, her eyes flashing open. The Dark Forest poured into view as faint light filtered through thick leaves rimming the colossal trees. She sat up slowly, a wave of her brown hair catching the soft light and glowing coppery gold.

That dream was real, she thought assuredly, *there's no way I could have created that in my sleep.*

Although she had always possessed a distractingly vivid imagination, her creativity didn't ordinarily extend into the barriers of her dreams—and she could still feel the mysterious boy's grip around her wrist...

"Good morning, sleepyhead," Blade's voice abruptly sounded, that characteristic snide undertone infiltrating his words. Glancing to her side, she discovered him squatting beside her, wielding a mischievous grin. "'Bout time you woke up."

She glanced upward, finding her other companions standing at the edge of their makeshift campsite. They had doused the fire and gathered their belongings and were eyeing the village in the distance.

"I was awake earlier, ready to go!" she responded haughtily, standing up. "And *you* had fallen asleep while on look-out duty!"

Blade scowled, hurriedly climbing to his feet. "I was exhausted! It had been a long day. And it's not like anyone would come searching for us, and even if someone stumbled upon us, they would probably just assume we were rogue Nonae!"

Kiara raised her eyebrows critically. "Oh, *really*?" Her voice oozed disdainful sarcasm. "So you're telling me that if—*oh*, I don't know—Vyntrx or one of her minions were to find us, they wouldn't immediately recognize me and kill us in our sleep?"

He instantly unhinged his mouth to fire a curt reply, but Rissa's sudden interjection silenced him. "Enough jeering," she demanded, suddenly in-between the pair. "I'm going to transform into a Demmonai once we approach the village. I brought some rope from the castle—I figured it would come in handy—and I can use that to tie everyone together so it looks like I've captured you. Let's get going."

✶✶✶✶✶

Rissa led the brigade through the Dark Forest, distant sunlight dotting their skin as they walked beneath the densely covered trees. Kiara had discovered, after her spontaneous escapade to the village, that the duration of the walk was not lengthy. She fell into pace beside Blade, whose eyes were trailing Rissa's backside. "You know those legends about Veinya taking pity on young souls and making them her servants?" she whispered.

He blinked, glancing over at his friend. "Hmm?"

She rolled her eyes impatiently. "The legends of Veinya's servants—are they real or just stories?" Anyone who had read or been informed of Veinya's sacred texts understood the vague concept of her servants, but like the existence of the goddess herself, the validity behind these stories was thoroughly questioned.

He shrugged. "How should I know? I assume they're more than a myth. Naturally, I was skeptical of the goddess and her stories until my journeys into the forest. You can *feel* her power here."

She surveyed Blade's sincere expression, furrowing her brow in contemplation. "So you think if someone died as a child that Veinya would actually allow them to become her servant and thrive inside her mansion until their soul reached its maximum maturity?"

"Yeah, sure," he spoke cavalierly. "I mean, that's what the ancient texts say. Why are you so curious?"

She shook her head dismissively, dispersing their conversation. "Just a dream I had."

Regardless if Blade had desired to know about Kiara's dream or not, he didn't receive a chance to probe her further. They had reached the outskirts of the village.

The companions stopped walking instantly, watching Rissa expectantly. She smiled nervously at them. "I guess that's my cue," she said quietly, as if she were reflecting to herself. She cleared her throat, strengthening her voice. "Demmonai have a strange, intimidating appearance, so please—*please*—don't scream when I transform." Her eyes wandered to Blade, her gaze drastically hardening. "Or laugh."

"Rissa," he said lightly, unabashed by her ferocious glare, "Why would any of us laugh at such a deadly creature as a Demmonai?"

She rolled her eyes as her emerald irises abruptly turned the color of flames. Her skin darkened, the shadowy canvas of her flesh outlined by an ornate silvery pattern as though her body had been traced with grey ink. Her hair slunk inward toward the crown of her head and was replaced by a handful of pointed spikes. Two large fangs protruded from her snarling mouth, suggesting a mouth full of dangerously sharp incisors. Her battle-weathered hands had been replaced with claws, her nails blood red and hazardously long. Though Kiara had considered the thought entirely ludicrous, Rissa's height had noticeably increased.

Kiara's eyes had never fallen upon a more hideous, frightening creature. She forced down a startled yelp as she studied the monster that had stolen her comrade's body. Rissa's skin had become so dark, she nearly blended in with the forest—beside her bright red eyes and nails, she practically vanished into the darkness. Kiara recalled observing detailed paintings and sketches of Demmonai in the textbooks she had been issued by Aiden during her lessons over the Dark Forest's creatures. Although she had been informed of the Demmonai's appearance and capabilities throughout the course of her studies at her village academy, she had not seen an extensive representation of the creatures until beginning her lectures at the castle. While Rissa's frightening exterior perfectly matched the sketches in Kiara's books, the actual presence of a Demmonai was drastically intimidating.

A loud, obnoxious laugh disturbed Kiara's thoughts. She twisted her head around, finding Blade chortling, tears welling in his eyes. "Is that *you*, Rissa?" he wailed.

The transformed captain glared at Blade with her intimidating, bright red eyes, but he continued to snicker.

"Shut up, idiot!" Kiara demanded crossly. "Someone's going to hear you!"

"Sorry," he muttered, restraining himself from laughing any further. A constrained expression dashed across his face as strangled noises escaped his tightly clamped lips.

"Too bad I don't have my shackles," Rissa commented, a frightening chill leaking into her voice. "I hope they'll believe you're my prisoners."

Kiara, eyeing Rissa warily, was harassed by the notion that there was a gaping flaw in their plan. "What if it's a Nonae village?" she questioned. "How would they react to a Demmonai waltzing into their campsite with Evalseman prisoners?"

"If it's Nonae territory, we're at an even better advantage," Aiden chimed in. "Nonae have a direct link to Vyntrx, so they'll summon her. But if we've stumbled upon a Demmonai encampment, they'll inform a Nonae, who will fetch Vyntrx. And if, in the worst-case scenario, they decide to just execute us without Vyntrx's input, then, naturally, we fight."

Kiara's hand automatically flew to her neck, the cold metal of her hidden weapon biting into her fingers. Rissa eyed Kiara's instinctive action as she rummaged through the small sack attached to her belt. "I'll need to confiscate your weapons," she decided. "It would look suspicious if you still had them." She unearthed a tightly wound bundle of rope from her pouch, setting it down on the ground beside her as she held out her hands expectantly, waiting for her companions to resign their weapons. She fastened Aiden's sword to her side, strapped Ace's metal pole to her back, and slung Blade's crossbow and arrows across her shoulder. As Kiara's weapon was sheathed by the appearance of a harmless necklace, Rissa allowed her to keep it safely tucked away beneath the fabric of her blouse.

After the travelers had been stripped of their weapons, Rissa unwound the coil of rope and strung it around the wrists of her cohorts. Connected together by their restricting binds, the group became merely puppets as the captain tugged on the end of the rope, testing its reliability. Beaming at her handiwork, she continued down the path leading to the village with her friends trailing awkwardly behind her.

The thickets of the forest faded gradually, dispersing into a small clearing lined by narrow buildings. Kiara glanced around the town, discovering countless creatures flocking the streets, baring similar appearances to Rissa's monstrous disguise. Their skin was as wispy and unsettled as billowing smoke, their scarlet eyes alight with curious scrutiny. A throng of creatures was huddled around a smoldering fire pit, the flickering flames casting shadows across their apprehensive faces.

"Who are you?" a male Demmonai suddenly grumbled, approaching the group of strangers cautiously. The planes of his hideous face were crowded with rocky spikes; horns emerged directly from where his eyebrows should have been. His build was wide and stocky, towering over Rissa's tall figure.

"My name is of no importance to you," Rissa responded hotly. "I caught these trespassers and I wish to take them to the empress."

The Demmonai narrowed his eyes disbelievingly. "Why have I not seen you before?"

"I'm a rogue," she said stiffly.

He growled, a disdainful expression creasing the features of his thorny face. "You reek of Evalseman," he spat reproachfully.

Rissa's face remained heartlessly blank, lacking a single hint of emotion beneath her cold, blood red eyes. "I just fought Evalseman," she reminded him plainly. She roughly nudged Kiara in the ribs, issuing a gasp from her startled lips. Her torso involuntarily bent forward, her throat reeling for the air stolen from her lungs.

The Demmonai snatched Kiara's chin in-between his icy fingers. He abrasively steered her face upward, his red eyes burning into hers. Although his irises were consistent and did not portray emotion, she could easily discern a wealth of abhorrence and disgust swimming in the crimson depths of his glare. "Are you an Evalseman, girl?" he grumbled, the smell of his repugnant breath swarming her nostrils.

She nodded slowly, the action slightly hindered by the Demmonai's persistent grip on her chin. She felt her eyes blaze scarlet with reciprocated infuriation as she fought off the urge to duck downward and bite his fingers.

He harshly released his hold on Kiara's face, nearly thrusting her into Blade. He spat on the ground beside her feet. "Killer!" he screamed, his eyes bulging with fury. "Enemy of the forest! You deserve to die!"

"Are you any different?" she retorted menacingly.

The Demmonai's eyes flashed dangerously. An abrupt throbbing pain shot through Kiara's cheek as the monster's fist made contact with her face, forcefully sending her body backward as she slammed into Blade's chest. He steadied her footing, wrapping his fettered hands around her shoulder protectively.

"Enough!" Rissa interjected, a tinge of franticness coursing through her tone despite her attempt to mask it. "Who gave you permission to touch my prisoners?"

He scoffed in response. "I don't need permission to touch this scum."

"Oh, shove it—" Kiara began, but was hurriedly cut off as Blade nudged her side.

"Kiara, stop," he intervened, whispering into her ear. "He's *trying* to upset you."

She huffed in frustration, wiping away the line of blood trickling down her chin. "Has he been taking lessons from you?"

Blade, wearing a hurt expression, opened his mouth to reply, but was silenced as the Demmonai suddenly bellowed, "And who are you?"

He hurriedly looked up at the monster, disentangling Kiara from his arms and positioning her behind his body defensively. "Blade Crossingrose," he spoke monotonously, his sharp blue eyes sparking with caution.

"What type of creature are you?"

Blade raised his eyebrows. "That's none of your business," he responded slowly.

The Demmonai clicked his tongue, tossing his hands into the air dramatically. "I hate you foreign creatures. Be gone!"

"Where's the empress?" Rissa cut in, her hands tightening around the rope nervously. "I have to deliver these Evalseman to her. I'm not leaving until you summon her here."

"Oh, she's right here," a proverbial voice unexpectedly resonated through the clearing. Kiara swiftly twisted her head around as her eyes disastrously fell on the sight of her aunt. She was positioned several yards away—a pair of Demmonai bowed lowly by her side—with that deranged smirk pinned to her pale face.

"Vyntrx," Kiara snarled, unbridled rage pulsating through her veins. *Avian's murderer*, she thought bitterly, *the woman who must die for her reprehensible crime.*

Vyntrx's sadistic smile slid into a pleased, toothy grin. "Hello, niece," she cooed sardonically. "Where's your lover-boy? Oh," she paused for several seconds, chuckling madly, "that's right. I killed him."

Kiara's face burned scarlet with fury. Countless responses stormed her mind, but in her incensed frenzy, she could not manage to form a cohesive reply. Her words burned in the base of her throat, overwhelming her vocal chords and condemning her sulky silence.

"I suppose you're here to try and save his soul, aren't you, dear?" Vyntrx spoke presumptuously, flinging a curtain of her hair away from her gloating face.

The cloud of jumbled words bubbling in Kiara's throat abruptly burst forth from her lips as she was miraculously able to form a sentence. "Oh, so you *do* have a functioning brain."

"This won't work, niece," she said somberly, her tone strikingly misplaced as a cavalier smile slipped across her face. "I'm sure of it."

Kiara, undaunted by her aunt's callous banter, felt a wave of determination rise in the pit of her stomach. "It will work after I defeat you."

Vyntrx scoffed. "You don't have the strength required to overpower me."

"Prove it," she spoke boldly, the volume of her voice increasing as the amount of courage she managed to harness continued to multiply.

Her aunt waved her hand through the air absentmindedly, a look of sheer boredom crossing her face. The ropes grazing Kiara's wrist abruptly vanished into nothingness. The link that held her companions in tow subsequently fell away, severed from the sudden loss of Kiara's bonds.

Vyntrx tossed her head back, a vicious smirk contouring her lips. "Let's fight, niece."

Without pausing to examine her aunt's words, Kiara yanked

off her necklace, envision the weapon she wished it to become. The pendant rapidly expanded into a small, lethal knife, the crown-encrusted handle falling into her palms as she sprinted in the direction of her aunt.

Observing her niece's movement carefully, Vyntrx's form shimmered before dissolving into the backdrop of her surroundings.

While Kiara frantically searched the empty space around her, Rissa shifted back into her original form, hurriedly returning the confiscated weapons to her friends.

"Don't make a move," Kiara commanded. "I'll handle Vyntrx. If any of her *minions*—" she broke off, distrustfully eyeing the crowd of anxious Demmonai, "—take action, then fend them off."

Her comrades nodded compliantly, readying their weapons as the horde of bystander Demmonai observed the situation tensely.

"Stop hiding like a coward and fight me!" Kiara bellowed into the empty atmosphere. The noise of a twig being snapped in half sounded from behind Kiara, instantly alerting her. She spun around, intuitively lashing out her leg with the intent of miraculously making contact with her invisible aunt.

Luckily, she did—but just barely. Her calf slammed against Vyntrx's forearm, inflicting miniscule damage but effectively causing her to lose focus. Her inconsistent figure flashed in and out of invisibility, rampantly appearing and disappearing as though she had lost control over her own power. Kiara, deducing the situation to be an advantageous one, hurriedly lashed the edge of her blade toward her aunt's unguarded torso. Vyntrx expertly caught Kiara's movement, darting out of range from the intended infliction as she disbanded any attempt to stabilize her magic.

Standing firmly several yards away from her bewildered niece, Vyntrx skillfully weaved her hands through the air, summoning enough energy to dispel a torrent of flames from her palms. The fire slid past Kiara's body as she clumsily stumbled to the side, resulting in a minor burn on her forearm and the fraying of the edge of her cloak. Hindered by the sharp sensation of pain, she was unable to regain her unbalanced footing as she tumbled to the hard-packed ground. Before she was able to gather her bearings, Vyntrx blocked her path.

"If you miss Avian so badly, why don't you abandon this useless effort and join him?" she jeered, sliding a jagged dagger from the folds of her gown. She kneeled to the ground beside her niece, raising her blade high above her head, her pale hands tightly gripping the handle of her weapon with thrilled anticipation.

"Kiara!" Blade shouted. The desperation secreting from his tone suggested he had dismissed Kiara's orders to not take rash action. He suddenly appeared between Kiara and her crazed aunt, utilizing the element of surprise to successfully knock the dagger out of Vyntrx's hands. He swiftly readied his crossbow, leveling the point of an arrow directly above her black astonished eyes. He glared at Vyntrx menacingly, his voice escaping his throat in a guttural growl as he demanded to be taken to Veinya.

*****

Vyntrx led the way through a narrow path in the Dark Forest while Aiden and Ace tightly pinned her hands behind her back with extreme caution. Her ink black hair spilled into her face, covering her dull, unnatural eyes. She didn't require vision to navigate through the forest—she had lived there her entire life, played there as a child, sought solace in the carefully hidden caves as an adolescent teenager. In adulthood, she mourned the loss of her sister's death in the darkest crevices of the winding labyrinth of trees, murdered her husband beside the mouth of the grimy, gloomy black river that cut through the tightly compacted earth. The forest was her playground, her shelter, her home—and most importantly, her self-proclaimed empire. She did not want the daughter of that man she hated so terribly, the man who prematurely stole her sister away, to soil the ground rightfully owned by the Nonae with her filthy Evalseman blood—unless, of course, her blood could be wrought from her lifeless body by Vyntrx's blithe hands.

She grinned manically, her thoroughly developed plan running through her head as she counted down the minutes until they reached the fleet of warrior Demmonai waiting to overwhelm Kiara and her loyal friends. She didn't want her niece to die by the hands of the Demmonai—no, Kiara was far too strong to be struck down by a simple creature, and Vyntrx whole-heartedly wished for the time when she could personally reap the life out of her niece's undeserving Nonae eyes—but the monsters served as a sufficient distraction.

Tossing her head back, the Dark Forest spilled into view as Vyntrx's eyes were unobstructed from the veil of her tangled hair. Although paved roads and street signs were absent from the forest, Vyntrx thought of every trail as a street, each one inevitably leading to Veinya's mansion at the heart of the woods. Veinya's mansion was not easily entered by the living, however. Only Vyntrx possessed the knowledge required to open the gates leading to the estate. One other person had once managed to gain entry to Veinya's lair—and Vyntrx had exhaustedly attempted to wipe him out of existence until the whim of time returned him to her manor.

Something shimmered in Vyntrx's peripheral vision, catching her attention like a deadlock. She swung her head around, her eyes unbelievingly falling upon Avian. He was standing in the shadows of a tall tree merely a few feet away, refusing to pay even a sliver of attention to her. His eyes were locked on Kiara as she trailed behind the rest of the group in silence. Vyntrx narrowed her eyes, knowing fully well that Avian lacked the capability to leave Veinya's manor. *It's that idiot boy,* she thought bitterly. *He's not supposed to be here. I didn't give him any orders. He's already taken sides before we've even brought his pathetic soul back to life.*

Kain directed his gaze toward Vyntrx, working Avian's face into a glare. She returned his sour expression with one overflowing with contempt, staring at the boy until Aiden and Ace roughly pulled her forward, dashing her concentration as she was forced to stare blankly ahead.

*****

The chilled wind whipped Kiara's face violently as she tucked her hair away behind her cloak's hood. While the weather in Enevale had been heating up progressively, the section of the forest they had wandered into was bitterly cold— and was nearly unbearable coupled with the rigid atmosphere. Although they had successfully captured Vyntrx, Kiara could not shake the feeling that her aunt had surrendered too easily. Vyntrx was renowned for being maliciously unstoppable. Her swift submission was dangerously uncharacteristic.

Kiara's companions were so entertained by the fact that they had captured Vyntrx, they hadn't even considered the possibility that she had relinquished for a reason. But Kiara vividly recalled the sadistic gleam in her aunt's eyes as she drove her blade into Avian's exposed chest. A villainous woman like Vyntrx would not acquiesce willingly. *You know you haven't seen anything yet,* an ominous voice sang mockingly in the back of her mind.

A twig snapped in the distance, startling Kiara's mind out of its haze. She directed her attention to a small cluster of trees, where the noise had sounded, her eyes falling on Avian cowering in the shadows. He held his pointer finger over his closed lips, indicating for her to refrain from raising an alarm.

She slowed her pace, glancing at her friends. They were several yards ahead of her, talking amongst themselves so animatedly, they didn't bother turning around to make sure

Kiara's short legs had efficiently kept up with their fast pace.

Slipping silently off the trail, she waded through the thickets toward the fake Avian's location. She stopped in front of him, attempting to quell the churning of her stomach as she examined Avian's visage. "You're that boy," she whispered.

He rolled Avian's mismatched eyes, sighing. "Yeah, I'm *that boy*."

"You didn't give me your name," she retorted, "so what else am I supposed to call you?"

"Whatever," he grumbled. He folded his arms across his chest uncaringly, his upturned eyebrows and scowling mouth revealing his annoyance. "Listen up. Vyntrx is leading you into a trap."

Kiara cursed under her breath. "I knew it," she whispered, glancing at her companions as they began to descend down a knoll in the trail.

"She's leading you directly into a large group of soldier Demmonai. Just be alert. I don't know what you're capable of, but not a lot of creatures can face a small army and make it out alive."

Kiara swallowed hard, attempting to bottle down the onslaught of paralytic fear that had been roused in the back of her mind. "That's reassuring," she mumbled sarcastically. "Why do we have to rely on Vyntrx? Why can't *you* just tell me where Veinya resides?"

"It's a disability," he explained, shrugging apologetically. "I physically cannot tell you where she is. Besides, you'll have better luck convincing Veinya if you've cleared a ton of obstacles to get to her."

She sighed loudly, sweeping a curtain of hair out of her eyes. "This'll be fun," she muttered sarcastically.

A hint of a smirk shadowed the contours of the boy's lips. "Wish I could join you."

Kiara furrowed her brow, observing Avian's brother's miserable attempt at a whimsical expression. "I have yet to see you smile," she noted. "When you try, you look as though the action pains you."

The boy unlatched his eyes from their locked position on Kiara's visage, turning his entire face to toward the ground. A handful of Avian's hair tumbled into his face. "It's not my thing."

She chuckled lightly. "You really *are* the opposite of your brother."

His attention was instantly recaptured by her voice. He turned to face her, a frantic look crossing his face. "You need to go." He pointed to the trail; her friends had completely vanished from sight. "You're gonna get lost."

"I can't believe they haven't noticed I'm missing," she huffed under her breath, wading her way through the hedges toward the narrow trail. She tilted her head in the boy's direction as she reached the uneven rocky path. "I'll see you soon. Meet up with me after the battle, okay?" She could have sworn she heard him laugh, but she was certain her ears were simply playing a trick on her.

*****

"What happened to you, Kiara?" Blade wondered as she appeared at his side, breathing heavily. "Why're you out of breath?"

She took a deep breath, attempting to soothe her frantic lungs. By the time she had noticed her friend's absence, they had managed to travel several yards and she was forced to sprint in order to catch up with them. "I, uh..." she trailed off, uncertain whether or not she should inform Blade of her meetings with Avian's dead brother. She bit her lip nervously, racking her brain for a convincing lie. "I fell—I tripped over a branch and landed in the woods. I stopped to make sure I hadn't injured myself and became a little disoriented after you guys vanished from sight. I had to run to catch up with you."

Blade snickered, gingerly patting Kiara's shoulder as he shook his head. "Typical. Watch your step, will you?"

She scanned the dense forest surrounding the trail, waiting expectantly for a horde of Demmonai to burst through the foliage. "Blade," she whispered, "Vyntrx is leading us into a trap."

He shook his head in denial, strands of his silvery hair flinging into his skeptical eyes. "You're just paranoid."

"No, I'm not," she argued sternly, not bothering to fight off the hint of annoyance that had spilled into her voice.

"Yes, you are," he sneered. "We beat Vyntrx. She's cooperating or else we'll kill her. She knows that."

Kiara rolled her eyes impatiently, glowering at the back of her aunt's head as she was dragged through the forest by Aiden and Ace. "You really think Vyntrx would surrender so easily? She's been the self-proclaimed empress of the Dark Forest for years. She's slaughtered hundreds of Evalseman who have wandered into her territory. There're rumors that she's ventured beyond the forest and has battled foreign creatures. She is a master of magic. You honestly believe a woman of that caliber would allow herself to be foolishly captured by a group of young Evalseman if she didn't have something planned?" A wave of unfettered irritation swept through her words, her eyes shifting inconsistently between frustrated black and infuriated crimson.

Blade was silent for several minutes. Faintly, a sharp cry sounded in the distance. "Why didn't you say something sooner?" he asked quietly, his icy eyes wide and speculative.

"I suspected, but I wasn't certain," she explained. "Now I am."

"What *exactly* convinced you?"

She released a sigh, hesitantly deciding to enlighten Blade about the situation with Avian's brother, hoping the information would quell his disbelief. "Avian's brother told me," she said slowly. "He's been showing himself to me in dreams. He was sent to me by Avian."

"Avian's brother?" he repeated incredulously. "The one who died several years ago? Why is he speaking to you? His soul should have been reincarnated over a decade ago."

"He became Veinya's servant," she explained quickly. "Avian wants me to save his brother's soul, as well. He warned me about Vyntrx's plans to ambush us. Since he's close to Veinya, I trust his word."

Blade raised his eyebrows dubiously. "You're going to just mindlessly trust a ghost? You know they can't take their true forms outside of dreams, so they are able to appear as anyone they please, right? I'm sure this spirit has his own agenda. You're so naï—" His voice was immediately silenced as a slick dagger abruptly dashed out of the trees, skimming the edge of his shoulder and issuing a small cry of startled pain to escape his lips.

Kiara instantly turned toward the woods in one fluid motion, yanking her necklace from its position on her chest as she willed its form to shift into a knife. Throngs of Demmonai were shoving their way through the thickets, weapon-clad and battle ready. Their faces were twisted into demonic snarls, guttural growls escaping their gaping mouths.

Kiara glanced at her friends nervously, watching Vyntrx's body heave as she was overwhelmed by bouts of joyous laughter. Aiden and Ace, warily eyeing the approaching army, attempted to tighten their grip around the empress's wrists. She suddenly thrust her arms backward, knocking the dukes directly into the jagged bark of nearby tree trunks as though she had summoned a force of unmatchable power that had previously been bottled down.

Blade and Rissa hurriedly readied their weapons, standing back-to-back as their eyes nervously scanned the oncoming waves of Demmonai soldiers. Blade flicked the point of an arrow from his crossbow in Vyntrx's direction, but instead of shrinking in fear as she once had, she merely chuckled at

Blade's fruitless attempt to intimidate her.

The empress's unnatural black eyes lit up with pleasure as a wicked smirk slid across her pallid face. "You know I hate being rude, dear, but I'm in a bit of a rush—I don't want to be late for my meeting with Veinya. Don't worry, though, as you can tell, I've arranged a parting gift."

"Stay and fight, you coward!" Kiara screeched in response as a line of Demmonai trickled onto the trail. Aiden and Ace hurriedly recovered their strength, standing to attention with their weapons drawn. Ace's body had seemingly shifted—his nails had expanded into deadly claws, his eyes wild and bright, his body slightly hunched and noticeably more muscular. Kiara recalled that Avian had labeled Ace as a creature known as a Kyraix—a mysterious, rare creature harboring incredible capabilities—and wondered if Ace's strange change in appearance was simply one of the Kyraix's uncharted attributes. Her thoughts were shattered as a crowd of Demmonai blocked her view of Ace, sharply calling her back to reality.

An armor-clad Demmonai obstructed her vision, bearing its pointed teeth as it heaved a spiked weapon through the air toward Kiara's head. She ducked at the last possible second, her heart pounding as she lashed her knife across the monster's body as though the action were second nature. As she remembered Avian scolding her several months ago for working herself into immobility as she was overwhelmed with the anxiety of battle, she found herself satisfied with her noteworthy progress. The sensation of accomplishment tickled her pride, but as she eyed the dying monster on the floor, its body squirming as life fled from its scared eyes, she was harassed by the notion of murder. She had very little experience killing, and the action of stealing of a life was foreign, disturbing. Although her psyche was racked by a storm of guilt, she blatantly understood that she must continue the battle.

She tightly clamped the hilt of her knife, expertly swiping the blade across the creature's neck and demolishing its life with a flick of her wrist. Blood sprayed upward, staining her fingers red. She stared in horror at her hands momentarily before her aunt's sadistic voice startled her out of her reverie.

"See you in your second life, niece!" Vyntrx mocked sardonically, a shrill laugh accompanying her conclusive declaration.

The fringe of Kiara's hair tumbled into her eyes as she glared at her aunt, watching her bitterly as she vanished into the heavy atmosphere. "Coward!" she screamed hopelessly. Her knife shifted to a bow in her palm, the thin metal grip of the weapon oddly comforting. She swung the bow in a semi-circle, aiming at an approaching Demmonai as she expertly pulled back the string. Yanking her fingers away from the string and toward her face, she willed a pointed arrow to materialize from the weapon and arch through the air. The arrow dashed in a blur of silver directly into the Demmonai's chest, nestling perfectly into a small exposed area between two sheets of armor. Content and momentarily undaunted by her kill, Kiara scanned the battlefield, searching eagerly for her friends.

Rissa was altering forms rampantly—she was a raging, towering monster, wiping out hordes of Demmonai with strikes of her mace. She shifted into a fire-breathing creature burning the Demmonai to ashy crisps, a poisonous serpent biting her victims and strangling their necks with her scaly body. Then she became a winged animal, swooping down upon the Demmonai's heads and clawing out their eyes with her dangerously sharp talons.

Viewing Rissa's vivacious determination in combat, Kiara was regrettably able to understand why her abilities had unwittingly made her such a valuable soldier and irreplaceable captain—she could easily transform into a myriad of vicious creatures and readily steal the identity of whomever she pleased. She was a lethal warrior and an undeniable asset to the kingdom.

Kiara's observation was abruptly concluded as a large Demmonai dominated her sight. Her bow shifted into a sleek knife better suited for close-range attacks just in time for her to plunge the newly transformed blade into the monster's heart. Blood frothed from the creature's chest, but the crimson fluid was unable to stain the silvery metal of the knife. Suspecting an additional magical attribute of the weapon, Kiara reared the knife backward, withdrawing its blade from the Demmonai's writhing body.

As she spun around, readying herself for another assault, her eyes fell upon Blade—only a few yards away—as he crystallized arrows from his crossbow, shooting the deadly projectiles at his opponents. Aiden dashed past Blade, encircling his foes in flames as he danced across the battlefield, setting the Demmonai ablaze as they screamed. Ace, flickering in and out of sight as the crowds of Demmonai thinned, clawed and stabbed the Demmonai with his sharp nails, ripping their shadowy flesh from silvery bones with his dagger-like fangs.

An arrow whizzed past Kiara's cheek as a blur of blackness, the sharp blade grazing the flesh directly below her widened eye. She diverted her attention from her friends, her left hand instantly flying to her cheek as she wiped away the stream of blood spilling down her face.

A raging flood of Demmonai suddenly charged Kiara as though they had broken through some invisible barrier. As she eyed the snarling pack, a wave of annoyance spiked in her veins as her mind was overwhelmed by the sudden, hungry desire to halt the battle. The dagger shifted in her outstretched hand, the form shimmering until it began to possess the figure of a bow. Her fingers gripped the string, pulling it back tightly as she leveled her aim with an approaching Demmonai's head. A solemn twanging sound resonated across the battlefield as the materialized arrow hurled itself from the shaft, puncturing the skin in-between the eyes of the Demmonai. The monster's weapon fell from its hands, snapping under pressure as its owner's lifeless body slumped downward, disappearing beneath the marching feet of the unshaken army of nearing Demmonai.

Kiara fired off arrows aimlessly into the masses, gleefully realizing that the bow would never be burdened by an empty quiver. During training sessions in the village, Kiara had constantly worried about her continually depleting stock of arrows and the disadvantage it would cause in a real battle. She was immensely grateful for her magical bow and its unlimited supply of arrows—was grateful for the significant upper-hand the amenity provided.

One by one, as time ticked slowly by, the pack of Demmonai began to thin until a mere handful of creatures reached Kiara's side. The weapon changed before she had fully completed the command, her favorite knife emerging from the shrinking silver bow and readily claiming the lives of Demmonai as she spun the blade in a wide arc.

Minutes of intense, concentrated battle occupied Kiara's movements until a heap of fallen Demmonai littered the forest floor. Victory rang through her bones as she proudly waltzed across the battlefield, the flat heels of her boots sticking to the bloodied ground. Only a diminutive gathering remained of the once monstrous army and the residual soldiers were occupied by Kiara's companions' carefully implemented fighting skills.

As Kiara's attention was captivated by the ongoing battle, she failed to notice a Demmonai slinking toward her until it had rammed it sword straight through her back. A sharp, terrible pain tore through her torso, sending an involuntary scream gasping from her lips. Her knife cascaded from her hands, clanging against the ground as it immediately shifted back into a defenseless necklace.

Time ticked slowly to a standstill as Kiara's eyes flickered downward, drinking in the uncanny sight of a crimson-stained blade emerging from a gaping hole in her shirt, her flesh tarnished and damp with blood. The weapon had narrowly missed her spine, ripping through her torso and skimming the edge of her left ribcage. Hot pain shot through her veins, every inch of her body becoming unresponsive. She willed her neck to swivel around, to discover her attacker, but she was barely able to move. Out of the corner of her eye, a smirking Demmonai was visible, its red eyes alight with pleasure.

The monster abruptly withdrew its sword from Kiara's body with one sharp heave. She emitted a second scream—louder and strikingly more helpless than the first—as her body crumpled to the ground. She fell to her knees, her arms wrapping protectively around her bleeding wound. The raging sound of the battle faded in and out of Kiara's ears as she slipped into despondency, her friends' screams reaching her in restless waves.

Her limp hand scrambled across the battle-scarred ground, searching for her discarded weapon. Her fingers brushed against something solid, something cold. Her eyes fluttered downward, discovering a crown pendant in a puddle of blood— her knife had reverted to its necklace form, its powers failing without her touch to stabilize it. Her fingers gripping the cold chain, she pulled the item close to her chest, whispering a single word into the metal. A sword suddenly elongated from the pendant, the blade lashing forward and skewering the Demmonai looming in front of Kiara. She twisted her wrist forward, slashing the blade upward through the Demmonai's scaly throat. Releasing one last bloodcurdling scream, the creature toppled—in two, disembodied pieces—to the ground.

Hindered by racking tremors of pain, Kiara's body dispelled the capability to stay alert. She collapsed, bloodied and exhausted, a layer of dust and blood coating her cheeks as fell against the forest ground.

Blade immediately abandoned his participation in the battle, sending an arrow directly into the center of a

Demmonai's head as he sprinted toward Kiara's limp figure. Rissa, Aiden, and Ace—sending solemn glances in Kiara's direction—continued to viciously pillage the Demmonai's bodies of life, distracting the thinning onslaught as Blade managed to reach his fallen comrade.

Blade's hands frantically found Kiara's shoulders, lightly rolling her onto her injured back as he rested the nape of her neck against his folded legs. He pushed up the edge of her blouse, examining her wound, his fingers gently tracing her fractured skin. He grimaced, eyeing the gaping hole in her torso.

"H-hi, Blade," she stammered, her voice strained. "I-I was ca-careless..."

Blade stared at Kiara's wound, his face scrunched up in saddened anxiety. His response to her injury was noticeably uncharacteristic, and if torrents of pain hadn't been surging through her body, she would have made fun of him.

"She's badly injured," Rissa's voice abruptly sounded as she appeared behind Blade. She had apparently abandoned her post in the battle, which suggested the horde of Demmonai had been nearly diminished and simply required Aiden and Ace's conclusive efforts. She knelt on the ground beside the pair, wincing as she evaluated Kiara's wound. "The laceration tears completely through her torso," she said weakly, frowning. "It must have hit at least one organ."

Blade nodded slowly. "It's a miracle it missed her spinal cord."

"Just about an inch off," Rissa commented matter-of-factly. "She's lucky."

Kiara wiggled her legs, attempting to determine how paralytic her body had become. Blade's hands immediately clutched her shoulders, and although his grip was tight and steadfast, there was a sense of gentleness and caring beneath his touch. "Don't move," he commanded. "You'll only hurt yourself more."

Unable to form an argumentative response, she nodded slightly in compliance. Aiden and Ace materialized at her side as her eyes flickered to their crestfallen faces, her dry lips moving as she started to ask if they had finished the battle.

"We just killed the last Demmonai," Aiden hurriedly explained before she had fully posed her question. "Hopefully another wave of soldiers won't show up."

"D-doesn't ma-matter," she spluttered, her voice eerily frail. "Vy-Vyntrx escaped. We—we have to—go after h-her." It had become increasingly difficult for her to summon enough energy to speak. Her entire body was malfunctioning—beads of sweat poured down her forehead, her flesh turned numb as her nerves became unresponsive and her heart pulsated spasmodically. As her mind was overwhelmed by haziness, she began to wonder if she would *ever* escape the Dark Forest...

"We'll find her," Rissa said reassuringly, gently patting Kiara's shoulder. Her emerald eyes, brimming with helpless desperation, flickered upward as she stared at the boys. "Does anyone know how to heal her?"

"There's a plant that can heal her," a flat voice unexpectedly sounded from an unknown speaker.

The dukes and Rissa simultaneously twisted their necks around, sucking in their breath as their eyes absorbed the sight of Avian. Kiara's view of the battlefield no longer obstructed by the heads of her friends, she was able to discern—through the foggy film of her fading vision—Avian's form lurking beside a tree.

Rissa instantly sprang to the balls of her feet as she was overwhelmingly engulfed by the sensation of disbelief. "AVIAN?" she shrieked.

While Kiara immediately understood that the man she was staring at was actually the mysterious boy parading in Avian's form, she lacked the desire to spend her diminishing energy clarifying a situation Avian's brother could easily explain.

The fake Avian ambled toward the group of comrades, his

eyes dull and lifeless, a somber expression contouring his borrowed features. "No, I'm his brother. I can't take my own form outside of dreams."

"Why?" Blade questioned, his voice quavering. His silvery eyebrows narrowed as he glanced at Kiara wearily, visualizing the argument they had shared over Avian's brother and the Demmonai ambush. He couldn't stop himself from feeling guilty for Kiara's wound.

Avian's figure held out his hand, swiping it through the trunk of a tree as he neared the small gathering. His hand vanished inside the tree, as it if had been swallowed by the bark, and then slowly re-appeared as it materialized in front of the trunk. "I'm dead."

Silence encompassed the atmosphere, conveying the flabbergasted emotion swirling through the companions' minds. The boy sauntered past Rissa, her pale face too tightly embossed in bemusement to bother following his movement. He stopped directly in front of Kiara, the edge of Avian's boots lightly brushing against her trembling forearm. He stared down at her mangled body, a sliver of a scowl crossing his face.

"You're careless," he observed emotionlessly.

She smiled weakly at him, a line of sweat dripping down her temple. "T-tell me your n-name before I-I die?"

He sneered, folding his arms across his unmoving chest. "Since you're not going to, I won't."

"Wh-what's it l-like?" she whispered hoarsely. "D-dying, I mean."

"Some other time, princess," he muttered, shrugging dismissively. "You'll have to die another day."

"Y-you're going to save me?" she wondered, the dawn of a smile playing on her paling lips. "That's sweet."

He huffed in annoyance. "Don't take it personally," he said icily, striding toward an overgrown thicket winding its way over the roots of trees. He glanced down, extending his pointer finger toward a dull plant with an unusually thick stem. Light pink leaves blossomed from its vines, flecked by swooping leaves and dew-coated thorns. "See this plant? Its existence is one of the reasons the Nonae made this forest their home. It's known to cure nearly anything. It's completely common here, but they've hidden it from the Evalseman for ages."

Blade's cerulean eyes lit up with expectancy. "It will heal her?"

Avian's brother nodded impatiently. "Press one leaf from the plant over the wound on her stomach and one on her back," he directed. "It'll save her."

"Rissa," Blade spoke slowly, his voice filled with urgency as he glanced at Kiara's pallid face resting on his lap. He pointed toward the plant. "Bring that here."

Rissa nodded, forcing herself out of her startled reverie. "A-alright," she stammered, glancing over her shoulder at her companions as she hurried over to the plant. She gently tore off a stem of the herb, carefully avoiding contact with the sharp-edged thorns.

"I'm leaving now," the boy declared monotonously, watching Rissa as she quickly treaded toward her companions, clutching the pruned herb. "Try not to kill yourself, princess." He suddenly vanished from sight, as though the faint light of the forest had wrapped itself around his body and completely engulfed his figure.

Rissa and the dukes stared disbelievingly at the spot the fake Avian had vanished from, still unable to wrap their minds around the concept of Avian's dead brother unexpectedly appearing in the forest and rescuing Kiara's life from the cold hands of death.

"That was..." Ace trailed off, his golden eyes alight with wonder, "far too weird."

Rissa knelt beside Kiara, biting her lip as she laid down the uprooted plant. She industriously began robbing the herb of its leaves, flinching every time her finger poked the edge of a thorn.

"H-he's visited me before," Kiara whispered, turning her face toward the captain.

"Shh, don't try to talk," Rissa cooed, her voice unnaturally gentle. She shoved the hem of Kiara's blouse upward as far as she could without inciting embarrassment from exposure, rubbing a sheared leaf against the laceration.

Kiara grimaced, a sharp convulsion shooting through her torso as the plant's healing balm began to seep through her skin. Her hand tightened around the pendant of her necklace, her body writhing fitfully.

Blade watched Rissa calmly tend to Kiara's wounds, his hands gripping Kiara's shoulders as he steadied her quivering frame. "I guess I should have listened to you earlier, huh?" he whispered, attempting to mask his guilt with a twinge of nonchalant sarcasm.

Kiara's jaw clenching in torment, she was unable to respond to Blade's clumsy apology.

"Why didn't Vyntrx just tell the Demmonai to attack us in the village?" Aiden wondered, furrowing his brow. His hand gently caressed Kiara's shoulder.

Rissa's fingers lightly pressed the leaf on Kiara's stomach. "Probably to throw us off guard," she suggested.

Blade scoffed. "That wouldn't have worked, anyway. We fought off those weak Demmonai without any trouble. No one even got injured—" his voice stopped abruptly, his gaze falling on Kiara's gaping wound, "—'cept you, Kiara, but that's typical because you're such an unobservant klutz."

If not for the throbbing of her wound, she would have worked her mouth into a scowl and formed a curt response— but as rivets of pain racked her limbs, she was forced into uncomfortable silence.

"Look!" Rissa exclaimed, quickly removing the herb from Kiara's stomach. She used the edge of her cloak to soak up the small puddle of blood that had doused Kiara's torso, revealing unblemished skin. The dukes gasped in unison, staring disbelievingly at their companion's miraculously healed wound. The laceration had vanished entirely, and if it hadn't been for the intense pain enveloping Kiara's back, she would have believed the injury to be completely healed.

As if she had read Kiara's thoughts, Rissa gently removed Kiara's head from Blade's lap, rolling her weight onto her stomach. She lightly withdrew Kiara's pendant from her clenched hand, fastening the chain around her neck. Hurriedly repeating the procedure she had performed on Kiara's first wound, Rissa laid a second leaf against the deep gash in her back, frowning as her patient's body began to squirm.

"I wonder if it will heal any broken organs," Ace wondered.

"It should," Rissa responded thoughtfully. "I don't think Avian's brother would have shown us the plant if it didn't."

Kiara stared at the ground, tears spilling down her cheeks as the pain slowly subdued. Her vision was progressively healed of its grainy film; noise no longer reached her ears in diluted waves. Medicine from the herb passed through her body, repairing her broken skin and mending her tarnished muscles. After unending minutes of raw, unwavering anguish, Kiara's body turned numb. The pain coursing through her veins relinquished to the medication provided by the leaf. Her back tingled as Rissa gently brushed her fingers over the newly reformed skin.

"You're all healed," the captain announced, her arms winding around Kiara's shoulders as she helped her fallen comrade regain her footing.

"How do you feel?" Blade questioned. He and the dukes climbed to their feet, their faces bearing accidental expressions of anxious curiosity.

Kiara shrugged, faint tremors of pain radiating from her mended torso. Despite the residual aching, her entire form felt immensely rejuvenated. "I feel fine," she admitted, her voice finally unhindered by quivering lips. "We have to find Vyntrx, and—" her voice trailed off as her eyes flitted around the unfamiliar nook of the forest her aunt had deviously led them to. "Where are we?"

Rissa shrugged. "I haven't seen this part of the forest."

"Neither have we," Blade added. "I'm sure she intentionally led us to an unfamiliar location."

"Why don't you ask Avian's brother for help?" Ace suggested.

Kiara sighed, tucking a loose strand of her disheveled hair behind her ear. Dirt streaked her cheeks, mixing with flecks of blood and lines of tears. "I can't summon him or anything like that. He just appears," she explained, shrugging. "How are we doing in terms of time?"

"I'd say it's around late afternoon," Blade said informingly, eyeing the foliage-shrouded sky. "We still have about two days."

Rissa glanced at Kiara expectantly, her dark eyebrows furrowed. "What should we do? Try to find Vitaciel? Nonae claim most trails lead there."

During Kiara's studies she had learned about Vyntrx's primary citadel—Vitaciel. Being the largest Nonae fortress in the Dark Forest, Vitaciel progressively became recognized as both the capital of the forest and Vyntrx's self-proclaimed kingdom.

Blade immediately shook his head. "No, that would be far too dangerous. Rogue Demmonai wouldn't dare trek into that city—it's nothing like the encampments. And if Evalseman prisoners were brought into Vitaciel, they would be hanged immediately, no questions asked. It would be suicide."

Kiara nodded, comprehending Blade's concerns. Her eyes flashed a cool, collected brown. "Let's just walk until we come across another village. We're bound to find one eventually. Vyntrx will be alerted of our arrival."

Blade nodded in compliance, shouldering his crossbow. "To the nearest village, then."

hapter Fourteen

Distrust

Kain hovered over a crystalline orb, watching a scene unfurl from the depths of the swirling contents. Kiara's face poured into view as she spoke with her friends—she was no longer thrashing in pain as her body had been purged of its traumatic injury. "So it worked, then?" he mumbled, allowing a small twinge of relief to flood his chest.

"Why did you save her?" Veinya's pensive voice echoed through the room.

Kain immediately turned away from the orb, his eyes falling on the death goddess as she strode across the shadowy floor. "What?"

"You could have let her die," she said darkly, sliding her fingers across the smooth edge of the glass ball. Kiara's image faded from the backdrop, replaced by grey clouds. "If the princess were to perish, Avian would have failed his contract with her father, resulting in the immediate termination of his soul. That's why Vyntrx can't kill the child until she's crowned queen. You knew this. You could have let her die and then you would have received your revenge. Your brother would have been gone forever."

Kain shrugged. "Revenge isn't what I'm looking for. I just want Avian to suffer. Damning him to nothingness doesn't exactly sound painful, does it? If I keep the princess alive, I gain something. I get my life back. And then Avian is free to continue his tangled existence until it inevitably kills him."

A sharp crack resonated through the manor as Vyntrx and Avian materialized beside the goddess. Kain stepped away from the orb, casting his gaze at the floor in an attempt to avoid eye contact with his brother.

"Why did you summon me?" Avian implored, staring at Vyntrx with his sharp mismatched eyes.

"Watch your tone," she chided, tapping the base of the orb with her pointer finger. Kiara's face swarmed the contents once more, her expression locked in a state of determination. "The girl and her friends survived the ambush, so I'm planning another one. She suspected the last, so I'll really catch her off guard this time."

Avian scoffed. "Why are you even bothering? She's just going to keep winning. You're just wasting time and soldiers."

Vyntrx rolled her eyes, shouldering Avian's compliant. "This is supposed to be a realistic adventure for her. She can't suspect that I'm pulling the strings. I cannot simply turn myself over to her, she has to beat me—which she never could, so I will be forced to acquiesce in order to uphold the plan. Besides, I can use this as an opportunity to raze her morale. Perhaps I'll even murder one of her friends."

The empress's words echoed through Avian's head as a harrowing sensation swept through his chest. Despite his long-term allegiance with Vyntrx, he harbored genuine affection for the dukes. Having been raised together, he had considered them his own flesh and blood—his proverbial brothers—and if harm had been thrust upon them by his misguided actions, it would irreversibly devastate him. Jarring fear scripted his thundering heartbeat, worked his voice into silence.

Vyntrx, eyeing her rattled companion, tapped the orb, dissolving Kiara's smoky figure from the surface. "I need to make arrangements with Miriam. I may not be back for several hours—he's oddly protective of those Demmonai soldiers and won't take news of another scuffle lightly. When I return, Veinya, we'll discuss Kiara's arrival." Without waiting for a reaction, the shadows of the manor engulfed her form, leaving the Knight brothers alone with the company of the goddess.

"I'm departing, as well," Veinya said dully. "I have a heap of

Demmonai souls to evaluate. Try not to kill each other while I'm gone—oh, wait, you're both already dead." A sadistic snicker crept across her face as she turned away from the orb.

Kain watched the goddess depart the room as she was absorbed by darkness. Being a servant of Veinya for over half his life, Kain had grown accustomed to the goddess's multiple personalities, yet the gleam of malevolence in her eyes after being influenced by Vyntrx's presence never ceased to disturb him.

"Brother," Avian whispered, warily eyeing the sweeping shadows of the mansion as though he expected a monstrous creature to emerge from the darkness and rip out his heart. "I need you to help me."

"*Help* you?" Kain spat the sentence as though the words prickled his tongue. "Why would I do that?"

Avian's eyes latched on his brother's contemptuous expression. "Because," he said slowly, his voice brimming with desperation, "you're the only one who can."

"What are you talking about?"

"Vyntrx wants to kill my friends," he lamented. "If you could warn Kiara, they would be alert and not as careless. *Please* help me, Kain."

Kain scoffed. He stared straight into his brother's eyes—despite the uneasy feeling that swarmed his chest as he observed Avian's uncharacteristically somber face—working his lips into a scowl. "Did you ask anyone to save *my* life? Did you worry as you saw Vyntrx murder me? Of course you didn't. You never cared. You still don't. You have a real brother, yet you consider *them* more family than your own blood. You're despicable." Avian opened his mouth to respond, his eyes widening in guilt, but Kain hurriedly continued speaking, startling his brother into silence. "How dare you ask *me* for help?"

"Kain—" Avian started, his voice choking off as he was overwhelmed by a wave of hysteria.

Kain glowered at his brother as he flicked the glass of the orb. Kiara's face poured into view once again, her pallid cheeks flushed with exhaustion as she foraged the forest for Vyntrx. "This is who you'll have to ask for forgiveness—for help. Not me. If one of your friends die, it's your own damn fault. You'll have to answer to her for your crimes. Not immediately, but eventually she'll learn the truth. And then no one can help you but her. Just leave me out of this stupid mess you've worked yourself into and don't *ever* think you deserve *any* help from me." Concluding his heated speech, Kain hurriedly departed the area, disappearing into the spirit-infested shadows, leaving Avian staring at the orb encompassed by Kiara's pensive face.

As Kain's legs swiftly paced through the mansion, his mind was harassed by Avian's desperate pleading. If his brother had appeared nearly hysterical at the mere notion of his friends' deaths, he couldn't fathom the scope of Kiara's reaction to a slaughtered comrade. There was something about the sharp sapphire of her saddened eyes that had punctured his unmoving heart. He had known it since watching her eyes shift blue as she stared longingly at Avian's ghostly form—he would willingly do anything to prevent that desolate emotion from ever invading her eyes again.

He rashly decided he would warn her about Vyntrx's planned assault, but not because he wanted to appease Avian— no, he determined he must prevent the death of the dukes due to the influence of those wide, innocent eyes that had somehow—grudgingly—left an irreversible imprint on the folds of his mind.

*****

Unearthing a village in the midst of the Dark Forest surprisingly resulted to be a troublesome endeavor. Kiara, alongside her companions, wandered through the densely canopied woods for nearly half the day, their deprived stomachs rumbling as their exhausted legs wobbled with the prospect of buckling. She could not shake the sensation of being watched; chills of apprehension clung to her skin as she shouldered her friends' weary complaints. She walked steadily, staring pointedly ahead as though the revels of the hopeful future hung against the horizon.

"We need to stop and rest," Rissa pleaded, eyeing a diminutive patch of darkening sky visible through the compressive leaves.

"We haven't found a village yet," Kiara countered, ignoring the sharp pains of hunger shooting through her stomach.

"The Nonae could be using spells to shroud their villages from other creatures," Aiden suggested, scanning the cluster of trees for even the slimmest sign of life.

Kiara scowled, her hand clamping around her pendant as though the action diluted her aggravation. "*I* would be able to see it. I'm half-Nonae."

"Or maybe your Evalseman blood would prevent it," Rissa interposed thoughtfully.

Ace's hand fell on her shoulder tentatively. "Regardless, we're exhausted, Kiara," he slowly whispered.

"And starving," Blade added. He stomach growled loudly as if on cue, validating his claim.

Kiara shouldered Ace's hand, quickening her pace. "Rissa brought food. Walk and eat," she said hotly. She was ashamed of her unnecessary harshness, but she couldn't bottle the feeling of frustration her friends had incited.

"Maybe Avian's brother will contact you while you're sleeping," Rissa suggested, a convincing tone underlining her words. "He could tell you where to find Vyntrx."

Kiara's face fell into a pout, her hands crossing her chest as her feet slowed to a stop. The captain had been convincing, but a small voice in the back of her mind kept nagging at her to continue walking. "Fine," she decided tersely. "Let's stop."

*****

Aiden hurriedly gathered a pile of firewood, alighting the branches in the center of the small clearing they had designated for a campsite. While Aiden was nursing the flames, Rissa withdrew a chunk of meat and a loaf of bread from her pouch—the iconic meal of their journey—rationing the portions among the companions.

Kiara held her slab of meat over the fire. She eyed the flickering flames as she hovered over the smothered tree limbs, her body tickling with warmth. Her companions ravenously consumed their small meals, sprawled out around the blazing pit, their voices filling the silence of the forest as they conversed.

Satisfied with the temperature of her meat, Kiara crouched on the ground beside Ace, folding her legs under her. She didn't bother interjecting into the conversation. She sat in silence as she quickly consumed the chunk of meat, her mind reeling with the events of their escapade. She positioned the small loaf of bread against her lips, unable to summon enough energy to chew through the roll. Her stomach was growling relentlessly, but her lips would not part.

She could vaguely hear the rumble of her friend's voices, but her mind refused to interpret a single word. Her thoughts gravitated to Avian and his mysterious brother. She could distantly recall the first day she had met Avian—the day that seemed so strikingly long ago—when they had been sitting in the snow discussing his bloodstained past.

"It's common knowledge that my parents were brutally murdered when I was a child, but there are two additional points to the story that I have kept hidden from prying minds," Avian had solemnly explained. *"First, I had a younger half-brother who was also killed on that dreadful day. Second, my family was massacred by Vyntrx herself."*

Avian had admitted that Vyntrx had slaughtered his family,

but he hadn't elaborated on the situation. Kiara assumed her aunt would not murder without a motive, despite her malicious nature, as she appeared to be a woman of calculated intent. Curiosity prickled her nerves as a bout of cold wind rustled through the forest. *What could have happened?* she wondered, attempting to fathom a scenario in which Vyntrx would be prompted to kill and how Avian had managed to avoid suffering the same fate. This notion had never troubled her before, but after being introduced to Avian's bitterly deceased brother, she couldn't slow her mind's unyielding questioning.

"I'm not who you think I am at all," the words the fake Avian had ominously spoke echoed through her head. *"You think you know me, but you haven't even met the real me. I have dark secrets. You've only scratched the surface of my personality—the man cowering behind my facade is really just a monster."* His brother had acted as though Avian was hiding a part of his identity—a dark, carefully curtained portion of his life. She refused to naively believe his brother's insinuated accusations, as it was blatantly obvious that he despised Avian and would naturally possess a skewered conception of him—but she couldn't swallow the insatiable thirst for detailed knowledge of Avian's past.

"Kiara?" Aiden's voice reached her ears in a sudden rush of noise. She was immediately drawn from her mind-consuming thoughts, blinking hard in an attempt to clear her head of distracting contemplations.

The discussion that had recently occupied the companions' attention had apparently been concluded. They stared at Kiara expectantly, clutching the remnants of their half-eaten dinners. She deduced that someone had addressed her and she had failed to respond appropriately.

"What?" she stammered, her uneaten bread nearly toppling from her hands.

Aiden narrowed his thin, pale eyebrows. "I just asked you a question."

"Oh, did you?" she mumbled uncomfortably. "Would you repeat it?"

"What's Avian's brother's name?" he asked impatiently.

She shrugged, awkwardly averting her gaze. Her friends' glares were oppressive as they scrutinized her fallen face. "Why?" she countered. "Don't you all know about him? I thought Avian would have told you."

"He did," Blade affirmed. "We met his brother a few times, but we were all young. He's been dead for over a decade. We can't remember his name."

She sighed loudly, wrapping her fingers around the loaf of bread as she pulled her legs tightly against her chest. "I don't know his name," she admitted. "He won't tell me."

Rissa's emerald eyes were hard. She looked utterly offended; her face bore a strikingly opposite emotion than the one of empathy she had embraced on Kiara's supposed deathbed. A rigid atmosphere had leaked into the campsite, urging a spasm of chills to rattle Kiara's bones.

"Oh, *really*?" Rissa exclaimed disbelievingly. "Why?"

"I don't know."

"Maybe because he's not *really* Avian's brother?" Blade offered, his tone not nearly as condescending as Rissa's had been. He appeared merely conversational, as though he were offering a logical explanation.

Kiara's brow lowered. "He is," she said firmly. "Avian was with him in my dreams. Spirits can appear in dreams until Veinya decides what to do with them—don't you know that? Avian's brother took me to Avian, who plainly asked me to bring his brother back to life."

"Maybe this boy just created an illusion of Avian to trick you into bringing him back to life," Aiden offered, his face scrunched up in contemplation.

Kiara shook her head defiantly. "I *know* it was Avian. I would know if he were fake. Avian's brother—" she abruptly stopped herself from telling her friends about her first encounter with the mysterious boy. She didn't believe informing them about how he had impersonated Avian in an attempt to disgruntle her would convince them of his sincerity. "I'm not being deceived."

The companions unwaveringly stared at her with unconvinced expressions, but a suppressive silence was settling over them. The only sound was the wind whistling lowly, rattling the thin leaves of the trees. Although not a single person had emitted even a whisper, Kiara could hear the single word *naïve* shrieking through the whirling air as though the insult had been stolen from her friends' unmoving lips and released into the atmosphere.

Kiara glanced at her hands, stuffing the chunk of bread into her mouth. She lay down beside the fire, turned her back to the group of companions, and wrapped her cloak around her body as she swallowed the food in one gulp. Her friends began conversing in low whispers, but she didn't bother trying to listen. She closed her eyes, falling headfirst into her oppressive dreams.

hapter Fifteen

A Streak of Light in the Shadows

Kiara's dream was ubiquitously blank. Not a single image welled beneath her eyelids; she was entirely encompassed in darkness. While the dream was lacking the typical vividly horrific scenes her sleeping mind had grown accustomed to, the atmosphere possessed a definite echoing noise that gradually sounded through the silence until a distinct voice broke through the calm.

"I can't show myself right now," Avian's brother's voice reverberated through the shadows. "I have some news, though, so listen up. You're very close to Veinya's manor. Vyntrx is gathering an even bigger army of Demmonai to halt you. She was trying to use the element of surprise, but I'm warning you so you won't be caught off-guard. You can easily fight her fleet, but don't be careless. Don't get another sword through your stomach. Challenge Vyntrx immediately and leave the soldiers to your friends. Make a deal with her: if you win, she calls off her army and leads you to Veinya, but if she wins, she can take you prisoner.

"You can win. Attack her physically before she can use magic. It'll throw her off. If she manages to teleport or turn invisible, your gut feeling *should* tell you where she is. She's your aunt, so there's a blood connection that even she can't sever. After you've defeated her, she'll lead you to Veinya so long as you keep her from using magic. If you see her trying to use a spell, hurt her. She can't handle physical pain—it's her weakness. Remember that.

"If the battle goes the wrong way, and you lose, then I can't help you. It's all up to you, Kiara. Wake up, she's almost there."

The sound of the boy's voice was shattered as Kiara's mind was abruptly propelled out of the prophetic planes of her dreams. She jolted into consciousness, the landscape of the forest pouring into view in a muddled wave of shadows.

Her companions were still locked in slumber, the fire they encircled reduced to forlorn ashes. She hurriedly darted between each of her friends, shaking their shoulders until she managed to summon them back to reality. She instantly launched into a description of her latest dream, advising they ready their weapons in anticipation of the approaching battle.

"Avian's brother *is* helping us," she insisted, unlatching her necklace and commanding it to transform into a knife.

Rissa sighed, her emerald eyes surrounded by heavy shadows. "I don't know. If he's right, that means Vyntrx is nearby."

Kiara's mouth unhinged, a reply bubbling in her throat, but her voice was immediately silenced as an arrow narrowly slid past her head. The tip of the arrow burrowed into the bark of a tree, merely a few inches shy of Rissa's forearm.

Her heart pounding apprehensively, Kiara slowly turned her body around to face her aunt. Vyntrx was standing several yards away, a sadistic smile creeping across her features. She stood at the edge of the clearing, flanked by rows of soldier Demmonai snaking their way through the trees, wielding menacing weapons.

"Ready to play, princess?" Vyntrx's voice escaped her lips in a devious hiss, her black eyes glinting with malicious intent.

Kiara's knife felt heavy in her clenched palm. The burden of the oncoming battle—and the notion that success was dangerously imperative—weighed on her shoulders and chipped at her confidence. "Listen, Vyntrx," she spoke callously, her words clipped. "I want to fight you, one-on-one. Don't run away this time."

Her aunt smiled crookedly, her twisted face brimming with anticipation. "Alright," she breathed eagerly.

"But there's a catch," Kiara added hastily. "If I win, you take me to Veinya and call off your Demmonai fleet. In return, I won't kill you. If I lose, you can take me captive—only me; my friends are left unharmed—and you can do whatever you want with my soul." Although she attempted to speak in a gallant tone, her voice broke slightly, revealing her hidden anxiety.

Vyntrx's smirk enlarged, distorting her visage with a look of pure evil. "That sounds lovely," she decided, her voice crackling with excitement.

"Promise?" Kiara insisted, hesitantly stepping in the direction of her aunt. "You can't break your word."

Vyntrx's pale fingers traced two lines over her tightly clothed chest, marking the letter x as her long nails slid across the black fabric of her dress. "Cross my heart," she whispered sardonically.

Kiara's grip tightened around the handle of her knife as she prepared for battle. "Hope you die," she responded drily. She abruptly dashed forward, rearing the edge of her blade backward, but the distance between her and Vyntrx was too vast for her to cross before her aunt was alerted.

Vyntrx apprehended her niece's first move, grinning confidently. She lazily waved her hand, summoning a semi-transparent wall to engulf her figure. The tip of Kiara's knife scraped across the wall, issuing an unnerving grinding noise as the blade attempted to penetrate the unwavering force field. Kiara instinctively withdrew her weapon, eyeing the wall as it flickered inconsistently.

As the wall finally abandoned its struggle and succumbed to the shadows, Vyntrx moved her hand in a series of arches as crystallized daggers instantly appeared in the air behind her. Sweeping her hand forward, Vyntrx compelled the daggers to thrust forward, directly toward Kiara's heart.

Kiara hurriedly ducked down, maneuvering her body out of the daggers' range. The edge of an icy blade nearly sliced her cheek as she reclined her head, her heart pulsating nervously.

As the assault relented, she regained her footing, balling her left hand into a fist and swinging it toward her aunt's face. As she caught a flash of silver in the corner of her eye, she immediately halted her movement, sensing that Vyntrx's shield had been reinstated. Unsure of what uncanny fate her hand would have been subjected to had it made contact with the wall, she eyed the protective shield angrily, glowering at her aunt through the nearly translucent field.

Vyntrx returned her niece's contemptuous glare, a slight chuckle spilling from her parted, blood red lips. "Commence the battle!" she cried shrilly, addressing the fleet of monstrous Demmonai dutifully flanking her. The horde moved in one collective push toward Kiara's companions, trickling past Vyntrx and Kiara as they exchanged heated glances.

Vyntrx's precautionary wall timidly diminished. Her unnatural black eyes bore into her niece's, her arms tucked away behind her back as she slowly circled Kiara in a similar fashion as a monster cornering its prey.

Kiara followed her aunt's movement, her bright eyes red with unfettered fury. She could not swallow the unparalleled desire to vanquish her aunt's life—to aim directly for her heart and end it with a conclusive swipe of her knife—but she was sharply reminded of her initial goal of rescuing Avian's soul. She disastrously understood that in order to save Avian, she could not reap her aunt's body of life. *Remember Kain's advice,* she reminded herself critically, her grip tightening around the hilt of her weapon.

A low chuckle resonated in the base of Vyntrx's throat. "Well, well," she spoke slowly in a gravelly tone, "thought you could beat me, did you? Thought you could capture me and force me to lead you to Veinya's manor? Thought you would be able to save your precious Avian so easily?" she paused, chortling wildly, her eyes widening with deranged amusement. "Oh, it'll be more difficult than that, dear. Fighting me—right now, just the two of us without any interruptions—that's the boulder you must clear."

"Oh, I *will* clear that boulder," Kiara brazenly promised. "And not only will I clear it, I'll grind each broken stone into useless dust."

Without bothering to entertain pointless banter, Vyntrx lunged at her niece, wielding a jagged dagger. Understanding that Vyntrx's dagger possessed the potential of being smothered in the same fatal poison that had stolen Avian's life, Kiara warily ducked out of the blade's range. In the same instant that Kiara's body shifted out of the dagger's path, Vyntrx conjured a row of flames and hurled them in her niece's direction. As Vyntrx had just barely underestimated her niece's position, the fire avoided clashing directly into Kiara's figure, searing across her torso and slightly singeing her side. She cried out in pain, her hands automatically clutching her frayed blouse. She briefly glanced down at her wound, discovering disfigured skin blotted with bloodied burns.

Painfully forcing herself to bottle down the innate desire to succumb to the intense throbbing of her wounds, Kiara unsteadily regained her footing as she was struck with an idea. She recalled how naturally she had taken to Nonae magic, how easily she had been able to craft spells that had seemed unfathomable all her life. After Avian had asked her to heal the dying flowers beside her father's memorial, she had practiced summoning magic each day and had been able to memorize basic spells, but she had yet to conjure flames on purpose. She suspected mirroring her aunt's moves would be relatively simple, producing the same outcome and as an added bonus, would effectively startle Vyntrx into shock.

Kiara closely watched her aunt's hand movements as she summoned another bout of flames. Fire erupted from Vyntrx's palms, but Kiara predicted the assault, narrowly evading the row of flames sent in her direction. Without pausing to catch her breath, Kiara weaved her hands in a motion identical to her aunt's, envisioning the crackling flames of a fire spreading from her outstretched palms.

To her pleasant surprise, a line of flames billowed from her hands as a wave of heated energy escaped her veins. The fire shot through the air, heading directly toward her baffled aunt, who—in her stupor of horrific confusion—was scorched by the inferno. Her torso grotesquely charred, Vyntrx fell to her knees in pain, glaring at her niece with black eyes full of astounded terror. She placed a trembling hand on her stomach, her palm encompassed by a blue light as her disfigured flesh was quickly mended. Within seconds, her wound had been entirely healed—the only sign of disturbance found in the singed fabric of Vyntrx's dress. "How did you use magic?" she demanded an answer, unsteadily climbing to her feet.

"I've been practicing," Kiara responded drily. "I'm a quick learner. You'd better be careful or I'll inadvertently learn every spell you wield."

Vyntrx's lips parted to emit a callous riposte, but she was silenced as Kiara swung her fist directly into her face. Flung backwards by her niece's intense Evalseman strength, Vyntrx was slammed sharply against the tightly compacted ground of the forest.

Kiara was at her aunt's side in an instant—she knew fully well if she allowed Vyntrx even a second to regain her strength, the empress could easily shift the situation in her favor. Nearly tackling Vyntrx, Kiara's hands viciously wrapped around her aunt's neck, threatening to crush her windpipe. "Call off your Demmonai," she demanded through clenched teeth. Her tangled hair cascading into her eyes, darkly shadowing her solemn expression.

"You'll have to kill me first," Vyntrx spat in a deranged tone, chuckling wildly. Her dark irises cracked as flecks of crimson broke through, showcasing her red-hot anger. Kiara's grip tightened mercilessly around Vyntrx's neck, her patience wearing dangerously thin. She had to continually remind herself that killing her aunt would not bring Avian back to life, and would simply make his absence irrevocably concrete. "I beat you—I could kill you any second. You know the deal. You have to call off your army and take me to Veinya."

"Oh, but you haven't beat me," a haunting voice suddenly rang, sounding from behind Kiara. She turned her head apprehensively, her blood rushing as disbelief buzzed through her mind and terror captivated her heart. Several yards away, a second Vyntrx leaned casually against a tree, her arms folded across her chest. A devious smirk highlighted her face, her dark eyes glowing with excitement.

Her heart turning cold and heavy, Kiara slowly glanced down at the Vyntrx trapped beneath her constricting hands. The trapped Vyntrx smiled so wide her face split in two. Her flesh crackled and broke, deteriorating into a mound of dirt. Eerily startled, Kiara released her grip on the fake's throat as its body crumbled to dust.

Brushing the doppelganger's remains off her tattered clothes, Kiara faced her aunt with a hard, crimson stare. "How did you do that?"

"It's very advanced magic," Vyntrx cavalierly explained, sauntering toward her niece. "Let's see you try to copy *that*."

Kiara scowled, titling her head as she carefully planned the wisest course of action. After hastily evaluating the situation, she decided she would distract her aunt with physical pain, providing her with enough time to cultivate the hefty amount of energy needed to create her own clone.

Swiftly springing forward, Kiara successfully landed her fist against her aunt's jaw with a resonating *crack*. Vyntrx, horrified and utterly startled by the sudden sensation of pain, stumbled backwards into a tree. Kiara trailed the empress's staggering movement, repeatedly jabbing her exposed torso with harsh blows. Vyntrx emitted a loud cry, automatically crumpling to the ground as her arms wound around her stomach protectively.

While her aunt's eyes were diverted, staring at the ground

in a haze of pain, Kiara focused on the prospect of creating a replica of herself as she attempted to harness every ounce of her power into the spell. In the midst of Kiara's concentration, Vyntrx slowly began to raise her head from its slumped position, but was instantly sent sprawling to the ground as Kiara's booted foot slammed into her face.

As Kiara eyed her wounded aunt, pristine determination swarmed her chest and tickled her veins. A wave of power escaped her body in a torrent of chilling spasms as the ground below her feet shifted and swirled into plumes of dust. The storm built for several drawn-out minutes before it began molding itself into a definite shape—it was manifesting as the body of a human. Seconds warily crept by as the dusty figure solidified into an eerily perfect representation of Kiara.

Kiara stared at her twin with a profound mixture of fascination and incredulity. The second Kiara gaped at her creator with an identical expression, her shocked eyes shimmering bright yellow.

Lift up Vyntrx's face, Kiara silently commanded her doppelganger without verbal communication. The twin nodded in compliance as the original Kiara slinked behind the fake, ducking down and concealing her small form.

The double roughly grasped Vyntrx's chin, yanking her face upward. She stared directly into her aunt's callous eyes, a gloating expression sliding across her borrowed features.

"Y-you..." Vyntrx gasped, a line of blood trickling down her chin. "H-how...?"

The doppelganger sneered. "Look who won."

Kiara, cowering behind the figure of her twin, was amazed at how the fake was able to pull pieces of her creator's personality while acting on her own accord. Kiara felt as though she had unfastened a piece of her soul and temporarily provided it with a fleshy form.

A frustrated, throaty growl escaped Vyntrx's lips. Blood dripped off her chin and splattered against the pale hand of

Kiara's double.

As Vyntrx exchanged heated glares with her niece, a second figure slowly emerged from behind Kiara's head. Vyntrx's black eyes were slowly encompassed in incredulity as the realization that she was staring at an identical depiction of Kiara sank into her bewildered mind. "Impossible..." she muttered, her lips moving mechanically.

Kiara and her twin folded their arms across their chests simultaneously, sending each other pleased expressions dotted by mischievous grins. "The spell wasn't hard *or* advanced," the original Kiara jeered. "It was actually really simple."

"It takes *powerful* Nonae several years to—" Vyntrx's astounded words were interrupted by a spasm of uncontrollable coughing. Blood frothed from her lips, but she readily wiped at her mouth with the sleeve of her dress. She cast a dark, cold glare directly at her niece. "You must have learned magic somewhere."

The double shook her head in denial as the original opened her mouth to reply. "I haven't learned a single spell. There has been an occasion of accidental magic usage, and I have tried to train myself based on that experience, but I haven't been taught a thing."

"You were only taught very basic spells as a child and there is no possible way you could remember them!" Vyntrx snapped in a cry of frustration, her eyes welling with perplexity. "I was not aware that you had *any* experience with magic. Avian said—" her voice stopped mid-speech, her unfinished sentence hanging heavily in the tense air. She glanced downward sheepishly, using the back of her hand to mop up the puddle of blood that had coated her bottom lip.

Kiara inclined her head suspiciously, her eyes narrowing. "'Avian said'? What exactly did Avian say?" she probed quizzically. "And why did he say anything about me to you at all?"

"I overheard him," Vyntrx muttered unconvincingly. She

glared up at her niece from beneath a curtain of ink-black hair, her mouth twisting into a scowl. "Don't worry your pretty little head about it, dear," she spoke slowly, bitter sarcasm dripping from her words.

Kiara, ruffled by her aunt's strange comment and infuriatingly haughty demeanor, clicked her tongue. "Get up," she commanded harshly.

Vyntrx cringed at her niece's suggestion, uttering a sharp cry of displeasure—clearly, obeying the object of her obsessive rage was an unthinkable action and invited unbearable petulance.

Impatiently, Kiara and her doppelganger simultaneously clutched each of Vyntrx's arms, forcefully heaving her onto the balls of her unstable feet. Once she had managed to vaguely recall her balance, Vyntrx wavered slightly, the tips of her pale fingers lightly pressed against her temples. Kiara swatted at her aunt's hands, tightly grasping her wrists and pinning them against her back. Kiara's double clasped Vyntrx's shoulder, assisting her creator as she led the embarrassedly defeated empress toward the battlefield.

They slowly guided Vyntrx to the edge of a small hill, the sharply sloped ground below crowded with a throng of snarling Demmonai as they viciously assaulted the small group of Evalseman. Kiara's allies were back-to-back, expertly stealing the monsters' lives with masterfully executed maneuvers. They were clearly winning, but they were hopelessly outnumbered. Lacerations and bruises handicapped their inadequately armored bodies; their exhausted limbs lacked the luster and zealous power they had possessed during the previous battle.

Kiara's grip around her aunt's wrist tightened roughly. "Call off your Demmonai or I'll break your legs," she ordered through clenched teeth.

Vyntrx glowered at her niece through smoky black eyes streaked with scarlet fury. Hatred and frustration pulsated through her veins, threatening to convey her profound emotions through the revealing Nonae eyes she had taken such precaution to shroud with blackness.

Kiara raised her hand, ready to strike her aunt directly in the face. Vyntrx flinched, the sheer terror of pain forcing the doors of her mouth to unlock. Her voice bubbled in her throat, her cowardice serving as the insistent median between her vocal cords and tremulous lips. "Stop the battle!" she commanded shrilly, her voice magically echoing above the roar of clashing weapons and woeful screams.

Every soldier, utterly startled by the abrupt roaring of Vyntrx's voice, immediately halted his or her movement. The blade of Aiden's sword swung downward as his grip went limp, accidentally slicing through a nearby Demmonai. An eerie hush spread through the battlefield, the clanging of metal lapsing into silence.

"Stop fighting," Vyntrx mandated. "Return to the campsite immediately."

A confused Demmonai hovering near the sloped hill opened her mouth to protest, but Vyntrx's infuriated glare silenced the creature. "Do not question me. Questioning my motives would be questioning my authority. Leave now, or you all will die by my hand."

Hastily, the Demmonai dropped their fighting stances, shouldering their weapons. They departed the clearing in a massive heap, their heads hanging low with disappointment. Within several minutes, the army's thundering footsteps faded into the distance.

When the battleground had been completely abandoned by the Demmonai, Kiara's companions released a collective sigh of relief, dropping their weapons in exhaustion. With the assistance of her double, Kiara slowly maneuvered Vyntrx down the knoll.

"Kiara, there's two of you," Rissa said in a baffled tone, rubbing at her eyes. "I must've hit my head harder than I realized."

Kiara laughed lightly, halting in front of her frazzled friends. "You're seeing correctly. It's Nonae magic."

"You seriously beat her that quickly?" Blade asked incredulously. "I didn't think you were that powerful."

"Thank you for that boost of confidence, Blade. I appreciate it," she grumbled sarcastically.

"He means to say that he's impressed," Aiden interjected, chuckling. He eyed the captured Vyntrx, reaching past her head to approvingly pat Kiara's shoulder. "We all are. You did it, Kiara. We're saving Avian."

Kiara's companions beamed at her, a sense of pride and accomplishment radiating from their bright eyes. Her heart fluttered with excitement at Aiden's words. She was struck by a pang of confidence as she understood that they had successfully beaten Vyntrx and were one step closer to securing the lives of Avian and his mysterious brother.

Chapter Sixteen

The Death Goddess

Warm wind scurried through the forest, curling Kiara's hair as a line of sweat trickled down her spine. Heavy breath escaped her lips, her lungs unable to draw enough air. She wiped at her forehead with the edge of her cloak, suspiciously eyeing her solemn aunt. Vyntrx's face was angled at the ground, her hair hanging in black curtains around her face, her pinned hands quivering. She did not seem to notice her niece's strain.

Kiara peered at her double, eyeing her exhausted face. She walked just as wearily as her creator, her pace gradually slowing with each step. As the twins exchanged somber glances, they shared the same conclusion: Kiara's usage of advanced magic had begun to take a detrimental toll on her physical capacity.

"Are you alright, Kiara?" Blade's voice suddenly whispered in her ear, his cold palm falling against her shoulder. "You're paler than usual."

She shook her head in response. "N-no, I'm not. I'm losing energy. I need to dismiss my doppelganger."

Blade gestured at his companions to stop walking as Kiara's pace fell to stillness. He made a reach for her grip around Vyntrx's arm, but her protesting exclamation halted his movement. "What's wrong? I thought I would take over. Ace or Aiden can help me bind her."

"No, I need to do it. I'm afraid she'll try something if it isn't me."

Vyntrx scoffed, not bothering to turn toward her captors. "I won't try anything. I made a deal with you, niece. I may brandish many horrible titles, but I do not go back on my word."

Blade narrowed his eyebrows, his fingers wrapping around Kiara's wrist. "Let me. You're exhausted."

"I don't trust her," she whispered in response, stubbornly clutching her aunt's forearm.

He sighed, stealing a glance in the double's direction. "Fine. At least get rid of your twin. You can help me lead her, then, alright?"

She stared at Blade for several seconds, attempting to read the emotion welling beneath his irises. After a long silence, she finally acquiesced to his pleading. "Okay. You can help me."

Her doppelgänger sent her a worn, conclusive smile before her form slowly began to disintegrate into dust. Blade hurriedly snatched Vyntrx's briefly freed arm, sending Kiara a reassuring smile. Color seemed to flood back to her cheeks in a vitalizing wave, as though the sudden absence of her twin had immediately restored her energy.

"That's odd," she mumbled. "I feel perfectly fine now."

"What? Already?" Blade exclaimed in disbelief. "I don't know much about magic, but I figure it would take longer than a second to regain energy after having used a demanding spell."

Vyntrx's body flinched as though an electric current had passed through her veins. "It should have taken her an entire day to recover, maybe longer—" she muttered, pausing momentarily as though she lacked the capacity to sort out her baffled thoughts, "—especially being that inexperienced. I don't understand. She must be some sort of monster. Damn half-breeds." Her body heaved as she spat on the ground.

"Don't be jealous," Kiara huffed, shoving her aunt forward as she and her companions continued walking.

Vyntrx refrained from responding as they continued through the dimly lit forest, their heavy footsteps filling the silence. After several minutes encompassed in meticulous marching, the faint dirt road they had been trailing slowly faded into a paved stone walkway. As the trail transformed into a winding path, ironclad lanterns suddenly appeared in the dark sky, hovering magically and providing the road with dim illumination.

"This is it," Vyntrx whispered mournfully, breaking the bemused silence.

Kiara's heart hammered with apprehension as the light atmosphere thickened into anxious caution. She could not argue that they had stumbled across an intensely magical part of the forest, a part that was distinctly different from the unseen paths weaving through the thickets—but she could not heal the bite of skepticism that poisoned her trust in Vyntrx's honesty. "I hope it is," she muttered, sharing a foreboding glance with Blade.

The trail twisted and curved through the thinning woods, dark shadows enveloping the spaces between the trees. Kiara's boots clanked against the paved stones as she swiveled her gaze around her surroundings expectantly, hoping to discover Veinya's manor and dreading to be caught by another Demmonai assault. The seconds crawled by like inchworms, slowly accumulating into drawn-out minutes. As the anticipation building in Kiara's chest grew to an unbearable pressure, her eyes latched on the sight of a solid black wall progressively becoming distinguishable through the trees.

She hastened her pace, pushing her aunt forward as she hurried down the trail. Blade stumbled as he attempted to match her quickened speed, his eyes pinned to the shadowy manor as it grew nearer.

Within seconds, Kiara and her companions came face-to-face with the dark grey stone of the thick wall that sheltered Veinya's manor from wanderers. Kiara warily eyed the smooth stone, barely noticing a wooden door partly concealed by tufts of moss.

"I can open it," Vyntrx admitted somberly, "but I'll need my hands."

Kiara's grip immediately tightened around her aunt's wrist. "You'll flee."

Vyntrx languidly glanced at her niece over her shoulder. "You're already at her manor. I've taken you this far, why would I try to turn on you now? We made a deal."

Kiara sent Blade an uncertain expression. He met her gaze, shrugged, and slowly released his grip on Vyntrx's forearm.

Vyntrx turned to the side, facing her niece. Kiara's hand remained locked around her aunt's wrist, distrust swarming in her light red irises. "Come along, dear," Vyntrx's voice slithered from her throat. "You want to save Avian, don't you?"

Kiara started at the mention of Avian, her prudence overwhelmed by the prospect of reviving his soul. She reluctantly dropped her aunt's wrist, watching her freed hands fall limply to her side. "If you so much as—"

"I know," Vyntrx snapped. "I will uphold my part of the bargain so long as you do not go back on yours. Once you are inside the manor grounds, you will not try to kill me. That was our deal."

Kiara nodded slowly. "Alright. Get us inside the manor."

Vyntrx brushed past her niece, extending her hands to the entrance. The tips of her fingers slid over the wooden door as she muttered a phrase under her breath. As her hands danced in a pattern across the surface, streaks of bright light burned across the wood. The glistening lines twisted and curved as they expanded into the outline of a circle with an intricately written 'V' dominating the center. A crescent moon flanked by a twinkling star peaked out from behind the left side of the circle while a blazing sun erupted on the opposite side. An elaborate sword cut through the top of the orb, splitting the image in half as the double doors creaked open. The entrance swung inward, revealing the dark grounds of the manor hidden partially by clouds of fog. The outline of a mansion was slightly visible through the smog.

"It could be a trap," Rissa whispered, eyeing the ominous courtyard.

Vyntrx scoffed. "It's not. It would be disgraceful to arrange such a thing on the doorstep of the goddess herself. I'd be severely punished."

"Like it matters to you," Rissa coldly jeered. "We all know what's happening to your soul after death. You can't escape oblivion."

The Nonae empress smiled nastily, her pale cheeks flushing with anger. "You underestimate my influence over the goddess. Veinya favors evil just as strongly as she favors good."

"None of this matters, so shut up," Kiara snapped, glaring between her aunt and Rissa. "Lead the way to the manor, Vyntrx."

Swallowing a curt riposte, Vyntrx solemnly passed through the gates. Kiara and her companions trailed closely behind. As they crossed the grounds of Veinya's manor with trepidation, the fog parted beneath their shuffling feet, clearing the view of their surroundings. The entire estate appeared to be swathed in a silvery layer. Kiara glanced at the sky, discovering the absence of foliage. Without the cover of the forest's trees, the pale moonlight bled onto the grounds, providing bright illumination.

The mansion slowly emerged from the shadows, allowing Kiara to examine it in detail. It bore resemblance to a miniature castle adorned with lofty towers and sweeping archways. Heaps of ivy and moss wound their way across the silvery stone. Not a single window dotted the dark walls. A stone staircase led to a large, unattended doorway—the only visible entrance into the manor.

"She's inside," Vyntrx said hoarsely, nodding at the entrance.

Kiara had stopped in front of the doors, her hand hovering hesitantly over the doorknob. She could not decide if it would be wise to knock or simply turn the handle, but before she could determine her course of action, an icy voice slithered through her thoughts.

"You are a strange girl, indeed, Kiara Fable." The words infiltrated her head, echoing against the walls of her mind. The voice was unlike anything she had ever heard before—the sound of it filled her body with a contradicting mixture of security and fear—and the jovial, musical tone of the speaker was underlined by an unmistakable hint of harshness.

Kiara's eyes frantically darted around the grounds as she tried to discover the mysterious speaker, but her gaze simply fell upon her companion's questioning glances. She could tell from their quizzical expressions that they had not heard the voice.

"You will not find me, Kiara. I am inside," the hauntingly beautiful voice echoed through her head. "Come on in, then."

How are you talking to me? Kiara silently wondered, her hand slowly clamping around the door handle.

A tinkling laugh chimed through Kiara's head—the sound was more intoxicating than the sweetest nectar, more comforting than the softest lullaby. "My dear," the voice spoke heartily, "I am a goddess."

Kiara hastily tore open the door, propelling herself inside the manor. Her body was immediately thrust into a cold, dank room—or *was* it a room? The darkness was so thick and suppressive, Kiara's eyes could not discern anything aside from shadows. Not only had her vision been impaired, but her limbs had been depraved of the ability to *feel*. Her body seemed eerily detached from her mind—she found it difficult to communicate between her thoughts and her limbs, and had to struggle to force her neck to move. She slowly glanced over her shoulder, expecting to see an open door leading to the mansion grounds—but her eyes absorbed nothing but blackness. She was unsure where in the manor she had been sent, but wherever she was, she understood that the atmosphere had been entirely drained of even the smallest trace of light.

Panic bubbled in her chest, her skin numbing with anxiety. Her heart thudded loudly, blurring her vision with each frantic beat. "Hello?" she called, her voice cracking. "Is anyone there?"

"Afraid, Kiara?" the icy voice sang tauntingly, suddenly possessing a much crueler tone.

Understanding that the voice could only belong to Veinya, Kiara's hands twitched with anticipation. Her eyes scanned the depths of the shadows, hoping for even a miniscule fracture of light to guide her in the direction of the goddess. "Where are you?" she asked hoarsely.

There was a beat of absolute, crushing silence. Just as the wave of quiet reached stifling heights, Veinya's voice broke through the emptiness. "Come closer," she commanded.

Before Kiara could follow the goddess' command, her body was involuntarily pulled forward, her feet scraping against the floor as she was propelled through the icy darkness. Goose bumps rose on her skin as her hair tumbled out behind her, billowing in coppery-brown waves. Her heart pulsated madly in her chest, shock and apprehension swelling in the pit of her stomach as her throat constricted tightly.

After several moments of being swept through the shadows, waves of chilled wind whipping against her face, Kiara's body was released of the goddess' thrall. The sudden halt skewered her equilibrium, nearly sending her plummeting to the shadowy ground. She scrambled to gain control of her footing, uncharacteristically preventing herself from tumbling.

As she overcame the initial shock of being unwillingly dragged through a lightless manor, her sense of awareness was slowly revived. She realized her surroundings were no longer enveloped in darkness but were submerged in faint silvery illumination.

She slowly raised her face upward, her eyes blinking as they were assaulted by harsh streams of light—a stark comparison to the dark shadows of the manor. As her eyes adjusted, she realized she was standing in front of a colossal, glossy mirror.

The glass was rimmed with silver, the metallic hues of the material casting ghostly beams through the shadows. Beside the mirror resided a lithe figure, a tall creature constructed of varying shades of white and black. Her pale porcelain face possessed every aspect of beauty. Coal-black hair framed her gently curved cheeks, hanging in loose curls across her back. Her bright eyes—the only splash of vibrancy and color amid her entire figure—were the lightest shade of blue. An ornate black gown adorned her sculpted body, the hem of her dress lightly grazing the dark floor.

This is the monster *Avian's brother warned me of?* Kiara silently wondered in disbelief.

The death goddess smiled at her guest, her perfectly contoured lips sliding across her unblemished face. As Kiara watched the goddess' mouth work into a grin, her worries and concerns instantly melted away as though Veinya's reassuring expression had eradicated every form of darkness from the world.

"Welcome, Kiara," the goddess spoke, her voice sweetly fluid.

"Am I dead?" the words erupted from her lips as though she could not contain her thoughts.

Veinya shook her head, chuckling softly. "No, you're still very much alive," she paused, her fingers stroking the edge of the mirror. "You are wise to think so, however. This place—this nonphysical realm—is where souls are sent after they depart their bodies. They undergo three days of examination, during which I decide their fate. I either send them through here," she inclined her head toward the mirror, her fingers dancing across the metallic rim, "or I destroy them." Her light eyes abruptly hardened, warmness fleeing every curve of her expression.

Kiara, abashed by the goddess' sudden change in disposition, struggled to unblock her swollen vocal chords. "Wh-what about your servants?" she spluttered.

Veinya's smile returned just as quickly as it had vanished.

Warmth emanated from her gentle expression, her eyes lightening with kindness. "They are surrounding us," she whispered, motioning around the room with her pale hands, "in the shadows."

"Really?" Kiara's tone displayed her bemusement. She imagined Avian's brother standing nearby, entirely shrouded in the depths of the shadows. The thought set her frayed nerves at ease, allowing her tense body to slightly recoil.

"I know why you're here, Kiara," the goddess disapprovingly revealed. "I know you want to bring the Knight brothers back from the dead."

Kiara had only heard Avian's surname spoken on a handful of occasions, but she had never associated the name with his brother. To speak of Avian and his sibling as though they were a single, collective group seemed utterly unnatural. To her, Avian and his brother were two vastly different people far too contrasting to be placed in the same category.

Having been so distracted by her contemplative thoughts, Kiara had forgotten to respond to the goddess and was simply staring blankly ahead. The goddess cleared her throat, drawing Kiara's mind back to reality. She nodded shyly, nervously tucking away a strand of loose hair behind her ear.

"Why do you wish to save them?" Veinya inquired.

"Because Avian is an important person to me," Kiara explained, her cheeks flushing as her thoughts lingered on Avian. She was so close to saving him, so close to bringing him back, she could vaguely feel his fingers brushing against her skin. "And I'm empathetic of his brother's situation—he barely experienced life."

Veinya carefully scrutinized Kiara as though she were attempting to determine the genuineness of her claim. She raised her thin eyebrows, her lips curling into an all-knowing grin. "Are you aware that Avian's brother is my servant?"

Kiara nodded slowly.

The goddess released a loud sigh, her face scrunched up in

thought as she contemplated the situation. After a deafening wave of heavy silence passed through the atmosphere, Veinya's furrowed eyebrows relaxed. "Kain!" her voice escaped her throat in a sharp, resonating burst of sound.

Avian's brother abruptly materialized beside the goddess, a perplexed expression dominating his features. "What?" he spoke irritably, his dark hair partially masking his glowing violet eyes.

"This young lady wishes to free your soul and provide you with a second chance at life," she explained objectively. She raised her eyebrows, her light eyes staring directly into the boy's. "Did you try to convince her of it?"

He stared up at the goddess with unrestrained disdain as he uncaringly folded his arms across his chest. "You know I didn't. Avian did."

The boy's words had been seemingly innocent, but Veinya's eyes flashed dangerously with unadulterated fury—luckily, the flame of her anger was unable to burn wildly before it was squelched just as quickly as it had been fueled. Calming her disposition, she turned her attention to Kiara, a soft smile playing on her lips. "Very well, Kiara, you may have this boy's soul."

The goddess waved her hand over Kain's head. The hollowness of his lavender eyes was suddenly filled with glistening light; faint strokes of pink caressed his pallid cheeks as liveliness was restored to his somber form. His thin legs trembled slightly, his lips quivered in disbelief. He took a clumsy step toward Kiara, his shoulder ungracefully bumping against hers. He stared at his manifested arm, utterly flabbergasted, as a prickle of feeling spread upward from his wrist. It had been thirteen years since had physically felt *anything*. Although his spirit had been able to touch objects inside dreams and the goddess' manor, his nerves had been blunted, had refused to communicate with his brain, and had subsequently starved him of sensations.

"Thank you," he muttered shyly into Kiara's ear. Loose strands of her tangled hair gently brushed against his nose, sending unfamiliar shivers creeping down his back.

She smiled at him, her eyes glowing light purple with jovial relief. "You don't need to thank me." As soon as the words had escaped her lips, her irises rapidly shifted color. At first glance, Kain believed her eyes were burning red with anger, but as he carefully examined the complex shade of her irises, he noticed the glint of orange accompanying the crimson hue. Her fire-like eyes reflected the determination coursing through her veins. "Now we need to save Avian," she whispered.

"Kiara," Veinya whispered gently, her voice as small and fragile as shards of punctured glass, "I'm afraid the restoration of Avian's soul requires a sacrifice."

"I'll do it," Kiara instantly decided, not bothering to pause for contemplation. "You can take my soul if it will bring Avian back to life."

Kain's wide eyes latched on her, confusion and incredulity evident in the furrow of his brow. "You'd do that for *him*?"

Her bright eyes, glistening maroon with fright, glanced in the boy's direction. "Yes," she said plainly. "Avian died because of my carelessness. I'm repaying his sacrifice." Distantly, she recalled a time, shortly after she and Avian had been reacquainted, when she had stated that she couldn't imagine sacrificing her life for any cause, for anyone. If the situation had not been so dire, she would have laughed at the irony.

Kain bit his lip in frustration, startled momentarily by the sharp pain that tore through his mouth. As Kiara smiled softly at him, guilt built in the pit of his stomach, the sickening acid of the sensation forcing him to relinquish his staidness. "But, he—"

"You are willing to give your life to save another's?" Veinya interrupted, her expression harsh as she glared at Kain. She slowly turned her gaze toward Kiara, the soft gleam in her irises eerily soothing.

"Yes," Kiara spoke bravely, but the maroon shade of her eyes undermined her courageous pretense.

Veinya's lips slid into a gratifying grin. "Then he is now free. You may depart my mansion with the Knight brothers' souls."

Kiara stared at the goddess in disbelief. "But you said a sacrifice was required."

"By offering to give your own life in order to save this young man, you displayed your kind soul and pure heart. I am not cruel, Kiara, as many of my followers believe," she paused, her eyes momentarily sweeping over Kain. "Because you proved to be genuine and selfless, I have decided to grant you Avian Knight's soul."

Just as the words had escaped the goddess' lips, Avian's body materialized out of the darkness. A look of profound relief crossed his handsome face, but he was unable to smooth the old lines of worry that had crept onto his features.

His eyes slowly fell on Kiara, that look he reserved solely for her spilling across his face. He dashed at her, tightly wrapping his arms around her and holding her in a tight embrace. Her hands automatically wound around his back as she was overwhelmed by his presence. Tears spilled down her cheeks, her heartbeat thudded noisily, her stomach swirled with disbelief. She had succeeded in rescuing his soul; she had brought him back to life. The realization of the notion was so astounding, so surreal, she could hardly believe she was breathing in the scent of reality.

"Now you may go," Veinya decided, her calm voice slithering through the heavy atmosphere. Kiara slowly pulled her face out of the fabric of Avian's shirt, but the cold room, swirling mirror, and suppressive darkness melted away before she could murmur her thanks.

Chapter Seventeen

A Bittersweet Return

"I *hate* Kyan!" Vyntrx screeched, picking up the crystalline orb resting on the goddess' mantle and smashing it on the ground. A sharp crack resonated through the silence as the glass shards scattered across the shadowy ground. "Even after his death, he mocks me. If he had not forced Avian to promise that he would crown Kiara queen, I could have easily ended her life when she brazenly walked into my forest. If it hadn't been for Kyan, my advisor would not have fallen into Kiara's influence and would've remained a loyal, heartless servant. Do you understand how demoralizing it would be to watch your sworn enemy prance into your territory—the most perfect condition conceivable for you to steal her life—and then dance away victoriously into safety because you are unable to make a serious move? It's a blow to the ego!"

Veinya's eyes bore into the fractured pieces of her orb. "How rude," she huffed. The glass vanished from the floor as a new sparkling orb appeared where its predecessor had fallen. "Honestly, Vyntrx, you should be more upset with Avian than Kyan. I understand you've always had your *differences* with the Evalseman king, but you act as though Avian shouldn't be blamed whatsoever. *He* jumped in front of your blade and put you in this tricky situation, not Kyan. I don't know if you've noticed, but that boy isn't just following Kyan's orders. He's buying time with the girl," she paused, eyeing her companion's livid expression shift into one of contemptuous understanding. "Have you taken precautions to eradicate any feelings he may possess for the princess?"

"You know I have," she responded immediately. "But he

finds a way around every single blockade I install. I am not naïve enough to believe I could forcibly alter his emotions, but I can very well try. I've ordered him to begin manipulating her mind—not only will this work to our advantage, but once she discovers that he has committed this indiscretion against her, she will never forgive him. It will crush his heart and obliterate his darkening soul and then he will become the moldable warrior we require."

Veinya sighed a heavy breath, her fingers dancing across the surface of her newly repaired orb. "I am not on your team, Vyntrx. You keep forgetting that. Our interests are not the same. Naturally, I cannot favor one side over the other. I have been sincerely beguiled by that young princess."

Vyntrx attempted to conceal her escalating rage with a sigh of indifference, but she simply succeeded in releasing a frustrated cry. "Why would you favor that brat? You have such a soft side for self-proclaimed heroes. First her idiot father, and now—"

"Don't be jealous, Vyntrx," Veinya interrupted coldly, her glazed eyes carefully raking her friend. "You granted me your soul in return for sustainability. I haven't taken anything from Kiara—except her mortality."

Vyntrx's eyes bulged with rage, streaks of red stabbing through her blackened irises. As part of her contract with the goddess, a dark filter had been placed over her inconsistent eyes in an attempt to conceal her emotions—but occasionally, especially at times when Kiara was concerned, her moods became too fervent to hide. "You..." her voice trailed off, overwhelmed by the wave of fury that swept through her limbs. "She can't die?"

Veinya slowly shook her head, confirming Vyntrx's worst fears. "If she happens to die, I'll just restore her life. She'd just simply visit my manor briefly before I allow her to soul to return to its fleshy home. If she were to perish, you'd automatically win this little game, wouldn't you? That's not fair."

"Not *fair*?" Vyntrx cried shrilly, her eyes wide and wild with deranged anger. "How is it fair to make her immortal while I remain entirely vulnerable?" Her strained, hoarse voice revealed the terror she felt tearing through her heart and paralyzing her body. For once, she was afraid. For once, she caught a jarring glimpse of her own mortality. She was beyond frightened.

"You forget how difficult it is to kill you, Vyntrx," Veinya reminded the empress critically. "You're practically indestructible. The difference between you and Kiara is that you gave your soul to me while her allegiance is solely to herself. I did not take anything from her because I favored her on my own accord—she didn't seek me out to gain fortitude. You understand the conditions of our agreement; you know your soul cannot be granted immortality, and you know what should happen to it if you perish. Shouldn't that weighty factor motivate you to avoid failing?"

Vyntrx's teeth ground together in violent aggravation. A wicked idea was frothing up from the depths of her imagination; thoughts were meshing together to form devious schemes as her brain ticked with activity. A sly smile spread across her lips, the dark depths of her eyes obscured with excitement as her notions wove together into the workings of a plan. "Yes," she spoke calmly, a mischievous tone breaking through her collected pretense, "yes, of course." She had devised a scheme to eradicate Kiara's presence from Menevilen forever—a scheme that involved maiming Veinya's benevolent side so disastrously, she would be unable to feel even the softest prick of sympathy.

*****

Kiara awoke with a start. Her eyes slowly flickered open, absorbing the sideway view of a shadowy courtyard. There was a faint pounding in the back of her head, as if something dull had sharply made contact with her skull. Blinking hard, she pushed her exhausted body off the cold ground and positioned herself into a seated stance.

Feeling the insistent countenances of her companions graze her skin, Kiara slowly wheeled her vision upward, discovering Rissa and the dukes standing above her. As she carefully observed her friends' bemused expressions, she realized they weren't staring *at* her—their eyes were steadily locked on something directly *behind* her. She slowly twisted her head around, expecting to find a crimson-stained Vyntrx wielding a deadly weapon, and was relieved when she discovered a healthy, breathing Avian sitting merely inches away from her. Kain sat silently beside his brother, a torrent of sheer joy flashing through his eyes as he bewilderedly held up his hand and examined its solidness.

"You did it..." Rissa mouthed, unable to summon her voice. She cleared her throat, regaining the ability to articulate. "You really did it."

Kiara nodded slowly, disbelievingly, her eyes unable to depart from Avian's face. He smiled at her tentatively, his mismatched eyes softening with a ring of blissful tears. Watching his perplexed face twist into a victorious grin, Kiara felt her body turn numb with relief. She fell listlessly to the side as Avian extended his arms, catching her against his chest.

"You're alive," she whispered breathlessly, wrapping her arms around his torso and breathing in his familiar scent. He bent forward, placing his lips against the crown of her head as his hand cupped the nape of her neck. She exhaled shakily, laying her ear against his chest and reveling in the sound of his consistently beating heart. "You're alive," she repeated, her voice rising several octaves.

"Because of you," he reminded her softly, running his hands through her disheveled hair. "It's all because of you."

Kiara could hear Avian's brother sneering loudly at their

heartfelt reunion, but she couldn't bring herself to care. She balled her hands into fists, bunching a handful of the fabric of Avian's blouse into her palms, clinging to him as though he could vanish at any second. In that moment, she didn't care that Kain despised his brother—and she certainly didn't worry about the secretive, untold reason behind his hatred. She was so enveloped in relief, it didn't matter that salvaging the Knight brothers' souls had been miraculously simple. She was so blissfully ecstatic, she was able to mindlessly bottle down the nagging sensation of suspicion swirling in the pit of her stomach.

After Avian and Kiara's reunion thrived for several drawn-out minutes, Kiara eventually harnessed enough strength to pull away from their embrace. She and Avian climbed to their feet, their hands interlocked as they leaned against each other's sides. She wiped at her eyes with a handful of her cloak's cloth, glancing at her companions. "What happened to me?" she wondered. "Where's Vyntrx?"

"She disappeared when you fainted," Aiden explained, his shocked expression directed at his revived companion. "You were knocked out for a couple of minutes and then these two showed up beside you."

"Is that really you, Avian?" Blade asked hoarsely, his face uncharacteristically awestruck. His hands, limp at his side, quivered.

Avian smirked, extending his arms as he welcomed his friend into a hug. "It really is." The dukes noisily crowded around their resurrected comrade as Rissa stood awkwardly to the side, laughing and crying with disbelief.

Kiara smiled, slowly peeling her gaze away from Avian and glancing down at Kain. He sat placidly on the ground, bitterly glaring at his brother as he was greeted by his friends. Kiara timidly lowered her hand, offering to help him up. "Are you going to grace me with the honor of knowing your name?" she lightly joked. She had heard Veinya speak the boy's name, but she wanted to force a formal introduction from his casual personality.

"It's Kain," he muttered, reluctantly taking Kiara's hand. He stared up at her skeptically as she pulled him onto his feet.

"That's a good name," she commented. "I'm Kiara."

He huffed, folding his arms across his chest. "I know who you are, princess—obviously."

She emitted a small chuckle, tucking a loose strand of tattered hair behind her ear. "Why wouldn't you tell me your name?"

His eyes narrowed as his hardened gaze wandered in the direction of his brother. "No reason," he said huskily.

"I'm sure," she mumbled sarcastically.

He released an exasperated sigh, shoving his hands deep into the pockets of his pants. "Look, you should just stop talking to me. Go spend time with your boyfriend. That girl's trying to get all over him."

Kiara's eyes shied away from the younger Knight brother, falling upon Avian as he battled against an exhaustingly insistent Rissa. Kiara bit her lip, fighting off the urge to pry the captain away from Avian. Luckily, Blade intervened, steering Rissa away as Avian released a sigh of relief.

"I think he's alright for now," she decided. "You're going back to the castle with us, aren't you?" she urged, changing the subject.

"What, with *him*?" he merely spat the words, disgust apparent in his strained expression.

"Yes, with him," she responded quickly. "Where else are you going to go? You owe me a favor, anyway."

Kain groaned in protest. "First of all, why would you even want me to go with you? Secondly, *you* owe *me* a favor since I saved your pathetic life. You just repaid it by bringing me back—which was Avian's favor to begin with. I don't owe you anything."

Kiara rolled her eyes, scowling at Kain's harsh tone. She

trapped his forearm in-between her hands, setting her grip like a lock. "You're coming to castle with us. Whatever dark history you share with Avian can be—and needs to be—resolved. I'm not taking no for an answer."

Kain immediately attempted to wrench his arm from Kiara's steadfast grip, but despite exerting every plausible aspect of his power, he could not force her hands to budge. "*What* are you?"

"Half-Nonae, half-Evalseman," she stated matter-of-factly, abruptly dropping her hold on Kain's arm and catching him mildly off-guard.

Stumbling slightly, he rolled his violet eyes and sneered. "I obviously know that, idiot," he grumbled. "We already talked about it. Your Evalseman Specialty is strength, then?"

"Yes, it is, but stop trying to change the subject," she responded wryly. "Whatever happened between you and Avian is obviously personal. If I can't wrestle it out of you, I'm sure Avian won't mind filling in the blanks for me. Just come with us to the castle and try to at least reconcile your broken brotherhood."

"Save the speech, princess," he snapped hotly, folding his arms across the black fabric of his shirt. "Avian would rather die than tell you the truth of our past and I'm sure as hell keeping it to myself. Bringing me back to the castle will just create a burden for you, since you'll be the one who has to put up with my attitude. Stay out of mine and Avian's business, princess. You can't save something that's beyond repair."

"*My* and Avian's," she corrected automatically, resting her fist against her outturned hip. She shook her head, sighing loudly. "At least come with us to the castle until you figure out how to live on your own. You've been dead for over a decade. You'll need help."

Kain closed his eyes, running his pale fingers over his contemplative expression. After several seconds of thoughtful silence, he emitted a low grunt. "Whatever. Fine. I'll go with you. But it's only temporary. And don't expect me to get along with my brother, because that sure as hell won't happen."

Through a tangled web of the duke's arms, Avian abruptly shouted, "We should get out of here. We need to leave enemy territory." He managed to disentangle his body from the clutches of his overly joyous friends, tossing his head back as he motioned for his companions to follow him. "I'll lead the way. I know a short-cut."

"I wonder why that is," Kain muttered sarcastically, his voice so quiet only Kiara could discern the words. She glanced at him briefly, deciding to ignore his comment—but she couldn't ignore the unquenchable feeling of suspicion digging deep into her heart.

*****

The companions hastily trudged through an offbeat trail in the forest, wading through waist-high weeds. Avian had pointed them in the direction of the Wall before leading them through a forlorn portion of the woods and claiming his short-cut would get them back to the castle before sundown.

They had been traveling for several minutes in hushed silence. Kain had maintained his stoic disposition while they walked, but Kiara could feel his eyes on her and Avian's interlocked hands like fire. The static, uncomfortable mood between Kain and Avian was so intense, the entire group had been condemned to awkward muteness. Not even Blade dared to breathe a comment.

Avian continued to smile blissfully as he steered Kiara through the forest, his grip on her hand never once relenting. During their escapade back to Enevale, they had luckily managed to stay clear of any foreign creatures. The section of the forest Avian had dragged them through was eerily dark; the leaves on the trees above them were so thick, only a handful of sunlight managed to filter through the canopy. Whenever the amount of illumination slowly began to increase, Kiara instinctively knew that they were nearing the Wall.

The Wall loomed out of the darkness, appearing in front of the companions as though it were a rescue ship recovering stranded souls from an unknown island. A communal sigh of relief shattered the silence. Avian gently dropped Kiara's hand, walking over to the hole and beckoning for his friends to escape from the forest. They climbed through one after another, Avian bringing up the rear. Once they had all successfully crossed into Enevale's territory, Avian carefully covered the small entrance with the leaves of a nearby bush.

The companions walked toward the castle in exhausted silence. The sun had slipped into the horizon, casting a red glow across the darkening sky. Kain stared at the castle curiously as they approached, his eyes alight with wonder.

"You've never seen the castle before?" Kiara inquired, glancing at his marveling expression.

He shook his head, peeling his gaze away from the towering building and staring at the ground. "'Course not. I lived in the Dark Forest."

"I'm sure you'll love it here."

"I don't *love* anything," he huffed indignantly.

She sent him a quizzical glance as they crossed the training fields and approached the back entrance. "That's a sad way to live."

He refrained from responding, slowing his pace and falling away from Kiara. He skirted around the edge of the group, distancing himself from the princess in an attempt to avoid conversing with her. For some strange reason he couldn't comprehend, he found it exhaustingly stifling to be around her.

Avian opened the small door positioned on the back wall of the castle that led directly to the soldier barracks. The companions followed him through the dank chambers, weaving through the darkened labyrinth of rooms. They climbed the steps out of barracks, entering into the warm halls of the castle's main level. After ducking through several archways, Avian brought the group to a halt beside a sprawling staircase. Dismissing Rissa and the dukes with friendly embraces and appreciative words, Avian stood before an exhausted Kiara and a distant Kain. "Please lead Kain to the suite, Ara. I take it he's decided to stay with us," he stated languidly. He attempted to smile at his brother, but he couldn't smother the hardened glare in his eyes. "I should visit the nurse so she isn't terrified when she discovers that my body is missing. After I'm finished speaking with her, I'll fetch us some dinner. Do you want anything, Kain?"

Kain's body automatically stiffened as his brother's eyes wandered in his direction. His aghast facial expression suggested he was utterly horrified that his brother had dared to communicate with him. After several uncomfortable seconds, he nodded his head laboriously, indicating his response.

"What do you want?" Avian inquired, seemingly unabashed by his brother's sharp glowers.

"I don't care," Kain said huskily, attempting to dig up the remnants of a conversational tone from his characteristically condescending voice. "Anything."

Avian smiled at his brother in response, turning his attention to Kiara as he bent down to place a soft kiss on the crown of her head. "I'll be back soon, Ara. Get Kain settled into my bedroom. I haven't slept in there in over a month and I would like to keep him close."

Kain clicked his tongue, sniggering. "*You* don't trust *me*? That's ironic."

Avian attempted to ignore his brother's snide remark, but Kiara noticed his hand clench tightly into a fist while his quivering knuckles turned white. In an effort to distract him from Kain's cryptic outburst, she nudged his ribs, pulling her face into an embarrassed grin. "I know you've been falling asleep in my room lately, but are you sure you want to actually share a bedroom?"

His hand clamped around Kiara's shoulder comfortingly,

but his fingers were trembling. "Of course. Being close to you makes me feel more at ease about your security, anyway. I slept at your father's bedside for years. I'm quite used to not having my own personal space."

She nodded in compliance. "Alright, then it's settled. We'll meet you back at the suite."

Avian—his mind buzzing with crowded, unwelcome thoughts—released a half-hearted response through a muffled voice. He walked dizzily down the hallway, his fingers trailing over the walls for guidance. His brother's revitalization had affected him profoundly, and while he felt that saving Kain's soul had been a necessary move in order to redeem his blackened soul, he could not cure the poison of guilt that spread through his being each time he met his brother's gaze.

As Kiara's gentle voice faded into silence in the distance, Avian was hit by a sharp blow of anxiety as he recalled Vyntrx's latest order. *Please don't make me do this,* he silently pleaded, stumbling down the hallway. He accidentally bumped into a passing maid, but she hurriedly murmured a fretful apology and scurried out of sight. *Please don't torture me like this.* His legs gave away, sending him sprawling to the ground. He lay there motionlessly, fully succumbing to the wave of desolation that had been slowly drowning his mentality. *I can't do it, I can't do it. I'll lose her forever. I can't. I can't.*

Oh, you can do it, that jarringly malicious voice echoed through his head, *and you will. You will, Avian, you will. Because if you haven't done it by this time tomorrow, you will have disobeyed me. And you know what happens if you don't follow my rules.*

He released a shaky puff of air, his wet eyelashes sticking to his flushed cheeks. His hand clenched his chest just over his quavering heart, yanking at the fabric so tightly, he nearly ripped his blouse. *Would it really be so terrible to disobey?* he wondered desperately. *Could I disobey—for her—knowing it would lead to my demise?*

No, the voice answered, *you couldn't do that. You're too selfish.*

Avian shook is head, his hand softly tracing the fake wedding ring encircling his finger. *For her, I would do anything,* he decided, his hand clamping the wall as he attempted to hoist himself back up on his feet. *But I can't die like this. She deserves the truth—she deserves everything. She deserves to decide my fate. And until I can give her that, I'll be forced to break her heart. But someday, hopefully, she'll understand that my heart has been shattering since before we were reunited. And right now, because of what I'm about to do, my conscious is being scorched with guilt.*

Chapter Eighteen

Manipulation

Beads of warm water pelted Kiara's grime-coated body as she reveled in the small luxury of a hot shower. She ran her hands through her damaged hair, working out the swirls of tangles and rinsing away the dirt that had been caking her scalp. After lathering her limbs with soap, she scrubbed at the smears of dried blood that flecked her skin. A small red mark on her torso would not vanish, and after scrubbing at it incessantly for several minutes, she realized it was simply a scar from the Demmonai's blade that had nearly stolen her life.

At the thought of her near-death experience, her mind trailed in the direction of Avian's brother. After Avian had departed, she and Kain had walked silently through the halls of the castle, producing a very small amount of conversation. Any time she had attempted to talk to him, he had shot her topics down with a conclusive one-liner, successfully convening his wish to avoid communication. She had shown him his bedroom, which he received with a nod of appreciation, and had left him to scour Avian's discarded wardrobe for a change of clothes. She couldn't understand how Kain's personality could be such a sharp contrast from his brother's. She understood they were half-siblings, but they still shared the same blood. In the span of time she had spent with Avian, she had mapped out nearly every aspect of his personality and deciphered the proper approach to handle each of his moods—but Kain was unmanageable. If she wished to befriend him—or at least be on good terms with him—she would have rethink her approach.

Her fingers pressed the button on the shower wall, abruptly

halting the flow of water that escaped the facets lining the ceiling. Wrapping a towel around her chilled body, she exited the bathroom, darting through her bedroom and into her closet.

After she had changed into a comfortable nightgown, she opened her bedroom door, expecting to find Avian waiting for her in the dining room—a startled Kain met her gaze instead. He was reclining on a couch in the living room, lazily flipping through the leaves of a book Kiara had picked out from the castle library. "Hello," he muttered.

"Avian isn't back yet?" she questioned, slowly closing her bedroom door behind her as she cautiously crossed the living room and sat on the couch opposite Kain.

He shook his head. "Not yet."

"Why do you hate him, Kain?" she probed, her curious hazel eyes staring attentively into his.

He scoffed. "I'm not going to tell you."

Her pensive expression hardened into a look of disappointment. "But I—"

The suite door opened loudly, startling Kiara so severely, she forgot to finish her sentence. Avian stood in the doorway, balancing two trays full of food in his hands, his ever-present smile beaming across his face.

"Oh, hello, Kain," he said exasperatedly, letting the door swing shut behind him as he crossed the dining room. He carefully set the tray down on the small table that rested in-between the couches, eyeing his brother. "I figured you would've slunk off your bedroom."

Kain averted his gaze, hungrily eyeing a plate of steaming meat. "Was waiting for my food," he said snappily, jumping up from the couch. "Which one's mine?"

Avian pointed to the meal his brother had been eyeing. "It was your favorite dish as a kid. I didn't think your preferences would have changed in Veinya's manor."

His eyes bulged at Avian's words as he swiped his plate off

the tray. He fought off the urge to chuck the meal against the wall in an act of defiant angst, allowing his fuming expression to be the sole median between the tense atmosphere and his darkened thoughts. "I'll be in my room." He brushed past his brother and Kiara in a series of wide strides, ducking into his bedroom and slamming the door loudly behind him.

Kiara sighed, rubbing at her temple in frustration. "He's so *rude*."

Avian ignored her comment, plopping down beside her on the couch and issuing a small grin. "I didn't think I would ever see you again."

She returned his smile, shyly tucking away a strand of wet hair behind her ear. His fingers danced across her shoulder, birthing chills along the ridges of her spine. "I can't believe I actually managed to tamper with life and death," she whispered. "I guess I'm full of surprises."

"That's what I've been telling you since we met, Ara," he responded heartily. "Was your journey very difficult?"

She shrugged, leaning her head against his chest and reveling in the steady rise and fall of his breathing. "It was a little challenging but I actually beat Vyntrx in combat."

His body jerked with surprise at Kiara's causally delivered statement. "Wait, you did *what*?"

"She kept attacking us with a fleet of Demmonai soldiers, so I challenged her to a duel," she explained, turning toward Avian with excitement as she retold her encounter with the Nonae empress. "She kept evading me with magic, so I attempted to copy her spells. She had created a doppelganger of herself in an attempt to confuse me, so I tried to emulate her actions and was instantly successful. She was so caught off guard, she lost the match."

Avian's face shifted into a dubious expression. "You created a double of yourself? You produced advanced Nonae magic?"

She nodded enthusiastically, laughing at his dumbfounded response. "I could show you if you don't believe me."

He shook his head, a smile breaking through his awestruck features. "No, I believe you. I'm sure creating a doppelganger requires a great deal of energy and I can tell you're already exhausted," he said softly, his fingers tussling the ends of her damp, curling hair. "I don't doubt your capabilities, I'm just astounded you were able to summon such profound power at a significantly early stage in your magic studies. Most Nonae are never able to harness enough power to sustain a temporary twin. You're really quite impressive."

She felt her cheeks heating with embarrassment. "Is that a compliment?"

Avian raised his arm, letting it fall over Kiara's shoulders as he pulled her body closer to his. "Of course it is," he breathed, gently brushing her cheek with the edge of his finger. "And now an opportunity has arisen for me to repay you for saving my life."

Kiara's rose-colored irises searched Avian's face. "I thought dinner was my reward?"

A mischievous smirk slid across his lips. "Of course not," he said quietly, lowering his mouth against her face and skimming his lips across hers as though he were tempting her with a half-given kiss. "Dinner can wait."

She wove her hands through his hair, interlacing her fingers behind his stooping neck. "Go on, then," she whispered, staring up at him through half-open lids rimmed by a curtain of dark lashes. His lips suddenly fell against hers with a fresh wave of passion, moving with a profound sense of urgency. The room was silent aside from the soft sound of stirring lips and thudding heartbeats, the intimacy of the environment sparking flames in the cores of each writhing body. Kiara's mouth was heavy with the weight of Avian's, her limbs moving to the flow of his touch. Each thickly perfumed minute that slowly ticked by dissolved every aspect of their singularity and joined their quivering bodies in unbreakable unison.

As the heat of their encounter spread into an unbearable

wildfire, Avian abruptly broke connection with Kiara's fast-paced lips, allowing a single sentence to escape his pulsating throat. "I love you," he hoarsely admitted.

His sweetly spoken words danced through the air, tingling and tickling Kiara's skin—but for him, the declaration had been dripping with hopeless desolation and tainted by the ugly disease of deception. He gravely understood that he and Kiara had shared one last sincere moment of euphoria, of romance—and he was disastrously aware that after he followed Vyntrx's malicious orders, Kiara's brain would be crippled of the ability to decipher true emotion, and then even her revealing eyes would produce fallacies. "I love you," he repeated. And although his words caused a pleasant smile to contour Kiara's pretty face, his voice echoed shapelessly through his punctured heart.

*****

Avian, that hauntingly familiar voice echoed through his dreams, disturbing the still darkness. *I require your assistance.*

The shore of his consciousness was abruptly splattered with unsettled waves as a current of despair rippled through his mind. The mirror-like substance of his psyche was suddenly disturbed by the pale white face of Vyntrx as she forcefully slithered into his thoughts.

Tomorrow, after you manipulate the girl's mind, I need you to return to the forest, the empress's malignant voice commanded. *This is non-negotiable, so don't even try to argue.*

The peaceful chambers of Avian's mind shook with rage. He was furious—furious at the situation, furious at Vyntrx, but most of all, he was furious with himself. *Kiara will be suspicious*, he replied hurriedly, evoking a casual tone in an attempt to shroud his reluctance.

She won't be if you control her mind, Vyntrx's callous tone cut through his thoughts like a knife. *I have gained an opportunity for you to travel outside of the forest—into the unknown lands—and secure a treaty with an Arlyn tribe. They're expecting your arrival within the next week. I can't go myself—I've already arranged meetings with three separate Demmonai villages. You understand how imperative it is that we cultivate a widespread army.*

Of course my top priority is making you stronger, he retorted bitterly, feeling the structure of his dreams tremble unsteadily as his master's words carved a hole of despair through the beams that held his mind intact.

I'm glad we see eye-to-eye, Vyntrx sneered jeeringly. Her sadistic, cackling laughter filled every chamber of Avian's mind—echoing off the walls, cracking the unstable floor, and chipping away the image of Kiara he had permanently plastered behind his eyes.

*****

Kiara awoke to the incessant sound of rustling. Someone was moving loudly through her bedroom, knocking into furniture pieces and toying with a plethora of objects. The lights in the room had been left unlit, but a pool of sunlight streamed in through the colossal window, bathing each curve of the room in golden illumination.

She slowly rolled her weight onto her backside as she pulled her body into a sitting position. Her eyes fell on Avian as he was scurrying through the bedroom, but he didn't notice that she had awakened.

"What're you doing?" she questioned loudly, rubbing sleep from her exhausted eyes.

He flinched slightly at the sound of her voice, nearly dropping the armful of clothes he was carrying. "Oh, hello," he said awkwardly, depositing the garments into the wide, greedy mouth of a tattered bag lying open on the edge of Kiara's bed. "Did you sleep well?"

"Never mind that," she snapped hotly. Although she couldn't discern an explanation, a sickening sensation had begun to spread through her stomach, warning her that some unknown force had severely troubled Avian. "I asked you a question."

He stopped moving. His hands fell listlessly to the side as he stared blankly ahead. "I—I have to return to the Dark Forest for reconnaissance."

A sharp cry of protest broke through Kiara's lips. She jumped up from the bed and landed at Avian's side in one swift motion, hot tears tinged in confusion and frustration stinging her eyes. "What do you mean?" she said hoarsely. "You've only just come back."

He timidly extended his hand, his palm falling against her stone-cold shoulder. "I know, Ara, I'm sorry," he whispered. "But I need to find out what Vyntrx's next move will be. I'm sure she's enraged about you defeating her. She'll most likely retaliate. Leaving you right now kills me—I swear—but I'm doing this for your safety."

She flinched away from his touch. "For my safety? Don't you always say you have to stay *by my side* to protect me?"

"Not always," he said slowly, furrowing his brow. "In this situation, I could prevent a disastrous situation from occurring. If I don't leave now, and she does plan something, I would indirectly put you in danger. I should only be gone a couple of days—"

"I don't understand why you're the one who has to go," she interrupted, her eyebrows set in a tight line. "You were *dead*, Avian. You're really going to prance back into the Dark Forest and risk your life—after everything I went through to save your soul? Can't the dukes handle this?"

Avian studied Kiara's wide eyes as they shimmered a rosy pink despite the tears outlining her solemn glare. He understood that love was the most potent emotion and would always pervade her irises so long as her gaze was fixated on him, but the sight was unnerving. As he examined her unwavering, determined expression, his mind was racked with the realization that he had reached a crucial, life-altering point—the moment he would manipulate Kiara's mind, reconstruct her emotions, and irreversibly damage her ability to love.

Kiara's sullen face slowly faded into a blank expression as he began repaving the walls of her mind. His influence swarmed every chamber of her brain, infected every element of her thoughts. The tightly locked room that held her overflowing affection for him was poisoned with a deadly strain of manipulation. Her free will was obliterated, sending sharp shards of shrapnel driving through every fiber of her brain. The pink hue of her eyes reluctantly retreated into a wave of blue that welled in her irises before it was mercilessly swallowed by a hauntingly unconcerned brown color. Her true emotions had been bottled down, captivated, tortured—and the fabricated feelings spurred by Avian's control had been tightly embedded in every dishonest shade of her eyes.

Tears streamed down Avian's face as he horrifically watched Kiara's transformation. He fought off the urge to repeal his influence from her mind, to liberate her emotions from the twisted vine that had begun to strangle them. He gurgled a sob as it rose in his throat, cupping his quivering mouth with a guilty hand.

She watched his mortified face with confusion, her eyebrows furrowing as she immediately forgot why she had been unsettled. "What's wrong, Avian?" her voice was soft but noticeably insincere. "I trust you to take care of yourself in the Dark Forest. If you believe this mission is necessary to the survival of the kingdom, then you must leave."

He didn't bother to wipe away the tears coating his glazed eyes. "Alright," he whispered hoarsely, timidly stroking his fingers across her unworried face. "I love you."

"I love you, too," she responded mechanically, her blank brown eyes staring up at him without a trace of affection.

He fell listlessly into her arms as his body was filled with paralytic numbness. She caught him in-between her hands, the gentleness of her touch depraved of genuine intimacy. He clung to her desperately—like a sick man on the brink of death clutching fading wisps of life—his palms bunching the fabric of her blouse in his steadfast grip. He felt her lightly pulling away from the embrace, felt his heart drop through his chest as she slipped through his fingers.

His ears ringing deafeningly with guilt, his body swaying powerlessly with emptiness, he slowly picked up his half-open pack, shouldered the strap, and walked out of the bedroom.

Without pausing to dwell on his absence, Kiara turned contentedly toward the closet, thumbing through her wardrobe as though she didn't harbor a single care or concern.

*****

Kain, lying sleepy-eyed and groggy in his bed, vaguely heard the suite door click shut. He sat up attentively, a confused expression crossing his features. Curiously, he slowly untangled himself from the bed sheets, creeping across his small room and cracking open the door. He peered through the sliver of space that divided the door from the wall, his eyes carefully observing the empty living room and dining room before he concluded that someone left the suite.

Hurriedly peeling off the pair of comfortable pants he had been sleeping in, he pulled down a dark shirt and grey trousers from his brother's forlorn wardrobe. Once he was fully dressed, he emerged from his bedroom, not bothering to run a brush through his unruly, disheveled hair.

For several rigidly awkward moments, he paused outside Kiara's bedroom door, his knuckles hovering over the smooth wood. After being subjected to silence for a handful of seconds, he finally heard a faint sigh escape through the small cracks on either end of the door, signaling someone's presence in the bedroom. The back of his hand fell against the door, issuing a low thumping sound and giving away his location.

"Hello?" Kiara's voice sounded small, as though it lacked the strength required to reverberate through the walls and echo in Kain's ears.

"It's me," he responded, wishing he could spin on his heel and retreat to his bedroom but knowing he would startle her if he left without an explanation. "Kain."

A muffled rustling sound filled the silence. "You can come in."

He reluctantly pushed open the door, finding Kiara sitting somberly on her bed in the dark. The only illumination streamed in from the window, falling upon her face as her golden-brown tresses glowed with fiery light. She had changed out of her nightgown and into a short, forest green dress—it was a strange sight for him to find her clothed in a dress, as in the small amount of time he had known her, she had continually been clothed in tight pants and knee-high boots—her pale, uncovered feet dangling off the edge of the bed. She wore an empty expression, her brown eyes searching the floor intently, as though her emotions were written across the threads of the carpet.

"Are you alright?" he asked, his palm slamming against the illuminator that rested on the nearby wall. Light flooded the room, causing Kiara to squint her eyes and blink with disorientation.

"I don't know," she admitted, her gaze flickering in his direction briefly before they continued staring at the ground. "My mind feels fuzzy."

Kain frowned in confusion, crossing the length of her room and timidly sitting down beside her on the bed. "Where's Avian?"

She shrugged half-heartedly. "I think he left to spy on Vyntrx in the Dark Forest."

He clicked his tongue. "That bastard," he muttered under his breath. "Are you upset?"

She shook her head slowly. "No, not really. It's strange. I *should* be upset, but I'm not."

"You alright, princess? You're being weird."

Kiara blinked rapidly, attempting to clear her mind of the fog that had diluted her thoughts. She turned to face Kain lethargically, finding an uncharacteristically concerned expression playing on his features. His violet eyes were wide and speculative, his mouth a tight, worried line. As she scrutinized his thoughtful gaze, a surge of life pulsated through her veins. The sensation coursing through the flames beneath her skin was undoubtedly a new feeling, yet it was paradoxically familiar. She felt instantly and unexplainably drawn to him, as though his undemanding presence and stoic demeanor served as an ailment to her newfound indolence.

"I'm alright," she decided, unable to draw her eyes away from Kain's contemplative face. "I just feel a bit different, that's all."

He sighed, his pensive expression fading as he was struck with an idea. "Let's go into the town and get breakfast," he casually suggested. "You can get your mind off things."

She nodded in agreement, allowing a small smile to curve her lips. She and Kain rose in sync, departing the bedroom in a shuffle of footsteps. As she led the way through the labyrinth castle halls, she could not bottle down the conflicting emotions rising in her chest. Although she felt dislocated and numb, Kain's eyes had melted the ice that had settled across her skin—and for a moment, it didn't matter that the thought of Avian had filled her mind with unfamiliarity and infused her heart with bitter pain.

Chapter Nineteen

The Bird's Shackles

"What's your Evalseman Specialty, Kain?" Kiara probed, her wide eyes shining hazel with curiosity. She sat across from him at a reclusive table hidden partially in shadows at a pub in Enevale that she and the dukes had visited on occasion. The only light in the cramped space radiated from dimly lit lamps, which were scarcely distributed on the walls of the tavern. Several windows flocked the stone walls, but thick curtains had been drawn around the glass to absorb the sunlight as it seeped in from outside. The air reeked of alcohol and the room buzzed with the gurgled sound of drunken customers. The rowdy atmosphere was uncharacteristic of Kiara's personality, but as she had enjoyed spending countless hours at the tavern laughing with the dukes and Avian, the place had been doused in the perfume of comforting nostalgia.

Kain gulped down a large swig of his beverage, wiping at the residual foam that had smeared across his lips. He had purchased an alcoholic drink—as he had never experienced the sensation and had beyond reached the legal age for drinking—and had already cleaned three glasses. "I can control things," he said quickly, slightly slurring his words, "with my mind."

Kiara swallowed a humored chuckle as it rose in the base of her throat. Her finger tapped the glass of her nillamee, her irises shifting yellow with shock as her mind slowly registered the words Kain had uttered. "Seriously? You can manipulate objects with your mind? Like that guy from the legends? He's been the only one in history to obtain that Specialty. Even Avian doesn't possess it." It was common Evalseman knowledge that amid the plethora of Specialties, there was one

274

that was incredibly rare and another that entirely impossible. While not a single Evalseman in history had ever been able to read minds, only one other Evalseman had shared Kain's unique gift—and he had been dead for hundreds of years.

Kain shrugged modestly. "Yeah, I guess."

She narrowed her eyebrows in consideration. "It's so strange that a half-Evalseman was able to be born with the rarest Specialty known to our kind," she said thoughtfully, carefully studying him. "And where is your name located?"

He sighed, yanking down the collar of his shirt. He pulled the fabric away until the entire right side of his bare chest was visible. His first name was clumsily sprawled across his peck, glistening there as though it had recently been drawn on with ink. "Do you always ask so many questions?" he wondered, releasing his grip on the shirt as his birthmark disappeared behind a wave of black cloth.

"I just have one more," she promised. "Why don't your eyes change color? You're half-Nonae, but for some reason, your eyes don't shift shades with your emotions like mine do."

He lifted his shoulders in an uncaring shrug. "I don't know. Maybe my eyes are just broken because of my lack of emotion. Or I guess my Evalseman side is stronger."

She shook her head, her thoughts whirling with countless possibilities. "Are you able to use magic normally?"

"No," he admitted, eyeing his empty glass with disapproval. "My mother tried to teach me as a child, but I never took to it. I haven't tried since. Why does it matter?"

An idea was forming in the back of her mind, slowly taking shape as it solidified into a logical theory. "What if your ability to use magic is handicapped and that's why your eyes don't change color?"

Kain's eyes widened in astounded wonder at Kiara's suggestion. "I've never thought of that," he admitted, nearly knocking over his glass as a waiter passed by to collect his empty mug. "You could be right."

She smiled shyly, hiding her proud face behind her steaming cup. "It'd be a little sad if you couldn't use magic, though, right?"

"No," he admitted. "I don't care much for magic," he paused, a frown slanting his lips downward. "But you said you were done asking me questions."

"I'm sorry," she blurted sheepishly. "I'll sto—"

"It's my turn to ask questions now, princess," he hurriedly interrupted. A waiter rushed past their table, placing Kain's refilled drink down in front of him and disappearing before Kain could utter his gratitude. He poured nearly half of the glass's contents down his throat, his eyes blinking rapidly as his body was assaulted by the alcohol. "Are you and Avian really married?"

Kiara, slightly astonished by Kain's inquiry, tentatively picked up his half-empty cup and set it down gingerly on her side of the table. "I think you've had quite enough to drink," she said sternly. "But I'll be honest with you—no, Avian and I are not married. He created the facade so the citizens of Enevale and the workers of the castle wouldn't be suspicious of my sudden appearance. He's keeping my true identity a secret until he believes I'm fit to be crowned."

He glanced at his stolen goblet bitterly, understanding— even in his hazy, semi-drunken state—that Kiara would not return his beverage despite any attempt at convincing. His gaze slowly climbed in the direction of her eyes, watching her irises flicker with Nonae emotion. He found it fascinating—and yet oddly imposing—that he could read her mental state just by glancing at the color of her eyes. His eyes bore directly into hers as he felt a question squirming upward from his chest, slithering through his throat, and forming along his tongue: "Do you really love him?"

His question caught her so severely off-guard that her hand twitched spasmodically, instantly knocking over her mug of nillamee and spewing hot liquid across the table. She released a startled gasp as she scrambled to retrieve the fallen cup, but before she could even start to wipe away the mess, Kain controlled the spilled contents, willing them to hover in the air momentarily before they splashed back down into Kiara's cup.

She stared in amazed wonder at the impressive speed in which he had summoned his Specialty. In her awed state, she momentarily forgot to answer his question, but was quickly reminded as he loudly repeated his inquiry.

"I-I don't know," she answered honestly. The truth escaped her lips in a heavy breath as though she had been holding in a mouthful of honest air for far too long. "If you would've asked me that question yesterday, I would have responded 'yes' without the tiniest pause or delay. B-but, today, I just...feel different..."

Kain closely examined her eyes, waiting for even the slightest flicker of pink to well in her irises. Regardless of the dim light of the tavern, he could clearly observe the color of eyes remain the dark amber of puzzlement. Although he had forgotten nearly everything from his childhood, he could still recall distinct memories—such as how he and his parents had been violently massacred by Vyntrx, or how soft and sincere his mother's voice had sounded whenever she sung him a lullaby. He could still remember how his mother had repeatedly told him that love and hate were the only emotions strong enough to overpower any other feelings. He could still vividly picture his mother's eyes shimmering pink whenever she glanced at her husband. He knew that enamored hue was the color Kiara's eyes should have adopted upon mentioning Avian and he was instantly troubled by her lack of emotion. "What exactly do you mean?" he probed.

She sighed, staring into the diminutive remains of her nillamee. "Yesterday, I was certain I loved him. I could *feel* it—with demonstrability. But, this morning—that's where everything started turning foggy. I feel as though I had been upset about something, and I'm almost certain we were fighting—but then, all of a sudden, I couldn't care less about Avian's business. And now, quite honestly, I'm not sure my feelings for him have persisted. I've just been straddled, it seems, with the responsibility of continuing to love him, because that's what I have been doing for months. But do I really love him? I just don't know anymore..."

Kain's brain slowly began to arrange the pieces of the situation together as he listened to Kiara speak. He had known Avian's darkest secret since that dreadful day Vyntrx had eradicated the Knight family, and he had never once doubted the extent of his brother's manipulative habits. He could list off all of Avian's Specialties—every single one. He was utterly aware of the horrors his brother was able to birth, the falsities he was capable of creating, the façades he was adept at playing. There was only one possible explanation to the symptoms Kiara had described, and Kain dreaded to accept it: her memories had been re-written, her thoughts had been violated, her feelings had been fabricated—and the culprit of this misconduct was Avian.

*****

The sprawling landscape of the forest blurred and darkened as Avian's eyes were drowned in tears. His legs quivered, his heart hammered loudly in his chest—he knew Vyntrx wouldn't hesitate to mock him if she found him in shambles, but he couldn't bring himself to care. His mind had been locked in such a miserable confinement, he hadn't realized he was merely a couple of strides away from the empress's main encampment until he nearly slammed into frowning woman.

"You look awful," a familiar voice critiqued. "What hell did you just escape from?"

Avian glanced at the speaker, dabbing at his clouded eyes with the back of his sleeve. A scowling redheaded girl poured into view, her sharp blue eyes studying his forlorn face.

"Demure," the girl's name escaped his lips in a rush of relieved air. Demure was, by definition, one of Vyntrx's most devoted followers and one of her closest companions—but by personality and character, she was one of the wisest and toughest people Avian had ever met. Despite having joined Vyntrx's ranks, Demure had been born a full-blooded Evalseman who harbored a passionate love for Nonae. She had been taken under Vyntrx's wing at a young age, after her own family had been slaughtered, and had been raised alongside Vyntrx's biological daughter since childhood. From Avian's observations, he had deduced that Demure harbored a larger sense of morality and conscience than the rest of Vyntrx's mindless followers, which instantly likened her to him and had been the initial basis of their sibling-like relationship.

"It's nothing," he muttered. "What are you doing here? Aren't you supposed to be leading a camp near the edge of the forest?"

Demure shrugged, tapping the edge of her blade-strewn belt. "Vyntrx asked me to journey with you beyond the forest, to secure the treaties with one of the Arlyn tribes. It's about a two-day walk, so we should get going."

He nodded, spinning on his heel and leading Demure away from the encampment, toward the edge of the forest. "At least this spares me from seeing Vyntrx for a couple of days," he grumbled.

"I'm not an idiot, Avian, I know something's wrong," she insisted, hurriedly following after him as he barreled through the woods.

He remained drenched in silence for several minutes, his mind slowly replaying his last encounter with Kiara. The image of her wide emotionless eyes bore through his thoughts, marred his bones, singed his skin, punctured his heart. His dry lips cracked open as his mouth worked itself into an honest reply, "Well, Demure," he explained hoarsely, "I have singlehandedly begun smothering the flame of my existence."

*****

After their excursion into the village, Kiara had helped a drunken Kain stumble back to the castle and into their suite. She had advised him to rest—she had been fearful he would injure himself or others in his hazy stupor—and carefully helped him climb into his bed. In a matter of seconds, he had acquiesced to slumber, and she had quietly tiptoed out of his bedroom and fell exhausted on the living room couch.

She had lounged around the suite for about an hour, thumbing through the leaves of a book, until she decided to steal down to the dining hall are share lunch with Sena.

Luckily, she found her friend sitting alone at an empty table and was greeted by that wide smile iconic of Sena's bubbly personality.

"I've missed you!" she exclaimed, jumping up from her chair and throwing her arms around Kiara's neck. "Where have you been the past four days? I haven't seen you at all!"

Kiara laughed lightly, disentangling herself from her friend's embrace. She sat down at the table across from her companion, placing her elbows against the wooden surface and leaning her chin upon her upturned palms. She sighed, hurriedly summarizing the events of the past week, starting with the tragic training session she had shared with Avian and Rissa. As she approached the end of the story, she skimmed over the hazy part of her memory that made her head feel as though it would split open with confusion, and simply concluded with the fact that Avian had left that morning for a reconnaissance mission.

Sena's green eyes widened with bemusement, her pale eyebrows raised high on her forehead. "Avian's *dead brother* is living in the castle now?" she questioned speculatively. "And you went up against Vyntrx entirely by yourself and came out victorious? This all sounds so surreal."

280

"I know," Kiara admitted, stifling an amused laugh as she surveyed her friend's astounded expression. "You can meet Kain soon. He's asleep now."

"Kiara, I have to be entirely honest with you," Sena suddenly blurted, her bronzed cheeks flushing scarlet with embarrassment. "One of my Evalseman Specialties is locating—I'm able to locate and target any Evalseman, Nonae, or other creature. Since you were gone for a couple of days, I began to worry about you, and when I used my Specialty to locate you, I was beyond surprised to find you in the Dark Forest. When I realized Rissa and the dukes were with you, I felt a little at ease, but I couldn't shake the fear that my friends were in danger. A rumor that Avian had died was spreading through the castle like wild fire, making the situation worse. The nurse kept swearing he was just ill, but I couldn't locate him at all until yesterday. When I noticed you were all returning home safely, I was finally able to breathe again."

Kiara smiled softly, eyeing her friend with compassion. "You're very thoughtful, Sena. I'm so sorry we caused you to worry. Had the situation been different, I would have sought you out and asked you to come with us—or at least told you where we were headed—but as I was so encumbered by Avian's death, I could not think outside of the mission, and made sure we left swiftly."

"You don't need to explain yourself," she gently assured her friend. She grinned, tucking a loose strand of blonde hair behind her ear. "I'm just glad you're back."

"Me too, Sena," Kiara responded softly, her eyes flickering downward as her mind swirled with fuzziness. She could not shake the profound feeling of dislocation—the feeling that she had lost herself amid a storm of estrangement and confusion. Although she had escaped the forest and had seemingly returned to normalcy, the strange feeling surging through her brain could not be defined as anything aside from abnormal. "Me too."

*****

Avian reclined on the padded mattress that rested on the floor of his tent, his watery eyes searching the fabric ceiling. He and Demure had been at the Arlyn tribe for two days but had been unsuccessful in their attempt to sway the brute creatures to serve Vyntrx's cause. The Arlyn were monstrous creatures in appearance—baring pointed fangs, muscular bodies covered in thick fur, and razor-sharp claws—but were uncannily articulate and opinionated. The tribe was proud and unwelcoming, and had barely allowed Avian and Demure to rest in spare tents on the edge of their village. Despite their flaws, it was apparent to Avian why Vyntrx wished to gain the military support of the Arlyn—the monster's strong bodies and merciless dispositions were admirable traits required for potential soldiers. But the monsters needed convincing, and Avian was failing miserably as his role as a persuader.

His thoughts were unfailingly rotating back to Kiara despite his efforts to focus on his mission. She appeared so often in his dreams, he had begun to think her image had been printed on the back of his eyelids. In the midst of the night, he would awake after being harassed by nightmares involving her death at his own hands, and was unable to fall back into the net of slumber. Each time he had tried to talk to the Arlyn, his mind had been unchangeably distracted. He found it impossible to evoke a convincing tone when the only emotion drumming through his mind was the overwhelming sensation of guilt. *How can I convince someone to join a cause I'm unwilling to serve myself?* he wondered silently, his eyes searching the ceiling as he envisioned Kiara's face smiling down at him.

His thoughts were disturbed as the curtained entrance to his tent was parted. Demure stuck her head in through the small opening, quizzically eyeing Avian's pensive expression. She had been abnormally patient with his sullen moods, but had expressed her concern at his uncharacteristic inability to persuade. "The Arlyn King wants to talk to you again," she explained. "Actually *try* to communicate with him this time so we can leave this place."

He released an exasperated sigh as he slowly climbed to his feet. He followed Demure out of the tent, squinting as his eyes were exposed to the immense sunlight while he attempted to harness the confidence and clear-mindedness required to efficiently deliver a convincing speech. But as he walked toward the king's wooden hall, the image of Kiara's emotionless countenance spread across his mind, and that familiar tinge of guilt swept through his chest.

Chapter Twenty

Slipping

Although Avian had been convinced his absence would spread across the hours of only a couple of days, the weeks slowly progressed into the span of nearly two months. Although Kiara knew she should have been growing paranoid, suspicious, and upset as each hour ticked by without him, she simply felt numb and dislocated. Every handful of days, she would ask Sena to locate him—to be sure he hadn't fallen prey to some disastrous accident—and she would report his whereabouts to either be at the edge of the Dark Forest or hidden somewhere in the streets of Vyntrx's fortress, Vitaciel.

"He's just doing his job," Sena assured her softly each time. Kiara would force a grimace and act as though his disappearance troubled her, but in reality, not a single pessimistic emotion welled in her chest as her thoughts lingered over Avian.

Kiara embraced a routine schedule that she followed obediently every day in an attempt to distract her mind from its perplexingly foggy thoughts. She awoke each morning in a sour mood, one that would persist incessantly until Kain's presence slowly revived her ability to laugh. She found herself continually wondering why she was so drawn to him, so reliant on his company. Unable to discern an explanation, she downplayed her increasing intrigue in Avian's mysterious brother as simple curiosity.

After consuming a small breakfast by herself in the suite's kitchen, she allotted the first few morning hours to time spent reading from various books she had pulled from the castle library. Around lunchtime, Kain would awake from his childlike slumber, and the pair of them would retreat to the dining hall to share a meal with Sena, Rissa, and the dukes. While Sena and Rissa were unable to force barely a syllable from Kain's mouth, he had taken to the dukes—with as much emotion as his stoic personality would allow—and was able to carry on small conversations with each of the boys by the end of the first week.

Every afternoon, Kain would sit and observe Kiara as she trained with the dukes at the practice fields behind the castle. The dukes had questioned Avian's whereabouts and were not shocked that he had already left to tend to matters in the Dark Forest. But as time quickly ticked by, Kiara could tell they were growing worried of his prolonged absence. The cool weather had been rapidly warming, and the daily humidity curled the ends of Kiara's hair and prompted a pool of sweat to continually coat her clothes. The dukes had noted a significant improvement in her sparring abilities, but chided her nearly every afternoon for her lack of control over her emotions. She had asked Kain to join her on multiple occasions, but he hadn't shown any interest in the matter.

Each night, she would sit cross-legged on the floor of her suite, harnessing her strength in an attempt to summon magic. Kain would watch, astounded, as she wove the elements into spells and bent the will of reality to her liking. She would laugh at his dumfounded incredulity, but she could feel a surge of power welling through her chest at the end of every exercise.

Although Kain had remained mildly distant, Kiara could vaguely sense his protective barrier fading into a thin wall of guarded awareness. On multiple occasions, she had managed to curve his scowling lips into the faint outline of a smile—yet as soon as he caught her gaping at his misplaced expression, he would cover up his humor with a snide comment and a forced frown. He had established a brand of dry humor in his speech and developed a faint look of gentleness in his eyes. While he had not been able to alleviate his stoicism, his temper, or his overall bitterness, he had managed to convey a wider range of emotion. For the first time he felt the tingling warmth of humor, exultant bond of friendship, and the irresistible thrall of attraction. As time steadily sped past, he felt the days he spent with Kiara turning into adventures. He found himself admitting she was beautiful as he watched her Nonae eyes spark with emotion and surveyed her good-natured personality bubble upward from her heart and play like shadows on her pretty face. He watched her with fascination and wonder as she sparred against the dukes, as she wove a sharp knife across a dummy with expert skill. In the mornings, he would watch hesitantly from his bedroom door as she flipped through books and wonder what coursed through her mind as she read, what words spoke out to her. When he had met her, he had been initially intrigued by her unique personality and determination, but he could never have predicted how swiftly he would find himself falling for her. Her smiling face was a beacon of light guiding him to the shores of contentment, but the treacherous waves of Avian's storm wrecked his ship and left him stranded.

As Kain had deduced that Kiara's mind had been the victim of Avian's manipulation, he could not say for certain if she had ever felt true love for his brother. This small uncertainty was enough to make him hesitant to express his affection for Kiara—that, and the prospect of failure—and yet it filled him with the desire to protect her from Avian's mischievous agenda. Occasionally, on accident, he would blurt out an allusion to Avian's secret alliance with Vyntrx, and would attempt to blame it on his imbedded hatred for his brother—but Kiara noticed. She would pry, probe, and use every angle to try and squeeze as much information out of him as she possibly could. Each time she grew suspicious of Avian, Kain liked to imagine that she had broken one of the links chaining her mentality to Avian's control. If Kain hadn't been so selfish and hadn't wished to preserve his recently redeveloped life, he would have immediately told her everything about his brother's villainy. After wrestling with every aspect of the situation, he finally decided his place was to stay alive in order to protect her from Avian's future plans—to protect her long after his brother had relinquished control over her mind.

As the first month of Avian's absence passed by in a blur of experiences, Kain managed to befriend Kiara and become as familiar with her personality as he was with his own characteristics. But occasionally, whenever she had succumbed to a particularly somber mood, he would peer into her eyes and see Avian's frowning face staring up at him from the bright-blue pools of her mind.

*****

Warm patches of sun leaked through the thick canopy of leaves, heating up Avian's cooled body as he strode through the forest with ease. To outsiders, the forest seemed haphazard and unconstructed. In reality, he knew there were carefully hidden trails leading to every town and campsite belonging to the Nonae and Demmonai races. He had been granted years of practice maneuvering the labyrinth paths of the forest, and pacing through the wooded trails had become second nature. He felt oddly comforted being back in the forest after spending far too long trapped in the Arlyn territory, and despite his burning desire to return back to the castle and into Kiara's arms, he was relieved to be in a familiar location.

He had just barely returned to Vyntrx's main encampment when a messenger had informed him of the empress's desire for him to meet her in Vitaciel to report the outcome of his mission. He had been thoroughly annoyed, considering Vyntrx could have just communicated to him through telepathy as he first entered the forest, but didn't bother wasting his energy over the issue. He parted ways with Demure, hurrying through the forest's secret trails as he formed an eloquent recollection of his time spent in the Arlyn territory. After passing several bloody and uncomfortable trails issued by the Arlyn king in an attempt to test Avian's fortitude, he had managed to win over the support of the monstrous beings. He had required nearly a week of rest to recover after his physically demanding evaluation, and the two-day walk back to the forest had frayed his strength.

The black tips of the tallest buildings contained inside Vyntrx's citadel appeared between the trees as though they were an illusion. Even after living in the forest for nearly all of his life, Avian still hadn't conquered the ominous feeling that always sunk into his chest whenever he examined the shadowy buildings of the Nonae capital. He hated entering the city—he knew he was secretly received unkindly by its inhabitants, and the cold place instilled his broken body with self-loathe and guilt—but he had been summoned. And he would be a fool to ignore Vyntrx's summoning.

"I warned you to stay away from the city," a familiar voice whispered through the trees, halting his brisk pace. "You know Cylis is always scouting for you."

"Why would Cylis risk his life by showing his despised face inside the capital city of the Nonae?" he retorted, refusing to face the speaker.

"You know why. Cylis wants both you and Vyntrx dead."

Avian laughed without humor, running his hands through his hair. "Not *you*, though?"

"I haven't done anything to offend him. I've simply been born into the wrong family," the speaker paused, as though she were allowing her thoughts to build in the back of her mind. Tentatively, she continued, "Actually, I support his cause."

He sighed, turning to face his addresser. She stood a yard away, her arms held in front of her body timidly. Her Nonae eyes flashed orange with panic as she realized she had been dangerously blunt. "I-I didn't mean—" she stumbled over her words.

"Of course you meant it," he interrupted, eyeing the gray hue of her irises as she attempted to fashion a lie. "I only wish I could be as free as you."

"Don't wish too hard or you'll get yourself killed," the girl spoke ominously, lowering her gaze to the floor. She folded her arms across her chest uncomfortably, shifting her weight between her booted feet. "My father made that mistake years ago."

"Is that why you haven't fled?"

She nodded slowly. "I'm waiting for my opportunity. I'm trusting in my cousin to save me from this place."

Avian scoffed. "She doesn't even know you exist."

"My mother can't keep us apart forever."

A thoughtful smirk crossed Avian's face as his brain ticked with activity. "I think, Kailx, if you still possess sympathy for my situation, you should be able to trust me. Because I just figured how I could ultimately free you from your mother's chains."

Kailx's eyes flashed turquoise with unprecedented excitement. "Tell me what to do."

*****

Through the darkness, the image of two listless bodies sprawled across a stone floor faded slowly into view. As the shadows slowly melted away, the figure's faces were revealed in a jarring burst of color. Brin and Anya were dead, lying lifelessly in a puddle of blood, their eyes staring blankly at the ceiling. Their necks had been freshly sliced open; fresh blood seeped from the gnarled wounds.

Vyntrx stood over the bodies, laughing dementedly, her pearl-white teeth dyed red with wet blood. Her deceivingly delicate hands were stained crimson, her pointed nails dripping with the scarlet ambrosia of stolen life. A shaded figure stood timidly behind the empress, bright blue eyes staring out from beneath its cloaked hood. "A warning," the figure spoke softly.

Vyntrx's eyes glowed viciously. "Do you like what I've done?" she asked in a shrill, unnerving voice. "Don't you just love how I've torn your world apart?"

Kiara's eyes snapped open. She felt a wave of breath escape her lips in a startled yelp. Her lungs craved oxygen. Her throat drew in air, replenishing her body with breath and drowning the ominous feeling that had followed her outside of her nightmare.

Avian's face poured into view as her vision slowly fell into focus. He was lying quietly next to her on the bed, peacefully asleep as though he had never departed from her side. Instinctively, she flinched away from him, nearly tumbling backwards off the mattress. The sudden sight of him startled her—his presence felt unnatural and unreal. Before she could fully gather her wits, he stirred in his sleep, his eyes flickering open slowly.

He caught her staring at him with unfamiliarity—the sight filled his heart with unbridled desolation. "I'm back," he said lightly, sitting up. Watching her apprehensively, he willed her mind to allow a tinge of emotion and love to seep back into her mentality. "I missed you."

Tears clouded her eyes as she clutched her head dizzily. "I'm a little overwhelmed," she admitted. The fogginess of her mind had been diluted slightly as a wave of affection swept through her thoughts. She was harassed by the urge to toss her arms around his neck, to plant a meaningful kiss on his lips— but something held her back.

"That's understandable," he commented quickly, gently caressing her shoulder. "It's safe to say Vyntrx won't retaliate against you for saving my soul. I followed her carefully for days and discovered that she's busy building an army. After your coronation, we should be weary of an attack."

She nodded comprehensively, allowing herself to fall weightlessly against Avian's chest. His arms immediately wound around her waist, his hands clinging to her body with desperation. She felt compelled to be near to him, yet her mind was buzzing with uncertainty and estrangement. She remained silent, unable to form words worthy of articulating.

"Speaking of your coronation, I've prepared a final test for you," he explained, running his hands through her tangled hair and reveling in the familiarity of her scent. "I've gathered information about an object that could help you destroy Vyntrx once and for all."

Kiara moved away from him as she processed his words. Despite the misplaced dullness that had captivated her mind, her burning hatred for Vyntrx had not been eradicated. "Please explain," she urged him to continue.

"There is an ancient Nonae spell book hidden in a temple in Vitaciel," he informed her as his fingers skimmed over her bare arms. "If you could obtain that book, you would hold the key to creating the most formidable spells known to the Nonae. You would be virtually unstoppable."

Kiara's glossy eyes sparked with delighted intrigue. "So I'll get the book," she decided rashly. "When can I leave?"

"The sooner the better," he declared. "I thought Kain could go with you. He wouldn't be recognized by the Nonae if you needed to slip by unnoticed. I, however, am infamously known throughout the Dark Forest."

She didn't bother protesting. Had he assigned this mission to her two months ago, she would have stubbornly fought for Avian's company in place of his brother's. Being around Avian was confusing, unnatural—entirely different than how she had felt around him before his death. "Alright," she said uncaringly.

"I have something to help you," he announced, gracefully sliding out of the sea of covers and waltzing over to Kiara's wooden armoire. A forlorn piece of yellowed paper rested against the wood, seemingly waiting for his touch. He snatched up the paper, waving it delicately in the air for Kiara to see. An intricate drawing had been inked onto the withered parchment. At first, she simply noticed thick black lines weaving together and forming complex swirls, but as she narrowed her gaze and closely examined the drawing, she realized the lines portrayed the hidden paths of the Dark Forest. "I looted Vyntrx's manor in Vitaciel for this," he explained, tossing the map in Kiara's direction. It swayed in the air, falling neatly against the embroidered blanket of her bed.

She hurriedly crawled across the mattress, insatiably snatching up the map. She clutched the worn parchment, her eyes carefully inspecting the elaborate lines inked across the page. Her fingers lovingly traced the markings. "It looks so old."

Avian chuckled softly. Watching her fret over the map, he momentarily allowed himself to forget about the misplaced influence he had issued upon her mind. "It is very old," he confirmed.

She glanced up at him, eyebrows raised. "Won't Vyntrx know you stole this?"

"It's yours, rightfully. Your great-great-grandfather drew that map. It was your mother's before her death."

She smiled softly, feeling as though she had obtained a small glimpse into her mother's life. "I wonder how often she would stare at this."

"Not as much as Vyntrx did. She knows even the most forgotten places in the forest."

Kiara furrowed her brow in skepticism. Her conscious was screaming at her to question his casual observation. A blot of suspicion darkened her thoughts. "Why do you know so much about Vyntrx?"

Avian didn't have to force a shocked expression to contour his features. His control over Kiara's mind should have been preventing speculation from harassing her thoughts, yet she

292

was clearly suspicious. He crossed the room hesitantly, sitting down beside her on the edge of the bed. "Is something the matter?" he paused, laughing nervously. "Has Kain been putting ideas in your head while I've been gone?"

"No, of course not," she lied quickly. "I know he doesn't appreciate your presence, but he wouldn't try to turn me against you..."

Kiara's tone was convincing, but Avian was far from fooled. The abrupt change in the color of her irises captured his attention, revealing her lie by the light grey hue replacing her previously light red eyes. "Then why do you doubt my loyalty? Have I done something to offend you?" he carried on as though he hadn't discovered her dishonesty.

"No," she mumbled shyly, her eyes falling toward the map. "You know so much about the forest and Vyntrx, I was just worried there's a reason behind that—other than recon missions."

"I did live in the forest for a while, you know," he explained, cautiously running his hand across her back. "After my mother died, my father moved our family into a manor house in the forest since his new wife was a Nonae."

Avian's gentle caress sent chills sprawling across her back, but she was not comforted by his touch. "Alright," she said quietly.

"You should leave tomorrow," he suggested. "After you absorb the contents of that book, Ara, you'll possess more than enough power to destroy Vyntrx."

She nodded, gingerly moving out of Avian's grasp as she stood up from the bed and turned her body away from his. "I hope so," she mumbled.

Trust me, he thought bitterly, *if anyone knows Vyntrx's weaknesses and abilities, it's me.*

*****

Kain's hand quivered on the doorknob. His ear was pressed to the wooden door, listening carefully to steady rhythmic sounds of Kiara and Avian's voices.

He woke up in a terrible mood and was able to sense his brother's presence without actually being alerted of his return. He debated for several minutes whether or not he should visit Kiara's room. He figured Avian would be attached to her side like a shadow, but that hadn't halted his legs from hurrying toward her bedroom. He hadn't planned what he was going to say, or what he was going to do—but had simply wanted to guard her from his brother desperately. It was as though Avian were stealing into her bedroom to put a knife through her heart.

"Is something the matter?" Avian's voice spilled out from behind the door, stopping Kain's hand from twisting the doorknob. "Has Kain been putting ideas in your head while I've been gone?"

"No, of course not." Kiara's voice was merely a whisper. "I know he doesn't appreciate your presence, but he wouldn't try to turn me against you..."

Kain's grip lost its motivation. His limp hand swung away from the door, falling to his side. His eyes raked the door as though he were intent on seeing through the wood. *Why?* he thought. *Why would she lie for me?*

Avian had always known that Kain possessed secretive information about his life. He had never doubted that Kain had despised him—and the feeling had more or less been mutual. When their souls had met in Veinya's manor, Kain had instantly figured out the entire scenario behind Avian's fake death, and Avian was completely aware of his brother's enlightenment. There was just one small factor to the story that Avian had managed to keep hidden from Kain—that was, until Kain had interrogated Kiara and divulged Avian's furtiveness. Avian was completely oblivious that Kain had discovered his manipulative scheme, but he didn't plan for him to remain in the dark. He had decided to confront his brother.

Kiara didn't understand the gravity of the situation she had been thrown into. She didn't realize how disastrous the vendetta between the Knight brothers could become. Kain had assumed she possessed a much greater sense of loyalty to Avian than him, yet she had blatantly been dishonest in order to preserve Avian's dwindling respect for his brother.

Kiara's notion of Avian's disloyalty and the caution she executed in revealing Kain's speculation proved merely one sentiment: she had somehow challenged Avian's manipulation and had begun to doubt the fortitude of his sincerity.

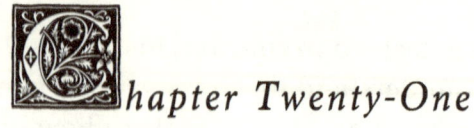

hapter Twenty-One

Return to the Forest

Kiara stared at the map, utterly dumbfounded. During the day leading up to their departure from the castle, and the time they had spent marching through the forest, she had never actually attempted to interpret the directions and had instead been distracted by the intricate designs winding their way across the parchment.

She glanced upward, looking around the forest hopefully. Regardless of the angle she titled her head, every visible part of the wooded area appeared identical. She sighed, handing the map to Kain. "I give up. This is ridiculous."

He brusquely acquired the piece of paper, skimming the contents. "You assume I'll be able to read it? What do you think I was doing during my stay in Veinya's manor? Attending an academy?"

"Don't get snappy with me," she responded dryly. "I basically failed my map-reading lessons with the dukes."

He shrugged dismissively, pointing north. "If I understand this correctly, the fortress is this way."

She glanced at him incredulously. "You figured it out?"

"It's not hard to decode."

She groaned, folding her arms across her chest. "You threw a fit for no reason."

"*I* threw a fit?"

"Let's just keep moving."

Kain sighed, shaking his head in annoyance. He headed in the direction he had pointed as Kiara trailed behind him quietly. The forest was ominously silent, lacking the typical noise of wildlife. Since they had left the castle during midmorning, the sunlight refrained from spilling in through the curtain of trees, condemning the forest to chilled temperatures despite the climate having nearly shifted into summer. Thankful for her cloak, Kiara tucked the fabric around her body, submerging herself in warmth.

She was amazed at Kain's alertness as he wove a path through the forest, his face set in a strikingly concentrated manner. He may not have been able to manipulate magic like a Nonae, but he was able to recognize trees and plants of the forest and distinguish locations that Kiara was utterly oblivious to.

"We're getting close," he muttered.

They had been walking for nearly an hour, and his declaration sparked anxiety and determination in Kiara's veins. "How much longer?"

"I'd say about five minutes. Can't you see the tips of the buildings ahead?" Kain's hand extended forward, his pointer finger directing her attention to a heap of shadows protruding from behind a filter of trees.

"I see it," she replied, her voice wobbling with anxiety. "Can we stop here and rest for a while? You know, to gather our wits?"

"You're nervous, aren't you?"

She sighed, stopping in her tracks. "Yes, and I'm thirsty. Can I have some water?"

He stopped beside her, unlatching a smooth, elastic bag from his belt. He handed her the sack as she sat down against the tightly compacted floor of the forest.

"Don't drink too much," he advised. "That has to last."

"You should have brought more," she rebuked, lightly sipping water from the mouth of the bag.

"Water weighs me down," he complained. "I have to be able to move quickly considering I can't use a weapon and have to rely on my Specialty."

"Here," she said dismissively, tossing him the sack of water as he sat down beside her on the ground. "Drink. You need to be hydrated in case we march into a battle."

Kain followed orders, timidly drinking from the bag. "They'll believe you're a full-blooded Nonae because of your eyes, but they'll suspect something's wrong with me. We need a story in case we're questioned."

"We'll just tell them the truth," she suggested. "You're emotionless and can't use magic."

Kain's eyes narrowed. "That never happens with Nonae. Emotions are very important to them. To be born without a vast array of feelings is unheard of."

"You have quite a knowledge of the Nonae. What were you doing in Veinya's manor, attending an academy?" she joked, a faint smirk brightening her face.

He scowled, suppressing his admiration for her humor. "If anyone asks, I'll be your servant. Say I owe you a life of servitude, or something..." his voice trailed off as he carefully secured the bag of water into place against his belt.

"Except I can't lie," she reminded him, her hands wrapping around her legs as she pulled her knees against her stomach. "So I'll just have to work around the truth."

"You can do it," he muttered shortly, climbing to his feet. "If you don't need anything else, let's get going."

She nodded, resuming her place beside him as they hurried along the path, an unsettling silence rising between them as they neared the city. As the black walls of the citadel crept over the foliage, Kain swore hotly under his breath. Kiara glanced at him quizzically. "What?" she whispered.

"There are guards at the gate. They may not let us in."

She stared straight ahead, discovering four armor-clad soldiers positioned beside a looming, iron-wrought gate. "Don't panic. We're sticking to our plan."

Kain glanced warily at the nearing fortress, his heartbeat accelerating with apprehension. The feeling of his heart fluttering madly in chest had remained a relatively new experience. He couldn't recall his heart ever beating so rapidly as a child—except for that dreadful day he had desperately fled from the sight of his murdered parents, only to have the drumming of his heartbeat cruelly silenced. The warm, rattling sensation spreading through his chest unfailingly terrified him and flooded his mind with unwelcome memories.

"*What* are you?" a guard demanded as Kain and Kiara reached the wall that closed off the city from the rest of the forest.

Kiara's yellow eyes flashed black with annoyance. "A Nonae, clearly."

The guard cocked his helmeted head, pulling his fingers through his coarse beard. "Well, you do have the eyes. I don't recognize you, but you look oddly familiar. What town are you from?"

"I don't belong to a town," she explained slowly. "I have business in the city."

"What kind of business?"

Kiara folded her arms across her chest, scowling. "None of yours."

"Your attitude is fiery and your courage definitely exceeds your small build. You must be acquainted with our empress."

"Vyntrx?" she assumed, her eyebrows rising. "Yes, we are *definitely* acquainted."

The guard pointed at Kain, who appeared heavily disgruntled as his purple eyes raked the soldiers. "Who's your companion?" the soldier inquired. "His eyes are violet but he doesn't appear gleeful."

"An Evalseman," she answered simply. "Don't worry. He serves my cause."

The guard appeared skeptical. He exchanged glances with the other soldiers, but their eyes were hidden in the shadows of their helmets, preventing Kiara from reading their emotions.

"We aren't carrying weapons," she added. "We obviously cannot do any harm."

The guard sighed, nodding at the soldier nearest the gate. "Very well. Since the empress has two full-blooded Evalseman in her innermost circle of trusted adversaries, it isn't my place to judge the company of other Nonae. You may proceed. Stay out of trouble, Evalseman."

The gates of the iron wall swung open with a screech as Kiara caught her first glimpse of her aunt's citadel. Every building in sight was seemingly constructed from shadows; every citizen wandering the streets of the city was draped in dull, black garments. A hauntingly ominous sensation weakened Kiara's limbs as she forced herself to step into the fortress.

The gates slammed shut, narrowly evading Kain's body as he reached Kiara's side. His eyes widened in amazement, his face paling. "This place..." he muttered.

"How does anyone stand to live here?" she wondered quietly.

"They're full-blooded Nonae. They probably aren't affected."

Her eyes narrowed, flashing red with anger. "Nonae aren't all evil, Kain. Our mothers' lives are all the validation you should need."

"Shut up, I know," he snapped, his fingers casually winding around Kiara's hand. "We need to find the temple."

"Does it show the way on the map?" she wondered as he led her along the bustling road.

He shook his head. "No, the instructions end here. It's up to us now."

"Where are we going, then?"

"We're getting out of this district. There are peasants for miles. I doubt Veinya's holy temple would share quarters with the filth of the city."

Kiara's free hand smacked Kain's shoulder. "Shh! They'll hear you."

"Calm down, princess. They wouldn't do anything."

"How will we know when the districts change?"

He laughed without humor. "Are you really that spacey? Don't you notice shared traits between Enevale and Vyntrx's citadel? The slums of the city are closer to the wall because the common people are more disposable in case of an attack. The higher-class quarters are located towards the middle of the city—" he broke off, pointing in the direction of a colossal manor in the distance that encompassed the immediate center of the fortress, "—in order to provide utmost protection. Of course, the layout here is slightly different than that of Enevale. There isn't much behind the castle besides training grounds, but here, the manor is heavily protected by rows upon rows of streets."

"You are incredibly observant," Kiara noticed, admiration teeming through the tone of her voice. "I would never have figured that out."

"I'm sure you would've—*anyone* would," he mumbled, pulling her through a gilded archway. The dirt road suddenly expanded into cobblestones, the weather-beaten houses replaced by finely crafted manors. "Notice the change in location, princess?"

"Actually, yes," she breathed, a dizzying sensation passing through her limbs as the dismal feeling associated with the slums was thankfully replaced by a piqued curiosity as her eyes darted from house to house.

Kain slowed his determined pace as they stumbled upon a stretch of the city reminiscent of a town square. Nobles wound their way through the crowds, their servants trailing behind as they struggled to maintain a grip on items their masters had purchased. Various stores lined the square; vendor stalls obscured the open space between buildings. In the center of the street, a charcoal clock tower stretched toward the open sky, a heavy curtain of dark grey clouds concealing the sun above.

"Excuse me," Kiara addressed a nearby noble, gently

releasing Kain's hand. "Could you point me in the direction of Veinya's temple?"

The noble scoffed, her heavily blackened eyes flashing the color of her eyeliner. "What sort of Nonae isn't aware of the location of the goddess' sanctuary?" she huffed, quickening her pace and disappearing into a crowd of citizens.

Kiara's irises burned scarlet, a sigh of frustration escaping her lips. Kain's mouth opened, an attempt at a comforting phrase forming along his lips, but he was silenced as the piercing sound of a siren resonated through the square.

"Attention, citizens," a booming, disembodied voice sounded. "Our beloved empress Vyntrx has returned to Vitaciel! She will be led through the city to Bloodstone Square, where she will deliver a speech before retreating to her manor. Attendance to this address is not optional!"

The little color left in Kiara's cheeks fled immediately. She shared a foreboding glance with Kain, whose hands were already flying toward his hood. He hid his face behind the fabric, hastily pushing Kiara's hood over her head and pulling her into the shadows of a nearby alleyway. A roar of delight surged across the square as Vyntrx—flanked by soldiers and four companions who wore cloaks identical to the empress's— paraded onto the scene. A maniacal smile cut across her pale face, her dark hair unusually braided away from her eyes. She waltzed into the square, reveling in each low bow she received. Waves of citizens poured in from conjoining streets, every one of them fighting to obtain the best view of the empress. She climbed the steps leading to the platform of the clock tower, her companions dutifully filing in behind her as the soldiers lined the circular stage, their weapons held forward, silently daring the crowd to move even an inch closer to the Nonae royalty.

"Hello, my loyal followers!" Vyntrx shouted, her voice managing to explode across the square and silence the rampant cheers. "Today is a cause for celebration! The Nonae race has officially obtained a new formidable ally—the Arlyn! These creatures live beyond the Dark Forest—in the unknown lands—and have been persuaded to offer us their military services in our conquest to expand our reign!" her declaration was rewarded with a wave of applause as smiles slipped across the faces of the two women and two men—one obviously a Demmonai—that stood behind the empress. "For this wonderful addition to our ranks, we have no one to thank but my beloved adversaries."

"Move, Kiara," Kain whispered suddenly, tightly grabbing Kiara's wrist. He led her out of the alleyway, scaling the edge of a nearby building. The crowd had grown so dense, he knew it would be utterly impossible for Vyntrx to spot Kiara's diminutive body from afar as they carefully wove their way through the crowds.

"*What* are we doing?" she whispered hotly.

"Just keep moving," he ordered. His eyes latched on a nearby inn, the wooden sign above the door wavering slightly in the persistent breeze.

"As you may have noticed, my most trusted advisor is missing from our ranks today," Vyntrx's voice sounded eerily. Kain's lock on Kiara's wrist increased heavily. She instinctively winced, fighting off the impulse to yank her arm free of his unrelenting clutch.

"Naturally, he is attending matters concerning the other side of his double life," her explanation was accompanied by a horrendous laugh that echoed through the crowd.

Kain quickened his pace, hastily yanking open the door of the inn and pushing Kiara inside. "But our beloved A—" Vyntrx's voice was abruptly silenced as Kain hurriedly sealed off the entrance to the empty tavern. He uncharacteristically embraced Kiara as his back fell against the door of the inn, his hands covering her ears and drowning her ability to hear in sheer silence.

Her eyes turned bright yellow with shock, her hands

automatically gripping Kain's, attempting to pry away his touch. Knowing he couldn't fight against Kiara's Evalseman strength, he invoked his own Specialty to control her hands. Her arms fell limply to her side, but he didn't anticipate the harsh kick she suddenly sent to his knees.

"*What* has come over you?" she demanded an explanation as he released her body, his hands dashing to his injured leg.

"The inn's empty," he explained, his hair falling into his eyes as he stared down at her. "It's a perfect time to use one of these rooms as a hide-out."

"It's just barely afternoon. We should continue looking."

"What happens when we don't find it and we need a place to stay the night? This is our only chance."

Kiara bit her lip, stealing a glance outside through a nearby window. Vyntrx was standing in the square, her hands waving as she spoke to the crowd. The thick walls of the inn reduced Vyntrx's booming voice to a mere whisper, but Kiara wasn't listening to the noise outside. "Why did you cover my ears?" she wondered.

"Let's go upstairs," Kain muttered dismissively. "We'll miss our chance if we don't hurry."

She wearily eyed the wooden staircase in the corner of the tavern that was partially hidden behind a wide pub. Half-drained drinks dotted the bar, padded stools pushed aside from the chaos that must have taken place before Vyntrx's appearance. "Why did you cover my ears?" she repeated firmly, setting her hands on her hips. "What did Vyntrx say that you didn't want me to hear?"

"I, uh, I thought she was going to say something rude about you."

"Oh, so, you just wanted to spare my feelings?" she huffed disbelievingly.

Kain nodded. *That's exactly what I was doing,* he thought sourly. *Protecting you.*

She sighed, shaking her head in astonishment. She crossed

the room, heading toward the staircase, the flat heel of her boots loudly clicking against the wooden floors.

He smirked slightly as he watched her pout; her arms were crossed tightly across her chest, her face set in a frustrated expression.

He followed after her hastily, climbing the steps and reaching the second floor of the inn. Several doors were thrown open, revealing that they had been in use before Vyntrx's apparition. Kiara discovered an unopened door at the end of the dimly lit hallway, but tried the handle and found it locked. She sighed, her head falling against the darkly painted doorway with a thud. "All of the open rooms are being used but we can't get inside the locked ones. Your plan failed."

"Did not," he argued, twisting the knob. The door swung open and Kiara nearly fell into the room. She caught herself, staring at him in astonishment.

"How did you—" she started.

"I just had to control the lock," he explained, striding into the bedroom. He shut and locked the door behind them, disdainfully eyeing the large window at the edge of the room. Through the thick glass, the crowded square was visible. Vyntrx had dismounted the platform and was being led to her manor by the parade of soldiers. The sun hung low in the sky, masked by hoards of swirling, grey clouds.

Kain quickly drew the curtains across the window, the faint light filling the bedroom instantly chased away by shadows. "We should keep the lights off," he advised. "Otherwise someone may see the light from under the door and grow suspicious."

She nodded slowly, but Kain couldn't decipher her figure through the darkness. "Are you hungry?" she inquired. "I brought bread."

"That's all?" he rebuffed, fumbling through the room in an attempt to discover her location. His leg rammed into a nearby dresser as he swore loudly in pain.

"I'm over here," she called. "I'm sitting on the bed."

"How did you manage to get there without tripping?"

She frowned, unlatching the food pouch from her belt. "It was close to the door."

Kain blindly stepped forward, his legs rubbing against the woolen blanket of the bed. He graciously jumped onto the mattress, startling Kiara as she scoured the sack for two pieces of bread.

"Here," she whispered, carefully handing him a piece of bread. "I have dried meat, too, if you want some."

"Of course I do," he mumbled, taking a bite of his roll.

Kiara's hands clumsily clutched the piece of meat as she reached toward Kain, placing the food into his outstretched hand. He ate quickly, asking for another piece of meat before he had completely finished his first. She complied, but warned him that if they ran out of rations, they would be forced to steal food from one of the vendors in the square.

"That'd be easy," he muttered, finishing his meal in one large gulp. He lay on his side and rolled away from her. "Now we wait."

"We should sneak out early tomorrow morning if we don't want to be noticed," she advised, carefully setting the bag of food and her cloak on the ground below. She pulled down the woolen comforter, covering her body with the warm blankets. "Where are you going to sleep?"

Kain snickered. "On the bed. Obviously."

"But I'm sleeping here."

"What makes you so special?" he argued, tossing off his cloak. "Just because you snuggled up under the blankets first doesn't mean you've claimed the bed."

Kiara's eyebrows furrowed. "But I'm the princess."

He laughed without humor. "I didn't think you cared about status."

"I brought you back to life."

"I saved yours."

"I bent the truth to get us into Vitaciel."

He sighed, pushing back the bedspread and joining Kiara under the covers. His heart thudded with embarrassment as he brushed his arm across hers, but he attempted to appear calm. "It was my idea to sneak into the inn while no one was around."

"Then it's your fault we're in this mess, so you should sleep on the floor."

"You're just afraid it'd make Avian mad if we fell asleep in the same bed," he countered, turning in her direction.

Kiara's cheeks flushed and she was suddenly grateful for the darkness of the room. "He wouldn't be upset. Nothing's going to happen."

"Then it shouldn't be an issue."

She sighed in defeat, pulling the covers over her blushing face. "Fine. Whatever. We can share the bed."

"Thank you."

"Why did you cover my ears earlier?"

Kain groaned irritably, rolling on his side and turning his entire body away from her. "Go to sleep."

"No, I'm not tired. It's midday."

"What else are we supposed to do? We're stuck here until morning."

Kiara's eyes peeked out from under the covers. She could just vaguely distinguish the outline of Kain's body in the darkness. "And whose fault is that? We could still be searching."

"I didn't want us to be stuck outside in the chilly wind through the entire night. I didn't feel like listening to you gripe and I don't think I could fend you off if you tried to cuddle with me to keep warm."

"Whatever," Kiara muttered. "You just wanted an excuse to share a bed with me."

"If I wanted you in bed with me, you'd know."

"Tough talk for someone who was dead through puberty."

Kain stifled an uncontrollable laugh, a choking noise bubbling in the base of his throat. He involuntarily sat up, staring at Kiara through the dense shadows. "Th-that doesn't mean it didn't happen!"

Kiara curved her torso upward, resting her weight on her elbows as she leaned into a sitting position. "Struck a nerve, have I?"

"N-no!" he spluttered. "Of course not!"

"Maybe *that's* why you're so unemotional. I haven't caught you staring at any of the girls in the castle and you seem uninterested in pursuing any sort of romantic relationship with anyone. You're still stuck in that little boy stage where girls are icky, huh?"

He scowled, pushing Kiara's shoulder and sending her off balance. Her back fell against the mattress as she erupted into laughter.

"It's not like that!" he shouted defensively, blushing furiously.

She stared up at him through strands of her disheveled hair. His light purple eyes were his only feature she could readily discriminate through the shadows. "Kain," she whispered, "it's funny. I can't picture Avian and I just sitting here laughing and talking. I used to be able to picture my entire life with him by my side, but now, the thought seems foreign and unreal. I fell in love with him quickly after I arrived in Enevale, but now I'm not sure what I feel. My head's a jumbled mess. You're the only one I can freely speak to, the only one I can be myself around. I'm just so confused. I don't know what's happening to me..."

He sighed, lying down closer to her than he had been before his outburst. He held his hand forward experimentally, lightly touching her tangled hair. He had only known her for two short months, but in that diminutive span of time, she had forced her way into his head and stuck there as if she had tattooed her name across the sensitive, exposed tissue of his heart. He felt a burning desire to protect her—and he had always been too selfish to protect anyone. His entire life, until the day he met Kiara, had been encompassed by death, regret, and revenge. She was a bright, blazing sun in the center of his shadowy world; her rays of compassion relentlessly chased away the darkness that had continually soiled his mentality. The thought of a portentous cloud unjustly darkening his sun fueled his body with rage and his hatred for Avian spiked with velocity. "I—I don't know what to say," he whispered delicately.

She shrugged, blinking hard. "Don't worry about it. You don't have to say anything."

"Alright," he mumbled.

"Good night, Kain," she said softly. "You can keep playing with my hair, if you want." She rolled over on her side, her back facing him. Her long, unpinned hair swept across the pillow, inviting him to gently stroke his fingers through her wavy tresses.

"Night, princess," he muttered huskily. And although Kiara's breathing was steady and docile as her mind slipped into rest, Kain knew with profound certainty that she was crying. She was crying from confusion, ambiguity—and more than anything—because all of the emotions she was bitterly experiencing were transpiring because of Avian.

Chapter Twenty-Two

The Clandestine Temple

The sun crept over the horizon, bathing Menevilen in a faint dull light. In the depths of the Dark Forest, the minute sunlight vaguely broke through the trees. The Nonae capitol of Vitaciel was shrouded in shadows, a minimal amount of light trickling through the omnipresent clouds that constantly darkened Vyntrx's citadel.

Kain stirred in his sleep, his mind slowly lurching into consciousness. There was a light pressure on his chest and arm, disturbing his slumber and disrupting his comfort. His eyes gradually flickered open; there was a very slight difference in the darkness behind his closed eyelids and the darkness of the bedroom.

"Kiara?" he called softly, turning his face in her direction. His chin bumped against something solid—he glanced down, barely distinguishing her head against his chest. Her shoulder lay on top of his arm, trapping him between her body and the mattress. He smiled, absentmindedly skimming his fingers across the fabric of her shirt. She grumbled in her sleep, shattering his reverie and drawing him back to his senses. He expertly detangled his body from hers, accidentally slamming his back into the nearby dresser as he dismounted the bed.

Kain's abrupt movement and the ruckus he caused aroused Kiara from her slumber. Her eyes opened slowly as she sat up, hugging the covers around her small frame and groggily staring around the dark room.

"Kain?" she called hoarsely. "Where are you?"

"O-Over here," he spluttered.

"What're you doing over there?"

"I, uh, fell off the bed."

She laughed quietly. "And we all think *I'm* the klutz," she muttered. "Do you want to eat some breakfast before we sneak out?"

"I'm not hungry," he replied shortly.

She nodded, suggesting that they should commence preparations for departure. He didn't reply and she took his silence as compliance. She carefully scrambled around the floor of the bedroom, gathering her discarded cloak and the sack carrying the provisions. "You're awfully quiet this morning," she noted, tying her cloak into place over her shoulders.

"Sorry," he mumbled, retrieving his own cloak from the floor.

She frowned, securing the bag against her belt. "Did something happen?"

"We're trapped in a pitch-black bedroom in the ungodly hours of the morning in a foreign Nonae village in the Dark Forest. Yes, I think something drastic happened—like, oh, I know, my girlfriend burst into the room and broke up with me for laying in a bed with another woman."

Kiara scowled at his sarcasm, but he couldn't discern the change in her facial expression through the shadows. "*Lying,*" she snapped matter-of-factly. "You were *lying* with me."

"I don't remember lying about anything. Except for when I said I have a girlfriend."

Kiara yelled in frustration, tossing her hands into the air dramatically. "You're unbelievable!"

"And *you're* going to get us discovered. Shut up!"

"You're really pissing me off," she derided. "You should stay here. I'll go look for the book myself."

"You're directionally challenged. You won't find anything except trouble."

She scoffed, fiddling around the room as she attempted to discover the door. "You're deficient of emotion."

"At least I'm not a love-sick idiot."

"You're a bastard." Her hands rammed into the biting cold metal of the doorknob as she industriously unlatched the lock. "You should have eaten breakfast earlier because I'm taking the food with me," she said coldly, thrusting open the door. A waterfall of light flooded the bedroom, highlighting her livid face as her flaming red eyes scanned the shadows for Kain. He stood in-between the bed and the dresser, blinking rapidly from the unannounced presence of light.

"I have the water," he reminded her, sweeping back the edge of his cloak to reveal the smooth container latched to his belt.

Her eyebrows knitted together, her grip tightened around the edge of the door so ferociously, her knuckles turned white. "You finally found something that can actually stand to be around you. You two will be very happy together." And with a conclusive, incensed countenance, Kiara slammed the door shut, condemning Kain to the shadows and dividing the pair as though they were as separate as night and day.

*****

"She's so stupid!" Kain released an indignant cry, angrily kicking the bedside dresser. *How does she manage to twist my emotions around?* he wondered silently. *Am I nothing but a helpless puppet?*

He had replayed their argument in his mind a hundred times, but he still couldn't understand how she had secured the audacity to abandon him. He had admitted to himself that their conflict had been the effect of his own stubbornness, but he had stupidly bitten his tongue as he watched her leave. He knew it wasn't too late to run after her and explain why he had misbehaved so significantly. He wanted to protect her from whatever dangerous situation she was unavoidably going to thrust herself into. He chided himself for allowing an accident-prone, unobservant klutz to wander off into the streets of an unfamiliar city on her own. But his pride had chained his feet to the ground during her departure and he was still fighting his dignity for the key to his freedom.

He suddenly heard his name. It had been shrieked desperately, helplessly, the high pitch of the exclamation conveying peril as the voice sprinted up the staircase of the inn and blasted through the doorway of the concealed bedroom. He knew instantly—by the lump in his throat, the sinking sensation in his chest, the cold chills that ran down his spine, and the furious, scathing hot blood that boiled through his veins—that Kiara's safety had been propelled into jeopardy.

*****

Kiara's eyes burned; she could *feel* the blazing crimson of her irises as her head pounded with perpetual anger. She had always possessed a short temper and gotten her feelings hurt far too easily. She couldn't comprehend Kain's sudden snappiness. She didn't understand what she had done to offend him. Her chest ached as though the precautionary bandage she had placed over her heart had been violently ripped away. The walls of solitude she had relied on throughout her childhood had been stripped away since entering Enevale. She no longer possessed the innate ability to wallow in isolation—she relied too heavily on Avian or Kain's presence. And she abhorred it. She hated relying on anyone else for her own happiness. More than anything, she hated Kain for lowering her guard and herself for being upset over a minuscule dispute.

She bounded down the staircase, no longer bothering to be discreet. She had abandoned the effort of secrecy. The desire to invoke a battle bubbled in her chest—she figured it was the only action to take could take to placate her frustration.

The staircase leaked into the foyer of the inn, but she didn't yield before passing through. Three men were positioned at the bar, two of them swigging down drinks while the bartender yawned sleepily in the corner of the room. The two men's heads swiveled automatically, their eyes simultaneously flashing light pink with lust as they drank in the sight of a young woman waltzing through the pub.

"'Ey, pretty miss," one of the inebriated men slurred. "Wha' ya doin' here?"

"Leaving," she huffed, refusing to slow her pace as she hurried toward the door.

One of the men moved quicker than what she would have deemed capable by an intoxicated person, suddenly blocking her path. "Only pleasure girls are out this early in the mornin'," he whispered, repugnant breath reeking off his lips and spilling into Kiara's face. She gagged. "They usually abandon their companions at this time. You a pleasure girl, lass?"

"No," she answered firmly, pushing the man aside. "I'm leaving."

"None of us will judge ya," he assured her, wrapping his arms around her shoulders. "We got lotsa money to spend, though, pet."

"Get off me!" she cried, pooling her Evalseman strength to detach the man's arms from her body. He stumbled away, a curious expression playing on his unshaven face.

"You..." he muttered. "How'd you do that?"

She rolled her eyes, turning toward the exit once more. The two drunken men sent each other knowing glances, devious smirks crawling across their lips. They raised their hands simultaneously, casting a spell at Kiara's retreating form.

She was suddenly writhing in pain, her body slinking toward the ground as she lost control over her limbs. Her eyes widened as the men peered over her unmoving body, but she could not will her limbs to cooperate. She wanted to kick, to claw, to bite—but she couldn't do anything except stare in horror as they knelt on the ground beside her body. She screamed, surprised her vocal cords had not been shut off, as one of the men forcefully ripped her cloak away from her shoulders. He laughed at her desperate scream, promising her that her efforts were pointless.

The other man was sitting beside her waist, toying with the leather belt around her hips. Her eyes welled with perturbed, vulnerable tears as she shrieked hopelessly. She caught a glimpse of the man's visage as he unbuckled her belt, his eyes wide and violet, portraying his glee. The deep purple of his irises were unlike Kain's, but the sight provoked a thought of potential hope inside her mind. She screamed Kain's name, straining her voice to volumes she had never achieved. She managed to call his name three times before the man at her waist caught on, his hand flying toward her face as she was struck with a spell that silenced her cries.

One of the men had untied her vest and was slowly sliding his hand under her shirt whenever she noticed Kain's head above the man's shoulder. Her rescuer's face possessed a look of sheer fury as he raised his hand high above his head, swinging his fist across the man's neck with the most force she had ever seen him execute. Without stopping for a second, his booted foot flew forward, violently making contact with the other man. Neither of the intoxicated men accepted defeat, and even though they were nursing bruised and bleeding wounds, stood up readily.

The spell over Kiara's body relented and she gratefully regained jurisdiction of her limbs. She inhaled loudly, scrambling around on the floor as she tried to decide her course of action.

"Stay out of this fight, Kiara," Kain instructed sternly, eyeing her attackers as though they were worst form of scum in the worlds. "I'll be with you in a minute."

Under normal conditions, she would have stubbornly argued with Kain's advice and forced her way into the battle, but she was still shaken up from the vileness of the drunken men. Her skin crawled with disgust, the feeling of violation and filthiness sinking through her flesh and poisoning her blood.

She stood up, hastily re-buckling her belt as she sprinted to the other side of the room, abandoning her torn cloak on the ground—she knew she would have to trash the ruined article of clothing, anyway. The bartender stood at the edge of the room, his eyes shut and body slumped against the wall. She had wondered why he hadn't initially come to her rescue and she was relieved to discover that he hadn't simply ignored her cries.

Without warning, Kain controlled a nearby table, smashing the object into the nearest Nonae. The man yelled in surprise, crashing to the ground as the piece of furniture sharply fell on top of his body, shattering his consciousness.

"Wha' kind of magic is tha'?" the other man questioned, staring at Kain incredulously.

"Evalseman," he answered shortly, darting forward and striking the standing Nonae's stomach.

He ignored the pain, sending a blow toward Kain's head. Kain ducked, ramming his leg upward into the Nonae's groin. He screamed loudly as his body was overwhelmed by the injury, staring at Kain with red eyes full of anger. "You evil Evalseman," he cursed.

"Got a knife, have you?" Kain wondered, eyeing a handle protruding from the Nonae's pocket. He reached toward the weapon, quickly withdrawing it from the folds of fabric that had concealed its unsheathed blade. "Would you like to do the honors, or should I?"

"Don't kill them, Kain," Kiara spoke hoarsely. "They're very drunk."

The man attempted to swipe the weapon out of Kain's grip, but he was suddenly pushed against the wall by an invisible force. He kicked his legs in protest, but Kain's control over the man allowed him to forcibly pin his enemy's back to the stone.

Kain glanced over at Kiara through a waterfall of his dark hair. "I don't care how drunk they are," he said simply.

"They're the enemy and they harmed you. Who knows what would have happened if I hadn't stopped them."

"But—" her voice faltered.

"You've killed Demmonai because they're monsters," Kain reasoned, eyeing the sharp blade in his hand. "This man is a monster. Close your eyes if you don't want to watch."

The Nonae's pupils widened with fear as Kain turned toward him. "No!" he pleaded. "Don't kill me! I don't want to die!"

"Should've thought about the consequences to your actions, then," Kain said darkly, striding toward the trapped man. He handed the handle of the dagger to the Nonae, but the man's body was completely under Kain's control. The Nonae watched in horror as Kain's eyes urged his hand forward, drawing the blade inevitably closer to his own chest.

"No—no—please—I can't—!" he implored, his hands quivering as Kain sent the knife closer and closer to the man's heart.

"Tell her you're sorry," Kain demanded, the blade prickling against the fabric of the Nonae's shirt.

"Sorry—I'm sorry!" he spluttered.

He stared at the Nonae disdainfully. "Pathetic."

The knife twisted inside the Nonae's hands, the sharp edge of the blade tearing through his shirt as he unwillingly stabbed through his own flesh. His eyes were dilated and maroon with fright, his mouth gaping open in a silent, broken scream.

Kiara whimpered slightly at the ghastly sight, shutting her eyes as she turned her head away from the scene. Kain waited until the last inch of life had fled from the Nonae's eyes before he released his control over the man's hands. The knife fell to the floor with a small clatter, splattering the fabric of Kain's pants with blood.

"Murderer!" the other Nonae exclaimed. He had regained consciousness just as the knife had passed through his comrade's chest and had been struggling to break free from the constraint of the heavy table.

Kain turned to the man. Kiara opened her eyes, directing her attention to the Nonae.

"You saw what happened," Kain said dully. "He killed himself."

The table flew away from the Nonae in a fit of rage, his hands glowing red with flames as he jumped to his feet. Refraining from continuing with aimless banter, he flung an unidentifiable spell in Kain's direction. He managed to duck out of the way, but the wall behind him subsequently caught fire. His gaze immediately locked on the flames, that familiar scent of ashes striking a chord of unwanted familiarity within his heart.

Mummy, it smells like smoke, a chilling voice crept through Kain's brain, instantly paralyzing him with horror.

The Nonae took Kain's moment of vulnerability as a gift. He sprung forward, pulling the stunned young man to the ground. The man's fists pounded Kain's blank face relentlessly, but his mind—reeling with the haunting scenes of his past— was unable to translate the pain.

Kiara dashed into action. She kicked the Nonae's stomach— sending him sprawling to the ground—as she raced toward the billowing flames. She captured her cloak, momentarily ignoring the lifeless body of Kain's victim as she fumbled with the fabric. She carefully smoldered the flames, coughing hysterically as she unintentionally inhaled the smoke.

With Kiara distracted, the Nonae continued to pillage the wellness from Kain's body, continually tarnishing his face with ferocious attacks. Kain couldn't feel the pain. He couldn't feel anything. His mind had faded from reality since the smoke had welled inside his nostrils. He could only picture those scarlet, deadly flames and Vyntrx's menacing smile as she received a lavish feast of terror. The image of his brother's desperate, guilty expression along with the the body of his dead mother— her chest empty, her eyes blank and lifeless, the color drained from her irises—flashed beneath his eyelids.

The flames were slowly subdued by Kiara's efforts. She sighed in relief, staring at the charred wood-and-stone wall. Kain's groan of pain captured her attention. She discarded her ruined cloak, tackling the Nonae and pushing him away from Kain's body. She fell on top of the man, repeatedly punching his face. Distracted by the pain, the Nonae's ability to summon magic was handicapped, rendering his defenses hopeless.

Kiara continued bludgeoning the man until her sore knuckles signaled for her to relent. She complied, eyeing the bruises that were already forming along the pale skin of her hands. She stood up wearily, sending a sharp kick to the Nonae's side. His face was bloodied, his hands covering his eyes in dismay. She spat at the ground beside him, cursing.

Kain was still lying on the ground, slowly returning from his relapse. She hurried to his side, gently placing his head over her lap. She brushed his hair out of his eyes, staring down at him concernedly. His face had taken a nasty beating. Blood caked his nostrils, his lips. His tresses were matted together, plastered to his forehead in a combination of sweat and blood.

"Kain," she cooed. "Are you alright?"

His eyelids fluttered slightly. "Mother," he whispered. "Don't be dead..."

"Shh," she spoke soothingly, running her palm across his cheek. Tears clouded his eyes, dampening his face. "The fire's gone. You're okay."

"Ki-Kiara," he stuttered, a twinge of fear underlining the tone of his voice. "Is Kiara okay?"

"She's fine," she assured him, lightly kissing his forehead. "She's fine."

"Have to—" he coughed, blood spewing from his mouth. "—protect her."

Kiara opened her mouth to reply, but she was suddenly lifted into the air, Kain's safety slipping from her fingertips. She screamed, twisting around to discover the Nonae, his face drenched in blood. His hands had captured her underneath her armpits, deeming her arms useless. He hadn't been smart enough to lock her legs, however, and she readily took advantage of his carelessness. She swung her foot backward, harshly colliding with the man's groin.

The Nonae yelled in response, dropping Kiara against the wooden floor. She scrambled to her feet, rushing to the bar and obtaining one of the half-drained bottles. As the Nonae lurched toward her, she swung the bottle heavily, smashing the glass sharply against his head. The bottle shattered alongside the Nonae's consciousness as he slid to the ground with a definite thud.

The bartender, still miraculously inebriated and unresponsive, snored in his sleep. Kiara eyed him bitterly, wondering whose side he would have chosen had he been awake. Before she had managed to peel her gaze away from the pub, the door to the inn suddenly flew open, instantly captivating her attention.

The faint light of the morning sky spilled into the dimly lit room, heightening the dark outline of a cloaked figure as it dominated the doorway. It was evident of the intruder's gender by her stance and stature. Her cloak gently hugged her curves, the hood just barely concealing her shoulder-length hair. Kiara knew instantly that the mysterious woman was not Vyntrx—the mysterious woman was slightly shorter and narrower in stature than the empress, and as the dull light fell on the intruder's hair, it glistened the color of honey.

"Are you Kiara?" she spoke hurriedly. Kiara was instantly taken aback by the strange familiarity of the voice.

"Yes," she said hesitantly. "Who are you?"

"I've been looking everywhere for you," she explained, removing her hood with a toss of her head. Light brown hair spilled around her shoulders, her Nonae eyes flashing turquoise with excitement. "The smoke sent me in this direction. My name's Kailx. I'm here to rescue you."

*****

Kailx carefully lit the lamps in the kitchen without using a match. Kiara watched in awe as she gracefully summoned a small flicker of flame, placing the fire against the wick of the candle with expert skill.

Kiara sat comfortably in an upholstered chair, her eyes occasionally wandering in Kain's direction. He had slipped into rest before they had even reached Kailx's flat and had been asleep nearly all morning. Kiara had taken the liberty of washing away the soot, sweat, and blood from his face, even though Kailx had insisted that she help. Kailx had been tremendously gracious, and had even helped Kiara drag Kain from the inn and into her nearby apartment by the faint light of sunrise.

"Now that we're all settled in, will you please explain who you are?" Kiara inquired politely, drawing her attention away from Kain long enough to stare Kailx directly in the eyes. There was something about her—something blatantly familiar—that Kiara couldn't quite pinpoint.

"I would prefer my identity to remain secret for the time being," she replied casually, sifting through her cabinets. "I assure you, though, you will know everything soon. I can also promise you that I am your friend, your supporter, and most importantly, your fan."

"Fan?" Kiara echoed. "What do you mean?"

Kailx smiled gently, withdrawing two teacups from the cupboard. "Your name is commonly heard in Vitaciel, Kiara. Actually, you're infamous all throughout the Dark Forest. You don't typically acquire fans, however—mainly just the opposite."

"Why did you develop a difference stance?"

She shrugged, her pin-straight hair bunching against her shoulders. "I was raised in the shadow of evil, so I desperately clung to the light. I once met Cylis Septimus," she broke off, filling the cups with water from a jar she withdrew from an ice-covered box, "he was battling one of my family members, but I couldn't help but cheer him on. Whenever I didn't rush to my mother's side, he questioned my motive. I couldn't articulate my feelings but he could see right through me. He smiled and promised me that if I stuck by my values, he would accept me into his society whenever I turned seventeen. That's still a year and a half away, and my mother would never allow it..."

"How old are you?"

Kailx smirked shyly. "I'm fifteen."

Kiara shook her head in disbelief, gaping at the young girl. "That's not possible! You're so much taller than me."

She chuckled slightly. "A lot of people are taller than you, Kiara."

Kiara disregarded the girl's comment, tucking away a persistent strand of hair behind her ear. "Cylis Septimus, huh? Avian and I came across his encampment when we were headed to Enevale from my village."

"Although he despises Enevale, he and Vyntrx are old enemies," Kailx explained, retrieving a small jar from the cabinet and lightly pouring herbs from its opening into the cups of water. "Cylis's story is renowned. His father died at the hands of King Kyan when Cylis was just three years old. He grew up by the whim of his nursemaid, harboring a hatred of Enevale for stealing his father away from him. Legend has it that on his tenth birthday, he was visited by his mother's sister. Apparently, it had taken her years to discover his location—since he was brought up in a manor house outside any of the Nonae villages—and she explained the entire situation of his mother's death. His hatred for Evalseman grew with velocity until she revealed a secret about his father that changed his outlook on Nonae entirely. No one knows what crime his father had committed, but it was enough to confuse Cylis." Fire erupted above her hands, directly warming up the contents of the teacups. "A few years later, a rumor about a secret society of rebellious Nonae spread among the masses. The leader was supposedly fourteen-year-old Cylis. Vyntrx, naturally, visited the rebels in an attempt to sway them away from their cause. According to her, neutrality is weakness, and she demanded they took a firm stance on the war. They refused and have been enemies of the empress ever since. Vyntrx has been hunting Cylis down for years but many think he's escaped from the Dark Forest and entered into unknown territory. I don't believe that, though, because he sends Vyntrx warning messages on a weekly basis," she concluded her story, gingerly handing Kiara a steaming cup of tea.

Kiara obtained the mug gratefully, the warmth of the china heating up her chilled fingers. "My father killed Cylis's father," she realized, staring into the honey-brown depths of tea. "Cylis probably wants me dead, too."

Kailx shook her head, slipping into the chair opposite the princess. "He has abandoned his hatred for the old king. Whatever happened between Kyan and Cylis's father was explainable and it was enough to deter Cylis's feeling of abhorrence for the king."

"Maybe I'll properly meet him," Kiara mused, sipping the warm beverage. "It will have to be after this war, though. I don't have time for pleasantries."

"You and I are speaking casually," Kailx reminded her. "Over tea, no less."

"I have a favor to ask of you," she responded hastily, withdrawing the cup from her parched lips. "Do you know where Veinya's temple is?"

Kailx sighed, nodding slowly. "I had a feeling you would inquire about that. The temple is hidden underground. Every citizen knows its location but the covered site eludes intruders. You're looking for the ancient spell book, yes?"

Kiara nodded in validation.

"That book is extremely old. Legend says it was written by

the first Nonae to enter the Dark Forest. If you want lessons on magic, I would comply."

Kiara quickly shook her head. "No, I need to learn magic that even Vyntrx doesn't comprehend. It's vital to the prosperity of my kingdom."

Kailx eyed the princess warily, her knuckles rapping against the edge of the teacup as she stared into the depths of her beverage thoughtfully. "It will be dangerous. The spell book is located within the deepest rooms of the temple. I'm sure drastic precautionary measures have been taken to ensure the book's safety. I cannot promise that your life won't be put into immediate risk."

"During the short span of time I have lived in Enevale, I have been thrust into more precarious situations than I had ever endured throughout the majority of my life," she responded tightly, recalling the hefty amount of times her vitality had been threatened in the past five months. "I assure you, Kailx, the prospect of danger no longer terrifies me."

Kailx's pale face broke into a smirk, her irises flashing a mixture of red and orange, conveying her determination. "Then let me show you the way to the clandestine temple."

*****

The wait for nightfall prickled Kiara's nerves and augmented her anxiety. She restlessly paced the hall of Kailx's confined loft, her eyes steadily observing the sky outside, willing time to rush forward.

Kain had finally awoken at midday and had taken Kailx's sworn alliance without complaint or an interrogation. The atmosphere between him and Kiara was no longer sour, but an unwanted sense of awkwardness had sealed their mouths shut without the drive for casual articulation.

Kailx had explained their plan to Kain, and he had embraced the wait with an uncharacteristic humbleness. He had sat on a wide plush chair in Kailx's living room, occasionally slipping in and out of consciousness, while Kiara uneasily paced up and down the length of the room.

"Soldiers have been running around town all day," Kailx observed, suddenly tugging shut the curtains the blotted the living room window and blinding Kiara's vision of the darkening sky above. "The scene you left at the inn did not go unnoticed."

"I'm not naïve enough to think it would," she replied coolly, biting at her fingernails nervously. "I shouldn't have left that Nonae alive. He'll recognize my face if he sees me."

Kailx nodded slowly. "Nightfall is the best cover. We should head out."

A tremendous sigh of relief poured from Kiara's lips. Kain stood up quickly from the chair, hurriedly tying his cloak into place.

"Here," Kailx whispered, handing Kiara her own cloak. "I noticed you didn't have one. You'll need it to hide your identity."

"What about you?" she wondered, lightly receiving the garment from the girl's eager hands.

"Trust me, I'm very well known in Vitaciel."

Kiara's eyebrows lowered skeptically, but she refrained from probing the girl. Regardless of her piqued interest in Kailx's identity, the young Nonae had been unassailable on the suggestion of divulging the secrets of her past.

"Alright," Kiara said skeptically, carefully latching the heavy cloak into place. She drew her hood over her head while brushing the stray hairs out of her eyes. "Lead the way."

Kailx smiled, crossing the foyer of her flat and quietly pulling open the front door. She stepped out onto the cobbled street, glancing around furtively before beckoning for Kain and Kiara to follow suit. They emerged from Kailx's apartment, Kain dutifully trailing behind the princess as they passed through the threshold.

The streets were nearly deserted, the soft red glow of the setting sun casting Kiara's shadow across the cobbled road as Kailx knowingly maneuvered their way through Vitaciel. A freshly printed sign on a nearby doorway captivated Kiara's attention as they passed. Large, bright red print bore the sentence *"murderer on the loose!"* Before she could read any further, Kain's hand was suddenly around her wrist, leading her through the city.

"Don't fall behind," he warned. "We'll never find you again."

The gentle brush of Kain's fingers against her skin flushed her cheeks and scripted her lips to ask the question she had been wondering since that morning. "Why did you save me?"

Kain averted his gaze, quickening his pace. He moved far enough away from Kiara as possible without loosening his grip, staring straight ahead and refusing to allow his facial expression to be studied. "Why wouldn't I?"

"We were fighting..."

He sneered. "Doesn't mean I would let you be defiled."

"I don't know why they thought I was a prostitute," she whispered, sighing.

"They were drunk," he reminded her coolly.

She nodded slowly. "You killed one of them."

Kain's eyes narrowed, his facial expression darkening, but he disallowed Kiara to notice the change in his demeanor. "I should have killed the other. That scum deserved it."

"Kain," she whispered cautiously, "why are you afraid of fire?"

His grip suddenly fell away from Kiara's hand, his muscles tightening with aggravation. "Ask Avian," he muttered hotly.

"Some day, Kain, you're going to tell me what all of these disdainful retorts about Avian mean."

"Oh, I won't be the one to do it."

Kiara opened her mouth to investigate the situation further, but Kailx's voice silenced her. "We're here," she said quietly, suddenly stopping in the middle of the uneven road. A set of ironclad gates opened upward from the cobblestones, a candle-lit stone staircase visible beneath the barred opening, the aged steps descending into shadows.

"I know we would have noticed this if only we had walked around town a little bit longer," Kiara rebuked, folding her arms across her chest as she stopped beside Kailx. "Then that entire situation at the inn could have been averted."

"Oh, whatever," Kain snapped. "You just don't want to admit that you actually enjoyed sharing a bed with me."

"What?" she demanded, appalled. "Who said—"

"Hey!" Kailx shouted, suffocating Kain and Kiara's bickering. "We need to focus. I will take you into the temple but I can't follow you to retrieve the book. I wouldn't be of much help and I would better serve your cause above ground, where I can be on the lookout for soldiers and Vyntrx."

"That's fine," Kiara assured her. "Your help is immensely appreciated."

Kailx smiled brightly. Her prominent chin and slightly up-turned nose were strikingly similar to Kiara's. Kiara studied her, eyebrows furrowed, as Kailx unlatched the gate. A cool, musty air spewed from the entrance, birthing chills of anticipation across Kiara's skin.

"We're related, aren't we?" Kiara spoke bluntly, startling the girl so profoundly, the gates slipped from her fingers and fell against the street with a loud crack.

"Wh-what makes you say that?" she wondered, taking a careful step onto the temple's staircase.

"You two are nearly identical," Kain interjected, beckoning for Kiara to follow after the Nonae. She did as he suggested, reaching over and grasping his hand for support as they descended into the temple.

"Are we sisters?" Kiara questioned, her other hand lightly grazing the cold stone wall.

"No, I promise, we're not," Kailx spoke sincerely, rounding

a corner as the staircase began to spiral.

"Cousins, then?" Kiara probed.

"We don't even look that much alike," Kailx argued stubbornly. "Honestly."

Kiara rolled her eyes, her foot slipping on the edge of an uneven step. Her tumbling body was suddenly steadied by Kain's hand, his fingers securely gripping her waist. Her eyes searched his face but he had purposely directed his gaze elsewhere. He gently helped her to her feet, muttering a derisive comment about her clumsiness.

Kiara mumbled her thanks, turning her body away from Kain as she continued down the staircase after Kailx. "We have a lot of the same features," she added to her accusation. "Our chins are the same, our noses are similar, we both have relatively high cheek bones, we're built the about the same—only you're taller—"

"Okay, fine!" Kailx shouted, gracefully spinning around on her heel. She faced Kiara, her eyes black and narrowed. It was still an oddity for Kiara to see someone else's eyes portray the emotions she had always been so familiar with. "You're my cousin."

"Worst kept secret," Kiara decided, smirking. "I can't believe it took me that long to figure it out."

"You're incredibly dense," Kain reminded her. "I figured something was up whenever I first saw her."

Kiara nudged him in the ribs, smiling at her cousin. "Which side do we share?" She understood that her cousin obviously possessed Nonae blood, but she wasn't certain if she were full-blooded or harboring some hidden Evalseman attributes.

Kailx's face fell, her eyes suddenly bright orange with panic. Her cheeks paled, her lips quivering slightly. "Don't think anything less of me," she warned, mumbling warily. "I'm Vyntrx's daughter."

Kiara drew in a sharp breath. She knew instantly that the color in her eyes had shifted to a bright yellow, distinctly transmitting her apparent astonishment. "Vyntrx is your *mother*?"

Kain shrugged nonchalantly. "I figured that was it."

Kiara swiveled around, smacking his shoulder in frustration. "You suspected that and you didn't tell me? Better yet, you didn't confront her about it?"

He brushed away Kiara's hand, a scowl dominating his face. "I don't judge people based on their family—with good reason. Clearly Kailx isn't anything like her mother, just like your mother wasn't anything like her sister."

Kiara bit her lip in stunned silence. Kailx stood three steps down from the pair, watching her cousin hesitantly through the shadows, her eyes penetratingly bright. "Can you understand why I wanted to keep my identity a secret?" she whispered. "I'm technically the princess of the Dark Forest but I despise my mother's cause. Instead, I'm seeking for peace with Enevale."

Kiara shook her head, chuckling slightly. "Kailx, Kain's right. There's no way I can judge you based on your mother's actions. I'm honestly more shocked that she actually had a child."

"My parents were married before my mother went insane. I was born afterward. I don't know what sparked the argument, but eight years ago, I witnessed my father's murder. My mother killed him. That night, she gave her soul to Veinya and I gave mine to Enevale."

Kiara bounded down the staircase, affectionately wrapping her arms around her cousin's shoulders. Kailx, startled, nearly toppled backward, but managed to maintain her footing on the sloped steps. It was so strange to Kiara that her cousin, two years her junior, appeared so much more mature—that she could be held by Kailx instead of being able to hold and comfort her. Kiara's blood burned with the desire to protect her young cousin, to shield her from Vyntrx's maniacal wrath, to embrace her alliance, to care for her as though she were the younger sister she never had.

"I'm so sorry you had to endure such hardships," Kiara whispered. "I promise, I will take you away from her."

Kailx gently pulled away from her cousin, her eyes shimmering purple with happiness. "I already have a plan to escape my manacles. It will happen soon, but not today. Today we're obtaining a spell book."

Kiara smiled, beckoning toward the darkness. "After you."

*****

Water dripped from the ceiling, splashing against the cold cave floor and dampening Kiara's boots. She trudged through the clandestine temple, nearing a candle-lit alter in the distance. "You know," she muttered, "when I hear the word 'temple', this is not what I envision."

Kailx threw Kiara a confused expression over her shoulder. "What else would you imagine?"

"The princess was raised in a remote Evalseman village," Kain explained, bumping his shoulder against Kiara's. "I don't think they have temples there."

"The book is hidden beyond that trail," Kailx said solemnly, pointing to the left of the alter. A dark, winding path was barely visible through the emanating candlelight. "This is as far as I dare go. If my mother appears, I will try my best to deter her. I cannot promise anything. You know how she is."

Kiara nodded gravely, her fingers lightly squeezing Kain's hand. "You ready?"

"You even have to ask?"

She abruptly darted forward, abandoning Kain's hand as she headed toward the dimly lit corridor. Kailx waved at Kain as he rushed after Kiara and entered the damp hall, leaving the remotely secure temple behind.

"You know a fire spell," Kain reminded Kiara shortly. "Can't you light the way?"

She sighed, attempting to stare through the thick shadows. She held her hand forward, picturing a ball of blazing flames circling inside her palm, the fire miraculously unable to scathe her vulnerable skin. Within seconds, flames had spread around her hand, illuminating the path and revealing jagged, black walls crawling with small, long-legged creatures. Kiara shrieked, nearly dousing the flame as she took an involuntary step closer to Kain.

"Watch it!" he mandated. "You know I don't like fire."

"I hate Ireti!"

He raised a skeptical eyebrow. "What's Ireti?"

Kiara shook her head, cautiously walking forward. She held her arms upward, avoiding contact with the infested walls. "They're a pest that riddled deserted corners of my village. I didn't know they lived in the Dark Forest."

"Shut up and keep walking."

"Stop being so testy," Kiara huffed, pushing the flames in his direction, "or I'll move the fire closer to you."

"Knock it off," he snapped irritably. "Seriously."

"Or what?"

Kain casually retrieved one of the unidentifiable insects from the cave wall, dangling it in front of Kiara's face. She squealed, involuntarily jumping backwards, landing against the wall, and exposing her back to the infested stone. She screamed loudly as the wall suddenly shifted, depositing her directly through a gaping hole in the floor. Kain yelled her name, diving after her through the fissure.

Kiara didn't fall long, but she hit the ground with a sharp thud. The flame growing inside her palm was extinguished by the abrupt contact with the cave floor, darkening her surroundings into incomprehensible shadows. Before she could examine her wounds, she was suddenly pinned against the ground as something fell from the ceiling and landed directly on top of her body. She cried out, repeatedly punching and clawing at the unidentified object.

"Hey—stop it—*Kiara!*" Kain's voice sounded, his hands desperately attempting to placate her violent thrashes.

"Kain," she spoke quietly. "Is that you?"

"Who else would it be, princess?" he questioned contemptuously, moving himself away from her body. "You okay?"

She breathed deeply, her lungs and back throbbing in protest. Her unexpected fall had stolen the air from her chest. "I think I injured my back and possibly my elbow."

"Idiot."

She scowled, gingerly pulling her body into a sitting position. She rubbed her sore arm, cringing. "It's not my fault. You did it."

"Whatever. Where are we?"

Kiara willed herself to manipulate the elements to create fire, but the act was twice as strenuous as it had been prior to her fall. Flames eventually erupted within her palm, showering the unknown room in light. "Wh-what are those?" she whispered, pointing to an array of slumped figures positioned in a circle merely a few feet away from where she and Kain had fallen.

He disdainfully examined the slumbering creatures. Deadly claws adorned their small, dark bodies; pointed fangs hung over their closed mouths, their snouts contoured into an irreplaceable snarl. Kain recognized their description from an old tale his mother had whispered to him on stormy nights— the story of a brave hero who had singularly slain a horde of the dangerously vicious Coronix.

"Coronix," Kain and Kiara muttered in sync as she came to the conclusion he had unearthed.

He shared an ominous look with her, whispering, "We need to move."

She furtively climbed to her feet, offering Kain her free hand. His palm fell into hers as she heaved his body forward, his weight rolling onto the balls of his feet. "What happens if they wake up?" she wondered quietly. "I've only ever read accounts of their attacks. I've never actually encountered one."

"Doesn't matter. Try to find an exit."

She pointed at the small crack in the ceiling. "The only way is up. This is an enclosed pit."

"I can control your body to push you through the fracture, but I can't control myself."

She shook her head. "I won't leave without you."

"No need to get all sentimental," he complained, although he couldn't fight the burning sensation rushing through his cheeks. "I'll be fine as long as the Coronix stay asleep. You'll get the book, learn a spell, and get me out of here."

"Too risky," she decided immediately. "Besides, you and I both know you don't trust me enough to actually save you."

He shrugged. "Can't argue that."

"What if you clung to me while you controlled my body? I can support your weight and you can send me—and, essentially, you—through the crevice."

Kain's violet eyes brightened at Kiara's suggestion. "That's not a bad idea," he praised.

She didn't have time to reply. Her hands automatically flew to her neck, retrieving her necklace as she hurriedly willed the weapon to shift into a crossbow. Kain stared at her in shocked horror, but she hurriedly pushed his shoulder, moving him out of range as she rapidly fired the weapon in the direction of the Coronix.

"*What* are you doing?" he exclaimed.

"One of them woke up. It was rushing toward your head." She lowered the bow, watching apprehensively as the horrendous creatures hovered in the darkness, abashed by the weapon's effects. "My crossbow abilities are remedial," she chided, glancing at the weapon derisively as it shifted into her favorite knife.

A chorus of offended, terrified growls resonated through the circular room. Kiara held her weapon forward, daring the

Coronix to attack. Their red eyes gleamed through the darkness, scrutinizing their opponent.

"Be careful!" Kain warned, suddenly controlling a nearby boulder and tossing it into the crowded group of Coronix.

The horde of monsters scattered. Several of the creatures were crushed by the onset of the heavy stone, but the majority of the Coronix darted away with impeccable agility. They sprung from the shadows, fangs bared, pouncing on the pair of intruders.

Kiara slashed her knife ferociously, scattering the monsters' disembodied limbs across the cave floor. Kain rapidly controlled the bodies of the creatures, willing their insides to erupt into a cloud of mangled flesh and bright red blood.

Kiara was stunned by the Coronix's advanced speed. Their quick, unpredictable movements eclipsed any attempt for blocking assaults. Regardless of the countless injuries she was receiving, Kiara desperately slashed her blade around the group of overwhelming monsters, reveling in the high amount of damage her steady attacks were issuing on the miniscule creatures.

Kain wasn't faring as fortunately. Because he was lacking the knowledge of weaponry, and had to merely rely on his Evalseman Specialty, he was rendered defenseless in close-range battles. He relentlessly manipulated the bodies of the Coronix, but their consistent activity distracted his eyes as he attempted to follow their speedy movements.

"Have any injuries?" Kiara gasped, running the tip of her blade directly through the momentarily exposed flesh of a pouncing Coronix.

"Seriously?" Kain exclaimed, fending off a wave of insistent monsters. "You're asking that now?"

She harrumphed, extending her palm as a row of flames incinerated an on-coming threat of Coronix. The pack of creatures was thinning and Kiara could now vividly locate each monster as it flew toward her—claws extended—and successfully drain its body of life with a mere flick of her wrist.

By the time she had cleared her opponents, the Coronix onslaught against Kain had barely diminished. Her eyes raked his bloodied body, the movement of his hands perpetuating determinedly. Without thinking, she rushed to his side, gently pushing him away as she tore her blade through the cloud of Coronix. He yelled in protest, but she ignored his complaints, shielding his body behind hers as she feverishly ambushed the seemingly inexorable monsters.

After merely seconds of unparalleled destruction, Kiara had successfully eradicated the last Coronix from the cave's depths. At the fall of the final monster, she turned to face Kain. Blood streamed down her forehead, spilling into her line of vision and causing her eyelid to involuntarily slide shut.

Kain sighed, wiping the blood off her face. "You took a beating," he observed.

She shrugged, scornfully eyeing her tarnished clothes. Her knife morphed back into her crown necklace as she hurriedly latched the hidden weapon into place against her collarbones. "So did you."

"You shouldn't have helped me."

"I've repaid my debt."

He shook his head. "Not even close."

She rolled her eyes, winding her hand around Kain's waist. "Let's get out of here."

He redirected his gaze upward, staring at the fissure in the ceiling. "Smartest suggestion you've ever made."

"Shut up," she barked, playfully smacking his chest with her free hand. "Let me pick you up."

He sneered, weaving his arm around her shoulders as she lightly pulled his body against her chest. "I hope this works," he muttered, unconvinced of the probability of success.

"It will," she said assuredly, snickering slightly as she envisioned how silly she appeared sustaining the weight of a man whose stature hovered over her diminutive height. "Just focus on lifting my body only."

"It will be hard for you to breathe," he warned, suddenly willing Kiara's small body to rush skyward. Determination hung heavy in the air, fueling Kain's lungs as he breathed deeply, his body exuding a colossal amount of power. Slowly but surely, Kiara's feet slid out from under her, dangling awkwardly in the air as her body was pulled toward the crack in the ceiling as though she and the fissure were magnets and the attraction between them had become irresistible.

Kain managed to maintain his control over Kiara as her grip on his body tightened. She clung to him desperately, but he was undaunted by the change in their location. They were nearing the exit, and he could taste freedom wetting his parched lips. With one last release of strength, he propelled Kiara's body through the fractured ceiling.

They collapsed in a tangled heap on the secure ground of the cave, Kain's body hovering over Kiara's as they simultaneously drew in breaths of relief. His limbs quivered with the sudden lack of vitality but he denied his body an extended rest.

"Good job," she praised, patting his head lovingly. "I knew you could do it."

His cheeks flushed. He expertly pushed himself away from Kiara's reach, running his hands through his tousled black hair. "Your idea."

She nodded, clumsily scrambling to her feet. She dusted off her cloak, sending clouds of dirt swirling through the air. She offered her hand to him—which he took uneasily—heaving his body off the ground as he rolled his weight to the balls of his feet.

"Are you badly injured?" she questioned softly.

He shook his head. "Just scratches. Looks like you took pretty heavy damage to your head. You okay?"

Her fingers curiously grazed her forehead and came away damp with blood. She dragged the edge of her cloak across her face, mopping away the excess blood.

Kain laughed at her, licking his thumb and rubbing her forehead with his extended finger. "You smeared blood all across your face, dummy."

Her cheeks burned as she hoped the dried blood caking her face would hide the pigmentation in her skin.

"Don't risk yourself for me again," he whispered solemnly, moving his hand away from her dirtied face and running his fingers through her matted hair. "I'm not worth it."

"Now isn't the time to try to romance me," she jeered, attempting to sound sarcastic but managing to only sound playful. Despite her words, she found her own hand weaving its way around Kain's.

"That's Avian's job, princess," he muttered, his hand falling away from her face. "Mine is to protect you."

She laughed lightly. "We're making progress. You wouldn't have admitted that yesterday."

"Not to you," he admitted. "There's a lot I won't admit to you."

Her eyes narrowed. "Why?" she probed.

He shrugged. "Because you're *you*. The only person I trust. I won't say something stupid to screw that up." His light eyes flashed to her face. She was suddenly penetrated by his intense stare.

Chills ran across Kiara's shoulders, a distant buzzing sounded through her ears. Her heart accelerated with velocity, blood rushed to her head, a dizzying sensation spread through her bones—and she suddenly realized what was happening. She was overwhelmed by the petrifying sensation of falling— and falling was exactly what she had unknowingly been guilty of. Kiara Fable was irrevocably falling in love with Kain Knight, and she disastrously knew that when she finally hit the ground of realization and reality, the aftermath would solely consist of broken bones and a fractured heart.

"Y-yeah," she stammered, clearing her throat. "We should,

um, continue searching."

Kain's eyebrows lowered as he evaluated her abrupt change in demeanor, but he nodded in compliance. She hurried along the corridor, Kain readily chasing after her and advising that she be weary of more trapdoors.

She ignited the flames within her hand once again, flooding the corridor with orange rays of light. After several minutes of walking in sheer silence, they divulged an unopened, elaborately carved door hidden against the walls of the cave.

Kain sent her a curious glance, but her eyes were locked on the doorway. She prudently ran her hand across the stone, pushing forward lightly. The door slowly crumbled at her touch, a torrent of dust detonating throughout the hall. She coughed, batting away the clouds of dirt.

"Kiara, look," Kain whispered.

She reared her head upward, attempting to see through the thick clouds of dust. Faint light was visible through the ubiquitous vapors, and once the dirt finally settled, Kiara's eyes fastened on a brightly lit room beyond the doorway. In the center of the colossal room, situated proudly on top of a stone platform, was an ancient, cast-iron chest. And inside the chest, Kiara instantly knew, lie the bane of their escapade: the highly appraised book of spells.

hapter Twenty-Three

Escape

Kiara rushed through the threshold, the sound of her pulsating heart drumming through her ears. Kain was at her heels, cautiously following her into the bright room. She ascended the steps leading to the platform, her palms growing sweaty with anxiety, her fingers itching to pull back the lid of the chest and reveal the spell book.

"Be careful," Kain advised. "It could be a trap."

She nodded, stopping in front of the iron trunk. She reached out experimentally, her fingers brushing against the top of the chest. She wallowed in anticipation, waiting for flames to burst from the sky or for water to swell upward from the ground or for any sort of magical phenomenon that was typically associated with the unveiling of legendary artifacts to transpire. When it became clear that no such occurrence was ordained, Kiara breathed a sigh of relief. Her hands gripped the top of the chest, prying open the trunk and sending a cloud of dust churning through the air.

Swathes of black, silk fabric draped the inside of the chest. A light film of dust tainted the material. Swaddled in the center of cloth lay an ancient, undisturbed book. The pages were uneven and yellowed with age; the dark binding had deteriorated slightly over the years, but the book's silver-inked title remained as glossy and shimmering as an unblemished diamond.

Kiara's hand reached forward, mesmerized. She gently procured the book, the rough material of the binding scraping across her bare hands. The sweet taste of victory bled along her tongue, relief stirring in the pit of her stomach as her worries rapidly dispersed. She turned to face Kain, but he was no longer paying attention to the spell book. He was staring around the room expectantly, waiting.

"Kain—" she started.

"Shh," he commanded. "I heard something."

"No—" her voice was silenced once again. A sudden bout of arrows sprang from the shadows, cutting through the room. She screamed, clutching the book to her chest with her right hand and securing Kain's wrist with her left as they hurriedly darted from the room.

She could feel arrows digging into her flesh, their sharp blades biting into her body, but she didn't stop. Safety was her top priority and she refused to weaken her grip on Kain's hand or slow her legs until she had passed through the threshold of the perilous room.

She jumped through the doorway of the room, yanking Kain through after her. She rounded the corner of the hallway, hurrying toward the entrance of the temple. Even though the onset of arrows had subsided, and even though her body ached with fresh wounds, she didn't dare risk any more precarious situations.

"Kiara," Kain moaned, "Kiara. Stop."

The tinge of pain in his voice stabbed her heart with anxiety. Her legs threatened to buckle. She knew automatically, before she had convinced herself to turn around, that Kain had been badly injured.

Slowly, her eyes crawled in his direction, her heart hammering as his body poured into view. His grip on her hand loosened. His arm fell limply to his blood-covered chest, revealing limbs heavily daunted by half-broken arrows. Nestled in the center of his chest, just an inch above his heart, was the feathered end of an arrow. Blood frothed from his chest, dampening his black shirt. His eyes were fluttering involuntarily, his pallid cheeks sallow and sunken. "*Now* I'm badly hurt," he whispered, his body crumpling to the ground.

Kiara gasped, rushing to prevent his fall. His body fell into her arms, his limbs strikingly frigid and stiff. "Kain," she whispered. "I'm so sorry, I didn't—"

"You..." he muttered. He squinted his eyes, the dull colors of the room darkening and swirling through a hazed film. Kiara's face was blurred, the slight darkness of her hair mixed with the paleness of her cheeks, two wide pink circles dotting the haphazard mess. "Your eyes..."

She frantically tore through the pages of the spell book, scouring for a healing spell. "It'll be okay," she promised, her voice breaking. "You'll be fine."

"T-take the arrow out," he commanded weakly.

She nodded in compliance, tears welling her eyes. The book gently fell into her lap as her hands securely gripped the end of the arrow that was horrifically poking out of Kain's chest. She grimaced, her hands stained with his blood, as she heaved the weapon out of his chest. He yelled in pain, his hands clenching into fists as his teeth smashed together violently. Fresh blood leaked from the wound as Kiara's crimson hands rapidly turned the pages of the spell book while she desperately searched for a healing spell. Finally, after what felt like hours of investigating, Kiara discovered four pages devoted to healing. She skimmed the first page, grateful for her ability to read swiftly.

Her hands cupped his wound, her eyes lingering on the contents of the page. The text advocated her movements but she wasn't convinced solely following directions could propel her abilities into victorious action. She focused on healing, on mending the broken muscles and tarnished skin. She pictured Kain's chest as though it were a torn shirt that possessed a necessity of strong thread to sew the broken pieces into one square of fabric. She allowed energy to flow from her body, to abandon the depths of her soul and crawl through her bones, out through her fingertips and into Kain's listless chest. She closed her eyes, pleading, praying silently to Veinya that she would spare Kain's soul one more time.

"Kiara," Kain's voice sounded suddenly, snapping her mind out of its trance.

Her eyes flickered open, his body pouring into view. His hand was wrapped around her wrist, his grip firm and strong. Color had drastically revisited his face. His limbs were no longer lying limply against the cave floor. He softly pushed Kiara's hands away from his chest, revealing bare, unblemished skin. Residual blood stained his flesh but he carefully swiped it away with the dark material of his cloak. "You saved me," he breathed. "You learned a new spell in a matter of seconds."

"I can't believe it," she gushed, her voice strained and nearly hysteric. Tears burned in the corner of her eyes but she refused to brush them away. Relief was slowly spilling through her veins, but after the arrow incident, she was weary to trust the initial sense of security.

Kain abruptly reached forward and pulled Kiara into his arms in one swift, spontaneous movement. Her eyes widened in surprise as she timidly drew her hands around his back. She was utterly baffled—Kain had never initiated any sort of affection and had always shied away from her attempts at intimacy. He denied the opportunity to speak and instead dwelled in silence, his steady breath cascading across Kiara's neck and sending chills across the planes of her exposed skin.

Kiara, her cheeks burning with flames of embarrassment, was the first to pull away. She gently released her grip on Kain, gathering the spell book in her hands and climbing to her feet. He stood up beside her, his gaze shyly averted. She instantly understood by the bashful expression playing on his face that he had no intention of recounting their embrace.

"You should heal yourself before we go," he muttered.

She glanced down at her body, injuries laced across the torn fabric of her clothes. The remnants of several arrows poked out from her legs and arms, but she hurriedly dislodged the weapons from her flesh, scowling. "They're just flesh wounds," she observed. "None of them were nestled too deeply."

"Vyntrx could be waiting for us at the exit," he argued rationally. "Those wounds will be troublesome in battle."

Kiara rolled her eyes, quickly executing a healing spell on her own injuries. She was amazed at how rapidly the magic worked. She could feel her muscles bending, her flesh repairing, her lost strength fervently returning.

"This way," she muttered, depositing the spell book into a wide pocket on the inside of her cloak.

She started down the hallway with Kain at her heels. The atmosphere enveloping the pair had become increasingly discomforted. An awkward silence settled among them as Kiara led the way through the halls, her hand alighted with magical fire held high above her head as a mock lantern.

"Thanks," Kain muttered, his voice spilling through the silence. His words cut through the tense ambiance as though they were knives constructed of compassion; Kiara could vaguely sense a twinge of sincerity hidden amid his husky tone. "For saving me."

She was overwhelmed by the desire to spin around and clasp her hands around his neck, finally succumbing to the exhausted tears her eyes were begging to spill. Her skin prickled with unbridled resistance as she forcefully fought off the urge. Kain's near-death experience had rattled her emotions, and—she judged by their careless embrace—had heavily bemused his.

"Of course," she whispered. "I think I've paid off my debt by now."

Kain snickered lightly, his eyes lingering on the back of her head as she wove her way through the constrictive hallways. Her wavy hair spilled over the back of her hood, the reddish-brown hue encircling the crown of her head fading slowly into a coppery gold at the ends of her tresses. Her narrow shoulders disappeared behind the over-sized cloak, her curved hips swaying as she clumsily rounded a corner. He cleared his throat, attempting to direct his attention elsewhere and failing miserably. "You're close. I saved you from two dangers and killed one of your attackers. That means you have one more favor to repay me."

Her profile was vaguely visible as she stole a glance at him over her shoulder, her small lips curved downward in a disappointed frown. "I saved you from the inn, though."

He shook his head. "Kailx did."

"Must we fight about everything?" she jeered jokingly. The bright entrance of the temple appeared in the distance as though it were a mirage and Kiara could barely comprehend the reality of its existence. They had only been inside the precarious chambers of the cave for a few hours, but the journey had felt much longer. Kiara's pace quickened as she raced toward the exit and Kain was forced to take wide steps in order to keep up with her hasty speed.

He didn't bother replying to her rhetorical question. He was replaying the arrow incident over and over in his mind. He could still vividly picture Kiara's eyes, wide and bright pink, as she frantically crouched over his decrepit body. He had automatically convinced himself that the sudden change of her eye color was merely a trick of the light. He knew what that color represented and he refused to believe she had succumbed to its meaning.

Kiara dashed through the exit, followed closely by Kain. The candle-lit room appeared oddly inviting after the cold, desolate chambers of the cave.

Kailx stood beside the shrine, worry evident in the lines cutting across her forehead. Her gaze fell upon the pair as they stumbled through the exit, her face lightening dramatically. She rushed to Kiara, pulling her into a back-shattering embrace. "Thank Veinya!" she exclaimed. "You've been gone for hours. Did you get the book?" She pulled away from her cousin, a grave look crossing her face. "My mother came searching for intruders. The survivor from the inn is leading her around town. If they see you, you'll be killed."

Kiara's eyes flashed yellow. "How did she know we would be here?"

"She didn't, although she suspects you're the intruder. She's scouring the entire city..." her voice wandered off as her face fell somberly.

"We have what we came for," Kiara replied, patting the cloak's pocket. "We should hurry out of Vitaciel."

Kailx nodded in agreement, hurriedly turning toward the stone staircase with Kain and Kiara at her heels. They clambered up the staircase so vivaciously, Kiara's tired legs began to protest. After what felt like hours, the gated entrance appeared through the shadows, moonlight spilling in through the checkered lattice. Kailx pushed open the gate, the star-lit sky visible above. She climbed out of the cave, pulling Kain and Kiara out of the earth after her.

"That's him!" a voice squealed hysterically as soon as Kain's feet landed safely on the cobbled road. "He's the murderer!"

Kiara spun her head around, discovering the drunken Nonae from the inn standing across the street, accompanied by two weapon-clad soldiers.

"Tch," Kain groaned, eyeing the man contemptuously. "Problematic asshole. You should've let me kill him, Kiara."

The soldiers abruptly dashed forward, weapons gleaming threateningly in their hands. The Nonae grinned deviously, his eyes flickering purple with delight as he awaited the capture and termination of his attackers.

"We should probably run," Kiara suggested thoughtfully, warily eyeing the approaching soldiers. "Just a suggestion."

"Whatever!" Kain scoffed, charging directly toward the gloating Nonae. "I need to kill that bastard!"

She hurriedly grabbed his arm before he had stepped out of her reach, yanking him toward her as she launched into a sprint. Kailx immediately rushed after them, glancing behind her shoulder anxiously as the soldiers neared.

"Hey! Let go!" Kain protested, swatting at Kiara's hand as she led him through the city. The dimly lit nighttime streets had been deserted, providing them with an unblocked path free of distractions and complications.

"They'll bring Vyntrx to us!" she argued, tugging Kain forward insistently.

"Not if we kill them first!" he retorted.

There was a sudden flash of black as a shadowy figure swirled upward from the ground, appearing in the middle of the road and blocking their path. Kiara instinctively halted and Kain nearly crashed into his companion's frozen body. Kailx slowed to a stop beside her cousin, staring angrily ahead.

Vyntrx placidly stood on the uneven road, her eyes glowing dangerously as patches of silver moonlight reflected in the darkness of her irises. Her red lips were parted in a menacing grin, her hands folded haughtily across her chest. "Well, well," she spoke loudly, tossing back her head, "look what I've caught."

The soldiers, flanked insistently by the Nonae from the inn, clattered down the street. They stopped behind Kailx, grinning excitedly as their eyes fell upon their empress.

"Kailx, I am thoroughly disappointed," Vyntrx said dejectedly, eyeing her daughter as though she were a disobedient Demmonai. "How could you betray your own mother?"

"I—" Kailx started, but Kiara's sharp voice instantly silenced her.

"She didn't betray you," she lied quickly, averting her gaze to conceal her grey eyes. "She was pursuing us."

Vyntrx cocked her head in contemplation, glaring at her niece. "You would lie for her? Why?"

"I'm not lying," she argued through clenched teeth, refusing to surrender her cousin's true agenda.

"Your pet killed one of my subjects," the Nonae empress changed the topic abruptly, her long pale finger pointing directly at Kain. "The penalty for the murder of a Nonae is death."

"Then he already served that sentence," Kiara snapped, "for thirteen years. Was his murderer ever caught? Oh—that's right, she's still stubbornly clinging to the ragged strands of her pathetic life."

Vyntrx's shrill laugh echoed loudly. "The real culprit behind Kain's death isn't *me*! *He's* still serving his sentence—until death parts us!" she crackled.

Kiara narrowed her dark amber eyes in confusion, staring at her aunt with incredulity. "What are you going on about?"

"Why did you come here?" the empress probed, flecks of red highlighting her soulless eyes.

"Reconnaissance," she replied shortly, her eyes flittering briefly in Kain's direction. "We were just leaving."

"Oh, is *that* what you think you're doing?" she chortled, her eyes flashing dangerously. "You're terribly mistaken." She darted forward without warning, procuring a jagged dagger from the folds of her dress. She lashed forward, aiming directly for Kiara's chest. Kiara narrowly dodged her aunt's attack, her hand instantly reaching for her necklace as it morphed into a knife beneath her touch.

While Kiara viciously battled her aunt, the soldiers sprang into action. Their eyes carefully scrutinizing the empress's daughter as she watched her mother and cousin battle, the soldiers reached forward, each grabbing one of Kailx's arms. She feverishly attempted to pull herself out of their constricting grip, scoffing indignantly. "Do you *know* who I am?" she shouted.

Kain automatically hurried to help her, but the Nonae from the inn suddenly blocked his path.

"We meet again, eh?" the man sneered, his breath reeking of alcohol. "This time I'll get my revenge."

Kain laughed derisively in response, shrugging his shoulders as though the Nonae's words could not be taken seriously. "You will? Yeah, *right*," he sneered sarcastically. "You're gonna pay for trying to defile that girl."

"She deserved it," the Nonae whispered feverishly. "Her filthy body deserved to be defiled."

Raw fury burned through Kain's chest—it was a strange emotion; he had never experienced anything so painful and prevalent. His rage was building so ferociously and heavily that he felt as though his body would explode from the sudden intake of unwanted emotion. He glared at the man, his wrath suddenly propelling from his chest, exploding through his fingertips in a frenzied rage.

The Nonae cried loudly. His body was suddenly split into two halves, as though an invisible sword had cut directly through the crown of his head. Blood oozed from his broken skin, splattering Kain's clothes and staining the cobbled stones red. The dismembered halves of the Nonae's body toppled in two different directions, startling Kailx so fervently she released a shaky whimper.

"You deserved it," Kain sneered sardonically, eyeing the man's tarnished limbs. "Your filthy body deserved to be defiled."

The soldiers stared at Kain in shocked terror, their grip on Kailx loosening timidly as though they were uncertain whether to stay very still or to release the girl and sprint to safety.

"Let her go or you'll meet the same fate," he demanded, glowering at the Nonae threateningly.

The soldiers shared an identical expression of sheer horror as they exchanged incredulous glances. Without speaking, they simultaneously released their hold on the Nonae princess before rushing down the uneven street. They didn't dare look behind them once, but kept running determinedly until they vanished from sight.

Kiara swung her knife angrily, the blade swiping through a

wave of her aunt's unnaturally long hair as she expertly ducked downward. Unfazed, Vyntrx lashed forward, her dagger aiming straight for her niece's face.

Kiara parried the attack. The dagger, its path redirected, tore through her cloak, clipping her shoulder and exposing bare, bloodied flesh. She held back a painful yelp, hurriedly driving her knife through Vyntrx's briefly unshielded stomach.

Vyntrx cried loudly, staring at the blade in terror. Her face turned ghostly white, her black eyes strikingly prominent against the backdrop of her cloudy flesh. A spell welled in the palm of her hand, but Kiara didn't have enough time to predict which enchantment her aunt had summoned. She quickly yanked the weapon out of her aunt's torso, ducking to the floor as a row of flames billowed through the air above her. Vyntrx stumbled backward from the sudden racking heave of pain, her hair falling into her eyes and darkening her irate expression.

Kailx suddenly appeared in the midst of the battle, standing bravely in-between her mother and her cousin. "Go, Kiara, *now*!" she pleaded. "This is your best chance!"

Kiara nodded at her cousin with gratitude, a hint of a smile curving her lips. As Kain approached, her eyes flittered in his direction, momentarily falling on the dead body of the Nonae, but he didn't allow her to examine the murder scene. His hand was suddenly interlocked with hers, their hearts pounding in sync, as he led her through the city.

*****

Sirens blared in the night, reverberating repeatedly through the abandoned streets of Vitaciel. Alarmed inhabitants of the city pressed their noses to their windows, handicapped by fear and unable to emerge from their houses, watching apprehensively as Kain and Kiara dashed across the cobbled roads pursued heavily by armed guards. Arrows whizzed past Kiara's ear, but the accuracy of the soldiers was utterly imprecise. The sound of thudding footsteps echoed through the empty roads as they were pursued, the noise filling Kiara's chest with anxious fear.

Kain's hand was tightly locked around hers, as though he was worried she would slip from his fingers and instantly be swallowed up by the wave of soldiers trailing them. He led her through the labyrinth streets of the city, the swiftness of their speed never once diminishing. He managed to discover the path to the city gate, expertly guiding Kiara through the slums of Vitaciel.

Countless incoherent spells were tossed toward the retreating trespassers. Kiara's leg had been hit with some strange enchantment and had consequently found herself limping involuntarily, unable to pause long enough to magically dissolve the numbness that had spread through her limb.

"Almost there," Kain spoke breathlessly, eyeing the gate as it crept out of the darkness before them. Four guards lined the perimeter, various weapons held at the ready. He eyed the soldiers disapprovingly, glaring in their direction. One by one, the guards' bodies abruptly exploded into a wave of crimson blood. Their listless figures fell to the road, startling the soldiers pursuing the pair so drastically that their attacks momentarily relented.

"H-how did you—" Kiara started, but Kain's voice cut her off.

"I can control people, remember?" he explained, quickening his pace as they neared the unguarded gate.

"Can't you just do that to Vyntrx?" she inquired, breathing heavily.

"It won't work. I tried," he responded breathlessly. "She probably has some magical repellent field surrounding her at all times."

Kiara glanced behind her shoulder, watching the horde of soldiers swarm through the streets after them. "Where did she go?"

"Probably with Kailx," he deducted as they passed the recently slain guards. "Who knows if we'll see her again."

Kiara's eyes shifted light blue with worry. "What do you mean?"

They reached the gate, desperately pushing against the iron and willing it to unhinge. At the whim of Kiara's strength, it slowly creaked open, revealing rows of trees in the distance. Kain pushed her through the small opening first, stealing a final glance at the nearing soldiers as he released his grip, swinging the door firmly shut.

They bounded through the densely canopied forest. Shadows caressed their pale skin as moonlight danced through the leaves, illuminating the pathway with a silvery glow. Soldiers poured from the mouth of the city, disturbing the quiet calm as they stubbornly chased after the trespassers.

Kain's speed was rapid and unrelenting. As Kiara struggled to not fall behind, her breathing became heavy and ragged. Running was not her forte—her legs quivered fervently despite her desperate attempt to steady her pace.

Unknown spells flew through the air, brightening the night sky with their dazzling colors. An explosion suddenly erupted less than a yard away from Kiara, instantly knocking her backwards. She screamed, but her voice was lost amongst the torrent of deafening explosions. Flames and unearthed dirt swirled through the air. She choked on the debris, screaming Kain's name.

After flailing blindly through the smog, he miraculously reached her side, drawing her dizzied body into his arms. He pulled her onto wobbling feet, fighting away the urge to fall into a relapse as the flames flickered deviously around them.

The soldiers jeered loudly as their footsteps rapidly approached. Kain's sweaty hand closed around Kiara's, pulling her forward through the churning clouds of smoke.

"Do you know which way to head?" she gasped, glancing

downward as a dark spell crept across the forest floor, eating away the dirt as though it were acid ravenously devouring the earth.

Kain shook his head. "I can't look at the map right now," he called over the thunderous roar of the soldier's footsteps and explosive spells.

"My sides—" she moaned. "I—hate—running!"

He snickered, yanking her forward as he increased his speed. She clung vivaciously to her cloak pocket, reassuring herself that the book was safely tucked away in the folds of the garment despite the intense thrashing her cloak had been subjected to in the midst of their flee.

Tree branches suddenly swept downward as though they had obtained a mind of their own, viciously swinging at the pair as they passed through the forest. Kiara screamed, her hand escaping Kain's grip as she narrowly avoided collision with a wall of sharp twigs. Dirt from the forest floor swirled upward, dancing around her body and hopelessly blinding her as she ran ahead screaming Kain's name.

Branches were swiping at Kain as if he were an insistent fly, but the dark Nonae magic powerlessly succumbed to his will as he controlled the trees with his Specialty, ending their violent rampage. He searched eagerly for Kiara, willing the clouds of dirt to relent.

She stumbled into view, coughing loudly, her face bloodied with cuts from the merciless branches. She sprinted toward him, her hand clasping around his forearm as she dragged him after her, yelling over the noise about finding a way to escape.

"How are they doing this?" she screamed, thrusting her body into the air as dirt suddenly fell away at her feet, revealing a black chasm of nothingness where she had momentarily been standing. She landed firmly on solid ground, her pace quickening in spite of the adamant trembling of her legs and the pain pulsating through her battered head.

"Magic!" Kain responded irritably as a row of arrows

suddenly flew through the air. He hurriedly sought refuge behind the sturdy bark of a tree, pulling Kiara's body against his as the arrows plummeted relentlessly against their temporary shelter.

"One person can do all of this?" she wondered, astounded. Blood dripped into her eyes as she stared up at Kain.

He quickly wiped her face, smearing the blood across her forehead. She flinched, his salty skin stinging her wounds. "No, I'm sure they're pooling their abilities into one powerful force."

The storm of arrows suddenly conceded. The soldiers were nearby and Kiara could distinctly hear the phrases they were loudly chanting. They seemed to be speaking another language—a dark, ancient Nonae tongue.

"Come on," Kain urged as she stared mesmerizingly from behind the tree at the approaching soldiers. "*Hurry!*"

He roughly pulled her forward, shattering her reverie and drawing her attention back to the chase. Her legs protested the movement, threatening to buckle at any moment. "Are we close?" she panted, wearily eyeing the film of black water that had suddenly swarmed the forest floor. Half of her leather boots were drowned in the murky water as the liquid rapidly expanded into a partially solidified substance. She struggled to lift her legs, desperately clinging onto Kain as he attempted to yank his ankles free from the muck.

Frustrated, she sent a row of wind directly into the dense liquid, breaking her free from the watery prison. She summoned a horde of powerful air, rapidly molding a path through the muddled water. Kain, who had been freed during Kiara's magical outbreak, sent her an appraising look, his hand tightening around hers. They rushed through the makeshift pathway, Kiara's free hand constantly spewing swirling wind, cutting through the escalating grime.

Thunder crackled ominously in the distance as rain began to pour from the sky. Kiara glanced upward, wondering if the storm was occurring naturally or if it had been induced by magic. Sheets of rain dampened her body, weighing down her clothes as they were soaked through with water. The murky substance spreading below her feet was replaced by sheets of rain as it smothered the ground, chasing away the spell-induced matter. Her hand fell to her pocket, her fingers gripping around the damp book and shielding it from the harsh weather conditions.

"We're nearly there!" Kain yelled, staring ahead determinedly. The Wall loomed on the horizon, the spires of Enevale's castle rising in the distance.

The sight of her kingdom sparked hope and relief inside Kiara's chest, fueling her body with enough energy to hasten the velocity of her legs. "Where's the hole?" she wondered, her eyes raking the nearing Wall. They had stumbled upon a part of the forest she wasn't familiar with, and she disastrously knew if they had to scramble around attempting to find an exit, they would be overwhelmed by the bloodthirsty Nonae soldiers.

"Doesn't matter!" Kain cried. "Pick me up!"

Kiara's eyes widened as she turned her gaze toward her companion. "*What*?"

"The way we got out of the cave, Kiara! *Hurry!*"

She groaned, slowing her pace just enough for Kain's hand to slide from hers. His arms wrapped around her neck as she pulled his body into her grasp, establishing a firm grip on his torso. She continued running until she was merely inches from colliding with the Wall. She started to slow her pace, but Kain yelled at her to keep sprinting. She closed her eyes, wincing, expecting to ram into the hard rock of the Wall—but her body was abruptly lifted into the air as though an invisible string had wrapped itself around her waist and yanked her into the sky. Her hands automatically tightened around Kain as a small gasp escaped her lips.

Kain focused on pushing her body upward, as though she were attached to a rope reeling her higher into the air. They successfully passed the Wall, and were carefully descending onto the other side when Kiara's eyes latched on the horde of ferocious soldiers. They reached the Wall in a massive wave of bodies, crying in outrage, desperately attempting to climb the smooth, twelve-foot high partition without triumph.

Kiara's feet landed softly on the grass inside Enevale's territory, the sweet nectar of safety thickening the blood rushing to her head. Kain's body fell from her arms as he jumped swiftly to the ground. He eyed her wearily, the cries of the defeated soldiers stinging his ears.

She smiled, shyly leaning toward him. They embraced, the rain soaking their bodies as they clung to one another, relief and security pulsating through their veins and dancing through their matching heartbeats.

A booming voice suddenly sounded over the roar of the thunderstorm, startling Kiara so badly, she jerked away from Kain's grasp.

"Enough!" Vyntrx's voice rumbled like thunder. "Relent! You know the plan!"

The soldiers complained loudly amongst themselves, cursing and shouting in protest. Nevertheless, Kiara could tell by the heavy sound of armored footsteps that they had abandoned their efforts and were reluctantly trudging away from the Wall.

Chapter Twenty-Four

Hell Unfurled

The skin on Kailx's back was viciously torn open. Cold metal bit deep into her flesh, skimming the surface of her bones. She cried loudly, her strained voice scathing through her throat, hot tears running down her cheeks. Her hands were manacled together by magic-draining shackles chained to a solid brick wall inside Vyntrx's torture chamber.

"You—insufferable—child!" Vyntrx screamed, lashing a metal whip against her daughter's body without the slightest tinge of restraint or remorse. "I—should—*kill*—you!"

"Why don't you?" Kailx demanded, her voice weak. Her body quivered precariously, her eyes bright maroon with apparent fear.

"It'd be a waste!" she spat, tossing the whip against the wall in a fit of rage. "Your magic is too strong. One day, you *will* take my place."

"Like hell I will," Kailx muttered, spitting blood in her mother's face. "I know the only reason you keep me alive is because if I were to die your power would wane, just like it did when you murdered my father."

Vyntrx's black eyes clouded with crimson rage as she impatiently wiped away the blood and spit mixture splattered on her cheek. She struck her daughter's face so forcefully, her frail body crumpled to the ground with an earsplitting crack, her chains creaking as they attempted to support her limp figure.

"You will learn to hold your tongue!" Vyntrx shrieked hoarsely.

Blood dripped off Kailx's swollen lips as she stared up at her mother through a curtain of sweat-drenched hair, hatred embodied in her glowering stare. "She'll defeat you, mother—she'll beat you," she gasped, struggling to breathe properly. Contusions dotted the skin over her ribs where Vyntrx had struck her with a blunt club. She inhaled deeply, flinching as her chest tightened in protest. "You know that, too—don't you?"

Vyntrx's eyes flashed dangerously. She snatched up a jagged dagger from its position on the wall beside various weapons, a demented smile spreading across her scarlet lips. "I thought I told you," she spoke in an eerily calm tone, "to hold your tongue."

Kailx stared at her mother in horror as she sauntered closer, sliding her pale fingers across the pointed blade.

Vyntrx's lips parted as she gathered a handful of her daughter's hair into her grip. Her eyes gleamed with sadistic glee. "You're going to wish you were never born by the time I'm through with you."

"Trust me," she muttered, her voice shaking, "I already do."

*****

"We're back!" Kiara announced, hurrying through the chambers of her suite. She flung open her bedroom door, finding Avian sprawled on his couch in the corner of the room, his pale hands covering his face. His fingers slowly fell to his side, revealing his startled expression.

"You're covered in blood!" he exclaimed, springing to his feet as Kiara and Kain crossed the threshold of the bedroom.

"I'm alright," she said quickly as Avian's hands wrapped around her shoulders. "What's important is that we found the book!" She fumbled through her pocket, her hands clasping the damp spell book as she procured it from the folds of her cloak. She held it proudly in front of Avian's face, watching his eyes widen disbelievingly as he stared at the worn black binding.

"You actually managed to thieve the highest appraised book in Nonae history?" he whispered incredulously. "And you circumvented the traps without severe injury? Did Vyntrx try to stop you?"

Kiara's eyes narrowed, her hands falling to her side, the book firmly clasped in her grip. She slid the artifact into the folds of her cloak, her gaze hardening suspiciously. "Of course I did," she muttered. "You doubted me?"

Avian shrugged, running his hands through his unusually tousled hair. "It was just a very dangerous mission and I'm impressed you completed it so efficiently. Did you have any trouble finding the temple?"

She set her hands against her hips, eyeing him distrustfully. "No, we found it easily," she spoke slowly, her voice tight, not certain if she should mention her meeting with Vyntrx's daughter or keep the information solely between her and Kain until the feeling of suspicion dissolved from her mind.

"I'm glad," he responded uneasily. He forced a smile. "I'm glad you're back!" He moved forward to wrap her in his arms, but she deliberately stepped backward, shoving his hand away.

"Just don't," she spoke tersely, her eyebrows furrowed. Her heart was pulsating so wildly, her vision started to blur. Her thoughts spun dizzily out of control, her emotions welling hysterically. "Don't touch me."

Kain gingerly reached forward, brushing her shoulder comfortingly. Unabashed by his touch, she stared at the floor enveloped in thought. Avian bitterly eyed his brother's hand as it stroked Kiara's arm, a wave of unfettered rage swelling through his chest.

"You two certainly became close," his voice escaped his lips in a harsh whisper.

"He's my best friend, Avian," Kiara responded coldly. Her hair cascaded into her face, shadowing her expression and concealing her inconsistent eyes.

He scoffed indignantly in response, tossing his head back

with vigorous rage. "You're the only friend he's *ever* had!"

Kain immediately flew at his brother, screaming, "Whose fault is that?" His hands balled into fists, ready to inflict damage.

Kiara was instantly in front of Kain, stubbornly blocking his path. Her hands clutched his arms tightly, slightly placating him. He stared down at her skeptically, watching her wide irises turn rosy pink as she turned her gaze on him.

"Go to your room for a little while, okay?" she said softly. "Stay there until you both calm down. I don't want anyone to end up hurt. *Please*, Kain," she whispered, her tone low as she pleaded with him.

"Fine," he said shortly, averting his eyes as he yanked his arm away from her grip.

"I'll come talk to you soon, okay?"

"Fine," he repeated mechanically, pushing past Kiara as he stormed out of the room, slamming the door shut behind him.

Something is terribly wrong, Avian thought miserably as he watched Kiara's pink eyes trailing Kain until he vanished behind the door. *Something has gone wrong. My manipulation is volatile—it's now beyond my control. All I've managed to do is screw up her head.*

He cleared his throat, drawing her attention to his face. The rosy hue faded from her eyes and was replaced by the light crimson of distrust. "Perhaps we should visit your family," he suggested. "It's been a while since you've seen them. I think it would be beneficial for you."

Despite her anger, an excitedly approving smile curved her lips as she processed Avian's proposal. "I would appreciate that."

He nodded, unable to summon his voice to continue the conversation. She stared blankly at the floor while he surveyed her, critically insulting his idiocy.

"I'm going to heal my wounds and bathe," she announced quietly, stepping hurriedly toward the bathroom.

"Kiara," he whispered as she passed him, his sullen voice momentarily halting her movement. "Something about you has changed."

She glanced at him through the corner of her eye. His expression was poignant, his eyes narrowed in contemplation as he studied her. She shrugged, turned away, and stomped loudly to the bathroom entrance. Her hand clasped the doorknob, her fingers quivering. "Well," she said huskily, "I guess I'm not the only one who noticed."

*****

Kiara stood outside the door to Kain's bedroom, her heart pounding wildly in her chest. Her damp hair hung in tangled waves down her back, falling against the satin fabric of her nightgown. The white scars of recently healed wounds laced her pallid face, her brown eyes unusually dark against her lightly freckled cheeks. Her hand moved slowly, carefully, through the darkness of the hallway. Her fingers lightly rapped against the wooden door.

Under normal circumstances, she would have casually thrown open the door and waltzed into his room uninvited, but after the intimidating tense moment he had shared with Avian, she was terrified of upsetting him further.

"If that's Avian, go away," his muffled voice sounded from within.

"It's me," she replied hoarsely, leaning her forehead against the door as she listened carefully for footsteps. "Do you honestly think Avian would come talk to you?"

The door opened abruptly. She stumbled, falling forward until her head bumped against Kain's shirtless chest—she immediately noticed his name sprawled across his left breast like an elaborate birthmark. She glanced up at him uneasily, watching his cheeks burn red with embarrassment.

"What do you want?" he mumbled, his hands gently raking

Kiara's shoulders as he moved her body away from his. He ushered her into the room, quietly shutting the door behind her.

"I wanted to talk to you," she replied honestly. She jumped onto his bed as though it were her own, resting her weight against her arms as she reclined casually.

"What about?" he inquired, sitting on the mattress beside her.

Her gaze followed his every movement, her rosy eyes slightly narrowed and curtained by dark lashes. "Nothing in particular. I just wanted to talk to you."

"Did you miss me or something?" he blurted.

She stared at him incredulously, the shadow of a smile playing on her lips. He appeared flustered, as if he had spoken his mind entirely by accident.

"Yes, actually," she admitted slowly. "I missed your company."

"How's your lover-boy?" he hurriedly changed the subject, standing up from the bed.

She rolled her eyes, resting her chin in the palm of her hand. "Don't call him that," she muttered.

"You don't love him," he whispered, glancing at her apprehensively.

"Why do you say that?" she stammered, taken aback by the bluntness of his comment.

He was silent for a moment, refusing to make eye contact with her. His gaze was inconsistent, darting around the room like a swiftly moving Coronix. "When you're in love, your eyes are supposed to turn pink, right?"

"Yes," she confirmed.

"I've not noticed your eyes turn pink when you look at him," Kain's tone was spiked with accusation, as though he expected an extensive explanation from her.

"I'm sure that's just because I'm feeling other emotions, as well," she explained quickly, stumbling over her words. "I just don't know—"

"No," he said firmly, cutting her off before she had a chance to fully elaborate on the situation. "Love is the strongest emotion, Kiara. You know that."

She sighed in defeat, her eyes locking with Kain's as he turned to look at her. "What color are my eyes when I look at you?"

He stared at her blankly, his eyebrows raised. His gaze burrowed into her bright pink irises. Her lips parted slightly as she quietly studied his dubious expression. "Um, they…" he paused, swallowing down the anxiety that was rising in his chest. "They change color. Like normal."

"Oh." She didn't mean to sound disappointed, but she managed to. Her eyes flickered away from Kain's stare, her irises automatically losing their pink tint as his face fled her vision.

He took a timid step toward Kiara, his hand out-stretched. She caught his movement from her peripheral vision, standing up hastily and pushing his hand away. She stood with her back facing him, her hands nervously gripping the icy metal of her necklace. "We're leaving tomorrow to travel to my home village," she whispered. "It would mean a lot to me if you would you accompany us."

"Did you talk to Avian about that?" Kain questioned softly, his voice somewhat choked as if he were restraining himself from speaking too much.

"I don't need to include him in the decision," she answered coolly. "The trip is for me."

"The princess is sticking up for me, huh?"

She nodded slowly, stubbornly refusing to face him. "I guess I am."

Kain sighed, his hands lightly gripping her shoulders as he spun her body around to face him. He stared down at her, examining her face carefully as her cheeks burned. "You're upset. What's wrong?"

"It's nothing," she lied. Kain's fingers moved slightly, his thumb running across the fabric of her nightgown. His touch automatically instilled her body with uncontrollable tension; her heart hammered loudly in her chest.

"Weird," he whispered, his fingers lightly pressing against her cheek. "You're lying but your eyes aren't grey."

"Maybe because I'm telling the truth," she replied.

He shook his head, his hand falling away from her face. "Hurry up. Go back to your room. I'm sure your lover-boy is missing you."

"Don't call him—"

"Right," Kain's voice silenced her as he pulled open the door. He grabbed her hand, walking her through the exit. "See you tomorrow, princess."

The door swung shut between them. Kain's back fell against the wood, his hands running through his hair as he attempted to placate his restlessly pulsating heart. *Stop it*, he thought bitterly, *you can't keep falling for her. You're not falling. Dammit, Kain, what have you gotten yourself into?*

*****

Sun filtered in through the colossal window in Kiara's bedroom. Avian was pacing the length of the room, waiting patiently for the princess to wake. She was snoring lightly, her legs pulled tightly against her chest. It was nearing midday and she still had not gathered the strength to depart the realm of slumber. He could understand—she had spent two days battling Nonae in the Dark Forest—but his patience was wearing thin. His torturing thoughts had grown to a catastrophic climax. He could no longer stand to be alone with his afflicting emotions.

He crossed the room hastily. He gently shook her shoulder, disturbing her peaceful sleep. She grumbled, her eyes fluttering as she battled unconsciousness. "Kiara," he whispered, arousing her from slumber. "We need to leave soon."

She opened her eyes wearily, finding Avian's face only inches from hers. "Morning," she whispered, pulling her body into a sitting position. "Where's Kain?"

The shadow of a repulsive scowl darkened Avian's expression. "In his room. Did you expect him to be here when you woke up?"

She shrugged, her hair cascading across her faintly freckled shoulders. "I forgot we were back from the forest," she admitted.

"Well, you are," he said shortly. "Get ready to leave, then fetch Kain. I'll be waiting for you both in the dining room. I've already compiled all of the supplies we should need. Don't," he added, eyeing her drooping eyelids, "fall back asleep."

Kiara hurried around her room, preparing for the journey. She tossed her hair into a messy bun, pulled on a pair of brown leather shorts and ankle-length boots, and covered her torso in a plain tunic whose baggy sleeves bunched around her elbows. Knowing the Dark Forest's weather was unruly, she selected a cloak from the depths of her closet, stuffing it into a small pack that she tied securely around her waist. After she deemed herself ready, she abandoned the chambers of her bedroom.

Without bothering to knock, she yanked open the door to Kain's room. He was sleeping soundlessly in his narrow bed, his black hair helplessly askew across his placid face.

"Wake up!" she shouted, shaking him into consciousness.

His murky eyes flashed open, staring up at her with a dumfounded expression. "Where's your lover-boy?" he asked, yawning.

"Don't call him that," she responded automatically. "He's waiting for us. We're leaving today to travel to my village, remember? It's about a two day walk."

"Fine," he muttered, disentangling his body from a web of blankets. "Do me a favor and don't look at me much while we travel. Don't think about me either. In fact, just ignore me completely."

She narrowed her line of vision. "What are you talking about? Why would I do that?"

"I just think Avian's annoyed that we've become friends," he explained quickly, unable to gather enough courage to tell her the true reason prompting his request.

"Alright," she said slowly, her eyes scrutinizing his face as she attempted to decipher his expression.

He cleared his throat. "You gonna leave or just stay there and gawk while I change?"

She rolled her eyes in response, her hand flying to the doorknob. "Oh, shut up," she chuckled slightly, opening his bedroom door. "I'll be waiting in the hall." She disappeared behind the wood and stood silently in the dimly lit hallway. She knew she could be waiting with Avian in the dining room, but she couldn't stop thinking that there was a newly discovered barrier between them—a cold, unassailable barrier.

The doorknob rattled, forcing Kiara's thoughts to return to reality. Kain emerged from his room, sporting a grey-and-black ensemble. As his hair was still helplessly disheveled, Kiara absentmindedly ran her fingers through the tousled tresses, smoothing his hair into place. He eyed her uneasily, his face flushing.

"Should we—" his voice trailed off as a lump rose in his throat. He eyed the dining room warily. "Should we go?"

Her hand fell away from his face as if she had suddenly been stunned by her actions. She clasped her hands together, averting her gaze. "Y-yeah, we should," she whispered, spinning around on the heel of her boot.

Kain followed her into the dining room, glaring critically at his brother as his figure poured into view. He was leaning against the wall, his hair neatly swept away from his mismatched eyes, a dull expression hovering on his face.

"Listen, boys," Kiara said loudly, stopping in-between the two of them. "No fighting allowed—*none*. If either of you so much as utter a sarcastic or derisive comment, you *will* be reprimanded. Understood?"

Kain and Avian nodded in unison but their glares were unrelenting.

*****

Before departing Enevale, Avian cleared his and Kiara's absence with the dukes, appointing Aiden to take over the position of temporary king should a disastrous situation arise. After Avian had finished discussing matters with Aiden, the dukes waved good-bye to the trio as they departed the castle gates and headed into the city.

As they paced steadily down the streets of Enevale, citizens gathered to watch in memorized wonder as the small group of royals passed through the village. Kain, uncomfortable with the attention he was receiving, slipped behind Kiara, allowing Avian to meet the citizen's beaming expressions with courteous waves.

After they had managed to pass through the large gate that separated Enevale from the Eustoripha Plains, they evoked a unanimous code of silence. Avian, naturally, did not wish to communicate with his brother and the feeling was blatantly mutual. He did, however, wish to speak to Kiara, but he found the action frustrating and guilt provoking while her mind remained in its crumbled state. He could tell she and Kain wished to speak to one another, but that they refrained to do so for a reason he could not discern.

They treaded through the Plains, wading through the tall grass with the humid heat of the approaching summer sweeping over their sweaty bodies. After crossing the vibrantly green land, they reached the edge of the Dark Forest, pausing momentarily before they took one deep collective breath and stepped into enemy territory.

Walking lightly and stealthily, they cautiously trucked

through the forest in silence. The forest wildlife remained eerily quiet; the only sound trickling through the woods was the soft crunch of boots on dirt and the rustling of leaves in the faint wind.

Slowly, the sun fell from the sky, casting shadows through the dimly lit forest. The darkness spread quickly, eventually encompassing the light so drastically, the companions were forced to stop walking and start a fire.

Avian offered to stay awake as a look-out while Kain and Kiara rested, but Kiara hurriedly suggested splitting the shift with him. Her mind had been harassed by such severe anticipation for seeing her family, she was certain she would be unable to rest for very long.

After Avian had prepared the makeshift campsite beside the glowing fire, Kain wrapped himself in a blanket and succumbed to slumber almost instantly. Avian reclined against the harsh bark of a tree, his eyes scanning the forest as his thoughts whirred. He heard Kiara shuffling closer to him and chided his heartbeat for accelerating from the mere reminder of her presence.

"See anything?" she whispered.

"No," he muttered. "You should get some rest."

She sighed, folding her legs against her chest and staring at Avian through the shadows. "My head feels like it's on fire," she said slowly. "When I look at you, when I'm near you, my body swirls and spins with confusion. A voice inside my head tells me to push you away, to distance myself from you—but a small part of me just wants to break down and sob. Why do I feel that way, Avian? Why have my emotions changed so much?"

He glanced away, his eyes locked on the lightless distance as tears slid down his cheeks. A lump of guilt rose in his throat as desolation smothered his heart. "Maybe someone out there just doesn't want us to be together," he choked.

His suggestion issued a wave of conflicting emotion to stir

in the pit of her stomach. She bit her lip, urging the sensation to pass—but it only grew stronger. "I'm not sure what to say," she admitted.

"There's something I want you to know and never forget," he spoke softly, his voice quavering. He refused to glance at her and allow her to see his tear-streaked face. "Regardless of what happens."

She furrowed her brow in confusion, attempting to discern his figure through the oppressive shadows. The gleam of the fire highlighted his body in an orange outline, but his face was deliberately turned from hers and even if he had been staring directly at her, she would not have been able to read his expression through the darkness. "What is it?"

He was silent for several seconds. In the distance, a bird squawked plaintively as though it had been attacked by a predator. "I love you," he declared. "I'll always love you."

An unexpected tear quickly fell down Kiara's cheek. Her hand automatically moved to wipe it away, but her fingers paused just before they could blot the liquid. Her hand curiously explored her wet cheek as she attempted to decipher the reasoning behind her sudden sullenness. Touched by the sincere atmosphere, she allowed her head to fall against Avian's back as tears uncontrollably streamed down her face. For a handful of meaningful minutes, they remained embossed in silence. They leaned on each other, listening to the broken sound of their breathing, of the air catching in their throats and escaping in the form of strangled sobs. The sadness they had bottled in their chests had overflown and spilled out through their eyes in the form of perplexed, unrelenting tears, and they were both suddenly very aware that their relationship had been far too damaged to ever return to its vibrant state.

Kiara released a shaky sigh as she gently reclined her head, lifting it from its position against Avian's shoulder. "I—I'm going to bed," she announced, her voice wobbling unevenly. "Good night, Avian. Wake me when it's my turn to be on look-out duty."

Rustling sounds filled the silence as she scavenged through the shadows for her blankets. After she had snuggled up in her quilts by the fire, Avian listened carefully for the steady rise and fall of her breathing to signal her lapse into slumber. "Good night, Ara," he murmured, his sobbing face falling limply into his hands as his mind burned with unwelcome thoughts. "Good night."

*****

The putrid smell of fire and blood smothered the air. A thick dark line of smoke billowed through the sky, visible through the thinning line of tees. Kiara's heart dropped as she realized the horrific odor was secreting from the direction of her village.

Avian stopped walking, staring ahead as he was struck with horrendous realization. Kain sent him a blameful glare, his hands balling into fists as his eyes bore into his brother's dumfounded expression.

Kiara emitted a sharp whimper, her limbs trembling with fear. Her heart thudded loudly in her chest, the sound ringing ominously through her ears. Her body felt numb and paralyzed, but a wave of unadulterated concern and uncertainty swept over her chest, urging her legs to start sprinting.

She thrashed through the underbrush, unaware of the sharp thorns and twigs stabbing at her calves. She desperately followed the trail of smoke until the ashy wind thickened into an oxygen-depraved void. She stumbled, her eyes clouded with the fiery discharge, her mind far too preoccupied to suggest summoning magic to safely guide her way. Avian and Kain reached her side, heaving and coughing loudly into their cupped palms. Kain grabbed her wrist while Avian evoked one of his countless Specialties to create a sweep of wind to battle the smoke. Kain hurriedly led the emotionally rattled girl through the outskirts of the forest while Avian ran ahead, wafting the billows of smoke away.

As the wisps of ashy clouds dissipated and the remainder of the forest passed by in a blur of smoky green, the jarring sight of a razed village poured into view. Charred houses and smoldering bodies littered the rubble, the repugnant odor of burned flesh swirling in the nostrils of the companions as they stared in disbelieving horror at the horrendous sight.

"NO!" Kiara shrieked, her voice exploding from her throat in the form of a broken wail. She fell listlessly to her knees as her maroon eyes scanned the sight with terror. "NO!"

Avian scanned the horizon, his heart assaulted by a pang of shocked dismay. "H-how did this..." his voice trailed off as a storm of hysterics rose in his throat. "H-how did this happen?"

Kiara half-crawled, half-ran through the scarred streets of her village. Kain hurried after her, but Avian stood strikingly still as though the sight had paralyzed his limbs.

She stumbled over the rubble, coughed on the toxic fumes, but her desperate determination to uncover her family did not relent.

The remains of her flattened house would have been unidentifiable to an outsider but Kiara recognized the building even in its demolished state. A plaintive cry escaped her lips as she neared her childhood home. She tore hysterically through the debris, discarding familiar objects that had been disfigured beyond repair. After several minutes of searching despairingly, she pulled away a half-crumbled wall to reveal the sallow, emaciated faces of Brin and Anya. Their lifeless eyes stared up at her, their mouths hanging open in soundless screams. Blood and ash smeared their faces but the fire that had destroyed their house had not stolen their lives—their throats had been mercilessly slashed open. The blade had been cut so deeply into their necks that their heads were just barely suspended by a thin thread of mangled flesh.

Kiara's mouth opened in horror, but no scream escaped her breathless lungs. Her listless body tumbled backwards and would have crashed sharply against the wreckage had Kain not made a swift move to catch her. He wrapped his arms around her as they slowly fell to their knees, her hysteric sobs echoing through the eerily silent village. She attempted to articulate her pain, to convey her muddled distress, but her voice was caught in her constricting throat.

"Brin and Anya—" Avian's weak voice sounded from behind them. He had slowly made his way through the ruined village and had witnessed from a distance Kiara's mournful reaction. "They're—they're—"

"It's your fault," Kain said darkly, holding Kiara's weeping face to his chest. "You killed them! You killed them just like you killed m—"

"Look at my face, Kain!" Avian screamed, his voice strained and hoarse. "Do I *look* guilty to you? Do I not appear startled and distressed? I *knew* these people!"

Kain glowered at his brother suspiciously. He scrutinized Avian's visage and found the only emotion chiseled on his face to be sincere anguish. Kain sighed, shaking his head. He turned his eyes to the singed house, his gaze briefly falling on Kiara's murdered family before he stared down at her tear-streaked face. He pressed his lips to the crown of her head while his hand cupped the back of her neck, his breathing ragged and unsteady. "I believe you, Avian," he admitted gruffly. "This time it was solely Vyntrx."

Avian nodded stiffly in response. "I'll kill her," he growled through clenched teeth. His entire body was trembling with unbridled rage, his vision blurring from the red tinge of fury that had clouded his mind. "Kain, take care of Kiara. Don't let her stay here. Take her into the woods and conceal her for the night. Travel back to Enevale and grieve with her. Console her until I return. I won't be gone long."

"You're seriously leaving her right now?" Kain questioned,

his voice rising as an accusing tone swept through his words. "Can't you see she's in pain?"

"She won't accept my comfort," he responded bitterly. "Only you can help her right now. I obviously didn't stay in the forest long enough to overhear her plans to raze Kiara's village. If I had, I could have prevented this. I'm going to make sure Vyntrx doesn't have another murderous spree planned."

Kain narrowed his eyes but he couldn't argue that his brother would be unable to quell Kiara's disastrous thoughts and placate her uncontrollable sobs. "Fine," he said shortly. "I'll comfort her, I'll take care of her. You go if you need to."

Avian's eyes lingered on Kiara's tremulous body as she clung to his brother's comforting arms. His heart shattered at the sight.

As though the smoky vapors had swathed his body and stolen him into the shadows, he vanished into the darkness of the charred village, leaving Kain and Kiara alone amid piles of mangled corpses.

hapter Twenty-Five

The Calm Before the Storm

Avian kicked open the double-doors of Vyntrx's throne room. The wooden doors violently slammed against the granite walls, a sharp crack resonating through the silence.

Vyntrx's head snapped upward, her attention instantly captured by Avian's dramatic entrance. Her four most trusted followers were positioned around the throne, their eyes trailing their companion as he stormed into the room. Avian could tell by Murdock's defensive stance that the five of them had been vehemently quarrelling over an issue prior to his abrupt appearance.

"What the hell have you done?" he demanded, brushing past Harlyt as she attempted to drape her arms around his neck. His furious mismatched eyes bore into Vyntrx's as she glared down at him from her reclined position on the throne.

"You're sexy when you're angry, Ave," Harlyt cooed, playfully skimming her nails across his shoulder. "Who should we thank?"

"The empress herself," he growled through clenched teeth.

A coy smile spread across Vyntrx's blood-red lips. "Oh, *whatever* are you speaking of, Avian?"

His eyes narrowed, his harsh glare seemingly turning his face to cold stone. "You massacred Kiara's village—you murdered her family!"

"Oh, yes," she admitted, interlacing her fingers as she rested her chin on her hands, "I remember *that*."

"I'm confused," Demure spoke quietly, brushing away a strand of her coppery hair. "I was under the impression that Avian knew of your plan."

Murdock shook his head, eyeing Harlyt disdainfully. "The bimbo forgot to inform him. Never allow a *blonde* to be a messenger, they will always—"

Harlyt's lipstick-coated mouth unhinged, but before she could speak, Avian's furious voice dominated the room. "I should not have to hear of such detrimental events through one of your minions, Vyntrx! Am I not your second-in-command?"

"Yes," she answered callously, "you are. However, I recommend that you begin to act appropriately if you wish to maintain such a status. Might I remind you about our little agreement?" Her pointer finger traced her chest, marking an x over her heart.

Avian's eyes bulged with rage but he sealed his mouth shut. He nodded stiffly, his hand automatically flying to his chest as though Vyntrx's sharp reminder had stabbed his heart.

"I'm still confused," Demure mumbled. "Why does Avian care if they're dead?"

"Yes, Avian," Vyntrx taunted menacingly, "why *do* you care?"

"Because it concerns Raiyx's child?" Murdock guessed, patting Avian's back. His face featured a look of empathetic understanding. "You two were childhood friends, weren't you?"

Avian remained silent, staring blankly ahead. He wished to express his rage, to condemn Vyntrx for being so merciless, but he bit his tongue. Murdock watched the wave of wrath spill across Avian's face. He smiled weakly, whispering, "Stifle your emotions, boy, or Vyn will drain them."

"Kiara Fable and her cohorts killed many of my kind," Miriam interjected. His stoic demeanor unfailingly evaded him whenever the concern of the Demmonai race was present. "They wiped out two fleets."

"And we've killed plenty of Evalseman," Demure argued hotly. "And yet Avian and I are still here. Race doesn't matter in a war, Miriam. War is ruthless."

Vyntrx raised her eyebrows skeptically. "Taking Avian's side, are we, Demure?"

"He should have been notified," she deducted, lowering her gaze sheepishly.

"I'm done discussing this matter," the empress mandated. "Harlyt has secured a treaty with the Omes of Oruem. You should all be extremely grateful! They are an exceedingly unintelligent race and negotiations with them were undoubtedly exhausting. I wish to procure a few more allies before we launch the battle with Enevale—"

"You'd better hurry, then," Avian jeered. "The coronation ball is in three weeks."

Vyntrx's black eyes shone with unparalleled excitement. "How enthralling!" she exclaimed. "I'll be making an appearance, of course!"

Avian sighed shakily, resentment settling in the pit of his stomach as his heart thudded with sickening apprehension. "Yes," he said warily. "The night when everything changes."

*****

The wind stirred abruptly, sending a cold chill flooding through the evening air. The sun was in the process of being swallowed by the horizon, emanating a soft, red glow across the bustling city of Enevale. Kiara sat alone at the top of a hill near the castle, over-looking the Dark Forest. Her eyes were red and swollen from crying. Her expression was blank, her eyes glazed as she observed the heinous forest, imagining that grim line of smoke rising from the trees.

Kain had carried her out of the ruins of her village. She had sobbed hysterically and protested violently—but he refused to let her go. They had spent the night in a shallow cave on the outskirts of the forest. Kain's arm had wound around her torso and did not relent all throughout the night. Having been unable to succumb to the nightmares that were surely waiting for her, she stared blankly at the shadows crossing the rock wall until the faint light of morning spilled in through the creviced entrance.

They had walked numbly through the forest for endless hours until the bright marble of the Wall radiated through the distance. After they had returned sullenly to the castle, Kiara had retreated silently to her bedroom and had shut the door firmly behind her. She had remained locked in her room for several hours until she had managed to gather enough strength to trek outside of the castle to breathe in the revitalizing air of nature.

Before traveling to Enevale, Kiara had often succumbed to anxiety attacks while musing over the thought of death. The permanence of the concept struck a heavy chord of fear inside her chest. She had always been entirely baffled by the finality of mortality, but she had never been forced to contemplate the subject on a personal basis. In Menevilen, the world beyond death was as clear and crisp as life itself—but that notion didn't make the actual departure less terrifying.

Her eyes clouded with tears at the thought of her deceased family. She still couldn't fathom the fact that their lives ceased to thrive. Even though she had left their home months ago, she had been content knowing that they were alive. At the loss of her family, the miniscule thread that linked her previous life to reality had been viciously severed.

Guilt and grief hung vivaciously to the chambers of Kiara's mind. It swelled through her chest and spilled into her abdomen, twisting her stomach into uneasy knots. She ran her fingers through her hair, sighing. She trapped her cheeks in-between her knees and attempted to breathe steadily, to calm her nerves and squelch her anxiety, but her efforts were fruitless.

"How are you?" Kain's voice sounded abruptly. She had been so entangled in her thoughts, she hadn't even heard his footsteps as he approached.

She refrained from responding, tilting her head slightly as

her eyes searched his worried expression. He sat down timidly in the grass beside her, his gaze never once departing her face.

"Wh-what're you—" she started to speak, but her voice was siphoned by an abrupt bout of hysterics.

"I'm not gonna let you suffer alone," he mumbled. His hand gently caressed her cheek. His thumb caught a falling tear as it seeped across her chin, his violet eyes examining the substance skeptically. "So this is sadness."

"This isn't real!" she gasped, burying her face in her palms as Kain hurriedly retracted his hand. His grasp fell to her shoulder, comforting her as she sobbed. "It—it just *can't* be!"

"I'm sorry, princess," he whispered sincerely, gently pulling her shoulder against his chest as his arms wrapped around her small frame. "I don't know what to say. I'm so sorry."

She whimpered slightly, dabbing at her wet eyes. "It isn't your fault," she murmured. She reached out her hand, tentatively, discovering his cheek. "Please don't die, Kain. I can't lose you, too."

His hand wound around hers. "Who would rescue you from Coronix-filled pits if I wasn't around?"

She shook her head, muttering, "*Weren't*. If you *weren't* around."

"I'm not going to leave you, princess," he whispered. His fingers lightly skimmed her hair; his lips grazed her forehead. "I promise."

Kiara's quivering lips mimicked the basis of a small smile at Kain's declaration, but a strange feeling spread through her chest. She wanted to cling to him, yet a voice in the back of her head begged her to push him away. Unwittingly, her thoughts rotated to Avian as the words he had spoken to her before the death of her family swarmed her head: *I love you. I'll always love you.* While his words echoed loudly through her mind, her body turned numb beneath Kain's touch as a fresh bout of tears spilled down her cheeks.

*****

Kain gingerly set the spell book against Kiara's folded legs, watching goose bumps spread across her bare skin. The binding of the book rubbed against the cuff of her shorts, the sudden pressure against her leg snapping her mind out of its distracting daydreams and drawing her eyes away from the floor. She glanced up at Kain as he sat down across from her, her eyebrows lowering.

"You think this will help me?" she inquired, carefully fondling the spine of the book. She and Kain had retreated to the suite after departing their position on the hill and had been overwhelmed by exhaustion from their dismally eventful escapade. She had persuaded Kain to sleep on the couch in her bedroom, as she knew she could not bear to be alone with her disquieting thoughts, but he had slipped into the bed beside her after she succumbed to an uncontrollable wave of hysterics. After he had managed to ease her into slumber, he had been far too exhausted to climb out of her bed and had instead fallen asleep with her tightly wrapped in his arms. The following morning, he had immediately suggested she busy herself with an activity through the day so she would be unable to fall into a grief-induced relapse.

"Yeah," he said shortly, thoughtfully cupping his chin with his upturned palm. "Which spell are you gonna learn?"

"I dunno," she breathed, gently pulling open the worn, ancient pages of the spell book. Her eyes were puffy and pink but she had managed to avoid crying for the first half of the morning. "Maybe all of them."

He raised a skeptical eyebrow. "You can do it all today?"

She shrugged, skimming her fingers across the heavily inked text. "I can try."

"Need me to help?"

"I may need to use you," she responded coolly, half-heartedly eyeing the instructions for temporarily raising the dead to use as mindless soldiers. "As a target or something."

"Use me however you want," he advised. "Whatever it takes to cheer you up."

Kiara's eyes flickered to his face, a studious look highlighting her expression as she contemplated his words. She abruptly shut the book, setting it down on the floor beside her. "*However* I want?" she mused aloud, slowly drawing her face nearer to Kain's. His pallid face flushed crimson but he didn't move away from her approaching figure. "You'd really do *anything* to make me happy again?"

He attempted to swallow down his nerves as he adopted a calm, collected demeanor. "Of course," he spoke confidently, unable to mask the tinge of tension creeping through his voice.

"You're showing emotion," she critiqued, clasping her hand around his shoulder and slowly lowering his face toward hers. "You hate emotion."

"Not when it concerns you," he admitted quietly, his hand lightly gripping the side of her face. His thumb ran across the smooth planes of her cheek, sending chills down her spine. "I care about you."

"Do you?" she inquired, resting her head against Kain's. Their foreheads pressed together, their eyes locked as their noses brushed. "I thought you didn't care about anyone."

"No one but you," his voice was hushed and quivering with apprehension. "I didn't think I could care about anyone, but you—"

Kiara's pointer finger halted his moving lips. His voice died in his throat. "It's not nice to tease, Kain," she whispered. He could feel the warmth of her breath against his face, could see the insistent tears outlining her narrowed eyes. "Please don't lie to me."

"I'm not," he admitted slowly. "I would never lie to you, unlike that bastard Avian."

Kiara's eyes widened at his remark. Her hand fell away from his shoulder as she leaned back in puzzled aggravation. She hurriedly climbed to her feet, turning her back to Kain as she attempted to calm her rampant thoughts. "You always speak of Avian as though he has committed the worst crime in the world. You allude to some hidden secret as though it's an insider between the two of you. You treat him with contempt and you're always muttering snide remarks that don't make sense to me. Clearly Avian has done something, and obviously I'm in the dark." She spun around on the heels of her bare feet, her eyes heatedly falling on Kain's sheepish expression. "If you really care about me like you say you do, then you should tell me what Avian has done." She stared at him expectantly, observing his every move.

He sighed, running his hand through his tousled black hair. He stood up slowly, his hands awkwardly smashed into his pockets. "Kiara," he started, unable to meet her threatening gaze, "I can't."

Her face flushed red with frustration. Her lips parted but her voice faltered before she could form a sentence. She glanced at the floor awkwardly, attempting to gather her thoughts, her eyes momentarily flashing scarlet as she averted her gaze from Kain. "Then you don't care about me," she decided. She didn't wait for a reaction—she didn't even glance in his direction. She spun around, hurried to her closet, and slammed the door shut behind her.

Kain stared, awestruck, at the spot she had abandoned. The spell book lie forlornly on the floor, its pages crumpled and protruding stubbornly from the leather binding. *Idiot*, he chided himself, *you've made her upset. You're not any better than Avian.*

Stop insulting me, Kain, Avian's voice abruptly cut through his thoughts. His eyes widened, rage rampantly pouring through his veins. He knew of his brother's endless abilities, knew how easily he could invade other's thoughts—but he had never experienced Avian's aptitude firsthand and had never been a direct victim of his manipulative ways. He was furious at his brother for procuring the audacity to tamper with his mind.

Get the hell out of my head, bastard, Kain thought viciously, briskly striding out of Kiara's bedroom. He shut the door behind him, hoping Avian's voice had been trapped inside the confinement of her room.

Meet me in the hallway, Avian's voice demanded just as Kain's rage began to mitigate. He sighed, exasperated, as he hurried through the suite. He yanked open the door leading to the corridors of the castle, unsurprised as his eyes fell upon his brother's hooded figure. He was leaning against the wall, his hair falling across his eyes and casting shadows across his pale cheeks.

"Hello, brother," Avian spoke solemnly. His voice was so cold, Kain could feel a chill creeping through the unventilated air.

"Aren't you supposed to be in the Dark Forest?" he questioned accusingly, his hands unwillingly balling into fists.

Avian chuckled, his characteristic grin sliding across his lips. "Yes, but you know how easy it is for me to slip in and out of the forest." His voice was on the verge of taunting, and Kain could feel bitterness from his brother's tone prickling his skin.

"Kiara's devastated," Kain poured as much condescension into his words as he could possibly muster. "And you don't even care."

"Ah, Kiara," Avian's defensive exterior softened momentarily as Kiara's name danced across his tongue. He picked at a string hanging from his olive green shirt, twirling the thread around his finger. "You've fallen for her, haven't you?"

Kain's cheeks flushed scarlet as his heartbeat rapidly accelerated. "Wh-what are you—" he stammered, stumbling over his words.

He sneered at his brother's reaction. "I may not be able to read minds, brother, but I can read emotions."

"You came all the way back to the castle to taunt me, then?"

Avian dropped the string he was tampering with. He narrowed his eyes, the bright mismatched hues of his irises slicing through the shaded hall. "No," he said firmly.

"Don't tell me..." he muttered, staring at his brother in dismay. "You're supposedly only following orders by playing the role of Kiara's advisor. You're supposed to be Vyntrx's pathetically loyal slave. Yet you've actually fallen in love with Kiara, haven't you?"

Avian's face remained utterly collected, lacking even the slightest tinge of emotion. Not a hint of crimson dotted his pale, uncharacteristically serious face. "Feel clever now, do you?"

"You came here to tell me to back off of your girl," Kain observed, folding his arms across his chest.

Avian flicked his head forward in the motion of a slight nod. "Indeed."

"*Sorry*," Kain sneered sarcastically, "but I'm not going to let you hurt her anymore. She deserves something better. She deserves something real."

"Listen to me very carefully," he spoke slowly and sternly, as though he were lecturing a disobedient child. "If you dare steal away the only precious thing I have left in this dismal world, you will become my eternal nemesis. I will never forgive you. Given the chance, I would end your life a second time, and if that happens, I'll make sure you stay dead."

"You're delusional," Kain spat. "You've controlled Kiara's mind and forced her to love you. You really think she'll stand by your side after she finds out the truth? Her eyes still change color when she looks at you—they're not pink."

Avian rolled his eyes edgily. "She can't feel true emotions for me while I'm influencing her thoughts. It's one of the many setbacks accompanied with mind control. I'm only manipulating her because Vyntrx commanded me to, and you're fully aware of what would occur should I not follow orders." He drew a slim finger across his throat, mimicking death.

"That doesn't matter," he stubbornly decided. "Once she knows who you're really loyal to, she'll never forgive you."

Avian locked his jaw, his facial expression hardening. "I see you've decided to stand your ground."

Kain nodded stiffly.

"Very well. Let this meeting serve as a warning. As soon as Kiara discovers the truth—and she will, I'm certain—then you and I will begin our lawless battle to secure her heart. I will not hold back."

Kain snickered, tossing his head back and disheveling his black hair. "'Kay. I accept your challenge. I won't hold back either."

Avian's mouth curled at the corners, pulling his lips into a mocking smile. "Good. I'll be back tomorrow morning. Go spend time with *my* girl—while you can."

Kain unhinged his mouth to utter a harsh retort, but Avian vanished without warning, leaving his brother alone with his disquieting thoughts in the shadows of the dark hallway.

*****

Don't cry, Kiara thought determinedly, *it isn't worth it*. Her back slid down the smooth wood of her closet door as she pulled her face into her hands. She heard a door shut somewhere in the suite and instantly understood that Kain had left her room without protest.

Without standing, she quietly creaked open the door. She could see her room through a thin sliver between the door and her closet wall—Kain was nowhere in sight and the book of spells was lying in the spot she had discarded it.

She climbed to her feet, abandoning the secluded walls of her closet. She hurried through her room, rescuing the spell book from its dejected position on the floor. She reclined on the soft mattress of her bed, pushing away bittersweet thoughts of Kain as she absentmindedly fingered through the pages of the spell book. As she scanned the pages, she realized there were several spells she was itching to try, but they all appeared extremely complex for her novice status. She eventually decided to attempt a spell that pulled the moisture from the air, resulting in a colossal mass of water poised for exploitation. The concept wasn't entirely mind-boggling and the swift movement of her hands required to initiate the spell wasn't at all strenuous. She read through the directions several times, memorizing the steps.

After minutes of studying, she carefully balanced the open book on the edge of the bed, her eyes lingering over the leaves as she steadied herself. She took a deep breath, exhaling through her nostrils. Her hands moved mechanically, weaving around her body as she focused on drawing moisture from the air and transferring it into a ball of waves held precariously above her shoulders. As her wishful thoughts were drawn to the realm of reality, she was stunned by how rapidly she had managed to execute the spell and how easily she had gripped the concept. Curiously, she eyed the churning ball of water above her head, wondering if she could solidify the liquid into ice. Without bothering to concede the spell and search the book for instructions, she deftly pictured the torrents of water converting into a crystallized structure.

The sloshing sound of waves abruptly silenced, drawing Kiara out of her focused stupor. Her eyes widened in disbelief, her concentration snapping as the block of ice fell from her control and shattered against the floor of her suite.

Intrigued, she wondered if she could will the remnants of ice to vanish. Her eyes raked the collision site, envisioning the shards of ice seeping into the tufts of carpet and disintegrating. She didn't have to imagine anything for long—the ice began to disperse into liquid, pooling into a puddle of water as it was instantly absorbed by the ground.

A baffled smile crept across Kiara's face. She had managed to fully manipulate the water without memorizing different spells for each command. As her thoughts buzzed with prideful surprise, she kept reminding herself of Avian's informative declaration that spells didn't come so naturally—or so effortlessly—to everyone.

Fueled by a renewed sensation of exhilaration, Kiara excitedly tore through the spell book. She had planned on attempting the most complex spell the book could present, but her heart sank as soon as she flipped to the last page. Whatever the final spell had been, she would never know. The page had been hurriedly torn out of the book, jagged edges of the stolen leaf poking out from the binding.

*****

Kain had somehow managed to evade Kiara for the remainder of the night. Their estrangement had lasted into the drowsy hours of the morning, as he hadn't been able to shut down his rapidly speeding mind, and sleep had been an unattainable desire. After several disappointing hours of restless slumber, he crept out of his bedroom, secured a bottle of alcohol and hunk of meat from the suite's kitchen, and wandered aimlessly through the castle halls.

Eventually, he stumbled upon a stone walkway that connected the east end of the castle to the west wing. The path was lined with glassless windows, filling the chamber with cool morning air. A dull grey light illuminated the plain hall, casting shadows across Kain's pallid face as he slowly crossed the narrow room.

He stopped beside one of the windows, resting his elbows against the cold stone. He stared at the forest below, dangling the glass bottle out of the aperture and sighing loudly.

"You look somber," a voice called suddenly.

The speaker's identity was utterly obvious—instantly

recognizable by the accented village dialect that lilted her voice. He didn't turn around to face her, although every nerve in his body was screaming for him to move.

"Couldn't sleep, princess?" he asked drily.

A torrent of clumsily shuffling footsteps alerted Kain of Kiara's movement. She appeared beside him, sticking her arms through the glassless window and lacing her fingers together. She shook her head. "Apparently you couldn't either."

He stared straight ahead. "I've had some unsettling thoughts."

"Oh?" she wondered, her interested piqued. "What about?"

"Nothing," he muttered dismissively. "Why couldn't you sleep?"

She shrugged, her eyes lingering over the training fields below. A fire suddenly broke out on the grass, forming the letter 'a' with its flames. The fire shifted slowly until it had fully spelled out Avian's name. Kain turned to her, his eyebrows knit, just as the flames were squelched as quickly as they had erupted. The grass that had recently been scorched was immediately replaced by patches of new green grass as though flames had never damaged their vibrancy.

"I knew I could manipulate magic without learning spells, but it turns out I can manipulate enchantments and change their composition just by willing the magic to shift," she explained before he could pose the question forming on his lips. "Is that normal?"

"No, it's really not," he said slowly. "You mean you can do anything you think up?"

She raised her lightly freckled shoulders to her chin, cocking her head to one side. Her eyes studied the Dark Forest as her eyebrows furrowed. "Not anything. Ideally, I'd be able to locate my aunt right now and send a blade through her chest. Maybe her magic is blocking mine or maybe I'm just not that powerful. I guess I have limits. All I know is that I memorized every spell in that book in under an hour. I spent the rest of the night creating my own."

"Maybe it's an Evalseman Specialty," he offered helpfully. "Some Evalseman are born with more than one. Your lover-boy is a good example."

Kiara glanced in Kain's direction, allowing his words to fully sink in. "But in order for an Evalseman to be born with a magical Specialty, wouldn't he or she have to be half-Nonae?"

"Well, yeah. Specialties are linked with heredity, you know."

"Interesting," she spoke quietly, her eyes raking her small, delicate hands. "I guess I have two Specialties."

Kain tentatively extended his hand, resting his palm against her wrist. "That's amazing. You should tell Avian the good news. He'll be back tonight."

She skeptically raised her left eyebrow. "He will? How do you know?"

"Oh, um—it's just a hunch," he said quickly, mentally scolding himself for alluding to the private conversation he had shared with his brother. "Come on, let's go get some breakfast," he said dismissively, weaving his arms away from Kiara's hands and dragging them through the glassless window. He started down the hall, relief flooding his veins when he heard Kiara's footsteps behind him.

*****

The floorboards of Kailx's living room creaked as Avian passed through her disheveled flat. Her furniture had been overturned, the windows smashed. Shards of glass and fragments of torn paper littered the ground, crunching under his boots as he timidly stepped through the home. Vyntrx had clearly taken out her rage on more than Kailx's frail body.

"What're you doing here?" her small voice echoed through the dimly lit room.

His eyes swiveled to the side, discovering her slumped

lethargically in a wide chair. Her swollen, bruise-stained face stared up at him through the shadows.

"I came to check on you," he admitted, rushing to her side. He knelt on his knees beside the chair, his hand lightly clasping her lacerated fingers. "You look terrible."

"She barely let me out with my life," she spoke hoarsely. Her breath escaped her lips in a convoluted manor, as though the action of speaking caused her great pain. "But I'll heal. I've used minimal magic to hurry the process along but I'm too weak to summon enough power to fully revitalize my body."

He warily eyed the dark contusions dotting her pale skin. "Allow me to help you," he offered, tracing his fingers across her arm as he invoked one of his countless Specialties to heal her. "Your mother massacred Kiara's village."

Kailx's eyes, encircled by dark bruises, flashed dark sapphire with sadness. "I know," she admitted shakily. "I tried to stop her but she only worsened my injuries in response."

Avian's face fell as he moved to heal the bruises on her cheeks. "It's time you left your mother's grasp," he said slowly, his stomach knotting as he eyed a puddle of blood seeping through her dress and coating her torso. "Is our plan still intact?"

She nodded stiffly. "I will have certainly recovered my strength by the time of the coronation. Cylis's plans have not changed last I heard. I will keep you updated."

Avian's hands hovered over her stomach as he attempted to patch up the bleeding wound. She cringed, but did not cry out in pain. Her hands balled into fists as she stared blankly at the ceiling.

"Thank you for your help, Kailx," he said quietly.

Her body relaxed as Avian relented his efforts. The wound had been neatly healed and was no longer spurting blood down the front of her garment. She felt faintly rejuvenated but noticed she was still unable to gather enough energy to stand on her shaky legs. "We're simply helping each other," she decided. "I only wish I could save *you* from my mother's clutches."

He shook his head, a tinge of pain welling behind his mismatched eyes. "I'm afraid no one can do that," he murmured. "My unfortunate predicament was spurred by my own flawed actions. This is simply my punishment."

Kailx furrowed her brow, lightly patting her companion's shoulder. "You've suffered enough. You will be freed and forgiven eventually."

He was unable to reply. His mind thoroughly processed Kailx's words as he imagined an ideal, unachievable world. He pictured Kiara, her hearty smile overflowing with true emotion as her rosy eyes met his. He imagined Vyntrx dead—sslain by Kiara's willing hands—her merciless reign ended by the princess's gallant efforts. He felt his shackles dissolved, his heart light with the dizzying sensation of freedom. "Kiara is the only one who holds the key to my salvation," he whispered. "And after everything that has passed between us, I'm not certain she'll choose to unlock my cage."

*****

Kain's premonition about Avian's swift return had been correct. He had returned to the castle wearing a sullen expression and had immediately inquired about Kiara's emotional state. She promised him that she had begun to feel slightly better—although she understood that she would always bear the scar of her family's death—and had hurriedly informed him of her newfound realization that her advanced manipulation of magic could be identified as an Evalseman Specialty. He had been thoroughly impressed and slightly bemused by her announcement, but his somber mood prevented him from being overly enthused.

He had informed her that he had scheduled her coronation ball to take place in two weeks' time and had suggested that in the days leading up to the fateful event, she would continue her physical combat training while attempting to strengthen her control over Nonae magic. He warned her that until the coronation ball passed, the castle would be bustling with ceremony planners and that he would be continually in and out of the suite as he attended to different issues.

Just one day after Avian had announced the news of Kiara's coronation, Sena had entered the suite with a roll of measuring tape wrapped around her hand. Kiara had stared at her friend in baffled confusion, as she had been under the impression Sena was not aware of Kiara's true identity. Sena admitted shyly that Avian had informed her of the news that morning and had requested her help with the preparation of the coronation. As Avian could not ask the seamstresses of the castle to measure Kiara for her dress in fear of spreading a rumor about her identity, he had turned to a trusted friend for assistance. Sena had handled the news about her friend's secret identity with muddled shock but had quickly come to terms with the idea, claiming she had always pegged Kiara as a "respectable individual".

She had taken Kiara's measurements while chatting cheerfully about the upcoming coronation and had admitted that she had been charged with the duty of sketching the design for Kiara's dress. She assured her the garment would be finished in merely a week and that Avian had ordered the castle's blacksmith to forge a customized circlet for the crowning. He had gathered a planning crew of approximately forty citizens and castle workers who were charged with responsibilities ranging from handwriting the invitations to garnishing one of the castle's ballrooms with unique decorations for the event.

As the days sped past in a blur of fabrics, fittings, and finalizations, a crown of apprehension encircled Kiara's head while a cloud of disbelief flooded her lungs. She was unable to fathom that she would finally be crowned Queen of Enevale and be recognized by her citizens as Kyan's lost daughter. Having lived shrouded in the shadows of secrecy during her residency in Enevale, the notion of being exposed felt unsettling.

She was aware that once she was crowned, Vyntrx would be able to force her way into the kingdom—as Raiyx's preventative spell protecting the kingdom from malevolent forces would fade once the coronation commenced—and Kiara was not naïve enough to believe she would wait to launch an attack. Before she could advise Avian to prepare for the ceremony to be strictly monitored by soldiers, he had already taken precautionary measures by requiring every on-duty soldier to undergo extensive training before the coronation.

She understood that she should feel excited and thrilled by the notion of her crowning, but she had admitted wryly to herself that the thought of the coronation instilled her body with unparalleled apprehension and fear. She found herself wishing Brin and Anya were alive to witness her ascend to the throne, but she continually chided herself for longing for an unrealistic world she could not obtain.

As the two weeks leading up to the coronation faded into the past, Kiara attempted to mentally prepare herself for her changed role in society. She recalled that once she was crowned, her fake marriage with Avian would dissolve and they would no longer be obligated to one another. She initially felt relieved by this knowledge—it was evident her relationship with him had been severely broken—but as her thoughts deepened, a small voice echoing in the back of her head cried out in protest.

Chapter Twenty-Six

A Bird in a Cage

Kiara's heart fluttered in her chest. She clumsily found Kain's shoulder in the darkness and gripped it tightly as her eyes focused straight ahead on the back of Sena's blonde ponytail.

She had spent the entire day locked in her suite under Sena's watchful eye. Rissa had appeared and reappeared throughout the afternoon, occasionally assisting Sena with Kiara's hair or make-up, but Sena's presence had been constant. She had coated Kiara's face in a thick layer of powder and colored dusts before brushing the tangled rats out of her unkempt hair. She then lathered her dry skin in a smooth cocoon of moisturizing cream, and neatly polished her battle-weathered nails. She and Rissa had helped squeeze Kiara into her breathtakingly ornate sapphire and silver dress, tightly winding the silky strings that laced up the back of the gown.

After a day of insistent pampering, Kiara felt sickeningly frilly and fake. Her inconsistent eye color was barely noticeable under such a heavy curtain of black liner, bright eye shadow, and false lashes. Sena had painted Kiara's face with powder until it was a ghostly white, and as she examined her colorless skin and carefully pinned hair in the mirror, she felt as though she were staring at a gaudy stranger.

Regardless of Kiara's relentless protesting, Rissa did not allow her to wear her crown necklace. Kiara had stubbornly voiced every argument she could fathom, but Rissa had continually responded that the accessory "clashed" with the circlet Avian had planned to place on her head during the coronation.

Kiara had stormed out of the room an hour before the coronation ball commenced, grabbed Kain's arm, and dragged him into the windowless corridor for momentary solitude and a revitalizing fresh breath of air. She had trouble breathing in her tightly fitted dress, which was so molded to her skin she was afraid she would have to cut it off. She and Kain had not spoken to each other—they were so frazzled after a busily stressful day, it had been satisfactory to enjoy one another's silent presence.

Sena had been tasked with the job of delivering Kiara to the stage. After she had retrieved Kain and Kiara from the corridor, she had hurriedly marched them through the castle halls and directed them to a secret passageway designed for maids and servants that led to the ballroom. She positioned them off-stage, where they had hid silently behind a thick velvet curtain.

Sena had one manicured hand wrapped around the edge of the curtain, creating a small opening for her to peek out onto the stage. Complex orchestra music danced mystically through the air, accompanied by a low reverberating hum of chatting voices. Occasionally, a humorous note would influence the atmosphere and a roar of laughter would threaten to overpower the melodies. The pleasant smell of decadent food filled Kiara's nostrils, sending her starved stomach into a growling fit.

Avian's voice suddenly sprung to life over the buzzing roar of the party. Silence swept through the room. Kiara caught her breath, anticipation boiling through her veins.

"I hope you're all enjoying tonight's festivities," he spoke confidently. Kiara couldn't help being envious of his natural eloquence and charisma. "The food is delicious, is it not? Our kitchen staff worked for two days to prepare this feast—but the celebration of delectable food is not why we have all gathered here tonight." He paused dramatically, waiting for the anxious curiosity surging through the crowd to build to a near breaking point. "As you all know, our beloved King Kyan passed away over six months ago. After his death, I retrieved his lost daughter from a village on the outskirts of the Evalseman territory. She traveled to Enevale with me and has been living amongst you all for months," he spoke boldly, waving his hands as his addressed the audience, a sense of theatrical elaboration breathing through his presentation. "But before I introduce our queen, I ask you all to understand how amazing this young woman is. Although she is a near identical representation of Queen Raiyx, she embraces King Kyan's determined personality. She is brave, kind, witty, stubborn—but most importantly, she is strong. She will vehemently protect our kingdom from the treacheries of the Dark Forest. She has already gallantly combated Enevale's most hated adversary—the corrupt Nonae empress herself—and has even met the reverent goddess face-to-ghostly-face. Some of you may recognize the princess as my wife, but I assure you—despite our intimate relations—our marriage was a façade created to conceal her identity." He paused one final time, allowing the crowd to intake a collective breath of unbridled anticipation. "Ladies and gentlemen, I am pleased to introduce the Queen of Enevale: Kiara Fable!"

Kiara was not granted enough time to fully comprehend Avian's words. Sena quickly twisted around, grabbed Kiara's wrist, and launched her through the velvet curtain. She stumbled onto the stage, squinting her eyes as they adjusted to the bright lights. Below the raised platform that she occupied, a black-and-white checkered floor was obscured by thousands of citizens dressed in swathes of expensive materials. Large wooden tables laden with a plethora of food, desserts, and beverages were placed in each corner. An intricate, colossal fountain was rooted in the center of the ballroom, glistening as though it were a newly buffed diamond.

She could feel the crowd's eyes shift to her face. Her cheeks burnt with startled embarrassment and she was suddenly grateful for the thick coat of powder concealing her blushing face. Her hands grew sweaty with nerves as her knees wobbled so loudly she was sure the entire room could hear.

She forced her eyes to sweep in Avian's direction. He was standing in the center of the stage, a calm smile playing on his face. His light brown hair had been neatly combed out of his eyes, which—paired with an elaborately decorated formal outfit—infused his presence with an air of sophistication. His hands steadily clutched a dazzling silver circlet baring sapphire jewels that had been embossed into the thin metal. He sent a comforting smile in Kiara's direction, beckoning for her to move nearer.

She carefully hitched up the skirts of her dress to prevent a clumsy incident as she slowly maneuvered her way across the stage. She reached Avian's side in a whirl of rustling skirts and anxious breaths, dispelling husky murmurs and whispers from the crowd below as she bowed her head to the temporary king.

He began to lower the circlet onto her head, chuckling softly as she bit her lip in anticipation. She closed her eyes nervously, waiting for the soft thud of metal against her skull that would signal her admittance as the Queen of Enevale. Its arrival was accompanied by chaos.

The jarringly familiar clanging of metal alerted Kiara that something had gone awry. Her eyes flashed open instantly, finding Avian's hands mere inches from her head. His shaking palms clutched a hurriedly withdrawn knife, a deflected blade lying ominously at his feet as his eyes fixated on something to his left. Kiara's eyes slowly followed his gaze, a lump of anxiety welling in her throat. Poised on the edge of the stage—her soulless eyes as dark as black pools of ink—stood Vyntrx. She brandished a pointed dagger in her hand, her eyes lingering over the recently deposited circlet resting profoundly on Kiara's head.

"I came to crash your party, princess," she taunted jeeringly, raising the dagger high above her head as she sauntered toward her niece.

Kiara stared upward, stunned, her hand helplessly searching her chest for her missing necklace. Vyntrx abruptly swung the blade down, but before Kiara could react, Kain launched himself from the side of the stage, pinning Kiara to the ground a yard away from Vyntrx's reach.

Soldiers poured into the room from the halls. A fraction of the fleet ushered citizens into safe rooms and attempted to quell the pandemonium that had poisoned the atmosphere, while a group of soldiers headed by the dukes and bearing weapons sprinted toward the stage.

Vyntrx reared backward, eyeing the approaching soldiers with a threatening glare. She withdrew a second blade from the folds of her dress, lifting her hand back as she flung the pointed knife into the mass of soldiers. The blade struck an armored man directly in the neck, immediately sending him sprawling to the ground.

"Kain, Kiara is your responsibility!" Avian yelled over the roar of the chaos-stricken ballroom. "Hide her! I'll find you! *Go!*"

Without a moment's hesitation, Kain climbed to his feet and wrapped Kiara in his arms. They escaped through the offstage entrance just as Vyntrx fired a menacing spell into the wave of soldiers, sending blood-coated bodies flailing aimlessly through the air.

"Let me go!" Kiara cried, beating her fists against Kain's chest as he maneuvered his way through the hidden corridors behind the stage. "Let me fight her!"

"No," he said sternly, tightening his grip around her squirming body. He used his Specialty to numb her limbs and cease her thrashing. "It's my duty to protect you."

"Stop it!" she ordered loudly. "If I don't help fight Vyntrx, innocent people will die."

Kain huffed indignantly. "Avian's stronger than you, princess," he snapped, bursting through the hidden passageway's door. They were suddenly thrust into a dark corridor in a secluded section of the castle, and as Kiara's eyes attempted to search Kain's face for evidence of emotion, she realized the action had been hindered by the ubiquitous shadows. "You're not risking your life tonight." The voice that escaped his mouth was lilted by a wavering tone of apprehension and concern.

Kain's emotion-drenched declaration startled Kiara into silence. She sighed in defeat, watching the outlines of shaded doors pass by as they sped through the castle halls. After endless minutes wrought in ambiguity and frustration had slowly ticked by, Kain suddenly selected a random door to infiltrate. He stopped running and began fumbling with the doorknob, using his Specialty to gain entry to the darkened room.

The enclosure was mainly abandoned, obstructed only by a cold hearth and a handful of broken chairs. Kain carried Kiara into the room, using his foot to shut the door behind them. His eyes latched on a small door in the corner and he decided to hide the newly crowned queen behind another set of strong walls. He hurriedly opened the closet door and deposited Kiara inside. Smashing himself in the closet with her, he shut the door behind them, drenching them in shadows.

Although the closet was far from spacious, it was entirely empty. Kiara stood as far away from Kain as she could manage in the limited space, her arms folded across her chest as she pouted silently. Kain's violet eyes glowed at her through the darkness, but his expression was shrouded in shadows.

She released an outcry of fury as she slammed her fist against the side of the closet. Kain flinched at the sudden noise, noticing that half of her arm had been swallowed by the gaping hole in the wall she had accidentally created. She sent him a weary glance as she yanked her forearm free. Debris fell into the room, sending clouds of dust swirling through the air as she coughed loudly. Blood dripped from her scathed arm, the flesh encircling her wrist torn and broken. She eyed her wound, grimacing.

"Oh, you idiot," Kain's voice was soft despite his harsh words. He gently took Kiara's arm into his grip, running his fingers across her skin as he examined the wound. "You're so stupid," he chided, controlling her skin and forcing the broken cells to repair themselves. She cringed at the pain, eyeing him begrudgingly. "You're oddly stoic," he observed. "What's wrong?"

"I'm worried about everyone," she whispered, gingerly retrieving her healed arm from his grasp. "I need to help them." She made an abrupt move to open the door, but before her fingers could reach the knob, Kain's hand caught her wrist. He gently spun her toward him, twisting the skirts of her dress into a tangled mess of fabrics. She tripped, falling against his chest as his back collided with the wall. His body slid down the smooth wood, dragging Kiara's trembling limbs with him to the floor, their hearts accelerating with embarrassment.

Sitting on the floor, Kain's arms wrapped firmly around her waist, Kiara blinked in confusion as her cheeks flushed red. She glanced up at him shyly, her rosy irises peeking out from under a curtain of downcast eyelashes. She gently smoothed her fingers across the fabric of Kain's dress shirt, feeling his anxious heartbeat thudding under her touch.

Cautiously, as though he weren't entirely aware of his actions, Kain slowly dragged his hand across the exposed planes of Kiara's back. His fingers lightly danced across her shoulders, explored the curve of her neck. He tenderly cupped her cheek against the hollow of his palm, his eyes burrowing deep into hers.

"Wh-what're you—" she started, fumbling over her words.

"I love you," Kain declared. The sincerity of his quavering voice silenced her weak attempt at articulation. "I know it's crazy, but I do."

Kiara's lips automatically parted as she racked her brain for a response but her vocal chords were unwilling to cooperate. She had comprehended Kain's confession but she couldn't wrap her mind around the thought. She had admitted to herself that she possessed feelings for him, had realized she had undoubtedly been falling for him—but she had been trying so hopelessly to prevent her emotions from manifesting into an uncontrollable desire. Her efforts had, apparently, been futile.

"Your eyes are pink when you look at me," he continued, tucking a loose strand of Kiara's hair behind her ear. "But I want to hear it from you—if it's true."

"You lied," she said hoarsely, her hands stretching across his chest, clutching the fabric of his shirt in her grip. "You told me that my eyes change color when I look at you."

He nodded in accordance. "I didn't want to tell you the truth. You belong to Avian."

"I don't belong to anyone," she said snappily. Catching her harsh tone, she softened her voice, continuing, "But that's not the point. The point is I—I love you."

Kain's expression brightened at Kiara's confession. A content smirk curved his lips, but she wasn't allotted time to examine his features. His mouth suddenly brushed across hers, drawing her into a deep, passionate kiss. An intangible desire surged through her limbs as her eyes dreamily slid shut, her body finally succumbing to the emotion she had been battling for months. Kain's hands curved around the nape of her neck, holding her body firmly against his as their movements flowed to the beat of their exhilarated breath. She could feel the rise and fall of his chest, the rapid pulsating of his heart, the heated blush of his scarlet cheeks.

An insistent rattling noise broke through the silence of the closet, but Kiara vaguely heard the sound. She hadn't been able to unearth the strength necessary to detach her limbs from Kain's before the closet door loudly slammed open. The shrieking noise of shattered wood finally captured Kiara's attention, disturbing the correlation between her lips and

Kain's.

Standing in the entrance—staring in shocked disbelief, his hand clenched against the doorknob so tightly his fingers shook—was Avian.

"Avian!" Kiara shrieked, utterly mortified. She untangled her hands from Kain's blouse, her legs wavering unsteadily as she jumped to her feet. She stared directly at Avian, a guilty expression enveloping her face.

His grip tightened around the doorknob, his astounded expression smoothing into a collected glare. A mocking smile spread across his darkened face. "I guess you aren't as predictable as I thought," he spoke sardonically. "And I thought *I* was the one betraying you."

His insult stung like an untreated wound, but Kiara refused to allow her confusing emotions to play across her face. "What does that mean?" she asked, hardening her tone in an attempt to prevent her voice from trembling.

Kain hastily stood up beside Kiara, eying his brother evilly. He refrained from speaking as he watched the situation fully develop, silently wishing for Avian to reveal his shrouded loyalty to Vyntrx. Avian returned his brother's heated glare with such vehemence that Kain was momentarily frightened that he would spring forward and kill him on the spot. Despite Kain's fears, Avian simply spun on his heel, dashing out of the room without muttering another word.

Kiara angrily gathered the skirts of her dress, ripping viciously through the fabric. Frustration augmenting her movements, she tossed the residual cloth away, freeing her legs from the constrictive barrier of the heavy skirts. No longer hindered by the ruffled fabric of her long dress, she darted out of the closet, sprinting through the corridors after Avian. Thudding footsteps instantly sounded from behind her, signaling Kain's decision to follow after them.

Avian had managed to noticeably distance himself from Kiara, his swollen, protesting heart propelling his speed. She loudly trailed him, her heeled feet surging with pain and threatening to buckle. Despite her discomfort, she refused to slow her pace, and after what she deemed to be an eternity of running, Avian came to an abrupt halt. The outline of the ballroom door was barely visible in the distance, the shadows of the unlit room casting an ominous shade on the disquieted atmosphere. For a brief moment, he stood eerily still, unable to summon enough strength to turn and face Kiara. His punctured heart rattled in his chest, filling his body with unbridled dread. The harrowing sensation seeping through his limbs grew to unbearable heights, forcing him to spin around and conclusively face his fears head-on. His mouth unhinged, his lips poised to articulate his thoughts, but the sight of Kiara's helplessly perplexed expression cast his voice into silence.

"What the hell is wrong with me?" she yelled breathlessly. She clattered down the hallway, slowing her speed to a halt as she neared his sulking figure. "I'm not acting like myself! I would *never* do anything to hurt you! I—"

"Why didn't you tell me you had feelings for Kain?" he interrupted snappily. Fury radiated from his bright eyes, but his expression remained unnervingly blank. "Why would you keep that to yourself? Were we not a couple?"

She released a shaky breath, crossing her arms over her chest as she attempted to calm her raging thoughts. "I was confused," she explained uneasily. "I was so in love with you, Avian, and then one day, my mind just shifted. It was as if my feelings for you vanished over night. Since then, my thoughts have been conflicted and my mind has been fogged. All I know is that Kain has been the only one able to make me *feel* again. A small part of me keeps screaming at me to be close to you, but something just keeps preventing me from loving you."

He lowered his gaze, allowing a handful of hair to fall across his face and darken his expression. "Of course it feels like that," he said rancorously. "It *is* fake, after all."

Kiara's eyes narrowed as she evaluated his words. "What is?"

Kain's footsteps grew nearer as he sprinted down the hallway. His voice echoed through the hall as he loudly repeated Kiara's name, the tone underlying his words filled with desolation.

"Haven't you figured it out yet, Ara?" Avian asked derisively, sneering. He glanced down the hallway, his gaze briefly skimming his nearing brother before it darted back to the queen's face. "I thought you were *smart*."

Before she could form a response, Kain materialized at her side. His breathing was sharp and ragged, his eyes locked furiously on his brother.

"Of course you knew everything all along, didn't you, Kain?" Avian icily jeered, watching his brother rest a concerned hand on Kiara's trembling shoulder.

Anger welled across Kain's scowling expression. "Shut up! You know I would have told her immediately if you hadn't threatened me. And you would have controlled my mind if I had even tried to tell her the truth!"

"Mind control?" Kiara questioned hoarsely, glaring at Avian with sharp, accusing eyes. "Kain told me you could manipulate minds."

Avian tossed his head back proudly, revealing his shadowy eyes. "It's one of my many Specialties. I can force my own thoughts, memories, and emotions to infiltrate anyone's head and trick them into believing the lies I've fabricated. I—" his hurried, uncaring declaration was abruptly shattered as his voice broke into silence. He stared directly at Kiara, his callous eyes burrowing deep into her disbelieving stare. "I manipulated your emotions and made you fall in love with me. You never had real feelings for me. The only reason you felt conflicted was because—because I tried to prevent you from falling in love with my brother." Although his face had been roughly molded into a compassionless countenance, the voice that escaped his scowling lips wobbled unconfidently as a rush of unwanted emotion surged through his words.

Searing blood scalded through Kiara's veins as her body was overwhelmed by lividness. Her thoughts blurred as they were poisoned by wrath. Her lips moved mechanically as she stole the bitter sensation sweeping through her chest and injected it into her query. "Since we first met, my feelings for you have been fake?" she questioned, utterly aghast. "You *made* me love you?"

He nodded, a sadistically accomplished look plastered across his face. "I figured you'd catch on eventually, but I suppose I misjudged your intelligence. Kain's been aware of our delicate situation since his revival, which is why he has harbored such a passionate hatred for me. He'd have been sent straight back to Veinya's manor had he let the secret slip—although, on second thought, he was probably just too afraid you'd despise him if he told you the truth. *Pathetic.*"

"*He's* pathetic?" she echoed in bewilderment. "You're the one who had the audacity to manipulate my life! How the hell could you do that to me?" she demanded an explanation, fighting off the urge to swing her balled fists directly at Avian's smirking face. "How could you tamper with my head without a hint of remorse? How *dare* you manipulate me?"

Avian deflected Kiara's fury as though her words hadn't managed to trigger a tinge of guilt to handicap his mind. He remained coolly collected, crossing his arms casually across his chest. "Once I receive an order, my only option is to not rest until it's completed. You've actually caused me more trouble than anything. If I could have, I would've killed you the moment I laid my eyes on you. In fact, I would have just left you in your miserable village to rot."

"Why didn't you?" she asked through clenched teeth. Hot tears stung at her corner of her saddened cerulean eyes. Her mind felt jumbled and violated. She had wholeheartedly trusted Avian—had willingly watched him knock down the precautionary barriers surrounding her heart and eagerly let him inside. The love she had initially felt for him had seemed so *real*, so overpowering and passionate. She could not fathom that he had managed to craft her love for him out of nothingness, that their relationship had been fabricated. Despite his cruel disloyalty, he was still present in the deepest chambers of her heart—but instead of filling her body with dizzying warmth and tickling her mind with the prospect of love, his disturbing confession had smothered her heart in a cold layer of ice, shattering the tender ligaments of the organ and sending them stabbing through her numbing limbs.

"While I held your dying father's hand, he demanded I take an unbreakable oath. I was ordered to guide you to this dismal kingdom and ensure your rise to power as queen. If I failed to comply, my soul would be terminated and I would never reach Veinya's manor. Since you were officially crowned queen, my duties have been concluded." A devious smile curved the corners of his mouth, distorting his handsome face into the visage of a vicious fiend.

Kiara's mind began to stitch the evidence of Avian's deceit into a tangled network of verification. She recalled several moments of speculation, various times that she should have probed further but refrained from doing so in order to maintain a trustful relationship with Avian. She recounted a conversation she had shared with him about her father, and could distinctly hear his voice stating: *"He didn't necessarily...*trust *me."*

And she finally understood why.

"You *bastard*," the words escaped her mouth in a rush of exasperated air. She ignored the unwanted tear that slid across her cheek as she swallowed down a bout of hysterics rising in her throat. "What was your motive?"

"A little *persuasion* from an old friend," a chillingly familiar voice echoed through the corridor. The shadows swirling in the space behind Avian were momentarily disturbed as a dark figure materialized at the end of the hall. Vyntrx's pale, snarling face poured into view, her tongue sadistically lapping blood off the tips of her fingers. "Great little actor, isn't he? Pretending to be in love with you—*ha*! I'm sure faking emotions for you would be very difficult. I'm glad he follows my orders like a loyal servant should." She emitted a high, crackling laugh, tossing her head back in a fit of humor.

"Avian works for *you*?" Kiara bellowed, disbelief stinging through her chest. The harsh whiplash of betrayal racked her limbs, scattering her mentality into the realms of bitter incredulity. "But you *killed* his family!"

"He *begged* me to," Vyntrx explained deviously, her mouth stretched into a wide red grin. Her black eyes glowed with sadistic pleasure as she watched Kiara's tear-streaked face twist into a horrified expression. "He was tired of them, tired of living in the Dark Forest, and especially tired of living with the nuisance of a little brother who had been the cause of his mother's untimely death. I accommodated his wishes under one firm condition: he would have to swear his eternal loyalty to me."

Kiara's sharp eyes bore into Avian's unreadable face. A reproachful expression darkened her features as she critically examined the man she had so willingly and mindlessly trusted. "Why would you wish for your family's death?" she probed, scornful resentment dripping from each of the clipped words she had uttered. "How could you hate them so much that you would wish the irreversible fate of death upon them?"

"He was young," Vyntrx languidly stated before Avian could articulate his explanation. "I'm sure he's been subjected to moments of regret but there isn't anything he can do about it now. His parents are dead and he has sworn his allegiance to me."

Kiara's eyes welled with crimson fury. Her hand itched to grab her necklace and transform it into a weapon suitable for killing both Vyntrx and her loyal companion, but as her fingers traced the empty plane of her chest, she disastrously recalled how Rissa had demanded she abandon her necklace for a night. "Why did you kill Avian, then? Was that all part of your plan?" she questioned, her voice rising to hysterics.

Vyntrx appeared utterly disgruntled by Kiara's demanding inquiry. "I had two reasons for doing so," she responded, attempting to smooth the slight tone of uneasiness that enveloped her words as she sent an annoyed glance in Avian's direction. "First of all, I wished to trick you into thinking Avian was so dedicated to your cause that he would sacrifice himself for you. And secondly, I wished to test your capabilities in order to discern your weaknesses and strengths."

Kiara furrowed her brow, thoroughly evaluating Vyntrx's explanation. She admitted silently to herself that the empress's declaration appeared strikingly unconvincing, but she knew regardless of how fervently she probed, her aunt would not reveal whatever secret she was concealing. "I suppose you came here to kill me tonight—since Avian is no longer a prisoner to my cause."

Vyntrx scowled at Kiara's assumption, tossing her head back in annoyance. "It isn't that easy. Veinya has grown too fond of you. If I managed to steal your life, she would simply revive your soul. It wouldn't require a sacrifice, or any thorough examination—she would automatically save you. She was apparently *impressed* by your efforts and has decided to favor you," the sentence escaped her lips in the form of a resentful sneer. "But I have no idea why she would favor *you!*"

"I know why," Kain said thickly. The abrupt resonating of his voice jolted Kiara—her attention had been so captivated by Vyntrx's confession and Avian's betrayal that she had momentarily forgotten his presence. "She's inherited her father's best traits. She—"

"I understand all of that, idiot," Vyntrx snapped, cutting off Kain's incomplete declaration as she rolled her eyes in annoyance. "Obviously, in order to kill you and make sure you stay dead, Kiara, I'll have to destroy the benevolent side of Veinya's mind."

Kain's eyes bulged with bewilderment. "You can't do that!" he argued, his voice breaking with dismay. "You can't tamper with a goddess!"

Vyntrx snickered evilly, shaking her head in defiance. "I will do as I please," she replied drily. "I came here tonight to take Kiara prisoner. With her locked away, I will become the empress of Enevale and begin my conquest of the Evalseman territory."

A bout of mordant laughter welled in Kiara's throat. "You're going to *kidnap* me?"

"Why is she laughing?" Vyntrx whispered hotly, turning her dark gaze on Avian.

He shrugged half-heartedly. "Perhaps she doubts your capabilities. Honestly, I—oh! Milady!"

Vyntrx's black eyes widened as Avian's distressed tone echoed through the hall. "What is it?"

"Cylis—Cylis is nearby," he explained in a rushed, fearful tone. "He and his renegades have surrounded the main encampment. They've taken Kailx hostage. I told you she would have been safer in Vitaciel."

Despite the seriousness of the situation, Kiara's acrimonious emotions subsided briefly to allow a trickle of relief to flood her veins after she heard Kailx's name. She had been terrified of her cousin's plausible death, but had been unable to contact her to sort out the circumstances. Knowing Kailx had survived her mother's wrath instilled Kiara with a vague sense of hope amid the catastrophic events that had unfurled at the coronation.

"He's surrounded the encampment?" Terror escalated sharply through Vyntrx's tone, raising her voice several octaves. "Are you certain?"

Avian nodded gravely. "Yes," he spoke conclusively. "I suggest we abandon the mission and return immediately.

Miriam has returned to his village on the other side of the forest, Murdock and Demure are stationed at different locations, and Harlyt is the only capable person at the campsite. Do you think she could effectively fight off Cylis and his revolutionaries without our help?"

"There are well-trained soldiers at the encampment," Vyntrx snapped dismissively despite the unconvinced demeanor she had fruitlessly attempted to cover.

"Cylis's forces will overpower such a small group," he muttered austerely. "Most of them will be slaughtered. They will not effectively protect Kailx from being killed or kidnapped."

Vyntrx remained engulfed in silence for several moments as she diligently contemplated and examined the situation. As an ominously quiet stillness spread through the hall, Kiara was struck with the desire to launch an assault on her aunt while she was in a vulnerable state, but she was afraid the battle would escalate, and—being distracted by the prospect of capturing her niece—Vyntrx would abandon the notion of departure.

"Fine," the empress decided haughtily, the sound of her voice chiseling through the uneasy atmosphere of the quiet room. "Let's go, Avian—quickly." Her hand fell lightly on her comrade's shoulder as she surveyed her niece with eyes overflowing with hate.

Avian flinched at Vyntrx's touch. His eyes flickered in Kiara's direction, and for the split second that their eyes met, she could have sworn that she had discerned a raw form of sadness in the depths of his gaze. Before she had been allotted enough time to fully examine the emotion surging through his features, he and the empress were swallowed by thick shadows, leaving Kiara staring blankly at the dark, empty hallway.

Her body was abruptly racked by an overwhelming array of emotion as Avian's figure was drowned in darkness. Upon his disappearance, he had evidently released his control over her mind, causing her mentality to unravel with dizzying confliction.

She shakily tore off the fake wedding ring that had tied her to Avian, harshly hurling the rounded piece of silver against the ground. With a deafeningly quiet snap, the ring shattered into thousands of miniscule, unsalvageable pieces scattered on the cold floor as helplessly as Kiara's frazzled emotions.

"Kiara," Kain's voice resonated through the hall. "Are you okay?"

His words dimly reached her ears, barely penetrating the loud chaos that rushed through her head. The numbing fog that had tainted her thoughts during Avian's manipulation instantly evaporated from the persistent heat of her true emotions, but as the reign over her mind was rightfully returned to her, the sensation that swept through her chest was far from relieved.

Her legs wobbled unsteadily as her entire frame shook with crushing realization. *Of course I really loved Avian,* she admitted as the affection she had developed for her advisor captured her mind and stabbed mercilessly at her heart. The sudden awareness of her unyielding, suppressed love filled her lungs with apprehensive air as she recalled Avian's regretless betrayal.

As though an invisible force had knocked her off balance, she was suddenly sent sprawling to the ground, her body appearing eerily lifeless as she landed limply on her knees. *He bottled down my feelings and lied about doing so,* she critically reminded herself. *So I can't love him. He's a fiend. I can't love him. I won't love him. I don't.*

Fits of hysteric sobs caught in her chest as she dejectedly dropped her tear-streaked face into her trembling hands. *And Kain?* she wondered, scavenging through her diluted thoughts and muddled feelings in an attempt to uncover her honest feelings for the other Knight. *Fake,* she somberly revealed. *My feelings for him were fake. He is nothing more to me now than a close companion.*

Kain was suddenly at her side, wrapping his comforting arms around her tremulous shoulders. She sobbed pitifully into his blouse, her hands clinging to the fabric of his shirt desperately as she attempted to quell her exhausted thoughts. "I—I'm an—idiot—" she stammered, choking over her words so drastically, it was as though the emotion pulsating through her mind had handicapped her ability to articulate.

"Please don't cry," he begged, repeatedly stroking his fingers across her chilled back. "You'll be okay, I promise."

"Kiara?" a small voice suddenly called, the noise reverberating through the empty hall. Quick, decisive footsteps sounded in the near distance, rapidly approaching with each completed step.

The abrupt noise startled Kain out of his reverie. He jolted his head up from its downcast position, his eyes immediately falling on Kiara's exasperated cousin as she emerged from the shadows.

"Kailx?" he questioned disbelievingly. "I thought you were at the campsite."

Kiara's head reared upward at the mention of her cousin. Her eyes widened as she absorbed the curious sight, attempting to decipher Kailx's figure through the film of tears soiling her vision. She clumsily unhinged herself from Kain's grasp, tossing herself into Kailx's welcoming arms. She comfortingly stroked Kiara's hair, sending Kain a weary glance over her cousin's quivering head.

"Cylis *is* attacking the campsite as we speak," she informatively stated. "But I was never there. I had secretly followed my mother to Enevale and waited silently for the distraction that would force her to return to the forest." She paused, gingerly extending her arms as she held a sobbing Kiara out in front of her. "I've escaped my mother's clutches and I wish to stay with you, if you'll let me. I want to help you win this war, Kiara."

Kain raised a skeptical eyebrow. "Avian lied to Vyntrx," he observed.

"Yes," Kailx agreed hastily. "He and I had made a deal. He had offered to help me flee the forest if I would assist you in the future. He had heard from a reliable source that Cylis had been planning an attack on the campsite, so he strategically scheduled your coronation in accordance with the raid."

"Why would Avian do that?" he wondered huskily.

She shrugged. "Perhaps he was sympathetic of my situation."

"'Avian' and 'sympathy' don't belong in the same sentence," Kiara muttered callously, brushing away her cousin's concerned grasp. The thick layer of make-up that lathered Kiara's face had been damaged from the night's events—dark smears smudged under her eyes, disturbing the unnatural ghostly tint of her cheeks. She wiped at her heavily coated eyes with annoyance, attempting to bottle down the sadness that had welled in her tear ducts. "He's the enemy, so we should stop acting like we're familiar with him. We don't know the real him and we never will. We should hate him for the traitor that he is."

Kailx appeared entirely unconvinced by Kiara's brief speech, but she remained silent in an attempt to avoid conflict with her emotionally drained cousin.

Kain's face possessed not a single trace of emotion as he crossed the hall and lightly captured Kiara's hand in his. "We should go back to the ballroom," he suggested. She glanced in his direction, her eyes flashing between saddened blue and amber confusion. "Gotta make sure everyone's alright."

Kain's hand was warm against Kiara's chilled, stone-like fingers, but his touch was dull and felt utterly misplaced. Her body been subjected to irreversible numbness, and although Kain's palm was pressing tightly against hers, she couldn't feel anything. "Yeah," she frostily agreed. "Let's go."

*****

Avian felt as though a heavy stone had been lifted from his chest, overwhelming him with dizzying freedom. He permitted his body to fall against the mattress of his massive four-poster bed, disheveling his tidy hair as he thumped against the padding.

Vyntrx had fought off Cylis and his warriors and had mercilessly captured several hostages to torture for information on the rogue's future plans. The battle had been quick and painless with few casualties on the empress's side. Despite their victory, Kailx hadn't been found anywhere. After ordering a search party to ransack the forest for her daughter, Vyntrx had grudgingly left the campsite to conclude pleasantries with several territories outside of the forest in an attempt to secure last-minute alliances. In the empress's absence, Avian was left in charge. He typically spent this much-desired time locked in isolation, entirely engulfed by his confusingly torturous thoughts.

His eyes clouded with unwelcome tears as his mind reeled. Kiara's devastated, pain-stricken face welled beneath his eyelids, as though the image had been permanently burned into the conscious chambers of his mind. The recollection of witnessing her lips moving against Kain's continually resurfaced from behind the locked doors of his nightmarish memories—the envisioned sight knotted his stomach and sent shivers of jealousy rushing through his limbs.

He clenched his eyes shut, attempting to block out every figment of Kiara from his brain. Regardless of his tiresome efforts, she stubbornly clung to the depths of his mind, lingering there like a persistent ghost.

His body ached where she had once touched him; his hands desperately longed to explore her diminutive figure and hold her body as close to his as he could physically manage. His stomach lurched with emptiness as the shattering realization of her permanent absence painfully sank into his head.

And whose fault is that? a derisive subconscious rang through Avian's psyche.

Mine, he answered bitterly, *all mine.*

He had played the part of the villain well. He had momentarily wanted to inflict all of his bottled pain onto Kiara's vulnerable mentality—he had wanted her to feel something even remotely similar to that gnawing sensation that spread through his heart at the sight of her lips locked with Kain's. He had wanted her to yearn for him, to realize that she would no longer have him, and would somehow—in someway—need him. But why would she desire a deceitful, manipulating fiend when a loyal, honest boy stood steadfastly by her side?

He wanted so terribly to explain why he had acted the way he did and assure her that he had never meant to hurt her. He would swear that every word he had uttered had been a blatant lie. He knew Kiara well enough to know that, given the circumstances, she'd eventually forgive him. Her merciful demeanor had been a thick, reoccurring thread that had masterfully weaved his affections for her into a dazzling tapestry displaying true romance.

He sighed, peeling open his damp eyes. He had never allowed himself to cry—not since that day his family had been mercilessly slaughtered before his eyes. From what he could recall about those heart-wrenching, traumatic memories, he had discovered that the writhing pain he had felt on that tragic day and the incurable pain he felt from Kiara's permanent absence were nearly equal.

"I have lost the one thing I genuinely care about. I've lost the only person I could ever love," he spoke gruffly to himself, running his hand through his matted hair. "And it is entirely my fault."

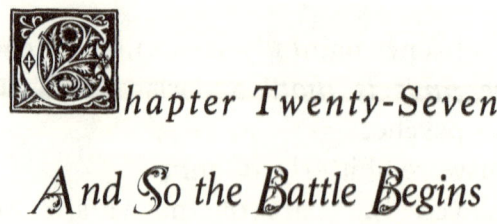

hapter Twenty-Seven

And So the Battle Begins

Kiara lay still beneath the security of an enormous, heavy blanket that swallowed her entire body. Her eyes paced the dark room, her lids glossed with drying tears. Even though she sensed Kain beside her, felt faint warmth radiating from his resting limbs, heard the soft rise and fall of his breathing, she felt completely alone.

The ballroom fiasco had been a disaster. Despite the soldier's determined efforts, a slew of unlucky villagers had been unable to escape to safety and had subsequently been violently massacred by Vyntrx. The checkered floor had been harrowingly splattered with crimson blood and strewn with dead bodies. After absorbing the jarring sight, Kiara had been overwhelmed with the desire to break down into inexorable tears, but she hadn't permitted herself to fall prey to her emotions—being the queen, it was her duty to remain strong for her people. She had given a weak speech in attempt to quell the crowds and had received outcries of protest when she had mentioned Avian's betrayal, but she had fortunately managed to slightly placate the citizens' frazzled emotions.

After exchanging solemn words with the dukes, Kiara had retreated to the suite with Kain and Kailx at her heels. Kailx had wished to stay awake and converse with her cousin about a topic that she considered "pressing", but Kiara's emotions had been worn dangerously thin. She had escorted Kailx to Kain's room and promised her they would talk immediately the following morning before silently retreating to her chambers.

Regardless of the exhaustion biting deep into Kiara's drooping eyelids, she could not shut down her rapidly pacing thoughts. Her mind clung to the memory of Brin and Anya— the emotions accompanying their sudden death had come sweeping back into her chest after Avian had relented his control of her mind and she had miserably succumbed to the mind-numbing, heartbreaking sadness that had recently been distilled from her mind. As her thoughts lingered over Avian's treachery, she couldn't help but wonder if he had been aware of her family's death prior to having prompted the spontaneous trip to her village. She had been so unhinged by despairing emotion that she had been unable to closely survey his features, but she could clearly recall the sight of poignant guilt seeping across his face.

Bitter tears stung at her eyes. She didn't bother wiping them away. There was no one to see her cry in the dark shadows of her bedroom with her head carefully hidden beneath the thick fabric of her blanket. Not a single person was around to call her weak, no one to expect of her an inhuman fortitude insusceptible to emotions and tribulations brought on by the cruel hands of fate.

Grey morning light filtered in through her bedroom's colossal window, alerting her that she had sustained consciousness well into the early hours of dawn. She sighed, abandoning her fruitless search for sleep.

She unraveled her body from the bed, careful not to arouse Kain. Her bare feet quietly padded across her bedroom floor, stopping momentarily as she unhinged the door and entered the living room. She hurried into the kitchen, ransacking the cabinets for even a small remnant of tea. Securing a tin box filled to the brim with green sweet-scented herbs, she recovered a large ceramic mug from the cupboard, filled it with water, and nestled herself into a padded chair at the dinning room table.

"Good morning," a pleasant voice called from the edge of the room.

She didn't need to divert her attention from fiddling with

the tea to realize the speaker was Kailx. "Morning," she answered bleakly, tipping the hot beverage past her lips. "You're up early."

Kailx gripped the headrest of the chair nearest her cousin, pulling it far enough away from the table that she could squeeze through. She rested her head in her hands, staring in Kiara's direction. "I'm used to it," She didn't offer an explanation and Kiara, not being in the type of mood that advocated banter, remained silent. "I wanted to talk to you about something."

After processing Kailx's seemingly significant words, Kiara felt the need to pursue a conversation. "Yes, I remember. What is it?"

"Vyntrx will attack Enevale in two weeks' time," Kailx said plainly, folding her arms across her chest. "Fourteen days from now, she'll gather a small faction of her endless army and knock down the Wall. She doesn't care about securing reign over Enevale—her war is with the Evalseman race. She's been beyond the forest, though. There are Evalseman kingdoms all throughout the foreign lands, but these unfamiliar territories are inhabited by strange creatures that we do not understand. She wishes to take control over the land beyond the forest and to become the supreme ruler of all Menevilen. The only reason she's attacking Enevale is to demoralize the citizens and capture you."

"Why don't we attack first?" Kiara immediately suggested, unabashed by the news. She had suspected that her aunt had been planning some sort of ambush since their meeting in Vitaciel, but she hadn't been given much time to fully ponder the idea. "A preemptive strike. We could sneak into the Dark Forest and utilize the element of surprise."

"You'd lose the advantage of home ground," Kailx reminded her readily, as though she had already thought through Kiara's suggestions and pinpointed every flaw. "Vyntrx plans to use just a mere fraction of her army, but if you provoke her, she may be tempted to summon more soldiers. She has erected thousands of campsites in the forest and handfuls of sites outside the Nonae territory. Besides, the forest is confusing for outsiders. Many soldiers would perish simply because they wouldn't know how to maneuver through the trees."

Kiara nodded grimly. "You're right. I should issue increased mandatory training for the soldiers throughout the week. We can at least be prepared whenever she comes."

"Of course. Would you like me to participate in the battle? I can't fight or handle a weapon, but I can use magic very effectively."

She shrugged, lightly setting her teacup against the table and wrapping her arms around her fleece nightgown. "I could use your help, but you don't have to risk your life for my cause."

"Of course I do," Kailx held her arm forward. The dining hall light caught the shadows creeping across her skin, displaying an array of new red scars that Kiara hadn't managed to notice before. Looking closely at her cousin, Kiara realized nearly every inch of her flesh was blotched with gnarled scars.

"She tortured me," Kailx said stiffly, catching her cousin's mortified expression. "She isn't a mother at all—she's a monster. She needs to be destroyed and I won't stand by and watch someone else pour their life into a cause I support with my entire essence."

Kiara's fingers softly traced the slowly healing wounds on Kailx's forearm, her stomach churning as she observed the lacerations. The marks were deep and jagged, climbing her arm until they disappeared underneath the collar of her nightgown. Multiple cuts lined her cheeks, her neck, her chest. Kiara was terrified of the undoubtedly horrific state the rest of her cousin's body could be in. "I'm so sorry," she spoke softly, sympathy flowing through her tone. "I really do appreciate all of your brave efforts."

"Don't thank me quite yet. We still have a battle to face."

Kiara's lips pulled into a humorless smile. She wasn't thrilled by the notion of battle, and she wasn't anticipating the jolt of adrenaline she would naturally endure as she relentlessly fought against Vyntrx's minions—no, the eagerness to reap her aunt's body of every despicable ounce of life she possessed urged Kiara's fingers to itch toward her necklace.

*****

Rissa had been compliant to Kiara's proposal. Upon the queen's request, she had immediately launched every able-bodied soldier into all-day training that she naturally oversaw with Sena dutifully at her side.

Kiara had prepared a uniquely structured training session for the dukes, however, and had summoned them to the edge of the training field alongside Kain and Kailx.

"I'm in need of a new advisor," she announced bluntly, pacing the length of the training fields. "The position should be filled by someone who has a working knowledge of Enevale and its military—someone who is willing to defend me at all costs."

"I'll do it," Blade's voice echoed loudly across the fields before Kiara had finished articulating her sentence. She turned to face him, flabbergasted, waiting for him to break out into laughter—but his face remained uncharacteristically calm. "I know a lot about this place."

Aiden and Ace appeared equally as shocked as Kiara. They stared at their comrade, gaping, expecting him to break his collected demeanor and succumb to amusement.

"Kiara's advisor has to actually *care* about her well-being, Blade," Aiden reminded him drily. "I would think after what happened with Avian, even your twisted sense of humor would have taken a damaging blow."

Blade scowled, awkwardly folding his arms across his armored chest. "You think I would joke around about this?

Avian put us in a shitty situation and I won't be able to forgive him for it. With Avian gone, it is our duty as the remaining dukes to look after the princess. So, yes, I care about her."

A unanimous gasp resonated amongst Kiara and the dukes. Kain stared at the ground in quiet contemplation while Kailx, being unfamiliar with Blade and his cynical characteristics, listened to the conversation in confusion.

"Did I hear him correctly?" Kiara wondered, dramatically clutching her chest as though she had suffered some sort of stroke. "Blade actually *cares* about me?"

"I won't for long if you don't shut up!" he barked, averting his gaze as his cheeks flushed.

She attempted to wipe the smirk off her face, but was partially unsuccessful, resulting in a humorously constrained expression. "Are you entirely convinced that you want this position? There's no backing out once you've accepted."

Blade nodded stiffly, not bothering to wipe away the curtain of silvery hair that cascaded into his eyes. He held his hand forward timidly, waiting for Kiara to return his gesture. "I'm sure," he spoke assuredly, his voice firm. "Let me be your advisor."

Kiara's hand automatically jolted forward, clasping Blade's palm against hers. A smile broke out across her face, her bright green eyes conveying the first stroke of happiness she had felt since Brin and Anya's death. "Thank you, Blade," she said softly. "Honestly."

He scowled, avoiding eye contact with her as he pulled his hand back to its place at his side. "What's my first assignment?"

"I want you to train Aiden, Ace, and Kain. Kain hasn't ever had any lessons in weapons or physical combat, so you might want to take it a little easier on him and make sure you cover the basics. Aiden and Ace should be given a strenuous workout. We've got to be as physically fit as possible before Vyntrx's assault," she explained, resting her hand upon her hip.

Sporting her silver circlet amid the auburn-brown tresses of her plaited hair, her body swathed in tight fabric paired with silver armor and leather boots laced all the way up to her knees, Blade couldn't help but believe Kiara resembled some sort of warrior queen.

He nodded in accordance, eying the other dukes. "Let's get to work. We've got to get you two into shape," he joked, forcing his voice into a mockingly gruff tone. The boys sent Kiara begrudging glances, but obediently followed Blade as he walked across the training field. Kain sent her an especially menacing look, his fear of social situations rising in the depths of his violet eyes. Kiara smirked, waving him away.

"Well, Kailx," she said, clasping her hands together as she turned her attention to her cousin. "Let's get started."

Kiara had mused over the idea of Kailx solely relying on magic in battle, but the thought perturbed her. She decided that she would introduce her cousin to at least the basics in physical combat and weapon control, as she firmly believed that in order to be successful in combat, her cousin needed to be capable of fighting in any situation or scenario. Brin had taught Kiara how to wield multiple weapons, but she had favored two: a bow and a dagger. She possessed a working knowledge of several other weapons but she figured Kailx would only need to be sufficient with one.

Throughout the course of the day, Kiara walked Kailx through the basics of each weapon, carefully examining her cousin's motions to identify which weapon she naturally familiarized with. She started with the bow and arrow, but Kailx couldn't even shoot the arrow half-way to the target, and most of the time, the arrow fell off the grip before she could even release the string. She couldn't properly handle the sword, let alone swing it. Her hands couldn't maintain a firm enough grasp around the hilt of the dagger and she felt uncomfortable being so close to her target. She couldn't fire a crossbow even semi-accurately. She wouldn't go near a mace, exclaiming that it was too brutal. Exhaustedly, Kiara abandoned her initial plan of handing Kailx a new weapon as she failed the last, and instead led her to the castle armory where she could select her own.

Kailx's eyes raked the endless supply of deadly weapons, her face set in a hardened visage. She studied the blunt staffs for several minutes before finally deciding they weren't an efficient item. Kiara suggested a spear, prompting Kailx to release some small cry of exhilaration. She selected her spear—a metal number with a four-inch blade tacked on to the rounded end—and exited the armory with a satisfied grin nestled between her cheeks.

While Kailx trained with her spear, Kiara focused on strengthening her magic. She recollected the book of spells from the suite, easily implementing every incantation ten times each. She would occasionally embrace her creativity and attempt to create her own spell, which habitually resulted in an outpour of success.

Aside from memorizing and manipulating spells, Kiara focused on exercising her body. She and Kailx ran laps around the fields, swam against the strong current in the Kahliar Sea, and sparred against one another. Kiara familiarized herself with the weapons she could summon from her necklace. She shot arrows through the dead center of targets, shredded dummies with swords, and employed the knife so fervently her hand started to grow sore.

When the heavy sun finally dipped beneath the horizon, dousing the training fields in shadows, Kiara, along with the other soldiers, lethargically retreated into the familiar halls of the castle, the ripe scent of a day spent bathed in success dripping from their exhausted bodies.

Kiara repeated such a similar routine throughout the duration of the two weeks leading up to the fated attack, she could barely decipher one day from the other. On the eve of the prophesized assault, anxiety swept through her body, nearly

paralyzing her legs with terror. Enevale was ready for battle—
there was no doubt about that—but her heart still raced as if it
were determined to exploit all of its vitality before it gained the
chance to be violently halted.

Kain and Kailx's combat abilities had progressed greatly,
but unsurprisingly, they weren't close to matching any of the
soldiers' talents. Despite their noticeable lack of skill, Kiara felt
relieved that they had at least gripped the basics of weaponry
and physical combat.

Rissa and Sena had driven the soldiers into over-time,
strengthening their muscles and greatly improving their
capabilities. The dukes had done wonderfully under Blade's
command and had cut the amount of arguments between the
three of them by half the previous amount.

After a final exhausting day of relentless training, Kailx
groggily retreated to the suite and fell asleep. Kain was
strangely absent from the room, but Kiara hadn't seen him
depart the training fields. A ball of apprehension sunk into her
stomach as she attempted to uncover his location.

Her feet automatically carried her off the castle grounds
and through the village. Shops were closing early since the
entire kingdom had been issued a lock-down order during the
night and the following day. She followed the city streets until
the paved roads faded into grass that slowly dispersed into
sand. She slid off her boots, clutching them in her hands as she
made her way across the beach. Her toes melted into the warm,
powdery sand as the wind swept her unpinned hair across her
back.

She reached the waves, watching the silvery water seep
across the shore as sea foam frothed against her ankles. The
sun had just been eclipsed by the horizon, darkening the sky in
a bluish hue that cast a dull light across the beach. Kiara
pushed up the hem of her pants until they bunched around the
middle of her thighs. She sloshed through the water, allowing
the waves to crash over her knees. The salty spray tickled her

bare skin and dampened her loose hair. Momentarily, she felt free. She felt as though her entire life lay sprawled out before her, undaunted by the ominous presence of the oncoming battle.

She shook her head, chiding herself for briefly rejecting reality. Her peripheral vision caught motion to her left, immediately grasping her attention. She spun around, discovering Kain standing in the sand several yards away, his face turned in her direction.

She quickly dashed out of the water, nearly tripping over the clumps of wet sand that clung to the soles of her feet as she ran. "Kain!"

He shuffled backward, his eyes hidden beneath his messy hair. "Kiara, stop!" he demanded. "Don't come any closer."

She slowed her pace, staring at him in confusion. "What's wrong?"

"I don't want you to see me like this," the voice that escaped his lips was husky, matching his darkened expression.

"Like *this*?" she repeated. "What do you mean?"

He remained silent for a while, his violet eyes scanning the waves as though his thoughts were strewn across the shore. "I'm..." he started, his expression softening as the façade he wore to mask his emotions abruptly faded into an honest face displaying unbridled terror, "scared."

"Scared?" Kiara repeated, taking a cautious step forward. "What're you scared of?"

"Vyntrx's ambush," he spoke quietly, reluctantly. She couldn't decipher his shaded expression but she could easily identify the uneasiness in his quavering voice. "What if she's stronger than we anticipated? What if she wipes out our entire fleet? What if you die, but I don't? What if..." his voice choked off. He kicked the ground, sending a cloud of sand blasting through the crisp evening air. "What if I lose you forever?"

"Oh, Kain," she gushed, her heart sinking through her stomach. She hurried over to where he stood, lightly grasping his shoulder. He flinched at her touch, averting his gaze. Her palm cupped his chin, gently twirling his face toward hers. She carefully wrapped her hands around his cheeks, attempting to force him to meet her stare, but his eyes were stubbornly downcast. "That won't happen. I'm not going to die."

He scowled, furrowing his brow. "How could you possibly know that?"

"Do you remember what Vyntrx told me? Veinya won't let me die," she cooed, brushing Kain's hair out of his tearful eyes. "We can win this battle." She managed to sound confident, but on the inside, her skepticism was on a rampage. *Be strong*, she reminded herself critically, *be strong for everyone else.*

"We can't win," he snapped pessimistically. "You're the best fighter we have but you can't beat Avian."

The thought of Avian shackled Kiara's body with a compilation of conflicting and confusion emotions highlighted by rage. Despite her uncertain feelings, she could not refrain from admitting Kain's observation was correct—Avian was far too strong, his vast array of Specialties too overwhelming. His physical strength could match Kiara's and he was definitely more cunning. But luckily, he was lacking that stubborn, furious drive his betrayal had so concretely instilled into Kiara's psyche. "You're right," she said quietly, releasing her grip on Kain's face. Her hands fell limply to her side. "Theoretically, I can't beat him—but I can still try."

Kain sighed, bending down and clutching the sides of Kiara's head as his fingers wove through her hair. He pulled her face close to his, bumping their foreheads together. Her hair cascaded into her light blue eyes, her eyelashes sweeping across her pale cheeks as she glanced at the ground. "You're so stupid," he breathed, his voice shaking. "How can someone so physically small be so spiritually vast?"

"I'm not," she mumbled, attempting to drown the voice screaming through her mind to back away from his touch. "I'm just obstinate."

Kain's lips pulled at the corners. He laughed, kissing the top of her head. "I'll try to fight, too. For you."

"Good," she whispered, her gaze flashing to his face. "We need to go home and get some rest before tomorrow."

He snickered, leaning his head to the side as his lips fell upon Kiara's. Startled by his abrupt directness, she was uncertain how to react to his act of affection. She remained still, lacking the drive required to reciprocate the action with verve.

"Kiara..." he mumbled between kisses. There was a sharp sadness in his voice that urged her to pull away from his grasp. She eyed him skeptically, waiting for him to speak.

"I love you," he said conclusively. His tone was final, as though he truly believed he had taken advantage of the last chance he would have to remind her of his feelings. His face was lined with worry and pain, his eyes locked with Kiara's.

"Don't say that like it's the last time you'll be able to," she commanded, "because it's not."

"You're right," he said lightly. "I love you."

She laughed, shaking her head. "That's not what I meant."

"I know," he said gently, pulling her body against his. "I love you," he whispered into her ear. Although his body was warm against hers, and although his heart was beating in sync with her own, she couldn't help but feel oddly displaced. She leaned her head against his shoulder, too afraid to draw away and send him spiraling into another fearful fit. As her small frame was tightly nestled between his wide arms, his chest rising and falling with vitality, she couldn't help but wonder if that moment could really be the last time she would hold him so close.

*****

The notion of the upcoming battle prickled Avian's nerves and jabbed mercilessly at his heart. Reclining against the headboard of his narrow bed, he turned over the fake wedding ring in his hand, his tear-drenched eyes watching the silver flicker as it reflected the dim firelight.

He had refused to participate in Vyntrx's "mandatory" training sessions. She had asked him to lead the practice, but he had managed to wiggle his way out of the duties by claiming his skills were better suited to be utilized in the strategic warfare planning room. He had sat quietly beside Demure as she and a handful of Vyntrx's cleverest soldiers poured over a map of Enevale, but he had refrained from participating.

On the eve of battle, Vyntrx's attention had been so heavily diverted by last minute preparations, he had managed to slip away to his tent without being noticed. He had been sitting somberly in his room for hours, staring at the wedding ring in silent contemplation.

I won't be able to kill anyone, he thought sullenly. *I'll be useless in battle—I can't kill Enevale's soldiers and if I killed Vyntrx's, she'd murder me.*

His thoughts lingered on the dukes as he was encompassed by the sickening sensation of unbridled guilt. He disastrously understood that given the chance, his friends would slaughter him for his betrayal, and because he could not effectively combat his proverbial brothers, they would undoubtedly be able to kill him.

And Kiara, his mind shifted to the thought of his childhood friend, issuing a fresh wave of tears to spill down his cheeks. *I'd rather have my body and soul put through everlasting torture than watch her die by my own hands.*

The approaching sound of thudding footsteps jolted Avian from his reverie. He glanced up at the hooded entrance to his tent just in time to watch Vyntrx stride into the room.

"You've done a thorough job of evading me today," she spoke callously. She clutched a small object in her pale hands, her black eyes glinting at her advisor with critical consideration.

426

"I'm not in the mood, Vyntrx," he muttered through clenched teeth, wiping angrily at his wet eyes. He abandoned his position on the bed, crossing the room while he glowered at the empress. "What do you want?"

She extended her fist forward, opening her clamped hand and revealing a small, strangely decorated ring. Her mouth twisted into a devious grin, her dark eyes lightening with excitement. "I have created something wonderful," she whispered breathlessly.

He furrowed his brow, staring down at the object in confusion. Power radiated from the odd piece of jewelry; a vague, bluish magical glow encircled the jewel-studded ring. "What is it?" he wondered.

"This will render Kiara completely powerless—it will suppress her Specialties, her magic, *everything*," she spoke enthusiastically, the sharp turquoise of excitement breaking through her black irises. "I have forged it out of the darkest magic. Once it is placed on her finger, only *I* can remove it—and trust me, I never will."

Avian stared down at the ring in stunned dismay. His heart pulsated wildly in his chest as fear darkened his thoughts and chilled his blood. If Vyntrx could manage to slip that ring on Kiara's finger, she would become a helpless victim to horrific assault. Staring at the object, he felt utterly defenseless. Terrible scenarios welled behind his eyelids. His finger inched toward the ring, to capture it and destroy it before it could inflict damage on Kiara's life—but Vyntrx promptly snatched her hand away, depositing the object in her pocket.

"You are unimpressed," she observed disappointedly. She huffed, abruptly rearing her hand back and harshly slapping her palm against her advisor's cheek. A sharp crack resonated through the quiet tent as a stab of pain flooded his face, but his body was far too numb to truly feel more than paralytic fear.

"You'd better shut down your feelings for the girl," she demanded coldly, furiously crossing the tent and hovering in the entrance, "or else I'll have to force you." She parted the curtains, stomped out of the tent, and subjected Avian to the dank, torturous conditions of his reeling mind.

*****

Kiara awoke before the sun had a chance to rise. Her dreams had managed to avoid collision with the hellish realm of nightmares, gratefully allotting her time to rest peacefully.

She ransacked her closet for attire suitable for battle, delighted when she discovered a pair of thin, elastic pants that did not hinder her movement. She pulled on a pair of durable brown boots, lacing them up to her mid-calf. She tucked her necklace away behind the fabric of her green shirt, rolling up the sleeves so they wouldn't interfere with her hands. She covered her clothes in a layer of lightweight but durable armor, grateful Enevale's blacksmith was capable of forging efficient equipment. Tying her hair out of her face, she swept the shorter strands of her tresses away from her sleepy eyes as she carefully secured the silver circlet around her head.

She woke Kain and Kailx, advising they consume a proper meal before heading to the battlefield. They groggily agreed, lethargically sauntering to the kitchen as Kiara slipped out of the suite.

An eerie silence encompassed the halls of the castle. Ominous shadows danced across the walls as the clouds shifted in the sky and altered the light filtered in through the large windows.

She quickly found Rissa's room and knocked loudly on the door. The noise reverberated off the wood, cutting through the silence like a sharp knife.

Within seconds, Rissa's emerald eyes poked out of the darkness. "Kiara," she breathed, "What's wrong?"

"I need you to gather the soldiers. We don't know what time she'll attack—we have to be ready."

Rissa sleepily rubbed her eyes. Her short black hair poked out in all directions. "Alright. We'll convene at the training fields in an hour. Is the plan still in action?"

Kiara had devised a battle plan in hopes of being highly prepared for Vyntrx's assault. She had decided her soldiers would split into four groups of 500 people in order to cover more ground. They were unsure how many warriors Vyntrx's army possessed or where she would strike first. And, of course, Vyntrx could teleport anywhere she wanted at any given time.

The first group would remain at the practice fields, beside the Wall; the second would stay inside the town and ensure the safety of the villagers; the third would reside outside the Wall, facing the Plains; and the fourth would guard the path between the castle and the village. Each group was given a leader capable of wielding fire—Kiara, Kailx, Aiden, and Kain (who could manipulate fire if it were already created)—and if Vyntrx were spotted, a bout of flames bursting through the sky would signal her appearance.

"Yes, of course," Kiara replied, her voice tight. "Thank you, Rissa. I'll meet you in an hour."

Kiara returned to her suite, walking slowly through the halls. Her body felt discouragingly weak and numb. Her mind had been held by the whim of anxiety more times than she could remember, but that familiar feeling of dread sinking through her chest never felt any less disastrous.

She quickly gathered Kain and Kailx, forcing herself to consume a piece of meat. Her stomach was too heavily knotted to endorse hunger, but she knew she would require the energy in battle.

With Kain and Kailx at her side, she hurried through the castle in the direction of the training grounds. The castle halls were seemingly deserted—the soldiers would have already been summoned to the rendezvous point and the other castle workers would still be clinging to the carefree comforts of sleep. Still, the empty castle was uncanny, and Kiara couldn't slow the brisk pace her anxious legs had adopted.

She broke through the doors of the castle at a light jog. Kain and Kailx were at her heels, trying desperately to keep up with her nervous pace. The soldiers were crowded around the training field, a low buzz of chatter filling the warm air. She took a deep breath, allowing the cool wind to billow through her throat and cut through the vines of apprehension strangling her lungs.

As the warriors noticed their queen's presence, a heavy silence instantly ensued. Kiara nervously bit her lip, fruitlessly searching the crowd for a familiar face. She locked eyes with several daring soldiers, but she couldn't gather the nerve to hold direct contact for more than a handful of seconds. She felt her cheeks flush, felt her hands grow sweaty the way they always had when her nerves had carelessly stolen the throne away from her psyche.

She swallowed, attempting to bottle her anxious demeanor. "Today is an important day," she started, pouring fabricated confidence into her tone as she used a spell to amplify her voice. "Today I hope to end this war. I plan to kill Vyntrx. I will not lie to you—this will be a bloody battle. Vyntrx's ranks will more than likely outnumber us. But if you'll stay by my side, we can show Enevale's enemies that we can achieve anything through the power and determination of real warriors! Who's with me?"

Cries of determination and appraisal emanated from the horde of soldiers lining the field. Several warriors enthusiastically thrust their weapons into the air, releasing low battle cries. Kiara smiled at the positive response, feeling her anxiety unravel into pride. "I believe Captain Rissa has already divided you into your groups. Aiden, wherever you are, will you please step forward to lead your faction?"

The silence assimilated into a chorus of low murmurs as soldiers shuffled around to make room for Aiden. His blonde head weaved through the thick crowd, emerging onto the empty span of land between Kiara and her army. He sent her a reassuring grin, taking his place beside Kain.

"Those of you assigned to the stay at the training grounds, Kain will be your leader. Those who have been ordered to protect the city, you'll come with me. Anyone guarding the path to the castle will be with Kailx, and those serving outside of the Wall will follow Aiden," the queen mandated, pointing at her companions as she addressed them. "Everyone, assume your positions. Let's go to war."

*****

Kiara's legs quivered as she attempted to stand still amid the deserted streets of Enevale. Her heart fluttered rampantly, an insistent drumming sounding through her ears. She had already transformed her necklace into a knife, hoping the company of a weapon would deter her anxiety. Combat itself was hell, but waiting in vain for an uncertain battle was an unwarranted evil that hung heavily in the deepest crevices of her mind—it was a breeding ground for apprehension and terror, a playground for nightmarish scenarios and disquieting conceptions.

"I can hear footsteps," Sena's voice broke through the tense atmosphere, jolting Kiara out of her stupor. "Thousands of people are running. Listen."

Kiara's alertness had been fogged by constricting fear. The drumming sound echoing through her ears hadn't been the pulse of her own heartbeat—it had been the rhythmic march of approaching warriors. "Are they nearby?" she whispered, her voice hoarse.

Sena shook her head, glancing at the castle. The overcast sky sent eerie shadows across her face, heightening her distressed expression. "The sound is too distant. They're approaching the Wall, near the castle."

"Kain's..." she started, her voice dying in her throat.

"That's his group, yes." A ground-shaking thump echoed ominously through the kingdom, startling Sena so profoundly, she could barely summon her voice to articulate her thoughts. "They've knocked down the Wall."

"I—I have to go over there," she rashly decided. She started to move in the direction of the castle, but Sena caught her arm.

"No, you don't. Her army may break down the Wall, but she can teleport anywhere she pleases. You're our only hope and she's our prime target. Where she goes, you go. Don't leave until you see the signal." As soon as the words fell from Sena's lips, a burst of flames lit up the dismal sky.

"She's been spotted," Kiara spoke, her eyes glued to the billowing flames. "Sena, you're in charge. Stay here with the army. I'll—"

"*Kiara!*" Sena's hoarse voice squeaked.

She spun on her heel, her eyes instantly falling on Vyntrx. The empress stood several yards away, her hand tight around Sena's neck. A wild expression dominated her face, her lips spreading into a crimson smile as she examined her niece's distraught demeanor.

"Let her go!" Kiara shrieked, willing her knife to shift into a bow. She quickly drew the string, aiming for her aunt's head. The arrow cut through the air with velocity, but Vyntrx managed to vanish before the projectile could make contact with her body.

An uncertain silence manifested from Vyntrx's absence. Kiara glanced around frantically, advising the soldiers to keep up their guard.

A twig snapped, signaling Vyntrx's sudden reappearance. Kiara rapidly sent a spell in her aunt's direction, releasing a burst of powerful wind. Vyntrx stumbled, involuntarily dropping Sena to the ground. Sena gasped desperately for air, crawling away from the vicious Nonae's reach.

"Go, Sena!" Kiara cried. "Take half of the soldiers and assist Kain's fleet but leave the rest to defend the town! I'll handle

Vyntrx!"

Sena didn't require further instruction. She quickly climbed to her feet, yelling orders at the soldiers as they raced toward the battle.

Vyntrx's face was pulled into a livid snarl. Her hair had fallen loose; ink-black strands covered her crimson eyes. "Where did you learn that? It wasn't in the book."

"I taught myself," Kiara boasted. "Advanced manipulation of magic is one of my Specialties."

Vyntrx sneered. "Lies!" she hissed. "The brat taught it to you, didn't she? She's here—somewhere—betraying me."

"Leave Kailx out of this," Kiara demanded through clenched teeth. "This is between you and me."

A devious grin slithered across Vyntrx's face. "We shall see," she grumbled. The air around her form suddenly shifted, as though it were being molded around her body. The atmosphere encompassed her figure, swallowing her entirely, leaving Kiara alone in the grim streets of a fortified city.

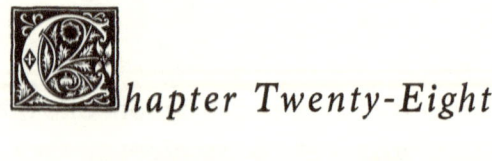

hapter Twenty-Eight

An Uncertain Finale

Avian cringed at the gruesome sight of Enevale's soldiers lying lifelessly in pools of blood on the battle-scarred ground, his stomach churning with grief as his heart was burdened by the weight of guilt. He was so busy attempting to recall the name and age of every dead soldier he observed that he was nearly struck head-on by a strange projectile.

He turned his attention away from the blood-strewn battlefield, his eyes immediately latching on his brother. Kain stood at the edge of the sparring field, a collection of jagged rocks under the thrall of his Evalseman Specialty floating above his head.

Avian released a shaky laugh, attempting to appear undaunted by the bloody battle. "I figured I would run into you, brother," he admitted, holding his sword forward jeeringly.

Kain glared at his brother, stepping toward him determinedly. "I'll kill you," he promised darkly. "I'm going to kill you."

He snickered in response, tossing his sword at the ground. He stretched his arms out, pushing his chest forward as though he were inviting Kain to drive a blade directly through his heart. "Go ahead, brother," he leered. The tone that escaped his lips appeared nonchalant, but his words were sharply tinged in saddened sincerity. "Kill me."

And it was then, while the wind stirred the putrid smell of blood across the field and storm clouds rolled eerily through the sky, the plaintive cries of battle penetrated the silence and Kain realized something utterly unexpected, unbelievable, and jarringly off-setting—Avian wanted to die.

*****

Kiara's body moved on its own, pulling her through the labyrinth streets of Enevale. Her legs were numb with tension, her mind whirling with neuroticism. The battle had spread across the training field and had begun to span across the steep hill that paved the path to the castle. Fleets of soldiers were being violently assaulted by foreign creatures wielding vicious weapons. Kiara didn't have time to examine the strange beings—she didn't feel the need to, as they were just as susceptible to her spells as any other mortal. Before she could fall into the range of any creature's weapons, she released a spell in their direction, blowing their bodies to miniscule pieces.

She was unaware of where she was headed, but she gravely understood that it was her duty to find Vyntrx. She couldn't relent her hasty pace or slow her sprinting legs even when her eyes raked the bloodstained ground littered with the bodies of her soldiers.

Her knife felt heavy in her tightly clenched grip as the prospect of a skirmish dawned nearer. She swiftly maneuvered her way across the battlefield, avoiding slashing blades and physical attacks. She expertly swiped her knife across her enemies, grateful for her diminutive form as she weaved her way through the smallest gaps between sparring bodies.

She reached the center of the battlefield—it was easily spotted due to the lack of warriors crowding around it. Creatures and soldiers migrated away from a small circle in the midst of the battle, as though there were an invisible field keeping them away—and as Kiara's eyes fell on Vyntrx, she suspected her aunt had implemented a spell to keep her detached from the rest of the battle.

Vyntrx was fighting Kailx, furiously exchanging countless

spells with her angered daughter. Kailx's hair had come undone, falling into her sweaty face. She stared angrily at her mother, but refrained from speaking, as though her insistent control over magic served as the confrontational tirade she was unable to voice.

Kiara timidly raised her hand through the invisible barrier she assumed her aunt had created. A faint shock coursed through her body but the force was not strong enough to repel her. She hurriedly jumped onto the barren field, reveling in the dazed expression that crossed Vyntrx's face as her eyes fell on her niece.

Before the empress could form the sentence perched on her tongue, Kiara sent a line of flames hurling toward her face. Vyntrx narrowly dodged the attack, a snarl escaping her curled lips. "You shouldn't have been able to get through the barrier. Only full-blooded Nonae can pass through the field."

"Maybe your magic is weak," Kiara suggested, a snide leer sliding across her face. "Leave Kailx alone."

Vyntrx scoffed. She grabbed her daughter's shoulders, her grip tight and constrictive. "Leave the traitor alone? Honestly, Kiara, you must be under some delusion that I'm considerate."

Kailx's hands wound around her mother's wrist. She didn't possess the strength required to escape Vyntrx's clutches, but Kiara could tell by her cousin's stance that she had other plans. Kailx's mouth darted toward Vyntrx's hand, her teeth chomping into sensitive flesh. The empress screamed, rearing backwards as Kailx quickly dashed from her range. She sprinted the length of the secluded circle, sending Kiara a reassuring grin as she passed through the invisible barrier and disappeared among the crowds of warriors.

"This is the last battle," Kiara decided, her hand extending forward as she tightened her grip on the knife. She leveled the weapon with her aunt's figure, staring down the edge of the gleaming blade. Vyntrx's scowling face was reflected across the mirror-like material of the knife, her black eyes strikingly apparent against the smooth silver of the blade.

"For *you*, it is," the empress replied coolly, raising her hand as she summoned a spell.

Kiara hastily lunged to the side, avoiding collision with the wall of jagged rock Vyntrx had suddenly created from the earth. Kiara had expected Vyntrx's first move to be a spell—in fact, she predicted the majority of her attacks would be rooted in magic. Magic was Vyntrx's strength but physical assaults were her weakness. Kiara reminded herself to avoid long-range attacks and bombard her aunt with direct assaults, which would ideally prevent her from wielding spells.

Kiara darted forward, her knife at the ready. She poured all of her Evalseman strength into the handle, aiming directly for Vyntrx's gut—but the empress vanished mere seconds before Kiara's blade could penetrate her briefly vulnerable body. As Kiara had been relying on the collision to steady her unbalanced stance, she stumbled, nearly tumbling to the ground. Before she could manage to fully gather her wits, Vyntrx sent a destructive spell hurtling in her direction. The ground below Kiara's feet was suddenly uprooted; dirt and rubble ripped through the air, pelting her body.

The dusty fallout of the spell momentarily blinded Vyntrx, but Kiara had memorized her aunt's location. She shifted her footing, careful not to venture too far or too close to her aunt in fear of losing her position. She imagined a terrible spell, one that would cloud the victim's mind with darkness and could resurface horrific memories and fears. With the notion of this spell still freshly present in Kiara's thoughts, she allowed magic to flow through her veins and escape her fingertips as she pointed in Vyntrx's direction.

The dust cleared just in time for Kiara to witness the white of her aunt's eyes turn black as ink. Vyntrx's pale face faded into a sickly gray hue, her eyes widening as her body trembled.

Kiara understood that her aunt was not weak. She knew the spell wouldn't last—Vyntrx would manage to maneuver her way through its dark clutches and escape its deadliness—she just had to strike before she regained consciousness.

Kiara's hand tightened around the knife's hilt. She plunged the blade straight through Vyntrx's heart, feeling an overwhelming surge of disbelieving accomplishment and relief. Her aunt's limbs shook uncontrollably as Kiara recoiled the blade from her chest, but her injured body did not tumble to the ground. Her figure suddenly exploded—but instead of releasing bodily fluids, a cloud of black dust erupted from the hole in her chest, caving inward and disintegrating her flesh into a heap of ashes that crumbled to the floor.

A cry of frustration and fury emanated from Kiara's mouth. She kicked the ground beside Vyntrx's decayed form, dreadfully understanding that she had merely eliminated a doppelganger—a very intricate doppelganger.

Where are you, really? Kiara thought. If Vyntrx hadn't even gathered enough courage to face her own daughter inside a protected barricade, surely she didn't possess the valor required to endure a vicious battle. There was really only place Vyntrx could be, and Kiara was so overwhelmed with disgust at her aunt's cowardice, she released a loud huff of incredulity. Vyntrx was undoubtedly hiding inside the Dark Forest, waiting eagerly for her niece to discover her plan—the Dark Forest was her territory, and if she was going to engage in a vital battle, she was going to do it on her terms.

Kiara escaped the confinement of the force field, breaking into enemy-infested land. She dashed toward the Wall, ducking around weapons and slashing her own across several bodies. As she neared the Wall, it became apparent that she didn't need to search for the miniscule hole that served as a hidden gateway between the forest and Enevale. Sena had been correct—Vyntrx's army had broken through the stone, creating a gaping crater where there had once been a minute crack in the granite partition.

Kiara frantically dashed through the jagged hole, leaping

over fallen debris. She crossed into Nonae territory, pushing away tree branches as she mindlessly sprinted through the forest. She would never understand how to navigate the mysterious realm of the Dark Forest, but she knew that her aunt would immediately sense her presence and teleport to her location.

"Vyntrx!" she panted, ducking under a thick tree limb. "Show yourself!"

A delirious laugh echoed through the forest. The piercing sound filled Kiara's ears, slipped deep into the pit of her stomach, spread through her flesh, and settled inside her bones. She was paralyzed her with fear. She stood in silence, scanning her surroundings, her breathing slow and faint. "Where are you?" she spoke weakly, drawing her eyebrows downward. "Aren't you going to fight me?"

Vyntrx's vicious laugh resonated a second time, and Kiara could sense by the intensity of the sound that her aunt had moved closer to her target. Curiously, she reared the weapon backwards, thrusting it into seemingly empty air. The blade stuck, forcing a sharp moan of pain to escape Vyntrx's throat.

Kiara cocked her head to the side, finding her knife protruding from Vyntrx's forearm. A twisted dagger fell from her aunt's hands, landing at her feet with a thud. An astonished expression lined her face, her dark eyes wide.

"You shouldn't play with your prey," Kiara retorted, forcefully withdrawing the edge of her knife from Vyntrx's arm. She spun around to face her aunt, pointing the blade at her chest.

A harsh smirk played on Vyntrx's blood-red lips. "I just thought I'd play a little game with you before you die. We don't spend much wholesome family time together anymore." Her fingers danced across her right arm, a bright light embodying her entire hand. Within seconds, the wound Kiara inflicted had been replaced with unblemished flesh.

"You've gotten stronger," Kiara remarked drily.

Residual blood dripped from Vyntrx's arm. She sadistically drew her tongue across her skin, lapping up the crimson liquid. Her eyes were wild and black, a demonic grin dehumanizing her features. "Did you see my new toys?" she wondered, excitement alight through her crackling voice.

"Those hideous monsters?" Kiara retorted, steadily holding the knife in a defensive stance. "Yeah, I killed a few."

Vyntrx frowned, her hand falling to her side. "Sadly, I can't kill you yet, Kiara," she whispered, her eyes flashing upward. "Veinya cannot yet be convinced."

"You're going to kill me anyway." It wasn't a question, or even a confirmation—it was simply a fact. Kiara understood her aunt's tainted personality enough to grasp her skewered concept on death. Vyntrx would kill her niece singularly for the pleasure and excitement the action would summon. It didn't matter that Kiara would immediately come back to life—Vyntrx would just murder her over and over in order to entertain her disturbed mentality.

"Of course I am," she spoke languidly, as though the notion of stealing Kiara's life was a topic her thoughts frequently visited. "I'm going to kill you repeatedly until you finally stay dead."

Kiara edged the knife closer to her aunt's chest. "Not if I kill you first."

"You can't," she declared, releasing a high-pitched, sadistic chuckle. "You're not the only one Veinya favors. She wouldn't allow my death to be permanent. You can't kill me."

Kiara's eyes widened in bewilderment, her heartbeat slowed to a nearly unresponsive pulse. She hadn't contemplated the possibility of Veinya favoring Vyntrx so passionately that she would impose the same conditions onto her that she had granted Kiara. Her mind was steadily unraveling with anxiety but she wouldn't allow her aunt to discover her failing strength.

She paused, uncertain of what her next move should be. If

she couldn't kill Vyntrx, she couldn't end the battle. If she couldn't end the battle, she would be undoubtedly overwhelmed by Vyntrx's army and her kingdom would be at the empress' mercy, which—Kiara had learnt from a slew of harrowing experiences—was a characteristic blatantly absent from her aunt's personality.

"Watch me," she said through clenched teeth. She jabbed the knife at her aunt's exposed torso, but Vyntrx had already predicted her niece's movement. The shadows instantly engulfed her body, shrouding her entirely in darkness. Within seconds, she reappeared several yards away, her back turned to her niece, her hair billowing out from behind her as she danced off into the distance, laughing fervently.

Kiara followed after her aunt begrudgingly, quickening her pace as she wove her way through the dense forest. After what felt like an eternity of mindless chasing, Vyntrx finally abandoned her attempt at fleeing. She stopped abruptly, swerving around to face her niece. "You know, I just recalled something," she said thoughtfully, a devious grin stretching her lips tightly across her pale face. "I haven't seen you since I killed your family. Tell me, was my gift well received?"

"Shut up!" Kiara screamed, her voice breaking unevenly. She instinctively lashed her foot forward as she extended her leg into a powerful round-kick. A loud, definite crack resounded through the forest as Kiara's calf made sharp contact with her aunt's startled face.

Vyntrx slunk to the ground, laughing maniacally despite the pain coursing through her injured nose. She lay motionless in the grass as blood trickled down her mouth and stained her teeth crimson.

Kiara expertly tucked the grip of her knife into the fold of her hand, positioning the blade away from her arm as she harshly punched her aunt's stomach. Vyntrx spat a wad of blood into the humid air, gasping momentarily. As the immediate shock of the injury progressively faded, she laughed excitedly, undaunted by the vague pain pulsating beneath her cheeks.

Frustrated by her aunt's sudden immunity to pain, Kiara repeatedly assaulted Vyntrx's bloodied face with her fists. She harnessed all of her Evalseman strength to inflict an unbearable amount of pain on Vyntrx, but as her fury was sifted down to sheer bewilderment at the lack of discomfort her aunt was displaying, she withdrew her hand, eying Vyntrx's swollen, unidentifiable face. She held her raised fist beside her cheek, watching blood trickle down her knuckles and splatter her aunt's black dress.

"Is that all you can do—" Vyntrx wailed, laughing like a deranged lunatic, "—make me bleed?" She stood shakily on unstable legs, smiling in spite of the smears of blood coating her disfigured face.

"You're even more insane now than you were the last time we met," Kiara noted condescendingly, stepping back from her aunt and shaking her head in disbelief.

Vyntrx stumbled toward her niece as though she were drunk on the violent atmosphere. "Isn't it wonderful?" she asked elatedly. She raised her hand, aiming directly at Kiara's face as she sent an unfamiliar spell churning through the air.

Kiara instantly jumped out of the line of fire, noticing her aunt's sudden movement from the corner of her eye. She mechanically raised her blade-wielding hand, deflecting an attack from a pointed dagger her aunt had procured from the folds of her dress. Frowning at the disappointing clank of metal meeting metal, Vyntrx harshly withdrew her weapon, grazing Kiara's arm with the blade in one sweeping motion.

She wasn't allotted time to recover. Vyntrx instantly lunged her dagger forward, aiming directly for her niece's stomach. Kiara, barely distinguishing her opponent's move, swept her knife across her aunt's forearm before the empress's blade was able to penetrate her torso. She leapt forward, closing the diminutive space between them and lashing the blade across

Vyntrx's ribs. The shadowy material of her dress was torn open, revealing a lengthy gash frothing with blood, but regardless of her wound, Vyntrx's content disposition was not vanquished.

The empress disdainfully tossed her weapon to the ground, directing a spell at her baffled niece. Caught completely off guard, the hex engulfed Kiara's entire form before she had found time to gather her wits.

Vyntrx had somehow managed to recreate the spell Kiara had inflicted upon the doppelganger empress. She was strikingly thrust into her worst nightmares as she entered a hellish dimension teeming with revulsion and terror. Her friends were dead. Her eyes latched on Blade's dying face through thick shadows, his silver hair matted with crimson blood. Kailx was chained in the basement of a torture chamber—Vyntrx stood beside her, wielding a sharp knife, tearing away her flesh inch by bloody inch. Kailx was screaming Kiara's name, pleading desperately for her cousin to rescue her. Kain's dead body littered the floor of Kiara's suite, his entire frame covered in lacerations. His purple eyes were wide and unblinking as he stared up at her, the last strain of unbridled terror he had felt before his death forever painted on his ghastly face. *You couldn't save me*, his voice echoed bitterly through his mind, *you let her kill me again.*

No! she screamed, her scratchy voice raking against the constricting walls of her throat. *It's just an illusion!*

Avian crept into Kiara's silent village equipped with a deadly sword. He stealthily approached Brin and Anya, reveling in their shocked expressions as he raised the weapon high above his head. Brin summoned every ounce of his power in an attempt to fight, but he was struck down almost immediately. Anya screamed, sobbing, crawling to the corner of the kitchen and covering her head in vain. Avian swung the sword down, splattering the wall with blood.

It's an illusion! It's an illusion! she repeated frantically, the poison of terror thickening dangerously in her wildly pounding chest.

"Kiara," Avian's voice was soft despite the traumatic events he had singlehandedly unfurled. Blood slid down his face, dripping off the edge of his chin as his mismatched eyes glowed sadistically. "Do you see how far I've gone to betray you?"

"It isn't real!" she screamed, finally able to gain control over her tightly wound vocal chords. Her nightmares dissipated as though they were smoke, fading slowly away into the clarity of reality. Her hands were positioned directly over her chest, the sharp edge of her knife's blade merely an inch away from plunging straight into her heart. She released a shaky huff of air, her hands falling to her side as she realized she had nearly fallen prey to the dark clutches of a spell she had so mindlessly created.

Vyntrx eyed her niece expectantly, sighing in discouragement. She bit her thumb, her features crestfallen. "That didn't take long."

"Sorry to disappoint," Kiara retorted cynically. Without pausing for even a beat, she sent a line of flames straight at her aunt's bleak face.

The empress waved her hand loftily, summoning a strong bout of wind to quickly disperse the flames. She subsequently launched a spell at her niece, a wicked gleam flashing through her eyes as the hex manifested into a torrent of crystallized spikes.

Kiara managed to narrowly evade the dangerous curse, ducking down as the fleet of spikes whirred past her head. Her knife shifted to a bow inside her sweaty hands as she hurriedly leveled her extended finger with her aunt's head. As she released the string, a silver arrow magically materialized from the empty shaft, slicing through the air as it attempted to meet its target.

Before Vyntrx could gauge her niece's actions, her forehead was directly struck by the point of the arrow. Her lips curled, releasing a quivering note of startled terror. She stared blankly at the sky, her eyes rolling unnaturally into the back of her head as she crumpled listlessly to the ground.

Silence resonated through the forest. Vyntrx's body was unmoving, but Kiara was innately suspicious of her aunt's trickery—her death had been too simple and easy. She cautiously approached the lifeless figure, her eyes trailing over the puddle of blood pooling beneath her injured head. Her eyes climbed her aunt's paling body, hovering over the ghastly image of the ashen face—a smile was impossibly pinned to her dead lips. Kiara emitted a sharp cry, stupefied by the jarring sight.

Another trap? she wondered incredulously, scanning her surroundings for even a vague sign of her crafty aunt. She wondered if Vyntrx's power had truly magnified significantly or if Kiara had merely grown dimwitted. Lost in thought, she didn't realize her aunt's unannounced appearance until an unbearable pain was pulsating wildly through her spine. She craned her neck around, watching her aunt smile wickedly.

Vyntrx was entirely unscathed, a smile plastered to her unsoiled face as she brandished a vial of poison. She waved the bottle playfully, snickering. "This will paralyze you temporarily, dearie," she explained icily.

As the empress's voice echoed through the shadowy woods, Kiara slowly began to lose control over her limbs. She fell the ground with a definite thud, her mind spinning dizzily as her body tingled and burned with numbness.

Vyntrx sauntered toward her niece, wrapping her hands around Kiara's dangling wrists. "Say goodbye to your dying friends," she whispered into her ear. Her breath reeked of blood.

Through the thick curtain of trees, Kiara could just barely decipher the battlefield on the other side of the half-destroyed Wall. She couldn't identify a single soldier's face from her position in the forest. Worry crept through her chest, increasing her heart rate ferociously and turning her blood to chilled shards of ice. She was harassed by the possibility of never knowing the fate of her friends—never knowing if they had survived the war or died among the countless emaciated bodies that littered the battlefield.

Tears welled in Kiara's eyes as she was overwhelmed by a profound sense of helplessness. She wanted to fight, wanted to claw, run, scream—but she couldn't do anything. She could only lay immobile, cocooned in a state of despondence. Silent tears spilling down her cheeks, she was abrasively dragged through the underbrush of the forest, twigs stabbing into her paralyzed skin, as she was led straight into the merciless clutches of Vyntrx.

To Be Continued

Enjoy this preview from the next book in the series,
Condemned...

Chapter One

Trapped

The sun rose timidly in the blackened sky, unseen through thick grey clouds intent on darkening the sunlight. A gloomy hue was cast upon the blood-soaked land, flickering uncanny shadows across the lifeless faces of fallen soldiers. Limp hands steered upward from emaciated bodies, forever reaching for weapons that lie forlornly in the sodden ground.

A sharp cry cut through the ominous atmosphere. Those scattered few who still clung to vitality glanced upward with half-hearted curiosity, even the smallest hint of hope absent from their solemn eyes.

Obedient footsteps sounded like thunder as Vyntrx's army marched toward the Dark Forest at their master's call. They thudded away in sync as though they were puppets dancing on a string, weaving through the wreckage of the scarred stage and exiting behind the curtain of foliage. Their numbers had barely dwindled, unabashed by the exhausted efforts of the slain soldiers. Despite their colossal coalition, they vanished within seconds.

Kain slumped downward, his damp hair falling into his bloodied face. He stared up at his retreating brother with unbridled hatred, wishing miserably that Avian's Specialties didn't block his ability to end his life with a flick of his wrist. He cursed loudly, falling to his knees. His body was heavily lacerated and he lacked the strength to continue fighting, yet he repeatedly chided himself for allowing his brother to disappear—unscathed—into the forest.

A mortified sob wailed amid the bitter silence, startling Kain so badly, he nearly toppled to the ground. He noticed one of the dukes, Ace, on his knees several yards away, flinging himself upon a headless body. A stone of apprehension sinking

448

through his stomach, Kain shakily climbed to his feet, slowly walking toward the hysteric duke.

A flash of yellow sped past Kain, sprinting toward the body. Aiden was beside his friend in seconds, staring down at the deceased with horror. His lips quivered. "N-no," he mumbled. "I-it's impossible."

Ace's arms wound around the girl's body, his eyes eerily glued to the spot her head should have rested. He didn't speak—he could barely whimper.

"Akanine?" Aiden asked frantically, touching his dead sister's shoulder. Flecks of blood dotted her pale skin. "Akanine! Akanine! Come back! *Akanine!*"

Kain bit his lip, unwanted sorrow compressing his chest. He hadn't known the girl. But it didn't matter. He could tell by Ace's reaction that he had been in love with her, and he knew Aiden had been her brother. To say Kain was familiar with grief was an understatement. He was overwhelmed by the desire to reach out and comfort Kiara's anguished friends, but he lacked the emotional capacity. He couldn't console someone else when his own mind was plagued with anxiety.

"Kain..."

He turned around instantly, expecting Kiara. Instead, his heart dropped from his chest at the sight of Kailx's bruised and mangled body. "Oh," he muttered. "There's been a fatality."

"There've been many," she said tensely, eyeing Akanine's corpse. "Are you alright?"

He shook his head mechanically. "Where's Kiara?"

Kailx's lips were a straight line of apprehension, her eyes wide and sapphire with saddened worry. "I-I don't—I haven't seen—She was—"

"Dead," Rissa choked morbidly. She appeared beside Kain, tears staining her cheeks. "Kiara's dead."

Kain's body instantly crumpled to the ground. He hadn't cried since that dreadful day his life had been mercilessly torn from the delicate seams of childhood, yet he couldn't stop the tears relentlessly pouring from his eyes. His chest ached, his heart throbbed unevenly, his lungs constricted, his stomach twisted into fettered knots—her absolute absence had seemingly stolen the vivacity from his veins, had stolen the desire to live from his reeling mind.

"Wh-what?" Kailx cried. "H-how do you—" her voice was

silenced as a fit of hysterics rose in her throat.

"I witnessed it," Rissa explained gravely. "Vyntrx killed her and dragged her into the forest."

Kailx's legs gave away. She fell beside Kain, staring at him hopelessly. "It can't be..." she whispered hoarsely. "It can't."

"Come on," Rissa bent down to the level of the pair of devastated soldiers, collectively wrapping her arms around their shoulders and heaving them upward. "Let's get inside. It's going to storm."

"No, Rissa," Kain spoke through clenched teeth. "It's already storming."

She inclined her head, tilting her gaze toward the dark sky. She understood that Kain wasn't referring to reality—she had comprehended his metaphor—but something about the gloomy sky above required a constant vigil. Before she could form a reply, Kain was on his feet. He had gathered his strength within seconds, racing toward the gaping hole in the Wall. She called after him, but her voice instantly died in her throat as her eyes fell on Akanine's bloodstained body.

Kain disappeared into the forest. Fatigue had nestled deep into the protesting muscles of his body, but the sense of despair fueled his bones with the capacity to flee. Although he couldn't navigate the labyrinth trails of the forest in his distraught state, he was determined to find Avian, or Vyntrx, or anyone—someone had to pay for Kiara's death. And he wasn't going to relent until he had successfully avenged her murder.

*****

Light welled beneath Kiara's eyelids, blotching through the darkness. She could feel her wet eyelashes glued to her cheeks, could feel sharp pains racking through her limbs. She was afraid to open her eyes, regardless of her conscious seeping back into reality. She was afraid of what she would see; afraid of the mangled state she would find her body.

She could distantly recall the battle. Most of it was a blur, but she could still picture Vyntrx's maniacal expression as she dragged her body through the underbrush of the forest. She recoiled unwillingly at the thought of the plausible state of her kingdom, at the possibility that her friends could be dead.

Cold air swept through the forest, rustling nearby leaves

and birthing chills across Kiara's skin. Her fingers itched to grab the edge of a warm blanket, to shield her body from the dangers of the world and to block out solemn reality.

It's quiet, Kiara realized, *maybe I'm alone.* Timidly, she peeled her damp eyelashes from her cheeks, watching the Dark Forest pour into view in a wave of dull green and dark brown. Dim sunlight filtered through the leaves of trees, heightening the shadows of the forest. The only sound present was the occasional chirp of a bird, but Kiara wasn't studying the foliage for a sight of wildlife—she was searching for Vyntrx.

She slowly lifted her torso, pulling her body into a sitting position, her wounds crying out in protest. She extended her arms and stared down at the crimson blood staining her pale skin. Grimacing, she glanced at her legs, finding countless lacerations winding their way around the dark fabric of her pants. She attempted to survey her injuries as though she were a medic, unbiased and without obligation to create falsified placations. She decided that her wounds were severe, but not entirely critical. The desire to heal herself with Nonae magic hung in the front of her mind, but she knew that she was far too weak to summon the strength required. She didn't lie and convince herself that she could run effectively. The best she could probably muster would be a light jog, and even that would be short-lived. Fleeing wasn't an option and fighting seemed strenuous. Still, if she came across trouble, she would have no other option but to bite her lip and endure the pain.

"Contemplating escape, Ara?" a snide voice suddenly disturbed her determined thoughts, shattering the small speck of hope she was so desperately clinging to.

"Avian," she growled through clenched teeth, shakily climbing to her feet as her eyes fell upon the man she so terribly despised—and bitterly loved.

He was standing several yards away, his arms folded across his chest as he rested his back against a tree. He possessed a haughty expression, filling Kiara's veins with heated rage. "You insufferable bastard!" she exclaimed, walking as quickly as she could in his direction. Her hands slammed against his chest, bunching his shirt into her palms. "How could you betray your kingdom? How could you fight against your friends?" She repeatedly slammed his back against the tree, her eyes red and wild. "How could you manipulate me?"

He coolly returned her gaze, unabashed by her physical assault. Although he appeared to be collected, Kiara could tell she had struck a nerve. His mismatched eyes shone with unrestrained sadness, his hands shaking as they wound their way around hers. "You wouldn't understand," he said thickly. "You couldn't possibly understand."

"Did Vyntrx call off the attack?" she questioned, ignoring his vague explanation. She flung her hands out of his grip, fighting off the urge to cling to the tree for assistance as she was overcome by a bout of dizziness spurred from sudden movement.

"Yes," he said tensely. "I'm afraid your soldiers didn't fare well."

Kiara folded her arms across her chest, smearing blood across the fabric of her shirt. "Don't say it like it pains you. You have only yourself to thank for that."

Avian's eyes lingered on the wounds weaving across her pale skin. He lightly touched her forearm, startling her. "Let me heal your injuries," he said softly.

"No," she snapped, jerking her arm away. "I don't want your help."

"You'll bleed to death," he deduced. "Then what use would you be?"

She hardened her gaze, distrust stubbornly clinging to the depths of her crimson eyes. "If you heal my wounds, I *will* escape."

He shrugged, gingerly retrieving her hand. "I doubt that." His fingers danced across her skin, instantly repairing the damaged flesh. A burning sensation swept through her entire body, urging her to whimper slightly. He wiped away the residual blood, moving on to her other arm. He continued to heal each and every wound that handicapped her body until her unblemished skin practically glistened.

"Thanks," she muttered, feeling much more formidable with unhindered limbs.

He shrugged modestly. "Anything for you."

"Avian," she spoke sternly. "Don't you dare reference the fake feelings you had for me."

"I'm not," he whispered. "I never fabricated *my* affections. And your feelings were never fals—" he abruptly stopped talking, clearing his throat. "Never mind."

Kiara shook her head mechanically, a stupefied expression dominating her features. "B-but—you said—" she fumbled over her words, chiding herself for allowing her apparent disbelief to diminish her articulation.

Before she could gather her wits and before Avian could convince himself to offer an explanation, a chilling voice broke through the tense atmosphere, sending waves of terror through Kiara's body, tightly constricting her lungs and urging her heartbeat to accelerate.

"Hello, niece," Vyntrx sneered.

Kiara's eyes instantly moved in her aunt's direction. Vyntrx was hovering beside a tree, a wicked smile on her face. Her black clothes were drenched in blood and she was holding three disembodied heads by the roots of their hair.

"Vyntrx," Kiara spoke through clenched teeth, her eyes instinctively flashing crimson with unparalleled resentment.

"I have a present for you, dear," her aunt cooed menacingly, sharply drawing her hand upward as she proudly displayed her collection of dismembered heads. "I brought one of your friends to play with us!"

Kiara's eyes unwittingly fell on the three lifeless faces Vyntrx had thrust into the air. Two heads belonged to unidentifiable men, but the third Kiara recognized with a sharp pang of sorrow. Akanine's disfigured face stared up at her with an empty expression, her mouth grotesquely open in a silent cry, her golden hair harshly pulled back from her forehead as Vyntrx clung to her tresses.

"You monster..." Kiara's voice quavered hoarsely, a storm of raw hatred swirling in the chambers of her heart. "You murderous bitch!" She lunged forward, fists at the ready, but her momentum was abruptly halted as Avian's arm blocked her path. His Evalseman strength rivaled hers, and he didn't need to use both of his arms to hold back her petite body. She scowled, yelling in frustration as she flung her clenched fist against his chest. His expression weakened, his eyes lined by undeniable tears, but he was otherwise unabashed by the action.

"I think you already understand that your efforts to escape are futile," Vyntrx sneered menacingly. "I already won once today, I could easily do it again—especially with Avian's strength on my side."

Kiara bit her lip, refusing to let her aunt's words ring true. Her grip tightened around Avian's forearm, attempting to bottle down the bitter flow of anger welling through her veins.

"Besides, dear, I *have* gotten stronger. You even said so yourself."

Kiara distinctly recalled watching her aunt heal her injuries in split seconds, remembered how she had appeared completely immune to pain, recollected the increased fortitude in Vyntrx's assaults. "How did you do it?"

A wicked grin slid across Vyntrx's eerily pale face. "Veinya entrusted me with a new power—every time I steal a life, I become stronger."

Kiara's tearful eyes widened in disbelief. "Th-that can't be true," she stammered, a stone of apprehension sinking through her stomach. "That's impossible!"

Vyntrx laughed deviously, her black eyes alight with sheer rapture. "I assure you, darling, it *is* possible! The best part of her gift was that she gave it to me mere hours before my little attack on your kingdom. I've never felt more alive!"

Kiara's head mechanically swung back in forth in denial. "N-no," she managed to choke. "That can't be..."

Her aunt abruptly clicked her tongue, the blissful expression suddenly wiped off her face. "What is *he* doing in the forest?"

"Cylis, milady?" Avian inquired, his curiosity piqued.

Vyntrx shook her head. "We'll talk about it later, Avian. For now, I must take care of this pest. Take Kiara to the campsite. I'll be back." Before her companion could protest, she suddenly vanished into the chilled air, leaving a gust of cold wind behind.

Kiara disentangled her body from Avian's, but he wouldn't relent his grip on her wrist. She tugged at her arm defiantly, but his hand tightened in response.

"We can't have you running away," he said unenthusiastically. "I can see thousands of questions running through your mind, Ara. Come quietly with me to the campsite and you'll have your answers."

"Don't call me that," she chided. Her tone was harsh, but she allowed Avian to gently pull her forward into the estranging shadows of her prison.

*****

Kain sprinted aimlessly, his eyes frantically raking the backdrop of the forest. His wounds were crying sharply for his body to rest, his heart rumbling like the steady *purr* of an engine—running mechanically, automatically, so dehumanized it could no longer feel anything aside from consistent stabs of guilt and sorrow.

"Come to rattle the bird's cage?" a sardonic voice cut through the silence. Kain slowed his pace, his eyebrows pulled tightly together as he studied his surroundings. There wasn't a living soul in sight and yet the voice had sounded as though someone were standing directly beside him.

Vyntrx, he concluded, *Kiara's murderer.*

"Was going to snap the bird's neck, actually," he retorted. "But yours will do just fine."

A low chuckle resonated, and if Kain's mind hadn't been fogged with desperation, he would have felt fear. Vyntrx's form flickered before him, as though she had materialized from the shadows. She was sporting that devilish grin she always wore, her unnaturally dark eyes gleaming.

"You impudent fool," she spoke callously, the edges of her mouth upturned in amusement. "You honestly think a weakling like you could defeat *me*?"

"How did you kill her?" he shrieked, his voice breaking. "She couldn't—she couldn't die!"

Vyntrx rolled her eyes, wiping a curtain of hair away from her face. "How else, imbecile? I destroyed Veinya's benevolent side."

"That would have destroyed her!" Kain argued. "You're lying!"

She huffed indignantly, her smile curving into a scowl. "How else would I have killed your pathetic girlfriend?"

"I don't—She didn't—You—" he stumbled over his words, unable to process a complete thought. His entire body ached from the absence of Kiara. His heart had been shattered into immeasurable pieces, shrapnel from the explosion nestling into the pit of his stomach. His legs gave away and he tumbled to the ground, landing on his hands and knees. Tears streamed from the eyes he believed were incapable of producing emotion. His fingers clawed the ground, his breath escaping his lips in trembling gasps.

"Pathetic," Vyntrx sneered. She spun on her heel, turning toward the depths of the forest.

"Aren't you going to kill me?" he whispered hoarsely. "I'm defenseless."

A sly smile cut across Vyntrx's face as she titled her head in Kain's direction. "You want to die," she observed. "I don't bestow favors."

The Nonae empress suddenly disappeared, leaving Kain staring after her with a dumfounded expression. He exhaled sharply, his face plummeting to the hard ground.

I should move, he encouraged himself. He attempted to push his body up with his hands, but his arms quivered and buckled, sending his stomach into sharp contact with the ground. *Eventually.*

*****

Avian's hand was tightly wrapped around Kiara's wrist, sending a strange mixture of anger and shyness creeping through her veins. She wanted to yank her hand away, to free herself from his confusing touch, but she knew he would take the action as a declaration of rebellion. She studied his steady figure, eyeing the curved slope connecting his neck to his wide shoulders. His muscular arms occasionally tightened with an emotion Kiara couldn't read, his grip constricting sharply before it would abruptly lessen. She carefully observed his posture and noticed the distraught slump of his typically proud stance. She could feel the irregular drumming of his pulse against her wrist, thudding wildly as though his veins had been injected with a powerful strain of adrenaline. Something had severely perturbed him—something recent—and she refused to believe it could simply be her presence.

"Who is Vyntrx chasing off?" she asked quietly as Avian led her through the densely canopied forest.

"Honestly, I can't be certain," he replied instantly, his voice unnaturally husky. "But I have a hunch."

Kiara's eyebrows furrowed. "You don't think it's Cylis?"

Avian shook his head, his brown hair sweeping across his neck. "No, Cylis is always in the forest. Vyntrx and Cylis aren't always at each other's throats—they both have other issues to attend to. Occasionally, one will grow annoyed and decide to assault the other. They've been playing a game of cat and mouse for years," he explained, refusing to even glance in Kiara's direction.

"What's your hunch, then?"

"I'd rather keep that information to myself."

Kiara rolled her eyes, scoffing. "You *are* good at not sharing your true thoughts. Had lots of practice through the years, didn't you?"

Avian suddenly stopped walking. He dropped his hold on Kiara's wrist, slowly turning around to face her. His visage was dark, partly masked by a handful of hair that had tumbled into his downcast eyes. "Let's get something straight," he spoke coldly. "What I did to you—how I acted—it wasn't because I wanted to."

Kiara's gaze hardened, her eyes flashing crimson. "I can't believe you, Avian. Stop trying to play your stupid mind games. That night, during the coronation ball, you told me that you manipulated my mind—that you *forced* me to fall in love with you," she spoke heatedly, allowing the anger and hurt she had felt from Avian's betrayal to seep through her words. A voice in the back of her head reminded her that she was certain Avian had never given her *fake* feelings for him, but she disallowed herself to reveal that to his undeserving ears. "You showed absolutely no sign of remorse. Don't pretend you've suddenly been struck with compassion."

Avian's eyes bulged with frustration, but he simply spun on his heel, turning his entire body away from Kiara. His hand reached back, sharply clasping around her forearm and pulling her forward as he continued to walk. "If only you knew..." he muttered, shaking his head. "We're approaching the campsite."

She titled her head to the side, allowing her eyes to glance over Avian's shoulder. Only a few yards away, countless rows of dark tents lined the forest floor, positioned in squadrons of ten around a massive, elaborate tent. *Vyntrx's tent,* she thought solemnly.

Avian quickened his pace, passing a pair of Demmonai soldiers as they paced the perimeter of the campsite. As Kiara walked by the soldiers, they sent her simultaneous glances of disgust, their hands tightening around the weapons they readily wielded. Kiara huffed, rolling her eyes at their weak attempt at intimidation, trailing Avian as he skillfully navigated his way around the encampment.

He led her to a black and red tent on the edge of the campsite, the distant location of the tent from the crowd of others suggesting its owner preferred solitude. He pulled back the curtained entrance, nodding at her to enter. She glanced at him with eyes full of curiosity, hesitantly walking inside and discovering a sleeping bag scattered across the floor beside a narrow bed that was rounded by a small table baring a plate of assorted food. She sat down timidly on the sleeping bag, watching Avian as he hovered awkwardly in the entrance.

"This is my tent," he informed her, his voice tight. "You'll be sharing it with me."

"What? No dungeon? No chains?" she replied mockingly, pulling her legs against her chest. "What kind of a prisoner am I?"

He shrugged, stepping forward and allowing the curtains to swing into place behind him. He sat down on the floor across from Kiara, resting his elbow on the table. "Vyntrx put me in charge of you. It's my decision where you sleep, what you wear, what you eat. She only cares about torturing you."

Kiara coyly peaked at him through her downcast eyelashes. "You're not going to harm me, then?"

He chuckled humorlessly. "Of course I'm not going to hurt you."

"Why are you being nice to me? We're enemies."

His eyes instantly hardened as he maneuvered his gaze toward the floor. "If only you knew everything," he muttered.

"So tell me," she ordered.

He shook his head. "You're not ready to hear it yet. You have other questions to ask me."

She pouted in rebuttal but proceeded to ask Avian the questions that had been forming inside her brain since she discovered herself captured in the Dark Forest. "Is Kain alive?"

Avian's gaze hardened as he studied Kiara's inquiry, his mouth stitched in a tight line as he worked his lips into the beginning of a sentence. "Yes," he said gruffly, as though her question had disastrously injured his body. "Kain is alive."

Relief flooded Kiara's veins, trimming away a layer of anxiety from her panic-stricken heart. The edges of her mouth curled upward in a grin, her mind far too enveloped in respite to notice Avian's drastic change in demeanor. "And Kailx? And the dukes? And Sena?"

"They're all fine," he responded mechanically, allowing his uncharacteristically unkempt hair to sweep across his brow and darken his eyes as he directed his gaze to the floor. "I wouldn't have been able to forgive myself if the dukes—" his words were abruptly swallowed by a hurricane of guilt that gushed through his chest and drowned his voice. His mouth hung open, as though he were attempting to articulate his thoughts, but after a pause entangled in desolation, he finally succumbed to the whim of silence.

"Don't play the helplessly misunderstood victim card," Kiara snapped, sharply eyeing his somber figure with distrust. "You think you can serve Vyntrx *and* protect Enevale's soldiers? You can't fool me, Avian. I know you don't care about anyone but yourself."

Avian's head snapped upward, his eyes blazing with unfettered fury. Tears welled in the corner of his lids, threatening to spill across his red-blotted cheeks. He locked his intense gaze with Kiara's, his body quivering as his breath escaped his lips in a wave of hot air. "Don't you *ever* say that again!" he sternly demanded, his hands clenching into fists. "In the past, I only ever thought about my own well being, but I've more than faced the consequences from the moronic mentality I once possessed. I may not be able to control the situation I so stupidly thrust myself into, but I *can* control my feelings! And I know I care about you—and the dukes—as though you were my own flesh and blood. I never lied about my feelings for you. I never *wanted* to harm you. So don't insult me, Kiara. You aren't aware of even a fracture of the torturous conditions my mind has been subjected to."

She bit her lip, holding back a defensive riposte as she carefully scrutinized Avian's sullen expression. His eyes bulged with shimmering tears, his face scrunched up in dejected contemplation. Unable to hold his gaze with Kiara's rapidly shifting irises, he cast his eyes in the direction of the ground, his hands clenching and unclenching as he wallowed in the paralytic silence.

"Avian..." Kiara started, unable to work her lips into a full-fledged sentence. She sighed, her mind whirling with conflicting and perplexing emotions. Her hand inflexibly itched to comfort him, but a vindictive voice radiating through her brain ordered her to remain undaunted by the traitor's plea for sympathy.

He abruptly stood up, unintentionally knocking over the small table at his bedside with a loud clatter. The bowl of fruit swiveled off the uneven surface, shattering against the ground and littering the small room with shards of ragged glass and punctured berries. "I need to be alone," he declared, his voice wavering unsteadily. He brushed past her, eyebrows narrowed in unsettled angst, hurrying toward the exit as though the prospect of his survival was hinged on the curve of the makeshift door. Just as his hand reached for the edge of the fabric, a Demmonai soldier suddenly drew back the curtain and stuck his head inside the tent. Avian, slightly startled, nearly struck the soldier in the face—but he managed to regain control of his spasmodic hands before he could inflict any damage to his subordinate.

"You shouldn't just *appear* like that," he chided angrily, refusing to steal even a glance in Kiara's direction. He rubbed his neck in aggravation, eyeing the soldier with disdain.

"Sorry, *sir*," the Demmonai responded sarcastically, as though it were a nuisance for him to show respect to an Evalseman. "The empress has returned. She's requested your presence."

Avian released a sigh tinged in frustration and contempt. "Of course she has," he muttered begrudgingly. His eyes instinctively flickered in Kiara's direction, briefly scanning her contemplative visage. He shook his head, forcing himself to glance away while his conscience scolded his eyes for raking her figure. "Watch the prisoner," he ordered the Demmonai, attempting to bottle down a sweltering surge of wrath as he anticipated his meeting with Vyntrx.

His eyes burning with the desire to climb in Kiara's direction, his body protesting as he headed to meet his foe, Avian ducked out of the tent, leaving his prisoner behind to contemplate a method of escape.

About the Author

MaKenzie McCroskey Jones has been writing since she was ten years old and started her first novel in fifth grade. Having been struck with the idea of the Fall of Menevilen series at age thirteen, the world of Menevilen and its residents have been a massive part of her life for over six years.

McCroskey Jones currently resides in Missouri and is attending college as an English major with a creative writing emphasis.

www.ingramcontent.com/pod-product-compliance
Lightning Source LLC
Chambersburg PA
CBHW030535260626
47157CB00006B/2037